A DEEP BROWN CRUCIBLE

The Third Mill Meacham Story

By

Carson A. Pierce

Library of Congress Cataloging-in-Publication Data is available from the Library of Congress

ISBN 978-0-9827537-4-3

2

Acknowledgements

A Deep Brown Crucible would never have been completed without the invaluable support of friends and family.

My wife, Cheryl, is my constant source of insight and encouragement. She serves ably as idea checker, proof reader, and editor.

Forest Service Law Enforcement Officers Ted Rainville and Javier Masiel gave me useful insights into the equipment used by Forest Service law enforcement and how they and their colleagues conduct operations.

Several people read the book in draft and provided me useful edits and comments. These caring critics include: Allen Gibbs, Ted and Christine Rainville, Jim Van Loan, and Javier Masiel.

My profound thanks to everyone.

Message from the Author

Is *A Deep Brown Crucible* a simple cops-and-robbers story? A love story? Is it about a young woman painfully working through the anguish of her life? About agencies and their cultures? About environmental politics and conflicts?

Is it an adventuresome narrative? A commentary on good and evil? On conflict and dispute resolution?

Maybe it's all of these things, a spicy cocktail blended for readers who want their literature to shake and shock them, to inform and intrigue them and, if they choose, to educate and uplift them.

Read! Enjoy!

Cap, 2012

Dedication

To
the
people
of America,
conned by the
media, led by the
greedy...still a beacon
of hope to folks worldwide.
I pray you the best in all ways,
always. *You readers there*! Lift your
glasses! Here's to wild places and to the
wild things that live in them! And here's to the
people who care for those wild places and things!
The freest ever!
Now
drink!

Table of Contents

Chapter 1 - Ahead, 2012 -- River of No Return

Special Agent Mill Meacham is on the Devil's trail. The Beast won't wait.

She sits behind the wheel of her plain-white, dusty-as-Hell, government pickup at the junction of Forest Service Road 20507 West and Idaho 55. The traffic is so heavy, she can't get across 55. She slams her hand against the steering wheel.

In the asphalt river before her swim huge metal whales and schools of faster, smaller fish. Their hurtling bodies swirl out dusty fume-currents that buffet her rig. Mill squints for an opening.

Her head pivots right, left, then right again.

A gap opens. She readies her foot to jump from brake to gas and then curses quietly as a red Miata accelerates around a wide, two-trailer Freightliner and steals her opportunity. Damn it!

Mill and her companion are supposed to keep a low profile on this trip, alert no one. But the temptation to turn on her siren and hidden cop lights grips her. Her hand moves unconsciously toward the toggles.

Beside her, Manny Suemez sees her movement and smiles, thin-lipped, "Mill, you see any *huesos* by the side of the road here?" Taking him seriously for a moment, Mill glances away from the traffic line to study the edges of the pavement and gravel. Ahhh! He's kidding.

She smiles, "No, Manny, no bones here!" Then, eyes crinkling, she throws her head back and laughs--her wonderful, four-note sound guaranteed to raise the mood of anyone nearby, even dry bones scattered by the roadside.

And, under Mill's spell, the usually dour Suemez grins and lets out a chuckle, "Just figured you might not know that nobody's ever starved to death here waitin' for a break in traffic. Otherwise, there'd be a burger joint or a taco stand on this corner." They both laugh again.

Then Manny sees a likely gap coming up, reaches over, and flips on the blue and red strobes. "We have business on the other side. Go when you can, Mill."

The cop lights work their magic. Departing traffic speeds away, trailing innocence like tail-pipe fumes. Intimidated, oncoming traffic slows…a shark's in their waters. The gap widens.

Mill hits the accelerator. Gravel spins from her rig's rear tires. The pickup shoots across 55's three lanes and skids onto 20507 East.

Mill turns off the strobes and accelerates to just what the truck can handle on the potholed road. The sea of traffic on Idaho 55 quickly disappears in the whirling cloud of dust behind the pickup.

A moment later, as the pickup vibrates across light washboard, she thinks of their gear in the back. The two law enforcement officers, or LEOs, are packing a full tactical gear load, from steel-toed boots to Kevlar helmets, Glock 40s, M-4 automatic rifles, and plenty of ammo. Will the jarring cause damage? No, the thickly padded cases should prevent that.

Manny and Mill are joining a rapidly gathering task force put together from the Federal Bureau of Investigation, the federal Bureau of Alcohol, Tobacco, Firearms, and Explosives, Homeland Security, Idaho State Police, and, their home agency, the Forest Service.

For the law enforcement officers coming in from outside the Forest Service, the mission is plain and simple police work. Find the bad guys and arrest them...or if they resist, put 'em down. For Manny and the other Forest Service LEOs, whatever happens here will be payback for horribly hurting their organization, their pride, and their own good officers.

But for Mill, it's personal--dark family stuff. Personal, too personal...Mom and Dad personal. In fact, she wouldn't be here if Manny hadn't vouched for her, told the task force commanders he would keep her under his wing...keep her from doing anything stupid.

No matter how the other cops think things will go, Mill and Manny know this will be a fight to the finish. In the minds of the Forest Service LEOs, this mission comes down to one idea. The eco-terrorist group, Mist, surrenders...or it dies.

Mill doesn't care which.

Chapter 2 - Cutter's Park

A few miles inside Idaho's River of No Return Wilderness, an old panel truck squats in the middle of Cutter's Park. Grasses grow though the truck's rusted floorboards and a willow climbs high from its empty, hoodless engine compartment. Who knows how it had got here…a mineral claim gone bust or a logging show shut down…some homesteader's broken dream.

However it arrived sometime in the 1920s or 30s, the tide of human greed had pushed it up to Cutter's Park. And later, Congressional decree made the land on which it sat Wilderness, to be forever "untrammeled by man".

So now the rusted-out truck sits, as out of place as a warty toad on a wedding cake.

Mist's War Clan Chief stoops inside the old truck. "You find this kind of junk all around the Rockies," Badger muses to herself, unsure if its presence offends Mother Nature. Or perhaps, as the Mother assimilates such junk back into the soil, She shows Her ultimate power over everything human. Yes, that thought satisfies Badger.

Well, for the next several days, the truck can continue to rust away. And pray that Mother protects the Mist warriors assembled here in Her Name, gives them power over Her enemies, the Greed Machine and its thug-lackeys, federal law enforcement.

Badger looks out through the empty window frames and around the 100-or-so acre high-mountain meadow called Cutter's Park. Aspen thinly edges the meadow's grasses and brush. An old forest circles the lovely gold-brown meadow, about half of the woods lodgepole pine and high-mountain firs dying from insects and disease.

Badger studies the landscape closely. She sees no sign of any of the law enforcement people she knows have to be hurtling her way.

She speaks quietly to the man next to her--a Mist assassin with extensive military experience--"Everything functioning properly, Chronos?"

The man checks the monitor in his hand, "Yes, Badger, all green."

She nods and points southwest, "Let's go then. We've got lots more to do before the thugs show up."

The pair ducks out of the rusting hulk and, staying low, they drop into the bottom of a little artesian creek that gushes from a wet rock outcrop ringed with mosses and ferns next to the truck. As the two move away, the little waterway conceals their tracks and provides them a low line of march.

Surrounded by the waist-deep, dry meadow, the Mist warriors splash downstream. What can be seen of them stands out--brown-green--camouflage to match the nearby forest, but out of place in the meadow. They crouch low, aware that surveillance drones, helicopters, and other equipment might be watching them.

In moments, the two reach the forested green line, and mist-like, vanish from hungry sky eyes.

Ten minutes later, a mouse-sized HeloEye buzzes into Cutter's Park. It zips past the old panel truck, then curves back and hovers to look inside. The HeloEye's wide-angle lens sees nothing. Two hundred miles away, the tiny helicopter's virtual pilot signals it to climb and start a spiral search outward from the rusty hulk.

Chapter 3 - Comes a Harbinger

Two months before the HeloEye buzzes into Cutter's Park, W.A. "Bull" Meacham had sat eyeing a handsome woman across the cluttered surface of the Pinchot Desk. The starkly beautiful woman had found her way into his office in the Jamie Whitten Building again, as she had done several times before, arriving mysteriously and always long before Bull's staff started showing up at 8 a.m.

Now, seated before him, she stared back, her smiling face mildly hostile, refusing to answer his repeated question of how she had gotten into the building without alerting security.

"Chief Meacham," she said firmly, "you know our bargain. We took care of the problem you had with Associate Chief Pizzaro and certain images. In return, the Aquasis Foundation expects you to do what we ask, when we ask it."

The Forest Service Chief stared even more rudely at the woman's unbound breasts tightly visible under her professionally tailored silk blouse. The woman stirred impatiently under his gaze and crossed her legs, causing his eyes to shift further south. His eyes slowly moved up her thighs and under her skirt.

"Chief Meacham, what's your answer?"

Bull leaned back in his tall, leather "executive service" chair and gazed up at the high ceiling of the Chief's Office. Thirteen feet, he'd heard it was, but he had never measured it with anything but wadded up paper and, once, Pizzaro's thong.

He'd been holding out on the Aquasis woman just to tease her, to keep her around to look at. So why not delay answering some more?

Ah yes, the thong. He smiled at the memory.

He had banged Angie on the couch in the corner until she dried up. Then he forced her to kneel in front of him and suck him while he pinched her nipples cruelly. Her whines and grunts of pain added to his pleasure.

After he finished, Angie had sat at his feet, hands over her throbbing nipples, humiliated. He picked up her thong from the pile of her clothes on the couch's arm, stretched it on his finger, and shot it at the ceiling. The rubber-band panty hit the plaster surface and fluttered down to catch on the high, five-bladed fan. Hanging there, it formed a bold scarlet "o" twelve feet from the floor, dangling where anyone could see it.

He laughed. The hanging thong was a fine trophy for his dominance over the trim little woman. But it had to come down. His staff would certainly see it in the morning and tongues would wag.

So he had made Pizzaro push the Pinchot desk under the fan. Then he made her jump, naked, up and down on the desk, swinging a ruler until she snagged the little bit of cloth. Quite a sight, watching the cold-blooded little bitch cry as she flailed.

Pizzaro deserved it. She had been the one who had trapped him on video, supposedly having gay sex with a male prostitute named Raoul. She did it to support her bid for Associate Chief and, eventually, his job.

Even if he didn't like what she had done, he could understand it.

But she had been caught…bested…by these Aquasis people. And that meant he was back on top. The naked leaping was part of Bull's pay back…the humiliating sex, too…like other situations he had enjoyed putting women in throughout his career.

Bull let go of the pleasant memory. He looked again at the tense Aquasis representative, "Okay, your people definitely did me a solid with the video stuff. So, what do you want? Tell me again."

The woman sighed with exasperation, "Chief, we want to know the name and location of every informant, paid or otherwise, who is assisting the federal government in its investigation of eco-terrorist organizations."

Bull shook his head ruefully, "I don't have access to that information. Maybe some for Forest Service cases, but certainly not for outfits like the Bureau of Land Management or the F, B, and I."

The woman spoke flatly, "Chief, we want it…all of it. You owe us. So get it."

The Chief's face took on a sly smile, "Well, maybe if you and I was to spend some time together…let me get an idea of what all this was for…you could impress me with the importance of what you want. Maybe we could meet tonight at the lounge over at the Marriott and talk awhile."

The woman pointed a finger at him, "That's not going to happen, Chief. You have two weeks to get the information to us."

She stood and handed him what appeared to be a thick, expensive pen, one her boss, Raven, Mist's Listening Clan Chief, had given her.

"Use this."

He took the pen and looked at it curiously, "You want me to write all this stuff down? Could be a long list. That might take forever."

She shook her head and took the pen back, "It's not actually a pen."

She demonstrated, twisting, "See, the cap pops open and releases a USB connector." She showed him twice how to open and close it, "Get the information for us on your computer, Chief, and then load it onto this jump drive. I'll tell you later where and when to deliver it."

"What if somebody sees me lookin' like an idiot sticking a pen in my computer? Gets hold of it? Figures it out?"

The woman spoke harshly, "So, Chief Meacham, you'll look a little foolish. But nothing will come of it. Whatever data you put on this drive goes in through an encryption lock. If someone without the encryption key tries to open it, everything on the drive will be erased. So no one can say you did anything wrong by having a jump drive concealed in a fancy pen. Just another techno gimmick for rich men."

The do-it-or-else tone in her voice softened, "And, as a gesture of good will, I brought you another leaf."

Her distraction worked. Bull forgot his questions about why the Aquasis Foundation went to such trouble to have him put encrypted data into a fake pen.

Each time he had provided information to Aquasis, the outfit gave him a heavy, green-on-gold cloisonné leaf big enough to cover his palm. Bull looked forward to getting his leaf. He had never had the others appraised but he knew they were worth thousands of dollars based on the weight of gold alone, not to mention the detailed engraving and perfect glasswork that made them beautiful works of art.

The Aquasis woman handed him a heavy velvet bag. He slid the leaf out into his hand where it glowed warmly in the sunlight streaming in through his office's high windows.

Was this leaf a little lighter than the others? No way to know until he checked it against the six others in his private safe.

She pointed to the leaf, "As I told you before, each leaf has unique engraving on it. The person meeting you will expect to see this leaf and this leaf only. If you fail to show up or show another leaf, our representative will leave and we will consider that you have broken our agreement. I will personally release your videos the press the next day."

Bull waved his hand irritably at her, "No reason to get pushy. And I don't know why you do this cloak and dagger stuff. 'Show the leaf and you will be approached' and all that shit. Nobody cares about the crap I give you. You could get most of it from our press releases and paperwork, for Christ's sake."

The woman nodded, smiling internally, and said, "Just humor us, please. Our 'sign-and counter-sign' procedure is meant to keep you safe by making sure you're meeting only our representative and not being set up by someone else."

The handsome woman felt no qualms about lying to this government slug. She knew her previous information requests had just been dress rehearsals--Raven's slow and exacting way of training this grotesque man, schooling him to comply with their orders.

Six times before, Mist had bribed this oaf to give very little. Now they were ready for the payoff. He would give them crucial information about Mist's enemies at a time when their plans required it.

The woman turned away from Bull and, bending away from Bull, picked up her large Gucci purse. As she bent, Bull's eyes followed the long curve of her back, rear, and legs.

My God, how he would like to "jump drive" this tightly wound heifer. Well, maybe someday he could trap her into it. He watched her sway gracefully out his office door.

He did not see her touch the switch hidden in the purse's strap, the one that turned off the high-resolution voice recorder in its base.

Picking up his phone, Bull dialed the Forest Service Law Enforcement Director, "Hey, Bill, I got somethin' to ask you. I know we've been talkin' about this Mist bunch and all the felonious crap they've been up to, but I'd like a briefing on all the eco-terrorista bastards you know about--individuals, organizations, where they're located—all that stuff. Can you do that in a couple of days?"

"Sure, boss. What do you need it for?"

"Got a phone call from the Hill and I just need to cover my ass for a meeting up there. Pull any stuff you have from other agencies, too, will you, including what the Bureau has?"

"Yeah, no problem. I'll have it for you tomorrow late."

"Okay…okay…great. And thanks, Bill. Hey, don't forgit about cee-gars and poke-her next week…" Bill's cackle filled the Chief's phone as he took the receiver from his ear.

Bull laughed out loud. If that Aquasis hottie only knew how easy it was for the Chief of the Forest Service to get the scoop.

Well, had she known, she'd be payin' him a lot less. So Bull would never tell her. Breed her maybe….

Chapter 4 - Comes a Reckoning

Two weeks after Bull made his phone call to the Director of Law Enforcement, Badger's tall, slender figure slipped through the back door of Esperanza Angelica Pizzaro's small, elegant condominium located off M Street in Georgetown.

An earlier break-in team had reprogrammed Pizzaro's alarm system so Badger could turn it off when she entered. Now inside, she squeezed the little controller-fob in the pocket of her loose-fitting jumpsuit. The alarm reactivated. Badger wanted Pizzaro to be completely at ease when she came home so the alarm had to be on and acting normally.

She ran a finger around the edge of the hood and face mask of the cool-suit she wore under the jumpsuit. Try as they would, the suit builders could not stop them from feeling damp or figure out how to make the liners less scratchy. But in a day when heat-sensing motion detectors monitored places like Pizzaro's, cool suits were essential for undetected break-ins.

Badger quickly checked the little two-story house filled with English antiques and gold-framed romantic-era paintings. The only living thing she found was a lazy calico cat sleeping on her owner's pillow. The cat raised her head, gave Badger a glassy-eyed stare, flicked her tail, and then snuggled back into Pizzaro's red satin pillow sham.

Badger checked the time on the military-styled watch on her wrist. If the Eyes and Ears surveillance team was right about Pizzaro's schedule, she would be home in an hour or so.

Past audio recordings of Pizzaro's movement in the house indicated her coming-home pattern was to walk from the front door to the kitchen and then upstairs to her bedroom. She would stay there long enough to change clothes and sometimes shower before returning to the first floor. Then she would spend a few minutes in the kitchen before going into her study. There she would read mail and work on her computer while sipping wine and listening to classical music.

The Strike plan called for Badger to hide in the study. But the entry team's photos showed that the smallish room had no closet or any obvious place where Badger might conceal herself.

Badger finished looking around the bedroom, went quickly downstairs, glanced into the kitchen, and then entered the study. In the far corner, a heavy table supported stacks of papers and journal articles. Pizzaro apparently used these sources for her work as an internationally known wildlife ecologist and occasional TV personality. The carpeted area under the table held a few boxes and, beyond the boxes, was a dark corner.

Badger pulled the corners of several rough silk scarves from a cargo pocket. She turned on the overhead light, bent, and quickly matched the dull color of one of the scarves to the dark corner's shadow.

This would work. She would curl up under the table, spread the scarf over her body, and wait until Pizzaro sat at the computer, back to Badger.

Now Badger turned to Pizzaro's computer. It had been hacked weeks before and a code inserted so that Badger could log into Pizzaro's personal Facebook account. Badger quickly connected, fumbling a little to type with gloved fingers.

"Hurry, you fool," she prompted herself, "This is crucial." In a moment, Pizzaro's Facebook account came up.

Badger let out a sigh of relief. The Wall post was there. It said simply, "Confirmed. Mist warriors gather. 450-804-6851 or 1496, x28785."

She typed in a reply message, "I will join my Mist brothers and sisters in spirit and rest in the Earth Mother's arms today." Then she stored the message in "drafts", blanked the screen, and moved away from the computer.

Twenty minutes later, Pizzaro opened the front door. Badger crouched by the desk and waited, tense, as the woman went into her kitchen and dropped her purse. Then Badger heard her muffled steps go upstairs.

Good. Pizzaro was following her normal pattern.

Badger woke the computer, pulled the message up from "drafts," pressed "send," and then shut the machine down by pressing the "off" button for ten seconds. Her computer work done, she slipped under the table to curl in the dark corner, a spider under silk.

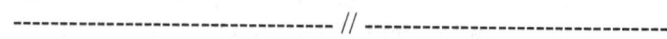

Just before 9 p.m., Bull Meacham sat on a bench in a park off Independence and L Streets NW. For a time after he arrived, hookers, male and female, had bee-buzzed him until his gruff insults had driven them away.

"Why the Hell did these Aquasis people have me meet them here?" he groused, "A bunch 'a workin' gals and druggie-queers tryin' to roll me."

If he had been truthful with himself, he would have admitted that sitting here with the gold leaf in his pocket made him nervous. He was a big, bluff Westerner by birth and inclination. Big spaces and few people was what he wanted, not these crowded Eastern cesspools.

If he hadn't been in DC where handguns were banned, he would have carried his Colt DA for protection. But getting caught with his long-barreled .45 would have been a bigger pain in the ass than losing the leaf to a hugger-mugger.

And then there was the call that he got just before sitting down on the bench, a message that made his head swim. Pizzaro had shot herself at her condo this evening!

In the head! Dead!

For a moment, feeling vaguely guilty, he wondered how much his sexual abuse of the little bitch had caused her to pull the trigger. He comforted himself with the thought that she had sure been willing to dish it to him. So she should have been willing to take it when it came her way.

Bill had mentioned something about a suicide note on her computer. Some reference to Mist and phone numbers. Nothing in it about Bull.

Still, her suicide made the shadowy park that much creepier. A dead-chill ran up his neck.

He shrugged it off with the same gruffness he had used on the whores, "Get a-hold a yourself, Meacham. Angie dyin' had nothin' to do with you."

Bull shifted uncomfortably on the bench, trying to avoid the smeared pigeon shit and hobo waste. He tried to get the image of Angie's head, bloody and open, out of his mind. He remembered that head going up and down a few days earlier on his horse-sized dong. Never again.

This was too much. He needed distraction…now.

"Jesus," he muttered under his breath, "where the Hell is the contact guy?"

He checked his watch. Nine straight up. Bull looked around quickly to see if any more street trash were approaching. No one.

He took the leaf out of his pocket and rested it on his knee, partially concealed by his hand. The leaf glowed in the dim light cast by a nearby street light.

He squinted at the ornate light post. It looked like it had been stolen from a bad English movie that had been set in the days of gaslights and garters. Here he was hiding in arty gloom with a fortune on his knee, surrounded by whores and dopers. What could the DC administration be thinking?

"Kee-rap," Bull muttered, "City!"

A big man strolled out of the shadows and nodded to Bull, "Nice night. Can you see the Washington Monument from here?"

Bull looked at the man closely. His words were the counter-sign to Bull's leaf display.

"Yeah," Bull boomed ironically, "Over there. The fuckin' thing is all lit up."

The paunchy, pleasant-faced man frowned and spoke quietly, "Just let me see the leaf, please. And keep your voice down, Chief. We don't want anyone to overhear us."

The Mist Enemies Chief, a long-time associate professor at the University of Texas, took the leaf and examined it. He recognized the engraving; it was the right one.

He nodded ponderously, "Very good, Chief. What I would expect from a man of your caliber. And next, good sir, please proffer your ersatz writing device."

For a moment, Bull wondered what the Hell this fancy-talking clown wanted. Then he realized it was the fake pen thing he had transferred the informant data onto. He reached into his shirt pocket and pulled it out, shoving it in the man's direction, "Here's the damn thing."

"Did anyone see you using it or help you download the information?" the Enemies Chief asked.

"No, no, fuck no," Bull answered irritably, "I got the pain-in-the-ass thing to work after about twenty tries. Kept forgetting that 'safely remove hardware' crap that you have to do to get it loose from the computer." As the man sat down next to him, Bull grumbled, "You guys are always asking me to do stupid shit like this."

"There, there," the man said, "After all, you got it done. Now just let me check this and you can be on your way like a good fella, off for drinks and a nice lady of the night if you want." He gestured genially around the park as he pulled a smart phone from his pocket, "Plenty to pick from around here."

Bull snorted, not amused.

"It'll be just a moment, dear chap," the Enemies Chief said to Bull, "And then you're done."

The genial man quickly inserted the pen-jump drive into the phone. Holding the screen at an angle away from Bull's gaze, he touched the screen three times in quick succession. The phone made a tinkling noise for a few seconds.

In a Michigan safe house, Raven took the call and routed the connection to her powerful PC. Encryption matched and the data rolled in. Once it had downloaded, she ran a search against Bull's list for the names of known informants, some of them were people Mist was operating as double-agents, and some were former Mist loyalists who she knew the FBI had turned. All but one informant showed up on Meacham's list.

Back in DC, the Enemies Chief's phone buzzed quietly. He lifted it to his ear, "Yes, this is Mr. L. Star, how may I help you?"

Raven's measured voice spoke in his ear. Her voice held an uncommon excitement below its habitually calm surface, "The information…appears legitimate. Proceed with…the next step. Call when…it has been accomplished."

"Yes, yes, my dear," he responded, "I will be glad to give Chief Meacham your respects. And thank you, too, for all your service to the Aquasis Foundation. All the best…"

The Enemies Chief ended the call with a flourish. He stood, pocketed the "ersatz writing device," and held the phone in his hand.

"Alright, Chief Meacham, time for you and me to be off. I'll go first if you don't mind. Wait a few minutes, dear chap, won't you, before you go. Better that we not be seen together, you know? There's a good man. Many thanks. Until we meet again."

With a small, aerie wave of his free hand, the man turned and strolled nonchalantly towards Independence Avenue.

Bull watched him disappear into the shadows between the nearest puny street light and the next. He turned away with a smile and muttered, "Stupid, faggoty bastard. I'm almost ashamed to take his gold…but I will."

Momentarily unafraid of the other predators in the park, Bull cradled the leaf and moved it back and forth so that the dim light rippled across its beautiful green-over-engraved-gold surface. "Beautiful, beautiful…," he mumbled quietly.

After a moment, he realized how crazy he was acting. Alarmed, he looked around quickly. No one near. No threat. He slipped the leaf into its velvet bag and then into his pants pocket.

He patted the hard object contentedly. If he kept getting these, he would be a rich man one day.

Smiling to himself, Bull decided he would head to the nearest bar for a stiff, three-fingers-'o-whiskey celebration. He started to get up.

That booze-hungry thought was his last.

-------------------------------- // --------------------------------

Before Bull could rise from the park bench, six ounces of concentrated "military' C-4 hidden in the green-gold leaf detonated. Gold fragments sleeted through Bull's body. The tiny, jagged fragments cut through the nearest parts first—penis, then legs, organs, and finally his disintegrating torso.

Thrown backwards over the bench, his torso tumbled down and fell flat, his back on the compacted earth of the drug-shooter' park. Oddly, the blast smashed and tore his body but left his head mostly untouched. His unseeing eyes stared up into the smoggy Foggy Bottom sky.

The blast nearly deafened two nearby junkies shooting up and knocked them flat. One took a pea-sized fragment of gold in the side of his head. He later pawned it for a fix.

Along nearby streets, john-cruising, scarecrow-thin dope whores craned their necks to see the grisly fall of Bull's body parts. Others watched the misty drift of his blood in the air.

They all turned and scuttled away. This was clearly trouble…none of their business. 5-0 would be arriving soon.

A block away, around the corner of a building, the Enemies Chief took his finger off his phone's touch screen. He mused to himself, "Gold makes such a nice antenna and collateral shrapnel for these sorts of things. I simply must compliment the War Chief for providing me such an efficient device."

As far-off sirens wailed, the man walked slowly to the nearest Metro station and disappeared down, down into Washington, DC's under-guts.

Chapter 5 - All the Blues that Fit

"Is this Millicent Meacham?" a tinny voice said into Mill's waking ear. "Yes, yes, it's Mill Meacham," she replied.

She glanced at the red-glowing numbers on her clock radio. 3 a.m.

She reminded herself of a cop's truth, "No good news comes at night."

She had been appointed as the most junior special agent in Montana after the crazy mess in Oregon two years ago, one where her boss, Bill Zumo, and her mentor, Jake Burns, had been killed by Mist eco-terrorists.

Fastest rise to special agent ever for a LEO. But after what she'd gone through, and her skilled, thoughtful performance, no one doubted she could do the special agent job. It didn't hurt that she was a fourth-generation Forest Service Legacy and daughter of the Chief. Still, even her critics would admit it had been her brains and guts that had gotten her the big promotion, not the Legacy nepotism so common in the Forest Service.

The now-urgent voice went on, "Mill, this is Harry Bitters. I'll be at your house in ten minutes with Deputy Regional Forester Redds. We have something important to see you about. Will that be okay?"

"Sure, sure," Mill muttered, "See you in ten minutes."

Bitters was her boss, Assistant Special Agent in Charge for the Northern Region stationed here in Missoula, and Redds was the DRF for Administration.

Mill bet their urgent visit was motivated by some kind of internal dust up. That must be it…something fast-moving like a threat by an employee ready to kill a supervisor, guns and pickup trucks blazing, or maybe a drug dealer working out of a Forest Service campground or employee housing.

She hung up the phone.

She would probably be on the road by five. Well, her bags were always packed, just the way they taught fledgling special agents at the Federal Law Enforcement Training Center, or FLETC, in Glynco, GA. "Fast response" was the watch-word.

Company coming! She jumped out of bed and darted into the bathroom. After a quick pee, she shrugged into a bra and pulled on jeans and a light sweater. Standing in front of her sink, she ran a quick brush through her hair, knocking down a few cowlicks with water.

Her image stared back—black hair around an oval face that just missed being beautiful. Brown eyes with green flecks and a few crow's feet around them from sun and smiles. Her habitual frown deepened as she pressed at the little wrinkles with her thumbs and wondered if any of those "age defying" skin products could help her now. Probably not.

Besides, she had no time to experiment with all that skin stuff. Leave that for the girly girls.

She looked down at her clothes and the body under it. Strong. Athletic.

Breasts a little large for her frame, hence the bra to receive visitors. She didn't want to wiggle "the girls" in faces of management as much as they might appreciate the display.

She turned and looked down. She still had her tight boy-butt. Although, nodding ruefully, she had to admit it had grown a little wider and rounder jockeying a chair at the regional office instead of working patrol in the field.

She looked back up and into her eyes. Once she had been afraid of what she might have seen there…dark hunger for sex, drugs, and booze…violent anger, hatred even, roiling just below the surface.

But now her eyes reminded her of the saving love she had found. Philip, childhood friend, husband, unconditional lover, and confident supporter. Philip, far away, the pastor of a large-ish church near Centralia, WA.

A chill ran up her neck, pushing out thoughts of Philip. This chill was something she had felt before when something wasn't quite right. Something about the two Forest Service men coming to her door so late at night tweaked her. "NO good news…" she whispered into to her fear-darkening eyes.

Should she call Philip, even at this early hour? Mill could talk to him, get some long-distance comfort. She wanted to feel the loving touch in his voice before the Forest Service bureaucrats crossed her doorstep.

She was just reaching for her iComm smart phone when the door bell rang.

--------------------------------- // ---------------------------------

22

An hour later, Mill used shaking hands to punch in Philip's number. She waited while the phone rang and rang, and then went to voicemail.

"Call me," she said curtly and ended the call.

Where could he be? She almost wept with rage, her grief at Bitters' news transmuted into anger towards Philip. Had he let his stupid phone battery run down again? Where was he? Was the bastard out cheating on her?

Her rage rose higher. A moment later, her phone rang.

"Sorry, sweetheart," comes Philip's voice, "I left my phone in the kitchen and had to scramble downstairs to get it. Tripped over the hassock in the living room and landed on the cat...." He chuckled.

"Philip," Mill broke in, "My father's been killed...in DC...a bomb or something. My boss and one of the Forest Service people who handle employee deaths just left. The paperwork stuff is nothing, but I need to go to DC, to go through Dad's stuff, to see what he might have been doing...you know, to cause this or whatever."

She drew a long, shuddering breath, and Philip started to console her, but she cut him off again, "I want you to meet me in DC. No, no. Wait. What I'd really like is for you to come here and then into DC with me. Can you do that? I mean come here...for me?"

Mill sobbed, less from grief than from anticipated rejection.

Mother deserted her at seven. Father saw her as just another fixture in the career monument he built to himself. Why would Philip be any different, any more supportive?

Suddenly, turning her mouth away from the phone, she wailed a long cry of pain. A moment later, her wail rose into an anguished scream.

Hundreds of miles to the west, Philip's heart ached for her. He spoke hastily into the phone, "Of course, I can get away. I'll be there as soon as I can get a flight out of SeaTac or Portland. Don't worry, Milly love, I'll be there."

Philip's pastor role had partially prepared him for his wife's pain. He had ushered many dying people into Eternity, led funeral services, consoled mourners, and hugged people feeling desperately vulnerable, mortal.

But Milly's loss was so close to the core of his love for her, he felt suddenly dizzy, off kilter. And they were so recently married...newlyweds really...living separately.

And he was instantly worried that this tragedy would send her down her old, dark, self-destructive paths. Her hard-won sobriety and chastity might be lost. If that happened, the life they were building together would disintegrate.

He spoke more quietly to her, "Sweetest, let me hang up for a moment and get my flight to Missoula arranged. I'll call right back."

Mill choked out, "O..kay" then pressed "end" on her iComm.

-------------------------------- // -------------------------------

Mill walked numbly towards the Missoula International Airport.

As she walked into the terminal, her thoughts bounced and rolled in rhymes, not reason.

"Must have been Mist." "Miss my Dad" "Sad Dad, too sad." "Glad and sad to have a Dad, no not that… glad."

All morning long while Philip traveled her way, her thoughts had tumbled through her head like this--bright pebbles in fast water--loose…disconnected. She would grab one thought, hold it for a moment, and then it would slip away to be replaced by another one, equally odd-shaped and off-colored.

Coffee hadn't helped settle this mental whirlwind. Buckets of tears hadn't either.

She stopped inside the airport's sliding doors, dazed.

Why had she come here? What was here? No, no…who?

Oh, Philip, of course!

She couldn't remember driving to the airport.

But here she was.

God, that loss of time was scary. Her counselor had told her that was a sure sign of high anxiety, distress taking her to her breaking point. She wondered if she should call the therapist. He had been such a help over the past year. But she couldn't seem to get organized enough to make the call.

That idea, just like the other bright pebbles, whirled away.

She walked further into the terminal and then just stood, her mind running with rhymes.

Philip walked into the baggage area. He spotted her and moved quickly to her. Reacting numbly, Mill stumbled into his arms and hugged him close. He led her off to a quiet spot well away from the thumping and whirring noises of the luggage dispensing machines. There, he simply stood and held her while she cried against him.

Eventually her knees began to buckle. He walked her over to a bench, sat with her there, and held her as she whispered and moaned in pain, tears and nose dripping.

Mill's well of grief gradually emptied. Her anxiety dropped. Her hyper-experience of time slowed. She suddenly became aware of her surroundings.

"What have I been doing? How did I get here?" she asked Philip dazedly.

"You've been mourning your father's death. And you drove here from your apartment to pick me up," he replied in his kind-but-direct counselor voice, "I'm going to be by your side as long as you want me."

She glanced at her husband shyly, "I feel like a regular nut-case. Why do you put up with my crazy shit?"

Philip laughed, "Well, I like both fruit and nuts. You're a bit of each...well, maybe a lot of each."

She punched him lightly on the arm. "Especially in the bedroom," she remarked tartly.

"Yeah, there, too," he shot back, smiling and slipping away from her next punch.

Philip felt a familiar internal twinge. His sexual experience was so minimal compared to Mill's. She had lived with varying degrees of sex addiction for almost a decade, had intercourse with a parade of mostly anonymous men and women. So, when she joked about sex, he felt so inexperienced and...well, clownishly angry. It was a very uncomfortable feeling.

And there was more.

Philip's guts twisted. He was certain that his neglect had lead to Milly's rape at fourteen. And, for all Mill's reassurances that it had not, his lingering guilt was so strong it almost smothered his heartbeats when it swept over him as it did now. Awful...awful...he was awful.

Sitting with his mourning wife, he tried to pull his thoughts away from the guilty abyss. If he was going to be able to act on the love and compassion he felt for Milly, he had to let go of the contempt and loathing he felt for himself.

He desperately rallied his thoughts. He rubbed his arm where Mill had tapped him. Having a wife who was a black belt in karate was a mixed blessing. Her punches hurt even when she didn't intend it. But if he was ever in a dark alley with muggers closing in, well.... Philip smiled at his goofiness and refocused on his wife.

He was pleased Mill had started reconnecting with reality. When her anxiety peaked as it had today, she was both incredibly vulnerable and incredibly dangerous. Lost in her mental fog, she could be blindsided and badly hurt or killed. And, with all the rage she felt, it was equally likely that she could kill someone without later remembering having done it.

Her counselor had been most specific with Philip on that point, "Do whatever you can to bring her down, even restrain her if you have to, before she acts out."

Philip thought ruefully, "Yeah, me…that's right, restrain Milly Meacham when she doesn't want to be…fat chance." Still he told the man, "I'll always do what I can, of course."

He was doing it now.

He hugged her close, "Okay if we get my luggage? I watched as it went round and round the carousel for the last hour or so. I think somebody finally hauled it away to sell at a yard sale."

Mill laughed a little at his silliness, "Okay, but I'm going with you to bid up your undies!"

They walked hand in hand to the luggage service office and crowded in. Even when she tried to pull her hand away from Philip's, Mill couldn't seem to let go.

Chapter 6 - The Root of All the Evil Is the Love...

Clipper Jones looks across the table at his administrative officer, "Everything go okay at Pillbox, Thyra?"

Thyra Dexter nods, "Sure did boss. My buying unit processed six purchases from Calico and eleven from FireFirst."

"What were the totals on those contracts?"

"Together, a little over $30,000 and each purchase was under $2,500."

"Good, good," the Forest Supervisor nods, "meets our guidelines exactly."

Unimpressed by the praise, Thyra smiles tightly at him, "Clipper, did you talk to the other Forest Supes about getting us grunts a bigger share?" Her jaw tightens and she spits her next words, "I mean we do all the work, take the risks, and, even after three fire seasons, you guys are still keeping half."

Clipper had heard this grumbling before, "Look, Thyra, the Green Rivers know that you guys pull your weight...process the paper and provide the cover...but we do our share, too. We have to make sure you don't get audited, watch for interest from the Inspector General or GAO. We set up the businesses. We make sure you get assigned to the right fires...call in favors from the incident commanders. All that's risky, too. Our necks are stuck out just as far...."

Thyra interrupts with quiet fury, "We don't give a damn about that stuff, Clipper! You do all that sitting in your chairs here at the office. We sit out there in the smoke, admin staff looking over our shoulders, wondering when some LEO'll be standing by our desk. Next thing, we'll be sitting in a cell while you guys cover your tracks. I'm telling you, we want seventy percent or the grunts are done!"

"Okay, okay, I'll talk to the other supes," he waves at Thyra soothingly, "but the Green Rivers don't get together again until fall. You'll have to get through the rest of the fire season under our present arrangement. That gonna work, or do we just shut everything down?"

Thyra growls, "You know damn well you could get something done before fire season ends if you tried, but, okay, I'll let the others know we go on like we are for now." She leans closer to the Forest Supervisor, "Look, Clipper, if we don't get a bigger cut next season, there'll *be* no 'next season' if you know what I mean."

For a moment, Clipper wonders if Thyra is threatening his life. His heart thumps. Then he realizes she is simply saying that her group of procurement and admin people wouldn't cooperate until they got what they wanted.

His heart slows and he smiles placatingly, "Okay, Thyra, let's just get through this season and then we'll work things out. I'm sure the Green Rivers will cooperate. I just don't know how much. Seventy percent seems really steep."

Thyra stands up and, always needing the last word, shakes an index finger at him, "They better cooperate, Clipper, or there'll be Hell to pay…"

With this last satisfying word spoken, Thyra turns and leaves his office.

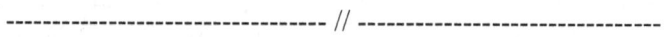

Clipper Jones leans back in his chair, hands behind his head. He thinks of himself, as he often says with sour humility, as being in "the twilight of a mediocre career." In this dissipated state, even clerks like Thyra could insult him…twist his arm for money or favors…and expect to get away with it.

He'd begun his Forest Service career with such enthusiasm and high hopes. Back then, he thought he would be one of the great ones, a recognized conservation leader, and a man with a big reputation.

But now, for all his years of service and more than a dozen assignments, he really had nothing significant to look back on or to be known for.

Two or three more years and he would retire. A couple of years after that and no one would remember he had ever served in the U.S. Forest Service.

His real first name is "Harold" but he'd been "Clipper" to his coworkers since he started with the Forest Service as a wildland firefighter. 1984 had been a slow fire year in his part of the world, so when his crew wasn't practicing drills or polishing the engine, he'd spent pretty much the whole time trimming bushes and painting fences around the Forest Service housing and administrative compound.

At the end of the season, he'd gotten a joke award from the ranger for working so hard on the shrubbery. The award had been made out to "Harold 'Clipper' Jones." The nickname stuck.

His next almost-thirty years had been somewhat like his first summer. He worked hard. But the glory jobs passed him by. He had advanced, sure enough, one slow step at a time…but often more mocked than respected by his superiors.

Forest Service leadership, dominated by Legacies and their toadies, had never fully taken to him. Still, as a capable African-American, he held a little edge in hiring. So, after an almost career-long wait, he had been assigned to supervise this backwater national forest with a small staff and little operations money.

Yes, Clipper is comfortably sitting in that mediocre twilight…or had been until four years ago.

His life had changed when he attended the national training for new forest supervisors. All newbie supes were put through a thirty-day "charm school" to get them settled in their new jobs.

Each charm-school class of ten was called a "Journey." After the training session was over, Journey-mates were expected to support one another, to provide the social network and encouragement that would never come from the Legacies.

Most Journeys only developed into bitchy cliques after graduation, wasting money on meaningless get-togethers. Some Journeys actually helped capable people advance and organized to work on tough policy issues shared among the national forests. And the others, perhaps most…well, they hoisted an infrequent, if empathetic beer with one another at the rare national meetings that brought them together.

Each class was asked to select a special Journey name. Clipper's Journey decided on the "Green Rivers." They chose this name after a team-building raft trip they'd taken, at government expense, down the Green River in Wyoming. The name had a touch of irony: a green river of agency money sending the trainees down waters bearing the same name.

Equally ironic, on that trip the "Green Rivers" found they shared a common experience. As one grey-haired member drawled, they were the "pissed-on and passed-over posse." And, even as they first laughed sourly at his comment, each one sit-circling that night's riverside campfire also realized it was true. Each really was a member of the "po-po posse", a twilighter hurtling into personal night, complete with an obscure retirement and an undistinguished death.

As this reality set in, the group grew quiet. They went to bed early.

Their Journey's focus had been on fire and fire management--about their new responsibilities as future "agency administrators" working with wildland-firefighter teams. And the next night, after a day-long presentation and discussion of fire costs and acquisition problems, the Green Rivers once again sat around a river-front campfire, drinking beer.

A wistful voice came out of the shadows, "You know, there are billions spent on fire every year. The Forest Service alone gets half a billion just for the organization. Then there are all the contractors and supplies...my God. If somebody was smart enough, I bet they could pull drops of money from that huge ocean of cash. Done right, no one would ever know."

Another voice said, "Yeah, sure. How would someone do that 'right'?"

Within a half an hour, disembodied voices offered a dozen ideas, some crazy...some practical. The Green Rivers realized one or two of those ideas could even work well. Their brains buzzed with thought.

Then, quite without anyone saying it, something else became clear to everyone around the campfire. The po-po posse saw a way to deliver a little payback, to stick it to their aloof Forest Service overlords...to do something significant in their time remaining, even if it was a little wicked. Suck some green rivulets from that vast fire-fund river.

They kept talking about it for the rest of the raft trip, half-jokingly testing their larcenous ideas on one another. After all, as long as the whole idea was a joke, it was just conjecture. Nothing needed to happen.

But, once home, the urge became action. Within a month of being back at their jobs, the Green Rivers had a plan in place.

First they carefully recruited clerks and administrators, promising them big money. Then each Green River set up a dozen fake businesses with post office box addresses and little else. The businesses appeared to offer humble things--toilet paper, bottled water, paper tablets and office supplies--things that no one ever really counts or cares about. But things that fire-fighting organizations run on.

Quickly, the businesses procured stationery, brochures, and official-sounding titles for fake owners. Then the Green Rivers moved pots of money around from bank account to bank account, filed the right forms, and got their fake firms certified as federal contractors.

They started working within the national fire organization to make sure their procurement clerks would be sent to moderate-sized fires where their activities wouldn't be noticed. And they made sure that, after the fire season, their audit clerks would review and approve the fires' bookkeeping and bill paying.

The 2010 fire season started and the procurement clerks went to work. Within a month, checks in small amounts, never more than $2,500 for each billing, began to arrive in post office boxes. And as more and more fake bills went out later in the season, those little check trickles became a flood.

The first year, the Green Rivers netted a little over a million dollars. In the next, just under two.

Half the money went to the ten Green Rivers and half to their twenty grunts. Nice money but not something the Green Rivers particularly cared much about that first year. No, that year, the Green Rivers were just the po-po posse quietly "stickin' it to the Chief".

It felt good.

But the second year the Green Rivers got just under a hundred thousand dollars each.

Their perceptions changed.

Being po-po posse members and in their twilight, they'd given up some of their retirement dreams. Now, with dollars this big flowing in, those dreams revived. The money itself got to be a lot more interesting than the joy of anonymously stickin' it to some far-off somebody.

And the same was true for the clerks and auditors. Between the extra pay they got for working long fire hours and the funds coming in from the Green Rivers, they could now dream of better college educations for their kids, vacation weeks in Las Vegas, new pickups, or, for Thyra, the chance to reroof her mother's home.

Pretty soon, no one, Green River forest supervisor or clerk, was "feelin' the luv" for anything other than the money.

------------------------------ // ------------------------------

Clipper sighs and picks up his phone. Time to start clueing the other Green Rivers in about the clerks' rebellion. Seventy percent. He could hear the what-the-Hells and the wah-wah-wahs now.

Chapter 7 – Dark Inquiry

Two days after Mill picked Philip up at the Missoula airport, she and Philip arrived at Bull's apartment in DC. They opened the door with the key the building manager had given them.

It was late in the day. Drenched dusk flowed in through rain-dotted windows.

Philip snapped on the light switch. Harsh light from a single-bulb, overhead fixture threw back the gloom.

Mill glanced around. She knew her father had a large, ten-room log house in California that he had prepared for his eventual retirement.

She would get out to his place in California sometime. Dad's stuff was in a locked storage room off the garage. An elderly couple rented the place long-term. She had no reason to disturb them.

Besides, what could be there that would matter anyway? Probably just old stuff to be thrown away.

But this apartment…what a contrast to the California place. Mill gestured at clothes and newspapers scattered around the small living room, "Philip, look at this pit. Do you think the FBI and Forest Service LEOs left it this way?"

Philip squinted at the dusty mess, "No, Manny Suemez said they went through here and tried not to disturb anything. He said there was nothing initially linking your Dad's apartment to his death. And after you gave your permission to come in, they found nothing here anyway."

He shrugged and looked at his exhausted wife, "Why don't we just check around a little tonight and then get to our hotel for some sleep? Hit it hard tomorrow."

Mill shook her head, "No, we need to gather up anything that might give us an idea of why he was killed…and anything of cash value, I guess. I have no idea what's here but we at least have to pull things together that Dad cared about…."

Tears came to her eyes. Her Dad had been such a pain in the ass for all of her life. So, she had avoided him as much as possible. Now that he was so suddenly gone, she had no idea what he valued.

Grief rippled through her. The conviction gripped her that she had to honor the things in her Dad's last place if only because she had not honored him.

She pointed towards the back bedrooms, "I'll search back there if you'll take this area—living room, dining room, and kitchen."

"Should I be throwing anything away as I go?"

"For sure. You know, old newspapers…food things that might spoil before we can get this place cleared out."

"Okay. Got it."

The two spilt up. Mill headed towards the bath and bedrooms.

Philip gingerly started to pick up scattered newspapers, trash, and clothing. Not a minute later, Philip found a few pieces of women's clothing by the couch and, a few feet away, underwear and an earring.

Suddenly blushing as if he'd been caught cheating on Mill, Philip hesitated. W.A. had died so horribly. Philip didn't want Mill to suffer more over his death because of her Dad's skirt-chasing lifestyle. He began to bag up the woman's clothes with the idea of just hiding them in the rest of the garbage.

He stopped himself. If Mill did not already know, she surely would find out about her father's habits as a result of the investigation into his death. Besides, she was a cop. She'd be upset with him if he tried to hide "evidence," even if it only pointed to her father's shallow, immoral life.

Shaking his head, he made a small pile of the women's clothes and accessories on one tattered, overstuffed chair.

An hour passed. Philip finished cleaning out the kitchen. He filled garbage bags with anything that might go bad in the next several weeks and took them out to the trash. He filled more bags with non-perishable items for a later haul to a homeless shelter or soup kitchen.

Finally he stood and looked around the rooms he had cleaned up. Nothing there but the dust-bunny leftovers of W.A.'s life.

Philip's heart sank. What a pitiful meaningless place W.A. had lived in when he died.

Philip walked back to the bedrooms, "So, Milly, what do you want me to do next? I found some…"

The look on Mill's face stopped him from continuing.

Mill was studying what appeared to be a list. She wore a frown so deep that the lines around her mouth looked carved in.

She glanced up at him and waved the paper, "Philip, this was stuck to the underside of Dad's laptop with two-sided tape. As near as I can make out, it's a list of Dad's sexual escapades with his Associate Chief, Esperanza Pizzaro."

"My goodness."

Mill looked up at Philip with a hurting, angry look, "And, Philip, it's…it's…awful stuff. As best I can tell, he abused her…forced her."

34

Tears started in the corners of Mill's eyes, "I know he was a ladies' man. Always had some woman around when I was growing up...maybe more than one at a time. But I had no idea he was a...a predator."

Her voice trailed off, "It doesn't seem to fit. I mean all Pizzaro would have to do is turn him in at the Forest Service and he'd be fired for this...sent to jail maybe." Having half-convinced herself that her father couldn't be as bad as the list implied, she finished, "So, there must be more to the story. Must be...."

Philip certainly hoped so, "What do you want to do with this list, Milly? Should we turn it over to law enforcement?"

Mill realized he had put his finger on the very question that had been nagging at her--one that she had tried to ignore.

Both Pizzaro and her Dad were dead. To law enforcement, the two deaths had no apparent connection.

If she turned in this list, the information about her Dad's sexual relationship with Pizzaro would get pulled into both investigations...almost certainly get leaked. And if the deaths turned out to be unrelated, both Pizzaro and her Dad would have their sex lives paraded publicly for nothing.

All else equal, they deserved better...particularly Pizzaro.

"No, Philip," Mill replied sadly, "We'll hold on to this for now."

As the words left her mouth, Mill realized with a shock that she was protecting her father...just as she had protected her mother two years before. Rebecca Theophile Meacham was a part of Mist, the violent eco-terrorist organization Mill had helped uncover.

Rebecca had been present when Mist operators killed Jake Burns and badly hurt Mill herself. And Mill had kept that information from Forest Service law enforcement and the FBI.

Her long-missing Mom...the chance of reconnection...Mill had no knowledge that Rebecca was a criminal anyways.... Back then, it had been one of those confusing non-choices...to let things be...just go along...and no one would know.

But now, if she held back the sex information about her Dad, she would be twice guilty of withholding information from federal investigators. Her spirit split between shame at not doing her duty and her passion to protect her family. Her heart ached.

She lowered her head. "Philip," she moaned, "I don't know what I'm doing...asking you to do, too. My parents...I can't get myself to talk to the other LEOs about their bad stuff. Mom and Mist. Now

Dad and Pizzaro. What the Hell am I doing? People need to know this stuff."

"Milly," he replied softly, rubbing her neck, "you're doing what any child would do--seeking her parents love. Thinking of W.A., you're not the first person to want a father's love, long absent in life and now far away in death. I understand that hunger, while I haven't a clue how you can get love from beyond the grave...."

Philip thought for a moment, chill on his spine, "No, it's usually something else that comes from that place." This was not his faith speaking, but his experience with loss.

Chapter 8 – Dark, Impending Storm

To the north of Cutter's Park, a large stand of old-growth spruce and fir trees sprawls across a broad landscape that rises from the park's edge to a tall ridge. Within the forest, high above the floor, arching branches and needles touch and form a canopy. The tight web of branches throws shade across hundreds of acres of small shrubs, ferns, and mosses growing below. Here and there, the canopy breaks. Light streams down into gaps where old trees once stretched their limbs to the sky, then died and fell. Or where winter storms broke their backs and snows pitilessly bore them down.

Under the old-growth forest, ninety-two members of Mist's War Clan sit on mossy logs and rock outcrops to listen to their War Chief speak. Badger says, "In a moment I will pass the Talking Stick so that all of you who have something to say may speak or, if you have questions, ask. But first, I have something to say to all of you." She takes two easy steps to the highest point of an enormous downed spruce log covered in a deep mossy blanket.

She smiles a grim smile, "You are all volunteers. You are also all the warriors Mist has, our finest. Most of you didn't even know one another until a few weeks ago. And yet to Cutter's Park you have come. I want you to know how much I respect your choice to be here. Many of us will bleed or even die in the next days as we confront the Greed Machine. But our sacrifice will be for a noble cause, the protection of our Earth Mother. What we of Mist do here will serve as a symbol of how much we care about this planet and its wildest places. If we must become martyrs, then so be it. Our sacrifice will send a signal everywhere that our dear Mother is worth giving up everything for, even dying. Green warriors, I salute you!"

The assembled warriors cheer.

Badger quickly signals for quiet with her hands, "Please, brothers and sisters, let's keep our voices down. The federal thugs may already have surveillance in the area."

Looking a little abashed, the warriors quickly hush.

Badger takes a stick she had carved and decorated with feathers the evening before, "Here is the Talking Stick. Pass it from person to person until all are satisfied."

She turns to her left and tosses the stick to Chronos, her second in command and the person most responsible for molding the assembled warriors into fighting units.

Chronos speaks quietly but distinctly, "I fought for the Greed Machine in the Iraq War called Desert Storm. But once I came to believe in our Mother's sanctity, I joined Mist to fight for Her survival. I am proud to be here."

He looks around the group, "And I, too, am proud of you. I know most of you are untested in battle. You have only the experience we've been able to give you in the last six months. That's why you are organized into small Prides of five or six warriors with an experienced fighter in charge. Badger and I have organized the Prides into two Fangs, so we can concentrate on supporting you and your Pride leaders during battle. Your Pride leader will get you through your assignments. Count on your Pridemates and your training."

He raises the Talking Stick and points it towards the east, "Trouble is on its way. So, when things look bad, dig deep and find the Mother's love within you. Then get angry and punish those who would hurt Her."

Heads nod agreement around the warriors' circle.

Chronos throws the Talking Stick to a small female warrior on his left.

She speaks in a high, clear voice, "I am Pride Leader Green Hawk, head of air defense. Badger, I have a question about when to use our weapons. I know we have to be careful in our timing because we don't have much capability. So, based on your latest intelligence, has anything changed about when we should be prepared to Strike?"

"Green Hawk," replies Badger gravely, "your Pride is critical to our success. We foresee two battle scenarios. The first is that the thugs will launch a ground attack without air support until we resist, and then aircraft will be sent to attack us."

"The second is the one I believe is most likely. The Greed Machine is proud of their weapons and technology. I counted on that arrogance when I worked out our second battle plan. In this scenario, the thugs arrive by air and establish a perimeter, then follow up with more personnel by air and ground. Once they've built up a lot of force close to or within Cutter's Park, they'll attack."

"So, in answer to your question, keep your air defenses hidden, on standby, until the first helicopters arrive. If the helicopters come first, land in Cutter's Park, and the thugs rush out to establish a perimeter, wait until Fang Commander Chronos and his Hellfire Pride complete their work. If the thugs come in on foot followed by helicopters, Strike the helicopters before they land."

Badger points at the young woman, "Green Hawk, you and your Pride have one of our toughest assignments. While other warriors are attacking and gaining victory, you will have to be patient and wait for Strike opportunities. This will be the hardest thing of all, waiting for the right moment while the other Prides are fighting."

Green Hawk grins through her camouflage face paint, "We will not fail the Mother, Badger." Green Hawk passes the Talking Stick to the next person.

Several warriors make comments. About halfway around the circle, an older warrior asks Badger, "I know we've talked about this, Badger, but I'm still not clear about why we're not using radios to communicate. Wouldn't we be able to coordinate our attacks better if we used them?"

Badger nods, "Yes, Stinger, it would be easier to use the radios. But we have to figure that the Greed Machine can monitor them…in fact, even if we used repeaters, would track us as we used them and even fire weapons at them. So, in this case, we answer their technology with a low-tech solution—no radios, but small, mobile Prides with clear objectives. Prides that operate independently, supported by well-trained medics and resupply warriors at known locations."

Badger looks around the group, "And we answer the Green Machine's thermal- and ferrous- tracking technology with high-tech of our own—with cool suits better than theirs' and with weapons containing little or no metal. Once again, we follow Mist's long-time ghost-force doctrine. We Strike invisibly and drift away, only to Strike again."

Stinger waves, "Understood, Badger…okay."

The Talking Stick passes around the circle once more and then again. Finally there are no more comments or questions. Badger speaks distinctly, "Okay, Mist Warriors, it's time to take your positions and wait for the thugs to arrive. I ask our Great Earth Mother to shelter and protect you. Strike hard!"

A few warriors cheer but then, regretting their noise, quickly quiet and join their Prides. The Prides trail out of the clearing to hidden locations.

A dozen hides lie close to Cutter's Park. Several more are dug in to the north and east along the timbered ridge lines above the Park and adjacent to huge Bear Valley.

Badger and Chronos watch as the Prides leave. Their own Prides wait several yards away while the two confer quietly.

Chronos asks Badger, "Do you think any of them know about the rest of Mist, how many other warriors there are?"

"No, I've listened closely to our warriors' talk. No one has mentioned the rest. These warriors were recruited from the most isolated cells, the ones that had never been supported by warriors from the other Clans, not even Movement. So, if any of these folks get captured and tortured by the federal thugs, they can only speculate about where support may have come from. The thugs will get nothing they can use."

Chronos nods and lowers his head to get closer to Badger's ear, "Badger, what if Millicent Meacham comes here? How will you handle that?"

"Chief Meacham is dead. Eyes and Ears reports that Milly mourns her loss, off-duty. And the feds would never let my daughter get this close to Mist after what happened before, too personal…against policy."

Rebecca Theophile Meacham smiles grimly under her green-and-brown painted face, "And if Milly does somehow show up, she will just have to take her chances with the rest of the thugs."

Chronos whispers, "Okay, but if she gets here, you have to be ready for tough choices."

"I am," Badger answers and makes the resolve in her voice metallic, hard--more to convince herself than Chronos that she would show her daughter no mercy.

The two turn away and start to walk towards their Prides. Just as they cross a large, mossy log, a HeloEye hums into the clearing.

Hearing the noise, the two leaders drop into ferny cover.

The ten other warriors don't notice the tiny camera until it orbits them for the second time.

Nine fall to the ground. The tenth stands, mouth agape, as the whirring device pauses and gets a clear picture of the warrior's painted face.

"Gotcha," the HeloEye pilot says to herself in Boise.

Raising her voice, she shouts, "Contact! Call Special Agent Tomlin and tell her we have a location."

"Okay, I'll make the call," her supervisor says, "You get ready to uplink the video to FBI Headquarters…."

Chapter 9 - Funeral Pyre

A day after cleaning out her Dad's apartment, Mill stared at the large TV screen in the Forest Service law enforcement offices, her mind whirling. First her father's homicide, and now this video of Esperanza Pizzaro's death shows up.

"This changes everything," she thought, "but also lets my Dad off the hook."

She turned to Manny Suemez, "Please play that again."

Manny cued the video recorder. Once again, Angie Pizzaro's face and torso appeared on the screen. Behind her were shelves, busy with books and stacks of paper, and, to her right side, a folding table with more paper stacks on top of it and boxes beneath. No sign of the ceiling, floor, or doors.

The bulk of a computer screen blocked the left side of Pizzaro's body from the lens. She stared into the screen, face intent. A few moments passed as her hands moved over the keys.

Then from behind Pizzaro's right side a dark object appeared. It looked something like the shaft and handle of a cane.

Pizzaro didn't react, perhaps because the object was outside her peripheral vision or perhaps because she was so focused on the screen.

Manny put the video into slow-mo.

The cane-like object swung wide and then whipped back to slam into Pizzaro's head. A donut-shaped spurt of flame and smoke erupted at the impact point.

Pizzaro's head and body jerked to her left and dropped out of sight.

Incredible! But what happened next was even more unbelievable. Seeming to rise out of nowhere, a slender, grey-clad human shape moved up into the picture.

Mill had an instant flashback to a similar person she had seen two years ago in the old Portland whorehouse where Jake Burns had died and she was badly injured. It was a painful, disjointed memory.

She had not recalled it before today. The docs had said that this sort of memory could pop up spontaneously. She shook the memory off, promising herself to rerun it later.

On the screen, the masked figure moved carefully. It took a small automatic handgun from a pocket. The figure then knelt and bent down.

Whatever contact there was between the killer and the dead woman could not be seen, cut off as it was by the plane of the desk's surface and the keyboard. A moment later the figure stood, leaped gracefully over what must have been Pizzaro's body and out of camera range. The video ran another sixty seconds, and then ended.

"Damn, Manny," Mill groaned, "these Mist bastards are everywhere. Didn't you say there was security on Pizzaro's place, no sign of unauthorized entry? And where did this video come from? It looked like this unsub didn't know about the camera."

When he didn't answer right away, Mill looked more closely at him.

Manny's eyes held his old-West sheriff look, the one that meant someone was in deep, deadly trouble.

He paused a moment longer, considering, and then spoke, "Mill, Pizzaro's security is one of the better home systems. But top-notch hackers can take 'em down, reprogram and later wipe 'em—and sometimes do all that remotely. So, no tellin' about how the Mist *asesino* got in or out. And, of course, when the crime-scene folks processed the site, they thought Pizzaro's death was suicide. You know, locked doors and windows, gun on the floor, contact wound on her temple. It all pointed to suicide."

"Anyway, they didn't know, so they missed the chance to really work Pizzaro's place over before it got trampled by cops and the Coroner's people. Then, a couple of days ago, one of our guys went in Pizzaro's place to look for gum'ent documents, equipment, and I don't know, rubber bands...whatever. The guy spots a clock radio on Pizzaro's desk. He recognizes it as a nanny cam, one of those heat- and motion-triggered video cameras people stick in their places to watch their hired help steal stuff and abuse the kids. Lucky for us our guy had the same one at home where he's been trying to catch his wife banging the plumber or something. "

"Okay, so he stops what he's doing and calls me. I get a tech over there. The tech brings the thing in here. We look at the recordings and call Freda Tomlin over at the FBI. Then the *mierda* lands in the *sarten*."

Mill had heard of shit hitting the fan before but never landing in a frying pan. This thought rolled around in her head for a moment and brought a faint smile to her face.

She looked at Manny and saw that his mouth was drawn into a severe, no-nonsense line.

Repressing her smile, she asked "So, did the Mist killer know about this nanny cam? I mean, if the unsub knew, why wouldn't they just shut if off or block the lens? Or maybe they *meant* for us to get the image. Oh crap, with these Mist bastards, you just can't tell."

"Well," Manny responded, "we know there's other stuff that's *extrano*, you know, weird, odd. Pizzaro got a Facebook post. She seems to have responded before she died. Maybe that's what we see her doing in the nanny cam footage. The timing fits more or less with when the security system says she was in the house and with her time of death."

He stares at the ceiling for a moment, "Her response could be read to mean she had plans to kill herself, you know, a suicide note. The big thing though is that her incoming message was from a supposed Mist source, one that gave her a phone number to call. We got her phone records and, as far as we can tell, she died before she could make that call."

Manny shoved a copy of the Facebook post across the table.

Mill read it quickly, "'Supposed Mist source' huh? You mean you believe the unsub might have *staged* the e-mails? But why? How? We don't see the unsub typing on the computer...just Pizzaro. Could it have been done remotely?"

Manny shook his head, "No, the tech folks say it was keyed in from Pizzaro's computer...no internet trace."

Mill threw her hands up, "Christ Almighty, this is just nuts. Nothing fits." Mill shook her head, "Manny what about the phone number? Did you call it?"

"Yeah, it goes to someplace in Quebec. Numbers given were not in service"

Mill looked closely at the numbers again, "These numbers look like some sort of business, even have an extension number. Did you find out where they'd been assigned before, get a location?"

Manny shook his head, "No, no help there. One had been assigned to a residence a while back. The other never had been assigned."

Mill frowned, "Phone numbers that are not in service. Another dead end or a dodge? Some kind of code?"

Manny smiled his sheriff's smile, "*Quien sabe, Chica*? Who the Hell knows?"

Once again, Mist had led them to a dead end, although clearly the eco-terrorists had tried to pin membership in their organization on Pizzaro.

How could that serve them? Would it somehow throw law enforcement off Mist's trail? If that was the idea, it wasn't real smart and it hadn't worked thanks partially to the nanny cam.

Mill was struck with another question, "Manny, what about this Quebec angle? For the last two years we've beat bushes all over the U.S. and we've had a Hell of a time finding Mist, let alone getting informants to cooperate. What if Mist has been hiding out in Canada all this time? Even after 9/11, the border's still pretty porous. Maybe they're hanging out in the People's Republic of Canadia."

Manny smiled slightly at Mill's joke about Canadians supposedly being more liberal than people in the U.S., "Could be. We've contacted the RCMP for some help. Nice part of working with the Mounties, they've got a lot more surveillance flexibility than we do even under the Patriot Act. And they have a much smaller population to watch. So, if Mist is hanging out in Canada's piney woods, they'll dig them up and out."

Mill sighed with frustration, "What a mess. Plenty of questions and no answers."

Moments later, Manny got interrupted and left the room to take a phone call from the FBI.

Mill dialed the Canadian numbers in the Facebook post.

Sure enough, no answers…dead end…again.

Chapter 10 – Digging Deeper

That afternoon, Manny and Mill arrived at the FBI headquarters across town from the Forest Service law enforcement offices. They waited until a group assembled and then their meeting began. Hours of reports and comments rolled by.

Finally, a frustrated Special Agent in Charge Frieda Tomlin pounded the table, "Goddamn it, you cherries, you better get this Mist case broken open before the unsubs start livin' in my basement without payin' rent."

The formidable little woman glared around the conference room table at a dozen or so FBI agents and the two Forest Service LEOs, "How the Hell do they get their information…go the places they do…and we have no clue about where they are or what they're up to?"

One of the senior FBI agents protested diffidently, "But, Frieda, our Mist sources have all dried up. Informants have gone missing or won't talk. The Quebec numbers are nothing. We have no idea what the unsubs plan to do next…nothing…no leads."

The red-faced Tomlin almost leaped onto the table, "What did I just say, Robbie? I don't care what you *don't* know. I want you to get this case working again. We have two fresh federal corpses here, job-related deaths. Pizzaro's killing is certainly a Mist kill. And the other is 99%-positive-fuckin'-tootly theirs as well. So you sherry-sippin,' FBI chair-boobs better get to work and find these Mist unsub bastards. Otherwise, for the next thousand parades down Constitution Avenue, you'll be in uniform shoveling up manure after all the politicians trot by."

She glared around the table, "Any more stupid comments? Okay, now get your weak asses back to work."

The task force members stood. Frieda pointed at Manny and Mill, "Not you two worthless cow cops. You stay put. I want words with you."

Manny and Mill dropped back into their seats as the others filed out.

Once the door closed behind the drooping group of FBI agents, Frieda walked briskly over to Mill and Manny. She sat down next to Mill and took her hand.

Frieda had been shocked when Mill had walked into the task force meeting a couple of hours earlier. Mill's face normally held a slight frown but now the frown was deep, lines etching her face. And she had been so clearly tired, shoulders drooping. Mill was not the woman filled with bursting energy that Frieda had remembered, an energy that had come through even when Mill had been hospitalized after a vicious attack by Mist killers.

In an uncharacteristically soft voice Tomlin asked, "Sorry if I mentioned your Dad, but I was just...you know...makin' a point. How you holding up, Meacham? Is that Bible-thumpin' husband of yours helping or do I need to pay him a visit?"

Mill smiled tiredly. She had come to love this gruff, belligerent FBI agent. After watching Frieda work, Mill thought Frieda's bluster and intimidation were merely clever theater meant to get fast and accurate results. For Frieda, there were so many bad guys in the world, all of them hurting people. And Frieda had made it her mission to bust them all before she died. So, no time to waste. Unless a friend needed help...as Mill did now.

"Philip is being the best support I could have, Frieda," Mill answered quietly, "Stays up all hours with me when I can't sleep. Right now he's off Milly duty and trying to catch up on sleep."

Frieda dropped Mill's hand and leaned back in her chair, "He may be great help, Meacham, but you still look like shit. You ought to be taking a month off, not trying to do police work."

Tomlin shook her head, "You sure you want to work this case? It's damn personal for you. In fact, FBI rules wouldn't allow an agent with your connection to work the case at all."

Manny leaned forward, "Agent Tomlin, I'm partnering with Mill on this. I guarantee she won't do anything crazy. And so far we're just consulting with the FBI, not running the case. So, Mill and I don't have the pressure on us the rest of you do."

Tomlin snorted, "The fuck you don't, Suemez! Look at this girl. Her dad's just been killed. Pizzaro's been murdered. In one day, the two leaders of a major federal agency have been killed. Meacham's brain's fried with trying to take it all in. She's worn out and sore. I don't think Mill Meacham might do something crazy. I *know* she'll do something crazy. You just make fuckin' sure she doesn't hurt herself or anyone else when she does."

Mill said evenly, a little of her old energy returning to her voice, "Frieda, look, I asked Manny to let me in. I can help. And...I really need to work. It's not some pride thing. Work keeps my anxiety down. Helps me focus. Otherwise, my brain really could explode."

46

Her voice took on a slight pleading note, "If I can't stay and help, I'm not sure I can survive...stay sane."

Frieda looked sharply at Mill, "Do you have help, Meacham? I don't mean your silly Saint Philip. I mean a counselor. Somebody to keep you out of the funny farm or, Goddamn me for mentioning it, from eating your gun."

Mill nodded reluctantly, "Yes, a good guy. I've been seeing him...well...for a lot of things."

"Okay, Meacham," Frieda said flatly, "You're on the case, but you go lightly. None of your damn feminist heroics."

Then, returning fully to her former style, Tomlin spat, "Okay, you fuckin' cow cops, you got anything a real law enforcement outfit can use? Or are you just here to drink the FBI's gourmet fuckin' cappuccinos?"

Two hours later, the three special agents sat staring at a long whiteboard that covered almost one wall of the room. The whiteboard showed a twisted mess of lists and diagrams that laid out everything the three knew about the recent deaths and any apparent connections to other Mist information their two agencies had.

Tomlin summed up, "Damn, that's a lot of crap, people. We have so little to go on."

She waved towards the board, "Look. No origins on the bomb materials. Everything seems to have been manufactured independently from base and untraceable chemical stocks. No markers in the C-4 or the electronics to lead us anywhere. No fingerprints that can't be explained. No DNA or fibers that don't fit. No visuals or witnesses. Pizzaro's unsub killer on video, but masked and covered...no voice. Let's fuckin' face it, cow cops, our basic forensics suck."

She stood and paced closer to the whiteboard. "The only thing hanging out at all is this Quebec phone number business...or better said, *no* phone number business 'cause they don't work."

Manny tapped the table, "You're right, Frieda. It's the only lead we got, and, it leads nowhere. Not in service. Typical Mist. Now you see 'em, now you don't."

Mill chimed in, "And we don't know if the phone numbers were a Mist plant... I mean above and beyond their apparent desire to conceal Pizzaro's murder as a suicide. But, as you said, Manny, the numbers mean nothing. Are they misdirection maybe, 'Out of service' and all that? Mocking us?"

A thought struck Suemez, "So, Frieda, what if they're not phone numbers? Did your analysts take a look at the numbers alone? Could they detect any code or pattern?"

Tomlin shook her head, "Yes, we looked at that angle. And, no, there was no code or pattern that we could tell. It could be an encryption, but without an algorithm or key, we could never break such a short number string. Just nineteen numbers is all there is to work with. And we never figured out any Mist codes, if they use any at all. Maybe it's just misdirection or mockery like Mill said. Or maybe it's a meet location, you know, a safe house or drop site."

Suddenly a chill ran down Mill's neck. There was something about these numbers that seemed subtly familiar. No, not the numbers themselves, or their sequence. No, it was something about the *number* of numbers.

The chill came back, stronger now.

Mill recognized the feeling. In the past, whenever she was on the edge of discovering something…something hidden, important, the chill would come. In fact, she had felt it when she found the first piece of evidence connecting a Mist killer to a Forest Service death…a tattered piece of cloth along a trail…a clue with no importance at the time.

Then it struck her. Mill said, "Manny, you may be on to something. And Frieda, it might actually be a code all right, but one hidden in plain sight."

With some of her old energy, Mill jumped up from her seat. She walked to the whiteboard and wrote, "450-804-6851 or 1496, x2878." She stared at the numbers for a moment, and then erased the word "or", the letter "x" and the dashes. The numbers now read "450 804 6851 1496 2878."

She turned to Frieda and Manny, "You guys know I used to run the field as a fisheries biologist. And you might remember I was on the Great Land Geo-Challenge, that crazy reality show thing where we ran all over Alaska using Global Positioning System equipment to find our way."

She shook her head, "What a nightmare."

Manny smiled at her comment. The Geo-Challenge time was when he met Mill, realized how brave and resourceful she was, and convinced her to become a LEO. And, yes, it had been a nightmare…mostly for Mill and her fellow racers.

48

Mill continued, "Well, I used to look at numbers like this all the time…on my eTrex GPS unit. These could be latitude and longitude. You can display lat-long in degrees, minutes, and seconds, or as a decimal number. These numbers wouldn't fit the minutes-seconds thing. But, see, if they were a decimal, they'd look something like this."

She quickly added periods and little "Os." Now the numbers looked like, "45.804685°" and "114.962878°".

Mill looked intently at Frieda, "You actually have to work backwards in the number sequences…six positions for the fraction, then two or three positions for the whole numbers. You wouldn't know this stuff unless you'd been running the field in places where there are no roads…places where you have to depend on maps and lat-long coordinates to get around. So, no reason your analysts could have known or even guessed."

Tomlin scowled, "Well, I pay the bastards to be better than that, Meacham. But, nooooo, if you're right, once again they let you cow pies beat them."

She shook her head ruefully and spat, "I'll take away their fuckin' Metro passes for goofing this one."

Mill and Manny laughed. Almost everyone rode the DC Metro to get around town. The FBI folks would not relish taking taxis at their own cost or, worse, walking to their various appointments.

Mill spotted the twinkle in Tomlin's eye, "Frieda, you could take away their shoes, too."

Frieda snapped back, "I like the way you think, Meacham. Maybe their feet."

The three laughed again.

"Okay, you forest freaks, to where or what do these numbers point us?" Frieda asked forcefully, "I swear, Meacham, if they point us to the middle of the Atlantic Ocean or downtown Bum Fuck, Egypt, I will never let you live it down."

Tomlin put a mock scowl on her face.

Mill laughed, "Yeah, look Frieda, I have no desire to go to Egypt for that or any other reason. So, I sequenced the numbers to fit in the U.S. But I'm not sure exactly where."

She looked up at the ceiling for a moment, considering, "But I'd say somewhere about where I-90 crosses the Rocky Mountains."

Mill drew a quick, rather turtle-shaped map of the U.S. on the whiteboard, "I'm no artist, but see, I-90 runs along the 45th parallel, more or less, and '114' means west of the Mississippi and east of Seattle, maybe about half way between. Guess your analysts could figure that out pretty quick. I could if I had my GPS here. Ah, maybe my iComm can do it...."

Before she could finish her sentence, the door had slammed behind Frieda.

Manny murmured admiringly, "Gotta give that woman credit, she never sits still when there's reason to move."

Mill almost kidded the man about being attracted to Frieda but she held back. Manny had always been strictly business with her and she did not want to offend him. Maybe another time when everyone was in a lighter mood.

Mill suddenly realized with a slight shock that her sense of humor and playfulness were returning. Her counselor had said that such emotions would be very good signs and to keep focusing on those thoughts and feelings for as long as she could.

Five minutes later, Frieda came back into the room with a wiry, but rather disheveled-looking little man in tow.

"Okay, Mr. What's Your Name," she yelled, "get that damn map up on the wall."

The guy looked nervously at Mill and Manny, and then shuffled by them to the whiteboard. He unrolled a map of the northern Rockies, and pointed to a red dot stuck to the map's surface. "Here's the location of the coordinates you gave us, Special Agent Meacham. Idaho. The Frank Church – River of No Return Wilderness."

The analyst gazed at the map for a moment, "Doesn't look like anything's there. I mean it's a Wilderness, right? Nothing's there is it?"

For a moment, the three special agents had no reply to his questions.

Mill thought, "Sure there's something there. Wilderness has all kinds of great things in it -- wild beauty...plants...animals...unique species and habitats."

But then she realized, the man was asking if there was some kind of town or buildings there.

She replied, "No, nothing there that would show up on your map. No towns, roads...pipelines. Nothing like that."

They all stared at the map a little longer.

Then Frieda Tomlin let out a low whistle, "There's something there all right. Mist. Mist is there. The phone numbers...whatever...were a cipher wrapped in a challenge. They killed our people...made our informants disappear...laid a big slap on us...and

50

then showed us numbers. They figured the shock of the killings would distract us...that it'd take us awhile to get their point. It did. And it gave 'em time to get ready for us."

Manny's face once again held his sheriff look, "So, they're ready."

He looked grimly at the two women, "They better be ready for *la danza de la muerte* because we're going to bring the music."

"You're a fuckin' poet, Suemez," Frieda grimaced in response, "a regular Roy Orbison among cops."

Manny didn't smile.

Mill thought, "Yes, poet or not, Manny's right, this fight will be 'the dance of death.' Mist and the Forest Service—like two knife fighters in a bad western, tied together by one wrist--only our music will come from gun barrels, not guitars and trumpets."

She shuddered, whether from fear or anticipation she did not know.

Chapter 11 - Puzzles

In the week after Mist's Idaho hideout had been discovered, Mill had little contact with Frieda and Manny. The two had been working to bring a multi-agency task force together that would sweep into the River of No Return Wilderness and root Mist out.

And Mill was getting settled in DC, working through some cases back home in Montana, and figuring our W.A.'s estate. All that took time.

Mill knew Frieda had sent significant surveillance to the area around the lat/long coordinates. In fact, more than 1,000 square miles was being tracked and analyzed by satellite, high-altitude fly-over's, and a few well-armed, ground-pounding "hikers" who seemed to be looking for that lost-in-the-wilderness experience. And more techno-sensors were due anytime.

Frieda promised Mill that she would call personally if anything was found. No calls so far.

Mill and Philip had rented a month-by-month "executive" apartment not far from Crystal City in DC's Virginia suburbs. It came complete with everything from linens to cookware and the building offered a food-delivery service. Given the intensity of their feelings and concerns, the apartment arrangement could not have been better.

Today, as Manny and Frieda labored on the other side of the Potomac, Mill sat looking through the pile of personal items she and Philip had brought over from her Dad's apartment before closing it out. Philip had sorted the stuff into three piles: "throw away", "look at some time", and "look now".

Mill had finished the look-now pile. She had set aside several items, including several pieces of women's jewelry, mostly earrings, a few datebooks and calendars, anything electronic, and several keys. She looked at the small pile, shrugged, and dug into the much larger, look-at-some-time pile.

She had burrowed about halfway through the pile when Philip came in. As she looked up, he smiled and immediately came across the room to kiss her.

As she had many times before, Mill thought, "There's something so good about this guy and, even better, he looks like a tall Johnny Depp. Such a deal!"

One kiss led to another and Mill soon gave up any thought of any more treasure hunting. They walked hand in hand into the bedroom.

Sex between them was complicated. It went beyond the reality that Mill had so much experience and Philip almost none. Much of Mill's experience had come while she was drunk or high. And, for many years, it was confused, driven, infused with rage. She hadn't cared whether her partner was male or female, as long as the person appeased Mill's demons for a time.

And then there was the truth that, at this stage in Mill's recovery from sex addiction, she mistrusted her sexual impulses and motives. She wanted tenderness and physical contact from Philip, not orgasmic release. In fact, she was very close to being asexual just now, edgily detached and almost disinterested.

Before they had become a couple, Philip had learned quite a bit about Mill's sexual history. This knowledge had profoundly shocked him. And when they first married, it hadn't seemed to matter. Now, feeling like he somehow had to measure up higher than all the partners she had been with before, he was almost obsessed with pleasing his wife sexually.

Philip tried too hard. Mill held back.

He wanted to try positions and behaviors he'd never done before. She pretended to be surprised at things that she had done innumerable times.

He watched her for signs of dissatisfaction. She tried not to disappoint him and forced herself to be enthusiastic.

If Mill had a favorite position any more, it was straddling Philip's lap while he rested against the head of their bed, back against a wedge of pillows. She would move her body against his, teasing his penis with her labia, and letting him taste her nipples. When he became firm, she would arch her back and slip him inside. After a few minutes, she would bring him to orgasm with long, slow, smooth movements of her hips.

If Mill could manage an orgasm for herself at all, it would be this way. Or, more often, she could fake one by pulling his face against her breasts, shuddering, and cooing triumphantly.

According to Philip's great-male-lover stereotype, men were to be active, forceful. So, he wanted to be on top.

Sex with Mill on top meant she was pleasuring him, not vice versa. He thought he should have Mill moving and moaning with pleasure beneath him.

But today, once again, he wound up under Mill with her in control.

54

A half hour after they walked into the bedroom, they lay covered in sweat and after-love dissatisfaction.

Mill turned on her side and pulled Philip closer with her right arm. He resisted.

A pang of fear shot through her. What if he wasn't satisfied? What if he left her because she wasn't pleasing him?

Didn't everyone betray her? Didn't they all leave her...Mom...Dad...her former partner, Tilly?

She almost couldn't speak. What if she asked the wrong question and sent him steaming out? Finally, after a desperate moment, she whispered hoarsely, "Philip, love, what's wrong? You seem angry about something and I can't figure out what it is."

Normally Philip was incredibly in tune with Mill's moods and quick to support her. But sex was such unknown territory for him. And he felt so inadequate with all those ghostly lovers wandering around his bedroom.

So Philip just said, "Nothing, Milly...nothing's wrong."

Mill's ears heard his words, but in her heart, where she wanted only Philip's tenderness, fear of losing him grew. Could he know that she was emotionally worn out...that she had faked her orgasm?

With a catch in her voice, she replied, "Okay. Let me know if there ever is."

After a few minutes, Philip fell asleep. Mill lay beside him, eyes searching the tiny hills and valleys of the ceiling for answers.

She found none.

Philip woke after an hour. Mill and he snuggled for a few minutes. Then they got up.

Philip went into the bathroom for a quick shower. Mill went out to the little kitchen and made a pot of tea.

A few minutes later, Philip came out of the bedroom, his hair towel-tousled, "Whatcha doing, Milly?"

"Well, I've been working through these piles you made for me. I've finished the 'look-now' stuff and I've almost finished the 'look-at-sometime' pile. It's kind of weird, but Dad had a bunch of women's earrings and small items, but pretty much no *pairs* of anything. Surely some of the women would have left a pair of something. You know, in the bathroom or on the nightstand, too hung over to remember where they were."

She realized Philip was staring at her unsmilingly. Oooooh, he could well be measuring her words for how accurately they revealed her innumerable one-night stands.

She blushed and mumbled lamely, "So, I would expect to see at least a few pairs of earrings among the single ones."

Philip thought for a moment, "Yeah that's kind of strange. Could W.A. have just picked these single earrings up off the pavement or something? You know some people do that…watch the ground for items like earrings that might be valuable, even find ones with diamonds in them."

Mill laughed, "No, Dad might bend over to pick up a dime…he was that tight…but I never saw him even look at something like an earring. And then there's this other stuff--a few lipsticks, manicure items—things like that. And I ask myself, why wouldn't he just return these things? Surely he knew where to find at least some of these women?"

Philip shrugged, "Beats me, Milly. I knew your Dad hardly at all. He was only at our wedding for a few hours, entertained everyone with crazy stories, and then left. We've spoken on the phone a few times since. About all the contact we've had."

"That's Dad, all right, a windy force of nature."

Mill paused for a moment, realizing she had mentioned her father as if he was still living. Tears started in her eyes and she lowered her head.

Philip moved to her side on the couch and hugged her close with one arm, "I love you, Milly."

She mumbled, "I love you, too, so much. Thanks for being here with me."

Mill sighed deeply and straightened up, "Okay, dear. Look at this bunch of keys. I couldn't tell you what they're for. See this label? These must be to Dad's house in California. The rest…well, I just don't know."

Philip looked through the pile of keys, some old and tarnished, and some comparatively bright and newer.

"Well, Milly," he said at length, "I'm not sure about most of these. Some seem to be security keys like we have for the church. You know, the kind that say 'do not replicate' on the side so no reputable locksmith will copy them. So those are probably for Forest Service buildings or whatever."

He grabbed and then held up two keys, "But these are for a safety deposit box at a bank. Yeah, see here on this little tab, it says 'First Independence Bank.' Maybe that's here in DC."

Before the last sentence was out of Philip's mouth, Mill was using the internet-locator function on her iComm to locate the First Independence Bank.

"Yup, there are ten branches here in DC. One's at Greer and 14th Streets Northwest. It's closest to Dad's office in the Whitten Building and pretty close to his old apartment. I say we start there in the morning. We'll see if we can locate the safety deposit box and find out if it has anything interesting in it."

Philip nodded, "Okay by me."

Searching for some kind of sunshine to lighten Mill's mood, he said, "Kinda like a treasure hunt, Milly."

Her face lit up. Thank God.

She dimpled at him. He looked at her face and the three dimples…one each in chin and cheeks…and fell in love with the girl of his young life all over again.

Chapter 12 - Gold, Cold Mine

Because of past work with grieving families, Philip thought Mill would have access to the safety deposit box only if she had a copy of W.A.'s death certificate and a court document naming her executor of his estate. He told her this over breakfast, saying "I just don't want you to be disappointed if they won't give you access."

After listening to his caution, she smiled, "This is when being a LEO pays off. I'll have the FBI fax the bank a Patriot Act search order and then, when we get there, show them my badge. They'll let me in to see what's there. Normally I couldn't remove anything under a search order, just look. Takes a court order to remove. But since I'm an heir, I bet I can even walk out with the contents."

Her voice dropped to a growl, "Sometimes, you just have to let the badge and your Glock do the talking."

Philip laughed delightedly, "Goodness, Milly, you sound like a detective on Law and Order, Criminal Intent. Maybe we should have a TV series named after you, 'Millicent Meacham, Have Glock Will Travel.' How about that?"

Mill groaned and held up a hand in protest, "No favors, please."

They got up from the little table and put their dishes in the sink. They grabbed their coats and left the apartment. Mill carried a large briefcase in her hand to fill up with items from the box if there was anything in it.

Twenty minutes later, Philip swung open the heavy door of the First Independence Bank and patted his wife's bottom as she walked past him into the bright interior.

Mill whispered to him, "Keep that up and I'll ravish you in the bank vault."

"Just what I was hoping for," he replied archly.

At his words, Mill felt a twinge of anxiety. She was just kidding. But was Philip going to want love making later?

After yesterday's ambiguous sex, she had even less interest than ever. Inside her, resistance and fear grew a little more. She started to make a mental note to ask her therapist what all this meant and then, nerves jangling, promptly forgot about it as a bank employee approached.

Ten minutes later, the three people were inside the vault and standing in front of a metal wall filled with numbered drawers.

"Here it is, officer," the bank manager said, "This is box C117. Just insert your key as I do mine, turn, and the locks will open."

The woman took a key from a ring in her hand and slid it into the lock on the right side. Mill did the same with the lock on the left. In a moment, they turned their keys, the lock clicked, and the box popped out an inch. The woman grabbed it by its small handle and pulled it out.

"Boy, this is heavy," she grunted, "Just let me get it to the table."

Philip and Mill stepped out of her way. She took a few quick, short steps and dropped the box with a slight thump to the tabletop.

"You know I have to watch while you open the box," the bank manager said, "It's the search order. I have to make sure everything gets put back once you look at it."

Mill took out her special agent credentials, "Ms. Castor, if you look closely, you'll see I'm not only representing the FBI here but I'm also W.A. Meacham's daughter and heir. Here's a copy of his death certificate showing me as his next of kin. I may decide to remove items and take them with me. So, you don't have to stay if you have other things to do."

The woman looked carefully at Mill's ID and the death certificate for moment. If she thought it odd that the FBI would send a Forest Service special agent who was also the daughter of a deceased renter to examine this box, she said nothing.

"Okay, Agent Meacham, I agree you should have full access. I'll just be on my way. Please press this buzzer when you're ready to leave or if I can help you any further."

With that, the woman turned and used a security fob to trigger the vault's gate. She quickly vanished through the gate, heels clicking across the metal bridge that spanned the base of the vault door.

The gate clanged shut behind her like a prison-cell door. A cold breeze flowed down across the couple from the vault's ceiling ventilation grill. Mill shuddered and pulled Philip's arm around her.

Mill turned slowly to the box. She put her hands on the lid.

That certain chill ran up her neck. This time it seemed to have a personal feel to it, not just evidence at a potential crime scene. Did she really want to know what was inside?

Mill squared her shoulders and grinned apprehensively at Philip.

He was looking at her, wondering why she hesitated. He smiled encouragingly, "I'm here, love. Treasure hunt, remember? Nothing in there can hurt you."

With no way to know how entirely wrong he was, Mill swung the lid open.

Mill began to "dig", layer by layer.

Let the treasure hunt begin.

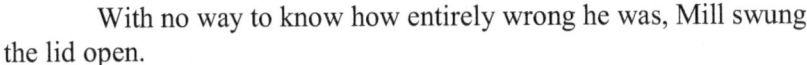

The items on top were startling but not surprising.

W.A.'s heavy revolver and a box with 100 rounds of .45 Long Colt ammunition. Those objects explained much of the box' weight. Mill put the weapon and ammunition in the briefcase.

The next items were mysterious, but not startling.

Six velvet bags containing green-on-gold cloisonné leafs, each beautifully wrought and engraved in different patterns.

"Did your Dad collect art?" Philip asked.

Mill grimaced and said mockingly, "Art for Dad was a half-naked girl on a billboard. He wouldn't have known a Monet from mayonnaise...or cared if there was a difference."

She picked up one of the leaves and rocked it so the light played across the surface.

"Wow," she whispered, "This is really beautiful. Nothing he would want...or could afford for that matter." She was struck by the thought that W.A. might not have come by these heavy gold leaves honestly or at least might have got them in some underhanded way.

Otherwise, wouldn't he have boasted to her about having them? And it seemed so odd for him to have them at all.

Not wanting any connection to them, she quickly slipped the leaf back in its bag and unconsciously wiped her fingerprints off it with the velvet. She placed the bags carefully in the brief case.

What lay under the velvet bags was intriguing, but not mysterious.

A DVD and a few jump drives with no labeling on them to tell what was recorded within. Next to them was a quart-sized plastic bag filled with many small objects—many earrings, a few compacts and lipsticks—reminiscent of similar items in her Dad's apartment.

Mill set aside the DVD and jump drives and looked sharply at the bag. Ideas from her FLETC training welled up in her head.

Sexual predators! Some sexual predators kept *trophies* to remind them of their attacks, of how they'd dominated and hurt others. Could that be what these things were?

She flashed on the note she'd found under her Dad's computer—the one that seemed to list his sexual contacts with Pizzaro. Did the contents of this bag add credibility to the idea that he liked sexually abusing women? A certain horror started to grow in her mind.

She lifted the bag out of the box and turned it in her hands. She looked closely but she saw few pairs of earrings...just singles like what was in the pile back at the apartment.

She lifted it and looked into Philips eyes, shaking the bag warningly, "This could be bad, Philip, real bad...."

Struggling to keep emotion off her face, she handed the bag, DVDs, and jump drives to Philip. He put them into the briefcase without a word.

He had not known W.A. Meacham that well. But his experience as a pastor had given him many examples of grotesque evil carried out by otherwise normal-seeming people. He didn't know what this bag meant, but Milly's reaction screamed a warning to him.

What Mill found next was horrifying, but not mysterious.

Mill bent to look into the drawer again and...her mind seized.

Her breath would not come.

She couldn't move.

Before her eyes was a pair of blue panties, cut through the seams at the hips...kid panties...blue with a rainbow across the butt.

The panties she had worn the day she was raped.

The panties her *rapist* had cut off her body before hurting her, spoiling her.

The knowledge stabbed her heart like the rapist's knife had once threatened to do.

Her rapist could only be--W.A. Meacham, *her father*.

That knowledge slammed her.

Her mind screamed but no words came.

Breath simply huffed out of her mouth, "Haaaaa, haaaaaa."

Mill's vision blurred and went dark. She dropped. Phillip just caught her just before her head hit the steel floor.

Her arms and legs twitched convulsively. Then she turned, thrust violently shaking arms around her husband, and jammed her face into his chest.

A banshee within her wailed a heart's-dying sound that carried out of the vault and across the bank.

People flinched to hear such pain.

Philip hugged her close.

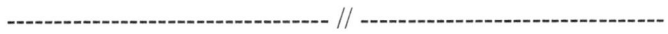

---------------------------------- // --------------------------------

A half hour later, Philip helped his still-sobbing wife out of the vault, past a few curious customers, and out the heavy glass door. In his hand was the large briefcase, loaded with everything from the safety deposit box.

The leather case hung heavily, weighed down with inexpressible, undeniable guilt.

Philip had heard enough from Milly to know that what needed to happen next was far beyond his capabilities as a pastor and as husband. He hailed a cab and told the cabbie the address of the therapist Mill's doctor in Missoula had given the couple.

Two hours later, back in their executive apartment, Mill was under IV sedation.

Dr. Canot wanted her relaxed and never more than just barely awake through the weekend.

He told Philip it might "let her unconscious mind start to sort things out" before he helped her waking mind tackle the horror she had unearthed in the bank vault.

64

Chapter 13 - Green Rivers, Troubled Waters

Clipper Jones stares at John Brinksman's handsome face on his computer screen. The two are connected using Skype and the picture is unusually clear.

Jones and Brinksman are the two Green Rivers most responsible for keeping the group working together in their quest to liberate excess fire funds. So, when the clerks had demanded increased shares, the two men divvied up the Green River roster and started meeting with the others as quickly as they were able to arrange. They'd agreed to be as discrete as they had always been—nothing by phone and no e-mails.

Clipper smiles carefully, "What did you just say, John? I'm not sure I heard you."

The other Green River frowns, "You heard me, Clipper, I said Charlie Cavendish made a speculum of himself. When I talked to him about setting up a different share for the clerks, he started cussing and then even cried right there in the Sizzler. It was embarrassing. When it comes to talking about money, he can't keep a grip."

Clipper had always been surprised by Brinksman's use of language. Somehow the man got his words mixed up, often in startling ways, particularly when he was upset. And John liked to use big, complicated words, which made his chance of error that much greater.

Worse, if you ever tried to correct him, Brinksman became even more adamant about his usage. And once the bad word got locked in his head, it was impossible to dislodge it during the conversation. Even opening a dictionary and pointing to the correct word and definition did no good.

Strangely, once he got over his "brain fart", as Brinksman's wife called his malapropisms, he usually didn't repeat the same mistake in later conversations. Really weird.

Clipper thought Brinksman had some kind of developmental disability. That trait and his defensive behavior probably had led to John's career being po-poed, much as Clipper's had been for other reasons.

For a moment Clipper considers John's words. Clipper's a visual thinker. The image of Charlie Cavendish's shaggy, saggy white head being shoved into one vagina after another sneaks into his mind.

He shudders. It's not an image he wants to remember.

"Okay, John," he replies, unable to completely suppress a chuckle even as he gives in, "so Charlie made a speculum of himself. Once he calmed down, did he agree to a different split or are we still stuck?"

Brinksman growls, "He agreed. But not seventy percent. He'll go sixty or, at most, sixty-five. Any amount over that will be a peckerdildo."

For a moment, Clipper's mind freezes.

What could "peckerdildo" mean? Oh, yeah, a "peccadillo."

Refusing this time to visualize Brinksman's word, Jones simply answers, "Okay, John, at least we know where Charlie's coming from. You keep working through your list. I should be done with mine by the end of next week. Some of the folks on my list are on leave."

Brinksman replies, "Yeah, one or two of those clerks, if they get sufficiently disgruntled, could turn us in to law enforcement in exchange for immunity from prostitution. That Thyra of yours, she'd be one of them."

Clipper immediately agrees. Thyra *is* a bitch. She'd probably turn them in.

But bigger than that, Jones doesn't want to spend his retirement years as a federal prostitute.

Being a passed-over, pissed-off ex-forest supervisor, albeit a wealthy one, would be just fine by comparison.

Chapter 14 - Cutter's Deep

Chronos surveys Cutter's Park carefully through Swarovski 35012 binoculars. He had chosen this model for its fabulous optics. The heavy binoculars could penetrate shady areas even under bright, sunny skies.

And today, Chronos carefully scans shady areas to see if the thugs had inserted surveillance teams around Cutter's Park. His military training told him the thugs could hide from the sun like cockroaches. And the excellent Swarovski's might just find them before they could spot him with their inferior equipment.

Chronos had help with his surveillance. As a part of preparing the Cutter's Park landscape for battle, Mist Eyes and Ears teams had planted hundreds of passive infrared and seismic sensors along paths and next to travel barriers. Experience showed that the devices had no problem detecting even small rodents, so the thug spies could be picked up easily.

And, indeed, over the past two days, a few "hikers" had come through the area and then moved on. None had returned. Their movements had been noisy, obvious.

Chronos assumes the hikers were advanced scouts for law enforcement. Probably carried equipment that detected and mapped Mist's sensors.

He also expects that much more sophisticated operators would be moving in at any time. This new wave of scouts would avoid common paths and Mist's sensors. They would be virtually undetectable because of their stealth and the counter-measures they carried.

Except maybe for his Swarovski's....

Chronos sees a flash of movement. His cool suit, visual camouflage, silver- and charcoal-impregnated body suit, and the absence of ferrous metals on his body make him almost invisible to any spy eyes or electronic noses. But his instinct to remain Mist-like, invisible, remains strong. He instinctively crouches a little.

Across the park, brush moves at the forest's edge. He tenses. His hand falls to the carbon-fiber crossbow hanging from a sling over his shoulder. He can almost see them....

Three cow elk burst into the clearing, a single calf with each. They trot out of cover and then amble out into the park, heads up, smelling the breeze. After a moment sensing for danger, the six buff, brown and white animals drop their heads and start to graze.

Chronos laughs quietly at his tense response to the elk.

He isn't afraid of battle. Too many days on patrol and in firefights in Iraq had driven that fear out of him.

No, he just wants the fight to start. So much preparation had gone into this operation---finding and preparing the Cutter's Park area, selecting and training the warriors, moving in their weapons and gear, developing the hides, both underground and aerial—and he had planned and led much of it.

Now Chronos is tired of the getting-ready part.

He wants the battle…the test…the moment when you prove your skills are better than the other guys'…when you kill him before he kills you.

Another HeloEye buzzes into Cutter's Park. Chronos hears it before he spots it.

Since one HeloEye had videoed some Mist warriors a few days ago, the little helicopters had flown through every hour or two. Larger surveillance drones had likely flown overhead. And a few light planes had cruised by at suspiciously low altitudes, probably loaded with cameras and other more sophisticated detection equipment. For all Chronos and Badger know, satellite orbits had been reassigned so Cutter's Park can be continuously monitored.

Chronos stays out of sight and lets the sky-eyes, real and imagined, buzz by. He remains achingly impatient for battle, while he searches the landscape minutely for enemy scouts.

Twenty minutes after the HeloEye disappears, Chronos climbs down from his observation post. He has seen nothing so far and wants to report in to Badger before something or someone really does show up.

After a ten minute walk, he squats in Badger's low hide, a small sandstone cave. The cave has two perks. A small clear stream runs from a rock pile at the cave's back and forms a little pond before gurgling out the entrance.

The stream's presence means Badger's Pride doesn't have to risk discovery to get freshwater. And the cave's otherwise dry floor is relatively level and just big enough for Badger's Pridemates to spread out their sleeping and other gear without crowding. Many other Prides are camped in underground dugouts, never as fully dry or comfortable as this one is.

Mist engineers had selected the best, driest sites, before excavating them. But soil walls and dampness mean that, after weeks of occupancy, the other underground hides are pretty dank.

"Any word from Raven?" Chronos asks Badger. Badger had their only connection to the rest of the far-flung Mist organization—an encrypted satellite phone.

"No, or rather not many more details than we had before. Thug security is very tight. But Raven has more and more evidence that law enforcement is on its way. Although this area is never mentioned specifically, Raven's drone-signal intercepts show that their surveillance is focused on a hundred square mile area roughly centered on Cutter's Park. The puzzle code on Pizzaro's computer and the HeloEye that circled our warriors must have done its job."

"Yes, I think being detected that way was all to the good," Chronos responds somberly, "They might have seen through the faked radio call in the clear that we had planned."

Badger nods, "Yes, they might have never figured that out and looked somewhere else. The Pizzaro code got them in the neighborhood; the HeloEye gave them our street address—both without looking too contrived."

"Did Raven turn up any more information about when the thugs are likely to arrive?"

Badger shakes her head, "No, but she estimates forty-eight hours. The thugs can't afford to let us slip away. I think our past performance colors the thugs' perceptions. To them, Mist appears and then vanishes, almost impossible to touch…or catch. They don't know we're here to stand and fight because we've never done it before. So they'll want to move in quickly."

"Yeah, sure, that'd be right," Chronos agrees. He climbs to his feet, "Well, look, I'm off to visit my Fang. I'll cover each hide one more time and tell them to sit tight…to wait for the signal. Are you going out to check on your Fang soon? If you are, how about waiting a half hour or so to start? That way, I'll have time to get done and we'll minimize any chance that the thugs will detect our movements."

Badger thinks for a moment, "I think I'll wait until dusk. The air will have cooled down enough to reduce battery drain on my cool suit. For some reason, my batteries aren't holding their charge as much as they should or the suit is drawing more."

Chronos frowns, "Anything to be concerned about? It's not good if our commander can't stay hidden. We could switch you out with someone else's suit. You know, switch with a woman of the same size and build."

"No, let's not rattle a warrior and her Pride just before battle. I've gathered a few extra battery packs so I can change out more frequently." Like the military's cool suits, Mist's "smart" suits give wearers status information, including low-battery and system failure signals. Badger points to her right ear where a small speaker had been built into the suit's hood, "If I hear the squeak, I'll change 'em right away."

She smiles, "I'll be all right."

Chronos hesitates and then asks gently, "Wouldn't it be great if Arrow could be with us. He would love this moment and what's to come."

Arrow had been the former War Chief and Badger's lover. He had died a year earlier of pancreatic cancer. Badger had been at his bedside for the last month of his life, tending him and going over endless details of the plan she and Chronos were now implementing.

No one knew of the intense relationship the two War Clan leaders had shared, except perhaps for Raven who knew everything. That relationship bloomed when Badger learned of Arrow's illness. It grew into a dark devotion based on their mutual hatred for the Greed Machine and their passion for maiming and killing it.

But in Arrow's last month, as he weakened daily, Rebecca finally experienced real tenderness from him. A forlorn love, bleak but with a tendril of real caring, replaced the dark-blood hate that had bonded them before.

So it had been that Arrow, as he died, whispered, "I love you, Rebecca. You are earth mother to me."

Tears flowing, she replied, "And you are my sky father, Arrow. Rest in the Mother until I join you. Then we will love and dance together again."

He had not spoken again after that.

She buried him by the big pond on his homestead near Anamosa, Iowa--the place that now belonged to her, Arrow's lifelong handiwork in every dig, joint, and stone.

Now Badger looks up at Chronos. Giving him no sign of her love for Arrow, she replies, "Yes, he would have loved being here. Now go and check on your Fang. My heart tells me our time is short. Your Prides must be ready."

Chronos slips out of the cave and begins his careful march to each Pride's hide. One unfortunate aspect of radio-silence is that this communication has to be by foot. As he moves from location to location, he takes care to stay in heavy cover and away from spying skies.

But Chronos' precautions have little value.

Two days before during the night, low-flying heli-drones had saturated the Cutter's Park landscape with eSeeds, tiny, natural-appearing burst transmitters that activated when stepped on.

Now, under Chronos' feet each little eSeed sends its tiny signal to receivers placed by the same heli-drones in grid patterns across the landscape. In turn, those receivers send data-bursts to surveillance analysts in Boise.

As Chronos moves, FBI experts triangulate Chronos' steps and plot a map of his route. Time sequencing tells the analysts when he stops to visit each hide and how long he spends there.

Although this is his last trip to visit his whole Fang, it is also his second trip after the eSeeds fell. So, when his trek is done, the FBI will have an accurate map of where more than half of Mist's Cutter's Park forces are hiding.

And a few hours later, Badger will unwittingly fill in the rest.

Chapter 15 - Psycho Hell

Friday night, Haldol took Mill down, deep down....

She begins to dream, vivid...real.

She finds herself slowly, slowly floating across an urban landscape—over smokestacks, roof tops, and parks. She sees people and vehicles.

Nothing below seems to be moving.

She coasts along, examining the texture beneath her as if she's seeing a large painting close up.

Then suddenly she realizes she is naked...horribly and completely naked.

Surely the unmoving people below must be able to see her. They have eyes, didn't they?

Her cheeks burn with embarrassment. Filled with shame, she glances away to the sky and stares at the peaceful clouds.

Finally, she looks back at the ground.

Unlike before, faces are now looking up at her, unblinking eyes staring, unmoving mouths murmuring.

They definitely can see her...are talking about her.

She writhes frantically, trying to cover her nakedness with her arms and hands.

But she is bound by thick, rough ropes. As she struggles, they scratch and chafe her skin. And each twist and turn of her body tightens the ropes and somehow forces her legs and arms wider and wider apart until her body is opened and revealed.

Below her, the people start moving. First one and then another begins to point at her.

They call to other people. Soon the streets fill with people staring and gesturing at Mill's naked body.

She begins to descend.

As she gets closer to the staring crowds, her shame deepens.

The people can see all of her. They could see between her legs, up inside her.

They know she has been raped.

Raped by her father.

They *all* know.

She can hear their voices telling her story, condemning her. She moans with grief, and then curses with frustration at not being able to escape, to hide.

Tears cascade down her face and run down her breasts. Her breasts glisten in the sunlight.

There! Her father stands in the crowd, bloodied…dead.

Dead or not, he still points and laughs at her with the rest.

She starts to gag.

The dream fades.

-------------------------------- // --------------------------------

Time passed--but under the Haldol, Mill had no perception of time.

The dream started again—the same cityscape, the same people.

The same horrible events rolled through her dreaming mind, always with the same results.

Then, around midnight Saturday, the doctor reduced the narcotic. Mill's mind slowly came off sedation.

-------------------------------- // --------------------------------

The dream changes. It's the same city, the same ropes.

But now she begins to see shapes—human shapes floating next to her like strange, white, wide-winged sea-birds. They hang just on the edge of her peripheral vision.

She tries to turn her head to get a good look at them but they always stay just out of full view.

Why are they there? Are they gawking at her like the crowds below? Examining her most private parts and innermost hurts?

She can't tell.

She begins to descend. The crowd starts to roar.

She realizes that the men below are lining up.

They laugh and grab their crotches, thrust their pelvises up at her, and make obscene gestures with their fingers and arms. Tongues thrust her way. A few expose themselves, dangling their penises.

Realization slams her.

The men are going to rape her…gang rape her…all of them.

And her father is first in line, laughing and encouraging the men around him.

Behind her father, the line of men stretches beyond view. And now a few women join the crowd, equally eager.

Mill struggles frantically. The ropes tighten and spread her arms and legs wider, wider.

She reaches tree-top level.

She knows she has only seconds before being horribly violated, over and over again.

Forced.

Humiliated.

Then, without notice, the shapes on the edge of her vision surround her.

A dozen white bodies move close, each with a tantalizingly familiar face.

Her distracted mind wonders momentarily who they can be. But her urgent need to escape takes her consciousness. Her eyes veer to the roaring crowd below.

The white beings' strong hands grab the ropes binding her and break them easily.

Bits of fiber rain down on the eager, grasping crowd.

Loose of the ropes, Mill begins to free-fall.

Panicked, she windmills her arms and legs.

The crowd roars approval.

She falls slower and slower…closer to the crowd…now feet, now inches.

The crowd reaches for her, fingers inches away.

But at the last possible second before she's grabbed and ripped down to be ruined, the white shapes catch her.

Together, Mill and her companions begin to rise slowly.

Below them, the crowd howls…frustrated, furious.

People leap high, trying to clutch her before she can get away.

Mill sees them rise. They almost touch her, but their hands miss and, strangely claw-like, fall away.

Different than the earlier dreams, Mill feels serene as the cool, supporting hands lift her higher. Soon she floats far above the crowd. The faces below have shrunk to tiny dots in the wide landscape's once-again painting-like surface.

A light breeze springs up and blows her away from the crowds and the city, wrapped in the arms of the white beings.

They travel long. The land beneath them rolls by, dreamlike and warm.

Finally, they drop gently into a grassy field--a place of no harm…a place beyond right and wrong, beyond justification, shame, and guilt.

Mill closes her eyes. When she opens them, she lies alone, at peace, in a sea of waving grass. Breeze puffs and soft seed heads gently caress her naked skin.

-------------------------------- // --------------------------------

6 a.m. Sunday morning. Mill woke with the last dream still a vivid memory. She ran through the dream's pieces.

City. Bound tight. Falling towards shame. Rapists.
The white beings carried her away from harm.
They had faces…whose faces?
The faces. Wait. She knew those faces.
The faces were…yes…*hers*…and, *yes…her mother's*!

-------------------------------- // --------------------------------

Doctor Canot spent four hours with Mill on Monday morning.

When Canot arrived, Mill was fully awake and having breakfast.

Without speaking to either doctor or patient, Philip kissed Mill's forehead and then left to give doctor and patient privacy.

When Philip returned at lunch time, Mill was in the bedroom, lying down.

Canot said he could go in, but Philip decided not to disturb her.

Canot motioned Philip out onto the little balcony.

He gestured to the two acrylic chairs there, "Let's sit for a few minutes. I'd like to go over some details of Mill's case with you. And I want to let you know what I see happening over the next several days."

"Of course," Philip replied, "anything I can do."

Canot looked at Philip with a reserved but happy smile, "Philip, your wife is a remarkable woman—mentally stronger and emotionally more resilient than most people I've known and treated."

Philip nodded, "Milly's incredible all right. Always has been, even as a girl."

Canot smiled more broadly, "I know you have an extensive counseling background, but probably nothing prepared you for your wife's experience of the past few days."

Philip nodded. Sudden pain etched lines into his face.

Canot spoke softly, "I imagine what happened to her was extremely difficult for you to experience. When people we love come apart at the seams, it can be unbearably frightening."

Philip nodded in agreement. A tear rolled down his left check. He let it stay.

Canot continued, "When I saw Mill on Friday, I was initially very troubled. The shock of finding out her rapist's identity...particularly that he had been her father...sent Mill to the edge of a serious psychotic break. When I first saw her, she had become marginally catatonic, cut off, uncommunicative, her consciousness adrift on the bare edge of reality."

He paused and looked into Philip's eyes for emphasis, "As a clinical psychologist, I would expect a person with her childhood background of maternal abandonment, paternal neglect and rape, and peer bullying to retreat from reality under such a shock. Your wife certainly did that."

The therapist cleared his throat, "And once catatonic, I would expect such a patient to take one of two paths. She could enter a complete, permanent catatonic state characterized by either no movement or frenetic movement, both without communications. Or, she could return to consciousness only to face prolonged, profound depression, a condition which would require significant intervention and medical support to overcome, if it could be at all."

Dr. Canot's words hit Philip hard.

Had he lost Milly to drift in some mental limbo?

Philip considered that what Dr. Canot described was what Christian Hell must be like.

Isolated from anyone's love, God's or her husband's.

Imprisoned in a cold, self-defined cell.

His Milly in Hell? He could not bear the thought.

He convulsively crossed his arms and hugged himself. His chest felt increasingly tight. His heart could barely squeeze blood through his constricted veins.

Black spots appeared in his vision.

His body began to weave slightly in the flimsy chair.

Dr. Canot looked at him with concern, "Are you okay, Philip? You look pretty bad."

Philip gasped, "No, I'll be...all right. Tell me...more...about Milly."

"Is she...is she," he sobbed, "g-gone...to me?"

"Philip, take deep breaths. Calm yourself. No, Mill didn't take either path. Instead, she did something I've rarely encountered. While sedated, she was somehow able to grapple with and integrate many of her key emotional contradictions. She didn't just cope with the shattering revelation about her rape, her love for her parent contradicted by his neglectful and violating treatment of her. No, she didn't just cope with it, she overcame it. You might even say she triumphed over it. A big part of her trauma history has been explained. And she internalized it…partially worked through it…even if the process was excruciatingly painful and unbearably lonely."

The doctor smiled, "Please don't misunderstand. She is still shocked and sad, but more or less normally so. She still has lots of work left to do. And certainly, she could regress. But her prognosis is as good as it could be."

Canot patted Philip on the arm and squeezed it reassuringly, "Your wife, Mill Meacham, should recover much of her normal emotional equilibrium over the next couple of weeks."

Seeing Philip's somber look continue, Canot smacked his hand gently against his chair arm for emphasis, "Philip, she's going to be okay, maybe on a better path to healing than before."

Finally the counselor's words sank in.

Relief flooded Philip.

Mill would be his once again.

He started to reach out to shake Canot's hand.

Then, perversely, having rallied through the bad news, he fainted at the good.

-------------------------------- // --------------------------------

That night, Philip lay awake, his mind coiling and raw.

Next to him, Mill slept peacefully under the influence of a mild sedative. A soft snore occasionally interrupted her smooth breathing.

Philip thought, "I was so close to losing Milly. I just can't forget the horror of what her father did to her. What kind of human being could do that to his own flesh and blood? To his own powerless daughter? Penetrate her? Damage her? Drive her to the edge of oblivion?"

The word "monster" kept rising in his mind. And he kept remembering his role in her rape, as unwitting as it had been.

Maybe the word "monster" applied to Philip as well.

78

And after hours of this painful thought, Philip began to get sleepy.

Erotic thoughts often crept into his mind at this point. He would enjoy them, toy with them, and then eventually reject them as inappropriate right before falling asleep—tell his mind to stop playing its Faustian game.

Faust had lusted after Helen of Troy. The Devil sent a demon disguised as Helen and, in return for having sex with her, Faust lost his soul to the Dark One forever.

Philip knew the Faust story well. He even had used it in some of his sermons to explain the power pornography and fantasy-thinking can have over some people. He also used the story to talk about mental traps people set for themselves and the consequences of such self-deception.

But even armed with that knowledge, Philip's sleepy mind often seemed intent on creating demons to serve his personal lusts--demons that toyed with him...enticed him.

Philip's dream women were dominating and yet caring. They would only seem to be in charge but they would actually do whatever he wanted, when he wanted it. He had dreamed this way since high school and the women, more often than not, were some version of Milly...virgin girl, adult temptress, brazen slut.

This Faustian impulse was strong. It pushed him to make it reality, even while he knew that many of the sexual things his mind wanted were perverse and manipulative, involving bondage and dominance, simulating his rape...or hers.

Guilt and lust warred within him.

Weren't sex and sins both in his mind? Connected...turning his soul black?

Dreaming the way, was he any better than W.A. Meacham?

Yes, there was a small difference. W.A. had acted on his fantasies. Philip had not...at least not so far.

But, by not harming others physically yet wanting to do it, was he really any better than Milly's Dad...or just more cowardly?

Shaken by these questions, he prayed sleepily for peace and healing...for demons to depart.

But he lost the urgency of his questions and the energy of his prayers in the body-calm that comes just before sleep. Instead of demons departing, another fantasy oozed seductively into his near-sleeping mind.

A dream began.

They are fourteen again and in the woods, far from town, and…completely naked. He lies tied and defenseless in front of Milly, stretched out along a log.

She moves close to him and rubs her body across his. He starts to moan with desire, but she dances away, teasing.

Then she returns and abruptly grabs him, forces his jaws open, and makes him swallow Ecstasy and other drugs. She takes some herself and then runs her hands up and down his erection, puts her mouth on it…warm…warm.

After a moment, Milly lets go and dances before him again. She opens her legs and mouth to him, spreads herself, climbs on him, and rubs her body on his.

Drug frenzy comes over her.

She twists and turns.

She takes him into every part of her body.

Philip's pleasure is so great it is almost painful.

He begins thrusting, over and over.

Faster and faster he thrusts and, with each thrust, his penis grows.

Milly takes it all, without protest.

Philip is approaching his orgasm when Milly's slack, drugged face changes.

She smiles. Dimples like stab wounds appear in her cheeks.

He sees her teeth—now needle sharp.

Her eyes glow and reflect like wild night eyes.

Her skin begins to scale.

She climbs off of him.

She flicks her tongue out of her mouth. It's long…so long.

It twines his penis, squeezing it painfully. She withdraws her tongue and hisses.

Demon!

He's still bound. He can't move…escape.

She mounts him again. He goes deep, deep into her.

He's suddenly desperate to pull out of her but he can't.

He keeps thrusting harder and harder, his body more machine than human now.

Panic takes him.

He has to find release before Milly turns all the way into a demon.

If she changes fully, he knows he will lose his soul.

He thrusts faster, faster, but no orgasm.

So close, so close, but now she is almost turned....

Philip woke, breath ragged, his skin shiny with sweat. He had a throbbing erection but no will whatsoever to wake his sleeping wife for love making.

Besides, he wasn't completely sure that, if he rolled her over, she wouldn't look at him with glowing demon eyes.

Gradually, he calmed down and grew sleepy again. As he fell back towards sleep, an idea that glittered, bright and fascinating, slipped into his mind.

Although his demonic dream had been scary and discomfiting, it now seemed to hold little threat.

It could be that the dream had touched on something he wanted...he needed...freedom to dominate while being dominated...to experiment with how drugs might help him achieve his fantasies...be his own, whole man sexually.

This idea felt nothing like how he had thought real men should behave...on top of their women, driving both lovers to raging release. No, his fantasy was perverse.

But, now at the edge of sleep, Philip found it...well...no, not threatening...enticing...enriching.

He wondered sleepily if perhaps it was the truth that Milly had binged on drugs and sex, on men and women, for years that had begun to create this fascination for him. He had no doubt he wanted to overwhelm her sexual experiences with more powerful ones that only he could provide. He wanted to pleasure her more than any other lover had done.

He wanted her to scream, "Oh, Sweet Jesus, Philip you are the best," at some future orgasmic peak.

And to do this, he knew he had to break out of the stale...the conventional...achieve something extraordinary.

Drugs...yes, drugs could be a key.

And the right mix of domination and control.... Yes, that could be it....

Lessons from the demon-lover dream whirled around his mind for a time and then lodged firmly as he dropped down, down...finally into full sleep.

Chapter 16 - Deep Work

Free of sedation and feeling a little more settled, Mill had taken time late Sunday to go through the contents of her Dad's safety deposit box again. She wanted to compare the bag of what she suspected were his sex-predator trophies to the similar objects Philip had found in the apartment.

But nothing significant leaped out at her from the jumbled piles, one big and one small. Though she looked closely at the objects with a magnifying glass, holding them up to the light in gloved hands, there were no names or any other identifying marks on the items.

Dead end.

At her direction, Philip had taken the blue panties and placed them in an evidence bag. A tight-jawed Mill had signed and dated the bag, noting when and where the panties had been discovered.

"Milly," a worried Philip questioned, "I'm not sure why you're doing this. Do you plan to give them to the FBI or Manny as evidence?"

Philip looked at her with care in his eyes, worried that she might be headed for another psychotic break.

"God help you," he whispered, "What happened to you took place so long ago. And, if I believe in anything, I believe W.A. is long since punished by a power higher than anything here in earth. Wouldn't it be better to just dispose of these and move on?"

Mill's eyes avoided his, "I don't know, Philip. Somehow treating my ruined panties as evidence makes it like I can be a cop and bring Dad to justice for what he did to me. And maybe it's helping me make sense of it somehow. You know, doing this might mean there could be some kind of resolution down the road....closure."

Mill's voice trailed off, her tone miserable.

Philip sat next to her and put his arm around her, "Okay, but at least let's store this bag somewhere you don't have to look at it every time you go through his stuff."

Choked up, Mill nodded agreement.

Philip took the evidence bag, went into the bedroom, and placed it in his empty suitcase. He thought, "Out of sight now, and hopefully out of Milly's mind soon."

When he returned to the living room, Mill was placing the small pile of earrings and other trophies they'd found in W.A.'s apartment in one evidence bag. He watched as she placed the larger bag from the safety deposit box in yet another. She sealed and signed both, setting them aside

Mill pointed to the DVD and two jump drives, "What are these things do you guess, Philip?"

He picked up the DVD and inspected it, "No way to tell unless we play it, I suppose."

With a sense of foreboding, he started Mill's laptop, opened the DVD player, and inserted the little disc. Mill and Philip looked at the screen.

A drunken W.A. Meacham appeared in a hotel hallway, his arm draped over the shoulder of a smaller person. After a lascivious kiss, the pair opened the door to a room and went inside, followed by the camera. Over the next half hour, husband and wife watched in fascinated horror as W.A. committed several acts of sodomy with the small person who turned out to be a man.

Philip had never seen anything like this before. Overwhelmed, he kept looking away.

Mill couldn't take her eyes off the screen, even though what she saw made her stomach churn.

When the DVD ended, Mill turned to Philip, "My God, what a mess! Dad was caught on video in a gay fling. Obviously someone gave him this DVD to show him he'd made an idiot of himself. But why would he keep it? It makes no sense. I mean, was he proud of looking like an idiot?"

Philip pointed to the jump drives, "Well, I almost hate to think of doing this, but what if the answers to your questions are on one of these? He obviously thought they were important, too."

Mill looked resigned, "Good guess, love. Okay, I suppose I can stand to see more, if viewing what is likely to turn out to be more family porn explains why Dad kept that awful DVD."

Philip took the first jump drive and inserted it the nearest USB port on Mill's laptop.

Several images were on the drive, some stills and a couple of short videos. The stills seemed to be excerpts from the DVD—close-ups of the most intimate contacts between W.A. and his male lover.

The videos were something entirely different.

They showed Esperanza Pizzaro having sex with W.A.

But instead of W.A. dominating and humiliating her as the notes Mill had found under her Dad's computer suggested, Pizzaro was clearly in charge.

84

In one sequence, Pizzaro was riding naked on W.A.'s back. He lurched around on all fours while she wiggled and rocked, occasionally snapping him on the buttocks and outer thighs with a little whip.

In another clip, Pizzaro reclined on her back across the venerable Pinchot Desk in the Chief's private office. W.A. knelt between her legs, face pressed into her vagina.

Pizzaro moaned with delight and moved her hips up and down. After she arched her back in an obvious orgasm, Esperanza turned towards the camera, grinned, and gave a thumbs-up.

After he satisfied her several times more, Pizzaro pushed him away with one foot and stood. She had him hold her panties while she stepped into them, then slapped him, saying, "Next time, you better use more tongue, Bull. We've got to work on your technique. Sloppy, too sloppy."

Mill rocked back on the couch, "Philip, I don't know what to think. One minute I'm sure Dad's a sexual predator and the next he's clearly some kind of victim. And why do we have all these videos of his wild, stupid stuff? Somebody wanted records of all his craziness, but why? And again, once he got them, why did he keep them? Didn't he realize I'd be looking at them someday?"

Philip shook his head. He was way beyond his comfort level and experience.

"I have no idea, Milly," he stammered, "Your Dad…uh…he did stuff…well, stuff that I…well, I just don't know. I…well, he kept those trophies. Maybe he just had some mental issue. Like maybe your Dad was narcissistic and he couldn't let go of sexual images of himself, no matter how demeaning or awful."

Mill looked at Philip's beet-red face and laughed kindly, "I bet you're wondering why you ever married into my totally messed up family. And now you're finding out that the 'totally messed up' part is far worse than you ever guessed!"

Her face clouded over, "I wouldn't blame you if you dropped me like a hot rock, Philip dear."

He quickly reassured her, "Oh, Milly, before this mess started, we both knew your Dad lived a wild life, what we Christians would call 'a life of wickedness.' And I'm shocked, sure. But, in a weird way, finding out about your father's behavior just makes me more impressed with how you've pulled your life together. You've had a lot to overcome."

He took her in his arms, "And besides, I love you no matter what. Seems like I always have. Always will, I guess."

Mill's dimples appeared. His words were what she hoped for but could not predict. She kissed him a long time before untangling.

Philip pointed to the second jump drive, "Should we stomach a look at that? I bet it's no better than the other stuff."

Mill looked him in the eyes. "Can you stand another walk down Nuthouse Lane? " They both laughed grimly.

The second jump drive contained perhaps the most shocking material of all.

It wasn't pornographic, but it was definitely obscene.

In it, a small man who called himself "Raoul" confessed that he had been W.A.'s lover in the DVD. Out of a battered, puffy face, Raoul stammered that W.A. Meacham had been drugged and that the person responsible was none other than "Dr. Esperanza Angelica Pizzaro." In fact, he repeated her full name and title over and over again throughout the short confessional video.

The only other item on the jump drive was a still photo of Raoul lying on a trash-strewn floor, bloodied and apparently dead.

Mill ran the Raoul video twice, making a few notes. Then she shut the laptop with a snap and, in her best cop voice, uttered the biggest understatement of the day, "Philip, I think we've determined that Dad's murder and Esperanza Pizzaro's are connected...."

On Monday, Mill dragged her weary body over to the FBI to meet with Tomlin. They were seated alone in Tomlin's office.

"Shit, Meacham," Frieda Tomlin spat when she saw her, "You look like death warmed over again. Did you get any sleep last weekend, or did you stay up fretting over all this crap going down around us?"

Mill reflected that, for most of four days, drugged or not, she had done almost nothing *but* sleep.

Silently, she took out the trophy-filled evidence bags, one containing the DVD and jump drives, and another that contained the note from under her father's computer. She pushed them across the table to Tomlin and explained what she thought they represented, adding that she was sorry she hadn't turned them in before.

Frieda Tomlin made her point but didn't press it, "So, Meacham, I guess you withheld that note from under your Dad's computer out of respect for the dead, right?"

Mill nodded ruefully at Frieda's question, "Dad's note was pretty cryptic. And...well, I guess I didn't want to believe what it seemed to say."

She pointed at the pile of DVDs, jump drives, and trophies, "But then all this stuff showed up. Once I had a look at it, I called you and came in."

Frieda snorted and replied grumpily, "Mill, did it occur to you that the note alone could have determined the unsub's ID, motive, and opportunity in both deaths? You're an investigator, though apparently a damned useless and green one. So even baby you should know this stuff. Or did they stop teaching evidence-management to you cherries over at the Glynco funny farm?"

Mill shrugged shakily, "I'm sorry, Frieda. I should 'a celled you as soon as we found the note Thursday evening, but...well...I didn't."

Tomlin got on the phone and, moments later a tech hustled into her office. She signed for the DVDs and jump drives and trotted out the door. Tomlin spent the next several minutes looking closely at the remaining evidence.

Mill still hadn't told Tomlin about the blue panties or about where she had spent the last four days. And Mill wouldn't tell her unless she had to for a reason not yet clear to her.

Frieda finally looked up. She shook her head resignedly and conceded the point, "Okay. Water over the dam, Meacham. I'll give you a pass on your fuckin' empty-brained oversights if you'll tell me what this pile of trash means because I can't figure out if it matters either."

Before Mill can answer, Frieda's phone buzzed and she picked up, "Okay, okay. Bring everything back up here as soon as possible."

Tomlin smiled grimly, "That was forensics. The lab folks say everything that's on the DVDs and jump drives is all straight footage, no electronic tampering that they could detect."

Mill grimaced, "Great. The family porn is legit. I'm so relieved."

She hugged herself tightly to prevent her arms from shaking. She gave Frieda a synopsis of what was on the DVDs and jump drives.

As she talked, Mill felt bile rising in her throat.

No breakfast and now this, "Okay, let's work the bags of earrings and personal effects. Looks like was a sexual predator…had been for a long time based on the trophy count. He must have picked those things up whenever he could. You know, from a night table in a motel room…out of some woman's jewelry box in her bedroom. Real creepy."

She gulped hard, "Also the video footage makes it look like Esperanza Pizzaro trapped Dad into making a gay-porn video with a guy who calls himself 'Raoul.' No idea if that's his real name. So, then Raoul confesses and Dad gets a copy of that video, maybe turns the table on Pizzaro. Dad starts abusing her and is dumb enough to write his crap down."

Frieda nodded, "Yeah, that'd be how I read it, too, although I'm more than a little fuzzy how your Dad got the videos of him and Raoul doin' the horizontal mambo and the one showing Raoul's confession. Did your Dad beat it out of him? Did he kill him? You said Raoul looked dead in a photo."

Mill sighed, "I don't know Frieda. After finding out so much about Dad's life this week, I guess he might have been capable of anything."

Her stomach churned again. She fought down a wave of anxiety using the method Dr. Canot had taught her—look at a neutral spot, breathe deeply, and relax her neck and upper body. It helped.

"Even murder."

Frieda grunted, "Well, absent any other evidence about Raoul, we can't hang his death on your Dad. And he didn't kill Dr. Pizzaro. Nanny cam says a skinny Mist operator did."

Tomlin's mouth widened in a grim smile, "And unless your Dad blew himself up with a bomb made out of gold, I'd bet my sainted mother's virginity he didn't kill himself either."

Mill's eyes widened, "What's that about gold, Frieda? Philip and I found some fancy gold leafs, you know, art pieces, in Dad's safety deposit box. Six of them."

Frieda's eyes widened, "Well, aren't you full of suppressed evidence today, Meacham! Goddamn gold leafs, huh? Well, FBI forensics lab says concentrated C-4 packed into a gold object killed your Dad. Professional job. Integrated circuits and antenna. Everything base sourced, meaning manufactured from common component parts. No trace. Electronics boys say it was likely triggered by cell phone."

Remembering the green glass surface on the leaves, Mill asked, "Did they find anything like green glass in with the gold? The surface of Dad's leafs are coated with cast green glass over beautiful etched patterns in the gold."

"As a matter of fact they did find green glass." Frieda thought over the preliminary autopsy report, deciding how much to tell Mill. "Let's just say they found some pieces in your Dad's upper body," she concluded, recalling that some of the green-glass material had been recovered from inside W.A. Meacham's skull.

Frieda shook her head, "So, Mist likely got Pizzaro. Nanny cam doesn't lie. And, looking at the sophistication of the bomb that took your Dad, I'd say they got him as well. No way to tell for sure, but everything points that way. Maybe they had a hand in this video business, too."

She stared at Mill, "We have a score to settle with Mist, Mill. You up for catching them... out in Idaho...Siberia...wherever?

Mill nodded. Her anxiety was spiking and she was afraid to open her mouth for fear of vomiting.

"Okay," Frieda smiled a rare warm smile, "We'll get them together."

Mill felt a little better.

"So, I want you to bring in the gold leafs you found. I won't have them placed in evidence, at least until we've had the lab test them. If they go into evidence, they'll probably get back to you later. I'll have the lab run the bedroom trophies, too. Have 'em look for indications of violence and check the computers for any reports of objects being lost or stolen. And I'll watch the DVDs and jump drive material with a team of analysts. Maybe we'll find something in them we can use. I'd guess you'd not want that stuff back. Right?"

Mill croaked out, "Right."

"And I just have to ask you, will that preacher-man husband of yours be able to keep all this sinful information confidential? I can just see him blurting out a 'this-deserves-Hellfire-and-damnation' sermon with a Mist rep sitting right there in his church, pious as a snake in a chicken coop."

Mill felt better answering for Philip, "No, he won't say anything, Frieda." She had listened to three of Philip's sermons after they were married. No Hellfire. No damnation. Just encouragement for his flock to lead better lives.

Mill almost fell asleep at the third one.

Thinking of his yawny-but-nice sermons, Mill remembered his loving remarks and arms around her that morning.

Before she could stop herself, she added, "Besides, he loves me too much to say anything."

Tomlin almost fell out of her chair laughing.

She choked out. "Oh my God, Meacham. I swear you are as naive as a Girl Scout selling cookies in a whore house."

Chapter 17 - Incident Corrupting Team

Clipper Jones has been waiting for a call back from Whitley Chalmers, Commander of Blue Mountain Two, for more than a day. Chalmers and Jones had been classmates at Oregon State University many years before. They had supported one another in little ways throughout the years--a favor here, a recommendation there. And one of the favors Forest Service administrators do for one another is to send each other good employees when needed.

Incident Command Team Blue Mountain Two is having a busy fire year. Chalmers' team is presently waiting for the "bubble to pop" and propel them off to their next fire assignment. Clipper wants to make sure that his partner-in-crime, Thyra, gets selected to serve with Whit's team for their next fire call-out.

Clipper and the other Green Rivers have everything arranged to milk the next fire of excess cash. But to do so, they have to get Thyra or her counterparts onto a team headed for a fire of the right large-but-not-huge size.

Blue Mountain Two is just such a "Type Two" team, handling smaller but challenging fires.

"Type One" Teams handle the really big fires.

The Green Rivers avoid those teams. They are too likely to have Incident Business Advisors, audit teams, and LEOs working on-site.

Too many knowing eyes on Type One fires.

Once called Fire Teams, Incident Command Teams lead the wildland firefighting effort across America. They model military organizations with a commander and deputy in charge. Specialists in subjects such as public affairs, meteorology, logistics, and fire behavior support the commanders. The teams also handle hundreds of on-the-fire-line firefighters. They support them with necessary resources, from helicopters and air tankers used to suppress the fires from above, to chow lines, toilets, and campsites waiting for the weary men and women at shift's end.

And procurement specialists like Thyra make the whole business happen.

She makes sure contract firefighters, heavy equipment, and everything else down to pencil sharpeners and toilet paper arrives at the Incident Command Headquarters when it's needed and in the right quantities.

Clipper's phone rings, "Jones."

"Clipper, this is Whit. Have you been trying to reach me? I've been on a week's leave…added a few days to my regular rest. The whole team needed it. We were worn out and half of us were smoke-sick."

Jones makes sympathetic noises as Chalmers goes on, "Looks like we're number one to dispatch. Half the West is on fire again, so we should go out soon. I'm hopin' you have some folks that want fire time because I'm runnin' short of good people."

It has been a long, hot fire season.

Now, at the season's ragged end, fewer and fewer employees are volunteering to dispatch, deciding to stay home for work and family instead.

Clipper answers, "Yeah, I've got a couple of folks who want to go out. Morris Middleton, my ranger at Coramond and Thyra Dexter, buying unit supervisor. I don't think you've met Morris. He's a good hand and he definitely needs fire experience. You've worked with Thyra before. She gets the job done and stays out of trouble."

"Sure, sure," Whit replies, "I will name-request them both, pronto. Thyra is great…nose to the grindstone and all that. What do you want me to do with the young ranger…what's his name…Morris Middle-something? Heck of a name. Reminds me of a chipmunk in a kid's book."

Clipper laughs, "Oh, I'd put him in Planning for his first go-round. He may as well be at the center of everything, get good and confused. He can figure everything out later."

Whit responds, "Okay. One new ranger, overwhelmed and worn out to order. I'll get the name-requests into the system."

The two men gossip a little while longer and then hang up.

Chapter 18 - Staging

After a long, bumpy ride in from Idaho 55, Mill and Manny reached the task force staging area just after dark. The two special agents parked their dusty Forest Service pickup at the end of a long row of vehicles at the edge of a large field. Next to the parking area, more than a hundred individual tents were scattered across several acres.

The FBI task force had commandeered a Forest Service work center and nearby fields to serve as staging area and base camp. The site was located at the end of one of the "cherry stem" roads that penetrate a few miles into the Frank Church-River of No Return Wilderness.

In previous weeks, high-capacity electrical lines had been strung to the staging area and a large satellite communications truck brought in, set up, and calibrated.

The LEO site was a little more than ten miles from Cutter's Park across a deep canyon and steeply rugged ground.

The two agents walked towards a well-lit cluster of large tents and a couple of yurts. Along the way, they heard snatches of conversation from people in the individual tent area, "Typical fuck up...no one knows what's going on."

"Hey, knock off the chatter and get some rest. We move up tomorrow."

"Pull your heads out ladies...lights out."

Excited laughter.

Manny shook his head, "It's always this way at the start of an operation...drug bust...SAR...everybody keyed up...wantin' to get the bad guys...be a hero. But that changes once bullets fly or we take some casualties. Then the conversation changes and they get down to serious business."

Mill looked around and pointed towards the well-lit area, "This is laid out like an incident command for a big wildfire. So the check-in should be that first large tent...over there...ahead on the right."

Manny grunted agreement.

Less than a minute later, the two found that there was one difference between this camp and a fire camp—much tighter security. They hadn't walked fifty feet before a heavily armed K-9 officer approached them, lit them up with a wide-lens patrol flashlight, and asked for their IDs.

They fumbled the IDs out of deep pockets and showed them to the tall LEO.

"Okay, Special Agents Meacham and…ah…Suemez, keep moving straight down this row until you get to the security check-point."

He pointed the direction with his left hand, "You have to go there first before you can go over to the workforce tent for check in. Oh…yeah, you'll want to display your IDs at all times here at camp. I guarantee you will get stopped if you're not wearing them and your supervisor will be notified."

Manny saluted him casually, "You bet, officer. Thanks for the heads up."

After running his light over Mill's trim, curvy figure one last time, the man and his dog strolled away.

Manny muttered dryly, "Sure glad he likes girls. Camp like this, 'gay' might not be a language anybody wants to speak."

Mill laughed, "You get used to it, Manny. Most guys take the first 'no' for an answer."

"Sure, but you're wearing a wedding ring. You'd think that big flashlight of his woulda showed him that instead of getting stiffer in his hand."

Mill laughs, "Manny, people think plenty of teepee creepin' goes on in fire camps. I imagine the same'd be true for a cop camp. So, true or not, most every guy here is hoping to get lucky. Just won't be with me."

Manny laughed respectfully, "No, I'm sure not. Did that husband of yours follow you out here? Stay in Boise or something?"

"No, Philip headed back to his flock in Centralia. It's not just Sundays he works. He really does a lot for them, all week long. And the volunteers who fill in for him when he's gone have other lives. If we have personal cell service here, I'll call him a couple times a day so we can stay caught up."

They arrived at the security check point. A pair of uniformed Idaho State Patrol officers looked up as they approached. One was seated at a small field desk. The other stood, looking at them closely, with a Remington Model 1100 Tac 4 tactical shotgun in his hands

"Names and organization please…."

"Special Agents Suemez and Meacham, Forest Service law enforcement."

The seated officer typed into a netbook, "Okay, I see you in the system. Here are your bracelets."

He reached across the table and offered them each a solid-feeling, rubberized band.

94

"Put it over your wrist. Squeeze it until it's snug but not tight. You'll keep it on until the op is over. We have a gizmo to remove it when you out-process."

Mill took the bracelet and waved it in front of the officer, "What is this thing? I've never seen one before."

The officer smiled, "I hadn't until yesterday. It's a combination life-signs monitor and transponder, called a LifeChec. With it on, the ops center knows where you are and how you're feeling. Better than the old transponders we had in our radios. If you lost the radio or it got blasted, ops couldn't find you. This lets them 4-1-1 you anytime."

"Great," Mill answers, "They can log every time I visit the ladies room or check my heartbeat when I'm reading a romance novel. Law enforcement has sunk so low...a bunch 'a peepin' e-toms".

The men laugh.

The tall officer with the shotgun said, "Yeah, Special Agent Meacham, if you don't mind me sayin' so, they'll be able to track your movements by the elevated heartbeats of the guys you'll be passing."

Mill peered at the man's name tag, "Why, Trooper Duncan, I do believe you are flirting with me."

The big man blushed, "Not really, ma'am, just pointin' out the obvious."

Mill smiled, dimples showing, "Does a girl's heart good, gentlemen. I'll give your regards to my husband."

At her last words, Duncan's cheeks got noticeably redder.

The seated trooper pointed towards the workforce reception tent, "You two better get on over there and sign in before Duncan here passes out from embarrassment. I haven't heard him say more than three words in a row...ever...before tonight. Good night, special agents."

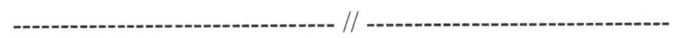

The next morning, Mill breakfasted mightily in the chow hall. French toast, a couple eggs, plenty of salsa, and lots of syrup and coffee. Now that was a breakfast.

Of course, she couldn't tell whether she was actually hungry or the butterflies in her stomach had swarmed. Either way, the breakfasters at the table next to hers were impressed.

One of them was Trooper Duncan from the night before.

Mill waved at him, "Hey Duncan, good to see you again. You doin' okay?"

As he had the night before, Duncan blushed, making the other men laugh, "Ah, sure, Meacham...I'm fine."

Mill smiled warmly at him, "Good. Eat hearty. If I get in a firefight, I want you to be the cavalry that comes to get me. That okay?"

He stammered a couple of times before speaking, "Yeah...uh...sure. I'd be proud...uh...you know."

"Okay then, it's a deal. I'll call for backup and you cover my backside."

At this, Duncan's face flamed.

Mill looked him levelly in the eyes, "Really, Duncan...all kidding aside, there's no one I'd rather have coming to help me out of a jam."

The big man just nodded, clearly pleased but completely unable to speak.

She finished up, stood, and carried her tray to the wash area. She separated the flatware and plates, put them in the wash rack and sprayed them until all the gunk came off.

"Regular little camper," she complimented herself. She hadn't done that kind of cleanup since scout camp almost twenty years before.

Mill beat feet to the 0700 briefing. A few people were already moving in to the large planning tent where the briefing was held. She got there before Manny. So she grabbed a seat in the back row right along the center aisle and dropped her ball cap on the seat next to hers to hold it for Manny.

By sitting here, they should both be able to see the people doing the briefing at the front of the tent. She figured the front rows were for the team leaders and unit commanders. A moment later, she saw a flash of gold braid up there that confirmed her suspicions.

Manny arrived about the same time as the cop horde began to pour in. He walked right past her, carried along by the flow.

She had to yell, "Manny...hey Suemez, over here!" before she could get his attention. He quickly made an about face and seconds later dropped into his seat.

"Thanks for saving me, *Chica*," he muttered, "So many big *bueyes* cops in this place, we *caballeros* of more modest size get edged out."

Mill looked around. Sure enough, there were plenty of big cops crowding into the tent, many already in the body armor that further swelled their bulk.

She had a mental image of the tall but slender Suemez and a comparatively tiny Mill trying to shove their ways through a crowd of "oxen" cops to the front. No way. She chuckled.

Someone yelled, "Atten-shun!" and the group came sloppily to its feet.

Forest Service law enforcement didn't practice paramilitary ceremony like many state patrols and city uniformed divisions did. That meant Mill and the other Forest Service LEOs straggled to their feet a half-beat behind LEOs from more practiced outfits.

In a mixed group like this one, Mill should have known that some ceremony and protocol would be followed. She took small comfort that Manny was even slower standing than she was.

Down the center aisle strode three figures, two tall and one short, all in camo and webbing, .40 caliber Glocks at their sides.

Mill couldn't help be a little proud of the shortest of the trio, Frieda Tomlin. Camo clearly was not Frieda's color. Mill smiled to herself, thinking of the FBI agent's usual fashionably severe clothing.

But Frieda more than made up for the size deficit and fabric choice with her tough bearing and straight posture. Mill remembered her FLETC briefings about self-control and "command presence," an almost indefinable and reassuring way a leader carried herself when among subordinates. Well, Frieda had self-control and command presence...bucket loads.

The tallest LEO of the trio stepped to the podium. "Good morning, everyone," his voice reverberated, "please sit. I'm Sid Ballantine, commander of the Southern Idaho Division of State Police. I've been designated the LEO task force incident commander. Putting a state person in charge may strike you federal law enforcement personnel as odd, but the decision was made by all cooperating agencies. As it turns out, I'm also a Brigadier General in the Idaho National Guard with two recent tours in the Middle East, so I can help us all out in ways others might not be able to do. Ease the way to share assets you might say."

A knowing laugh ran through the room. Most Forest Service cops felt better with this man in charge.

Forest Service law enforcement rarely got to be a part of such a big operation, particularly one to arrest sophisticated criminals like Mist. Marijuana eradication in the field could be very dangerous, but usually involved fewer than twenty guards, booby-traps, and various critters that bit and stung.

They could see that the paramilitary mission of this task force required high-level assets, from commander to equipment. Ballantine was an excellent choice.

Sid waved a big hand at a large topographic map that served a backdrop for the low stage on which he stood, "Okay, I'm going to get our plans chief up here in a minute to give you a full sit rep and preliminary field ops plan. He will also point out some of the important features of the area we're going into and where we might find Mist. Before he starts, though, I want to introduce two people who will be making your lives interesting until this operation is over."

A murmur came from the group. "Interesting" could describe a lot of things.

Sid smiled, "These two serve as my deputy commanders. Each will also command a division, so some of you will report directly to them and others of you will be within their command structure."

He put his hand on the shoulder of the broad, muscular man next to him, "This is Forest Service Special Agent Billy Branson, former military special ops and SEAL, now stationed in California. Heads up a multi-agency group working on border security with Mexico. Likes finding people who don't want to be found and working in the dark."

Branson stepped forward, smiled briefly, and waved to the group before saying, "I've got Red Team."

Mill looked at his powerful shoulders and muscular build that tightened the fabric of his camo. "Wow! Billy Branson could get lucky with me...eh, well, no!" she thought guiltily for a moment, then concluded, "So, I'm married and wouldn't stray...but, I can definitely look...."

She let her eyes linger on him.

Manny leaned over close to her ear, "So, don't drool all over yourself, Meacham."

She snorted and whispered back, "Okay, look, I have Branson for eye-candy and you have Frieda."

He chuckled, "Such a deal, *Dios mio*...."

Ballantine then pointed to Frieda Tomlin, "This is Special Agent Frieda Tomlin, works out of DC. She's the most decorated female officer in the FBI. Has the highest field operations rating in the Bureau, too."

Frieda stepped forward, "I'm Blue Team's division supervisor. Any of you cherries that serve under me should know two things. First, when I tell you to do something, do it. And second, if you do it to the best of your abilities, I'll have your six from here to Hell and back."

The small, stocky woman looked around the room, "Special Agent Meacham, are you here?" Mill instantly felt her pulse and panic rise. Her breath shortened. Her vision clouded around the edges until she could only see Frieda standing on the low stage.

What could Tomlin want? She shifted a little to her left, trying to hide behind the oxen cops in front of her.

Frieda spotted her, "There you are Meacham. Come up here please."

Mill reluctantly stood and walked forward, stiff legged.

Tomlin reached down and gave Mill a hand up to the stage. She stepped up awkwardly and turned to look at the crowd.

Cripes, she could only dimly see the mass of LEOs, their faces as blurry and obscure as if she was driving by them at sixty miles an hour. Mill's head spun a little.

"Meet Mill Meacham, recipient of the FBI's Distinguished Service Medal. Mill was the first person responsible for spotlighting Mist to law enforcement. She was also the first LEO to fight them. She survived hand-to-hand with a Mist killer who took out a friend of mine, Forest Service Special Agent Jake Burns. A couple of weeks ago, Mist killed Forest Service Chief W.A. Meacham with a bomb."

Murmurs filled the room.

"Yeah, Mill Meacham is Chief Meacham's daughter. Normally we wouldn't let someone with such a close connection come on this sort of operation. But Mill is a Mist fighter and a real professional. I'd trust her with my life, and I wouldn't say that about most of the rest of you cherries. So, when you get a chance, give Mill a 'hello' and get to know her a little. Be glad she's on your team."

Ballantine stepped across the stage and shook Mill's hand, "Glad you're with us, Meacham."

He turned to the group and said, "Let's get this operation done, people, for Mill, her Dad, and the American people who want and deserve a safe place to live."

The group applauded. Sid smiled at them, "Thanks. Okay, division supervisors, let's get off the stage and let the briefers up here. We have a lot to cover because mobilization begins tomorrow."

A few LEOs cheered.

Smiling, Sid held up his hand, "Oh yeah, one more guy to introduce. Stand up, Whit, and turn around so everyone can see you."

A tall man in a regular Forest Service uniform stood and turned to face the LEOs. "Folks, this is Whit Chalmers, Type Two Incident Commander and wildland firefighter. Whit's a Deputy Forest Supervisor on his day job and has worked closely with law enforcement for years. The Forest Service did us a big favor by mobilizing Whit."

Ballantine smiled broadly, "Whit's team is here to provide logistical and transportation support. They will also make sure this base camp and our forward field camp run properly. They won't do security or take part in our field operations. Whit reports to me but, since I'm likely to be busy with the bad guys, he says any unit leaders who need something should contact him directly. Thanks, Whit. You're making this easy for us."

The LEOs clapped their approval. Having an experienced Type Two team to handle all the mundane matters of operations in wild country would allow the LEOs to focus on capturing Mist members.

With that, Whit sat back down. Sid and his deputies left the stage.

The briefing began.

Chapter 19 - Landing

Chronos recognizes the chopper sound. It rapidly increases from a far-off tapping to a throaty turbine staccato. Two at least!

The choppers close on his position. He picks out the heavy thump of twin rotors...probably Chinooks.

His mind goes back to Iraq and missions he had been on, fast insertions with heavy impacts. His heartbeat picks up with excitement and...yes...a little dread.

The helo noise signals that the thugs mean business...that they plan to bring mayhem, special delivery, to the War Clan.

To Chronos, the fast-escalating sound also signals that the noisy helos had flown a diversion route, staying low and shielded behind the nearby Sawtooth Mountains. Out of sight and much sound until they could pop up, flair, and drop into Cutter's Field at the last moment.

The thugs must expect to be attacked as they approach to land. And they want to narrow Mist's window of opportunity.

Clearly they are taking the unknown Mist threat seriously.

He turns to his Pride, "Okay, gear up! We are plus five minutes for recon."

The six Mist warriors in front of him look variously nervous, sick, and excited. But, doing as they had been taught, each one first checks personal clothing, weapons, and other gear and then turns to a Pridemate to check their gear.

When they are done tightening and adjusting, Chronos walks around each of them, making his own survey. His steady hands on their gear and measured words calm them.

As he works through the group, he sees hands and limbs shaking. He figures one or two might run at the first shot.

Soon each Pridemate would come to that crossroads--cowardice or courage. Towards danger or away.

Whatever their choice was to be, these warriors would have to do. They are all he has; all Mist has chosen to send. No reinforcements.

"You're looking good, Cheetah," he says to one woman.

"Check your spare batteries," to another man.

"Make sure your quiver is secure," he says to a third.

And finally, back facing the whole Pride again, he orders, "Hold up a hand when you're ready"

After a few more adjustments, every hand comes up.

"Okay, Mist warriors," Chronos says quietly, "We leave here in two minutes. Go to your assigned positions and observe. No contact with the thugs until after the signal, unless you have to defend yourself to stay hidden."

He points to one of the gas-cocking crossbows each Pridemate carries, "Remember, you have only six bolts for this first recon. Until the signal, don't shoot at thugs unless you absolutely have to. The longer the thugs go without knowing where we are, the weapons we're using, or how many of us there are, the sloppier they'll be. We want to surprise them when they're good and relaxed. So let's give them nothing to worry about, keep them half asleep."

His eyes glitter in the gloomy hide, "We'll really wake 'em up with our first Strike."

He looks each warrior in turn, "Whatever happens today, and for as long as we fight here, don't come back to this hide. After we leave, nothing will be here except booby traps. You'll be blown up if you try to get back in. You each have your own cache. Go to your cache to resupply."

"And all of you know the rendezvous points. If you get separated from the Pride, check in at Rendez One the first day at 0100, Rendez Two the second day at 0200, and so on. Wait ten minutes, and then leave if no one else shows up."

"If your cool suit fails, or the thugs are hot on your trail, go to one of our Fang's clearing zones. Warriors guarding the zones will take out any thugs chasing you. The medics will patch you up. The supply people will get your gear repaired or replaced. Then you get back in the fight. Clear? Any questions?"

They'd been over these tactics a hundred times. Chronos is just drilling everything in one more time before letting them out on their own.

Cheetah holds up her hand. The tall, powerfully built young woman looks fiercely ready for a fight, "Chronos, what do you plan to do if you're wounded or captured? I mean you personally, not all of us together. You know, given our orders and all that."

Chronos had slept with Cheetah several times, including last night. And on the eve of battle, their coupling had been intense…satisfying…the best sort of morale boost. His groin tingled at the memory of her strong legs wrapped around him…hips pumping…twisting.

102

He pulls his mind away from the pleasant past and smiles grimly, "Cheetah, I won't be taken alive. Like you, I have a suicide pill. But I really would rather go out taking down thugs."

He looks into the faces of his Pride again, "You can't know what will happen in battle. The choice to live or die is one each of you may have to make. I know we've trained to accept death rather than defeat or capture. There's much honor for our Earth Mother in that. But there's also honor in living to fight another day."

He locks eyes with each Pridemate in turn, "Don't get me wrong. I expect you to follow Badger's orders. But you might fail to die for some reason. If that happens, honor yourself and the Mother by doubling your kill the next time you fight the Greed Machine. Any more questions?"

His words have been sobering. There are no more questions.

Chronos leads his Pride out of their underground hide. Blinking in the sunlight, they move out as a group.

A hundred feet from the hide, the Hellfire Pridemates disperse. The eSeeds track each one along game trails and over the tops of downed logs.

Then, minutes later, the warriors climb up into a network of ropes and ziplines running tree to tree. As their feet leave the ground, the eSeeds lose them.

In a few more minutes, the Hellfire Pride is strung like beads in a necklace high above and around the edge of Cutter's Park, invisible and watching.

Chronos stretches out along a wide branch, Swarovski binoculars in hand.

As he settles in to wait, the thundering Chinooks blast in and flair to land. Rotor wash flattens the tall grasses and blows dust and debris high in the air. The machines lower. Wheels dance against the ground. Finally, they settle. Flat-spinning rotors begin singing and sizzling as the pilots keep engines at full power, ready for immediate flight if incoming fire threatens the expensive aircraft.

Chronos grunts. He recognizes the insignia on the big machines. National Guard. The Green Dragons.

He wonders for a moment if the assault on Mist would come from the Guard. If true, he would regret it. He had served with Guard troops, respected them, and wouldn't like having to battle them.

But then he remembers that Raven had insisted the assault would be by federal law enforcement. And Raven was always right.

103

Camo-clad troops begin to drop out of the Chinooks' rear-bay doors. They move away from the big helos and create a ragged security perimeter. Chronos lifts the binoculars for a better look as more emerge. Yes, sloppy dismount, unpracticed in heli-assault.

Definitely law enforcement, not combat-hardened Guard. Good.

He looks at their firearms. Light but deadly enough.

Most thugs carry automatic rifles, mostly M-4s, some M-16s. A few carry shotguns. Each also wears a military-style pack heavy with ammo and gear.

No need to go light here. They don't have to walk far.

He watches as two sniper teams emerge, marked by cased .50 caliber rifles jutting high over the carriers' shoulders. They drop down into the tall grass and move quickly to the south. There, a tall, sharp rock outcrop gives them a high point from which to practice their lethal art.

Just what Badger and Chronos had figured—the FBI has sent quality shooters into the battle with Mist. High up on the rocks, they could cover any action in Cutter's Park.

As the last of the LEOs tumble out of the helos, they form three-person squads and move out in all directions to secure the Park's perimeter. As they straggle away, four vehicles roll out. First come two M249 SAW-machine-gun-mounted Humvees followed by two lightly-armored, tall-wheeled gun buggies built to carry four troops.

Perfuming the high altitude air with black diesel smoke, one of the Humvees moves to the center of Cutter's Park and parks near the old panel truck. Its commander pops up by the roof-mounted SAW and begins scanning the forest with fifty-power binoculars. Chronos sees the sunlight glint off the big lenses. The other Humvee moves south of the helos to guard against assault from that direction.

Chronos knows the .223 caliber Squad Automatic Weapons, or SAWs, can do real damage with their high rates of fire and laser sighting. Mist has no plans to provide human targets for those guns.

Unlike the deadly Humvees with their massive firepower, the gun buggies are used mostly for perimeter patrol. But if Mist tries a hit-and-run attack, Chronos figures the buggies will circle widely to flank and catch the attackers before they can get away. It's a successful mobile tactic developed by the Brits in Iraq that surprises and overwhelms attackers more often than not.

Taken together, the thugs' rifles and vehicles give them far more firepower and mobility than anything Mist has brought to this fight. And

104

who knew what else would show up as the thugs brought in more troops and equipment.

Chronos remembers the old adage about "never bring a knife to a gunfight." Well, Mist had done just that and, for most of the warriors, supplied even less than a "knife."

The thought makes Chronos wonder for the thousandth time what he would never mention to his Pride or to Badger.

Mist and the War Clan had their reasons, good ones, for a strategy of high-tech stealthy weapons and near-invisible force deployment.

Chronos would salute and execute.

But wouldn't being smart and well-gunned always be better than being brilliant and out-gunned?

If he survived it, this battle would give him the answer. When it was over, he would count Mist's wins and losses and decide if the strategy had worked.

War always worked that way.

Behind the four vehicles, two shallow flatbeds loaded with large pallets of equipment roll off the ramps and glide to the ground. The gun buggies hook up to the flatbeds. Engines roaring in low gear, they haul them south towards the tall outcrop where the sniper teams had gone to ground.

Mist war planners had predicted that the thugs would set up camp south of Cutter's Park. Good water, sniper cover, slightly higher ground for the camp, and open-savannah scrub cottonwood cover for a little shade and visual security made the location almost ideal.

The Green Dragon Chinooks increase rotor pitch for takeoff. Twin-turbine thunder begins to shake Cutter's Park again. One behind the other, the helos lift off and circle out to the southwest. Their noise fades quickly as the empty birds speed directly back to base in Boise, Idaho.

Chronos hears the laboring buggies roar towards the thugs' camp.

The Humvees idle--diesels rattling.

Hmmmm.

Chronos figures Cutter's Park won't be quiet again until Mist drives the thugs out.

Chapter 20 - Hellfire

A few minutes after the Chinooks depart three Blackhawks pop up over the south horizon. Chronos watches as they drop into Cutter's Park near the rapidly building thug nest. Two choppers disgorge more law enforcement people. Eager hands pull piles of gear out of the third.

Chronos sees several antennas and a satellite dish in the cargo mix. The thugs are setting up communications even before tents. Same as he would have done.

Perhaps they have better organization than he estimated from that first, sloppy landing. Unaware of Whit Chalmer's Incident Command Team, he admires the thug's apparent grasp of tactics and logistics.

He mutters grudgingly, "If you're gonna bring the people, you gotta bring the gear."

Minutes later, the empty Blackhawks rotate up and away. More thugs move out to establish a second perimeter, this a tighter one at the south end of the park close around their nest.

Chronos uses the binoculars to count heads. Close to a hundred thugs are on the ground, about half in or near the camp. That means Mist and the thugs are about equal in number for now, even if Mist is vastly outgunned.

A fast helo whirs overhead, coming in from the west. Chronos catches a glimpse of it through the tree canopy above.

Apache gunship!

Then another comes in fast from the east!

They must have been hovering off a mile or so, covering the Chinook and Blackhawk landings. Chronos looks at the helos insignias...also Green Dragons.

Now Mist is really outgunned.

In Iraq, gunships like these chewed up whole mechanized companies and battalions, right before Chronos' eyes. Chain-drive machine guns, anti-tank Gatling cannons, missiles, small bomb clusters—the Apaches had "deadly" built into them.

These ships are the varsity. The thugs must have called in many favors to get these deployed.

The Apaches flare and move in to hover over the center of Cutter's Park, one slightly west of the old truck and the other further east. The two helos swing slowly around 360 degrees, using their threat sensors and avionics to search for Mist trouble before they land.

Chronos prays to the Mother that none of his Fang's green warriors has disobeyed orders and emerged from their hides or that some warrior's batteries had failed on her cool suit. If the Apache crews catch even a hint of Mist presence, the warriors detected could be torn apart in a hail of munitions.

And, much worse, Mist would lose the advantage of surprise, the only "big" weapon they had brought to Cutter's Park.

The Apaches complete their surveillance turns. Sliding southward until they're inside the southern guard perimeter around the camp, the helos settle slowly onto honeycomb metal mats, part of the load the gun buggies dragged over from the Chinooks. Once they touch down, the pilots reduce power. Rotors spool down. The pilots cut the engines and the turbines grow quiet.

Chronos waits. Surely there's more to come.

Twenty minutes later, the three Blackhawks appear again. Each one has a bulky black bladder hanging under it. Chronos guesses that diesel fills one and kerosene another. These hold fuel for the Humvees, gun buggies, and helos.

Two Blackhawk pilots maneuver their bladders into position between the Apaches and gingerly land them.

The third drops its bladder at the LEO camp…probably water.

Then in precise order, the Blackhawks turn and land close to the thug nest. More troops and equipment deploy.

After ten minutes of unloading bits and pieces, two Blackhawks lift off and head southwest, leaving one for what Chronos guesses would be standby duties, quick movement of reinforcements, or medivac.

He searches the camp for more information, using the Swarovski's to probe the piles of gear and count noses.

Then he hears sounds like chain saws running.

What the Hell? Are the thugs cutting firewood?

A moment later, a column of twenty enduro motorcycles roars into Cutter's Park from the west.

Where could they have come from?

Chronos wonders if the trail bikes moved overland from one of the far-off roads. He wouldn't have thought the deep canyon to the west and rough country around here would have permitted even enduro bikes to come through.

Maybe some kind of river landing off the Salmon or Payette rivers?

No matter how, the bikes had come. The thugs now have a really mobile "light fighter" force in place, one that could move much faster than Mist warriors on foot.

Mist warriors equipped for stealth and evasion against fast-moving heavily armed motorcycle troops? Another test for Mist's tactics.

Chronos shakes his head. Cripes!

Well, okay, the bike troops were fast ground-movers, but they'd have a hard time getting those bikes through many places in the forest, particularly those parts heavily jackstrawed with down, dead trees.

Mist warriors could pick them off easily in that mess.

Chronos uses the binoculars to study the motorcycles. Two of the bikes have a sidecar containing a dog. K-9 units!

Really now, could it get any worse?

The Mist warriors will be initially protected against the dogs by their scent-suppressing clothing and by the anti-dog trails of CS powder, dried blood, and pepper extracts that Eyes and Ears teams had spread all through the woods and meadow.

But Chronos knows the Mist clothing will lose its suppression power as sweat and body odor builds up over days of battle.

And the dogs' handlers will figure out that their animals have "lost their noses" soon enough. They will rest and treat the dogs so they can smell again and, in the meantime, use electronic "sniffer" gear to detect and neutralize Mist's powders.

As he watches, the K-9 teams move into camp.

Hours pass.

The thugs finish setting up. As dusk nears, they begin to serve Meals Ready to Eat in foil packs. Chronos can see the troops sitting and eating under the oak trees and the occasional dull flash of a metalized meal cover. Perimeter guards begin to be relieved, rotating back through camp for grub and rest.

Chronos watches as recon patrols depart the nest and begin to circle out through the park and surrounding woods. He does not realize they have maps showing Mist's underground hides. If he had known earlier, he might have been alarmed enough to change the Hellfire plan, to try to warn the hidden Prides.

But now he gets ready to erase the danger and eliminate the need for warning.

Chronos tests the breeze. It's sharpening from the north as it did almost every day, heading strongly downslope and downriver to the southwest.

He waits as it builds stronger and stronger…and finally it's enough.

He reaches down into one of the large leg-pouches in his camo pants. He takes out a small transmitter and opens the cover.

Saying a short prayer to the Mother, he presses the button in the center of the little device.

Crummpp!

A brilliant white column shoots upwards from the derelict panel truck—fifty feet, then a hundred, then two.

Propelled by five hundred pounds of TNT, burning chunks of white phosphorous spread out over Cutter's Park.

The nearby Humvee disappears, shredded and shattered. Phosphorus pieces fall everywhere…on human and helicopter, on guard, dog, and gun buggy.

The fiercely burning, elemental metal cannot be quenched. It burns through everything. Screams and cries of warning fill the air.

The strong north breeze fans the thousands of little fires in the meadow grass into an instant inferno, a smoky-glowing mass of flame…a wall twenty feet high.

The wall rushes forward towards the thug nest…burning…running…burning.

In moments, the flames reach the three helicopters. And at about the same time, white phosphorous shards burn through the first fuel bladder's tough hide.

Kerosene! A column of flame and smoke blasts up a thousand feet. Flaming fuel rains over the Apaches and the Blackhawk.

Moments later, the second, diesel-filled bladder goes. Black-smoking fuel runs across the field.

Fuel tanks explode on the burning helos.

Munitions begin to "cook off," sending more hot metal across the park and beyond it, into the woods.

Metal rips through the foliage of the tree Chronos rests in.

He flinches and ducks involuntarily, murmuring, "No one's shot at me in a long time."

As he watches, the wind-driven flames hurtle towards the thug nest.

110

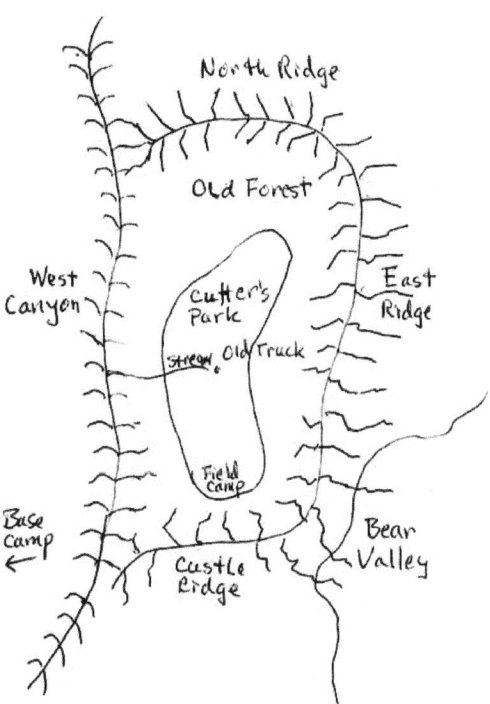

Map from Mill Meacham's after-action report

Chapter 21 - Contact Hot

Whit Chalmers hears the TNT blast and feels the shock wave ripple through his chest. He takes three running steps out of his Cutter's Park ops tent and looks towards the monstrous sound.

His practiced eye instantly takes in the mountain of smoke and flame to the north.

His cheek feels the steady north breeze.

His mind instantly calculates the fire-spread rate.

He has only a few minutes to get people out of the fire's path, or they will die or be horribly burned. When Whit had come up to this field camp, he brought several of his general staff with him, leaving his deputy back at the assembly area to manage things there.

Now, seeing his staffers standing a few feet away, gape-mouthed, Whit yells, "Get the LEO's moving! It's drop and run, guys. The LEO's have no fire shelters. So it has to be a bare-ground defense. Run 'em to that big rock pile to the northwest and get them face down in the rocks."

His firefighters stand there numbly, shaken momentarily by fuel bladders burning and helicopters exploding.

Whit rushes over to them and begins shaking and pushing them, "Get going! Do it now! Don't let the fire cut you off. Now, damn it, now!"

Years of Whit's leadership and fire training take over. Fire team members run to groups of LEOs, some standing, shocked, and others gathering to make a run into the fire in a vain attempt to save downed troops.

"No, no," the fire team yells, pointing, "We have to get out of here. Fire's on its way. Grab everyone you can and head to those rocks. We'll come back as soon as the fire gets past us and it's safe. Move, you people, move now!"

Some of the LEOs drop their gear and start to run. Others still stand, unmoving...undecided... perhaps unwilling to abandon fellow LEOs or unwilling to accept non-law-enforcement directions.

Whit begins to yell and gesture himself, pushing a few people towards the rocks, "Go! Go!"

Still, only a few more start to move.

Billy Branson roars up in a gun buggy. He hurls his massive body out of the phosphorus-fire damaged vehicle and yells, "Red Team, move out! Goddamn it, people, save yourselves! Do what the fire team is telling you to do."

Reality falls on the LEOs. The fire will consume them if they don't move.

In moments, they are rushing towards the rocks, shouting, encouraging others, and pulling a few of the slower ones along. At the urging of the fire team members, they dump gear as they run.

More a mob now than disciplined LEOs, yelling men and women sprint for safety, ravenous fire hurtling towards their flank.

As Billy runs at the rear of the LEOs, he keys his radio mike on the command channel, "Base...Branson. Mist attacked. We are evacuating northwest due to wildfire. Many burn casualties. Some dead. Send backup and medical. Branson clear."

His radio begins to crackle with questions coming in from base, but he has no time for them and switches the radio off. For now, base assets are of no use to him. He has to get his people clear...keep them safe.

Seconds after Billy and Whit reach the rocks and dive for cover, the fire chews through the camp and spits it out as heat, smoke, and ash.

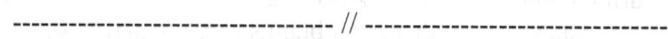

Watching the mad rush of flames burn through the helos and then the thug nest, Chronos smiles triumphantly. Mist has struck a heavy blow. The surprised thugs have lost vast resources.

There'd be dead and wounded to deal with. Thug troops would be demoralized and confused after being driven off by such a powerful, dramatic attack. They'd be doubly cautious when they regrouped and redeployed.

Out in Cutter's Park, Chronos sees figures in the smoke. A few surviving LEOs, many of them badly burned, stumble and lurch across blackened ground towards where their camp had been.

Chronos turns his field glasses on them. Oddly, he feels none of the fierce joy he expected at watching them drag along. Something about the scene reminds him of American convoys in Iraq caught by IEDs, or improvised explosive devices, mostly artillery shells concealed by roadsides and wired to explode by remote control.

Chronos remembers his friends blown up and cut apart by shrapnel.

Enemy fire teams and snipers picking off rescuers.

The smell of burning vehicles mixed with the stink of high explosives.

The smell…of burning battlefields and loss…of course, *that* smell.

It had robbed him of today's triumph…connected him to the wounded…to the stuttering pulse of the thugs' defeat.

A cold wave sweeps over Chronos. He angrily shakes it off. What could be wrong with him?

The coldness comes again. He shudders. The wave passes slowly and he warms.

He raises his binoculars again. Although he does not expect the thug's counter-strike soon, he has to be ready when it comes.

While Chronos and his Pridemates observe the wounded LEOs straggle off, Badger and the rest of the Mist warriors climb out of their hides. The Hellfire blast had been their signal to deploy. They are eager to get to their assigned positions.

Their movements are quick. They had been told their hides would be targets for thug forces… deathtraps if they stayed.

And who knew when the ground assault would come or even bombs rain down?

The surviving eSeeds began to track many Mist feet…spreading out into the forested hills around Cutter's Park.

--------------------------------- // ---------------------------------

Green Hawk and her Pridemates move quickly to their assigned Sky Strikes and slip into their firing seats.

Like the huge siege arrows of medieval warfare, the ten-foot-long, tungsten-reinforced ceramic Sky Strikes sit in sling-cradles waiting for a target. Each missile has an effective ceiling of about a hundred meters, although Mist designers had launched them accurately up to two hundred fifty.

Aiming is limited by the forest canopy and the gimbel mounts that hold the cradle…at best they tilt maybe fifteen degrees in any direction. Nearly straight overhead is the best shot.

As Badger had told them, Green Hawk's Pride has the most difficult job…to sit…bow hunters in a blind…and wait for dangerous game to fly by.

--------------------------------- // ---------------------------------

The hot face of fire chases Whit and Billy Branson into the rocks. They go to ground near one another on the long stretch of nearly bare volcanic rocks. As they wobble over shifting piles of rock, Whit yells, "Billy, get as far away as you can from any vegetation. It will probably burn and you don't want it close by when it does."

The big man gives him a thumbs up and drops down just as the fire reaches the rocky area. Whit takes one last look around. He sees that, last to arrive, he and Billy lie closest to the fire's edge. Good. He and the Red Team Commander are well away from the worst fuels so the others must be on even better ground.

Whit drops hard and shoves rocks aside, thrusting his face into a musty depression filled with otherwise cool, clear air.

A moment later the fire rips across the rock field. Intense heat touches Whit's bare skin and clothes. The fire is close, too close.

Had Billy and he waited too long…run too slowly…dropped too close to the fuels?

Whatever. There's nothing to be done about any of that now. Whit can't move and expect to live.

Whit holds still and keeps his head down, knowing that one breath of the superheated air above him could destroy his lungs…end his life.

A lick of flame from a nearby grass patch touches his wrist. He tucks that hand under him and screams into the dark crack below. A moment later, a hot cinder drops down on his neck and rolls under his collar. He throws the burned hand back up to slap it out. Damn, that hurts!

And then it's over…the fast-burning wave has eaten up the few fuels available on the rock field and passed on by.

Face down in the rocks, Whit feels the heat drop. He takes a deep, wet-leaf-smelling breath and raises his head for a quick peek.

Thick smoke hangs and cinders settle in the hot air. Flames glow to the south and southwest.

The smoke stings his eyes. The air is still too smoky for proper breathing.

He yells, "Stay down for a while longer, everyone! Pass the word. I'll tell you when you can get up."

Whit drops his head back down again for lungful of relatively clean air. He shoves his left hand down into the rocks so that he can see his watch. "Five minutes and I'll check again," he mutters to himself.

The time passes slowly.

When he raises his head again, the air has cleared significantly. The light fuels that fed the fire in Cutter's Park, mostly grasses and brush, have burned down to almost nothing. And the sharp north breeze has quickly pushed the fire and smoke south-southwestward.

Whit stands and takes a quick look around. Fifty or more prone LEO's and fire team members lie with their faces in the rocks, most at least partially covered in grey and black ash.

He yells, "Okay, folks, let's get up. Shake it off. Once you're up, regroup over here!"

Several heads pop up and bodies begin to rise stiffly to knees and feet. Whit stares at the eerie sight—bodies rising from ashy rugged ground—like a bad zombie movie. He cracks a grim smile.

Next to Whit, Billy Branson is also on his feet.

He peers out across the rock field and yells, "Everyone check around you. Make sure everyone's getting up. Help anyone who needs it."

Indeed, in a few minutes, several people are being helped. Some sprained ankles or knees scrambling over the rock field. Others "ate" a lot of smoke and, coughing and struggling for breath, have to be lifted over rougher spots.

As the LEOs straggle in, Whit notices several have burns, mainly on backs and legs where embers fell. Most are minor, but here and there Whit sees patches of red and blistered skin.

"Billy, if anyone has a first aid kit, we might want to get any of your troops who are EMTs working on the people who need some help. And I'd bet more bad news is coming from Mist…maybe soon."

Billy nods, "Okay, everyone who has a weapon, hold it up."

Everyone raises at least their handgun. Billy sees several M-4s, too.

"Okay, what about EMTs? Hands, please."

Six people hold up their hands, "Thanks, EMTs."

Billy smiles grimly, "Okay everyone, I want two groups. EMTs and people needing treatment stay here. Anyone who needs to see a doc and has an M-4, give it to someone who's well enough to secure the site. People not needing treatment grab any available M-4 and come with me."

In moments, the group needing medical attention squats or sits around the EMTs who had already started work. Billy's security group fans out and takes positions among the rocks, creating a protective perimeter.

Only when the guards are in place, and Billy has checked their positions, does he turn on his radio and key the mike, "Base…Branson…we have multiple casualties. Where's the cavalry?"

A relieved voice answers, "Branson, this is Sid Ballantine. Helos are five minutes out with reinforcements and a medical team. Give me a sit rep and a landing site."

Billy takes a deep breath and then reports his "situation," describing the fire, probable equipment losses, impacts on the troops, and concluding with, "We're sitting in the middle of a pile of rocks exposed to attack from an unseen enemy. About half of the Red Team LEOs are MIA, the rest with me and Whit's people. We have a few M-4s and handguns but no other means of defense."

Just as he utters these words, the sound of helicopters approaching reaches his ears, "Sid, the helos are here. Tell 'em we're northwest of the camp site on a big jumbled pile of reddish volcanic rock. Tell 'em to land just south of the rock pile and we'll get over to them."

"Roger that," Ballantine answers.

A few minutes later four Blackhawks are sitting on the ground, filled with grim-faced Blue Team cops ready to reinforce Branson's Red Team or pull them out if ordered.

Another Blackhawk orbits close overhead, a door gunner on each side of the aircraft watching the smoky ground below.

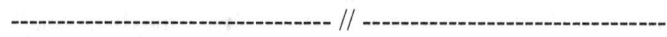

Mill and Manny had been at the base camp ready to be ferried up by helicopter when word reached them that the field camp had been attacked. The whole Blue Team was told to stand down while the commanders figured out the field situation.

So now, the two Forest Service LEOs sit with their squad…checking gear and weapons, sipping coffee and water, worrying and fidgeting…until Sid Ballantine and Frieda Tomlin approach. The LEOs stand up, shouldering their weapons, ready to go.

But Ballantine yells, "Blue Team, gather around. Deputy Commander Tomlin and I want to brief you on what's going on."

As almost a hundred LEOs hurry closer from several directions, he yells, "Okay, those in front sit. Those in the back, crowd in. This will take a few minutes and I want everybody to know what's what when we're done."

The LEOs close in on the two commanders and sit or stand so all can see and hear.

"Okay, Mist attacked the Cutter's Park camp with high explosives and Willie Pete...caused an instant wildfire that burned up two Apaches, a Blackhawk, and then went through camp."

A grumble of horrified anger runs through Blue Team.

"We're still getting the numbers but we have more than twenty personnel MIA, including the sniper teams that got caught on a rock outcrop and surrounded by fire. The camp's a total loss. Ground equipment has been hit hard. Humvees and crews were burnt out. Took out all but two vehicles, a gun buggy and a motorcycle."

Ballantine pauses for a moment and says, "Red Team is cut down to half strength at best. Many troops have burns or injuries. So, we're going to bring them out, then reinforce and redeploy."

"Blue Team, your job now is to bring them out. First in will be security teams and a medical unit. Then, the rest will go up for Search and Rescue and to help get Red Team folks back down to base."

He looked around the faces staring at him, "The Mist bastards surprised us. They had things figured out. We know they are out there in high numbers because of ground surveillance but we can't actually see them with our other equipment. From what we know now, they seem to have cool suits as good or better than our DoD recon troops have. We figure their weapons are probably equally stealthy. So, what happened today probably won't be the last surprise they pull on us. But, if I have anything to do with it, today's surprise will be the last one that costs us people."

"Some of you know about the Posse Comitatus Act. The Congress passed it after the Civil War to limit when and how the military can be used for police work. Social order has to pretty much break down to nothing before the military can come in, and if they do get involved, it's usually when the Governor of a state requests help. You know, like after Hurricane Katrina."

Several LEOs nod their understanding.

"Well, as you know, we had semi-official support from the National Guard for this operation already...transportation and air security mostly. But now I've asked the Governor to request more air assets from the regular military and get some Guard troops called up as reserves."

119

Sid looks around the group. He sees heads shaking, "Okay, I know we came out here to bust the bad guys and put them in jail. We came here to make arrests, not fight a war. But Mist...well...Mist has made it a war...or at least a pitched battle. So, I'm going to make sure we have the support we need to take 'em down. It's still our op. That won't change."

A few heads nod, pride for some taking a back seat to practicality, at least for the moment.

He gestures to Frieda, "Okay, Blue Team Commander, what do you want your folks to do?"

Chapter 22 - Contact Cold

The Blackhawk bucks and slews. Mill can't decide if the pilot is trying to evade ground fire or if she just enjoys trying to bounce Mill's squad around like teenagers on a theme-park thrill ride.

The helo makes three bumpy turns, and then Mill's stomach gets that empty, dropping-too-fast feeling. Through the tiny window next to her, Mill sees the ground coming up fast.

Blackhawk passengers sit below and to the rear of the huge turbine engines, so the helo's interior is incredibly, vibratingly noisy. There's no way to talk. She smacks Manny's shoulder and points out the window.

Manny smiles his tight sheriff's smile…narrow slit of white teeth, a stretch of cruel lips…and nods.

They both straighten up, waiting for the Blackhawk's big bush wheels to touch soil. In a moment, the two feel the aircraft's motion stop. The flight crew quickly slides the side doors open.

Pulling off their flight helmets, Mill and Manny put on their Kevlar "brain buckets" and leap out. Both Forest Service LEOs quickly take in their surroundings.

Above them, an Apache gunship orbits over the landing area and a Blackhawk circles looking for MIA LEOs. The air is slightly smoky and their grounded Blackhawk's rapidly turning blades sends smoke tendrils curling wildly.

A few fires still burn in the surrounding forest, even though the winds have driven the main fire at least a mile south. Mill can see the fire sputtering and "skunking around" across damper ground inside nearby forest areas.

These low, patchy fires might burn for days, irritating their lungs but posing little risk of spreading. Even so, the little hot spots in the forest could burn unwary feet and ankles. Mill resolves to look out for them.

A few "smokes" also rise from the blackened southern half of grassy Cutter's Park, little pockets of glowing coals drilling down into the roots of larger bushes. And, even with the strong north breeze, a low edge of fire creeps upwind, intent on slowly consuming the rest of the dry meadow's light fuels.

Mill's squad leader points to the northwest, "Okay, we're going to move out double time to the forest edge and form a security perimeter. Telemetry has tracked multiple targets to that area but exact perp locations are unknown. I want you in a skirmish line about twenty feet apart. We don't know what else these Mist people have waiting for us. So, keep your eyes out for any tripwires. Don't touch any suspicious things on the ground. And, look for any casualties. Check quickly to see if they're alive, radio your information, and pop a red smoke so the pick-up teams can come and get 'em. Don't wait for the teams. I need you on the line. And so do your buddies. Most of all, watch each others' backs. Everybody clear on what to do?"

Heads nod around the squad. The squad leader's words were pretty much identical to the things Frieda had told them, only without her punched-home, well-chosen cuss words.

Reading her better than most of the troops, Mill had figured Frieda was deeply concerned about suffering more LEO casualties on their "Goddamn better-never-fuckin'-happen-again search and rescue mission."

The squad leader gives one last order, "Okay, chamber a round in your M-4 and Glock if you haven't already done it. Then rifles on 'safety.' I want you to check both weapons. Remember 'safe and ready,' right?"

A few LEOs' faces redden with embarrassment. They either hadn't loaded a cartridge or hadn't "safed' their M-4. Either mistake could cost the squad a casualty.

Mill checks her guns again. Relief. Everything's okay…safe and ready.

The squad fans out and starts to jog forward. Mill finds trying to jog, watch the ground under her feet, and look ahead at the forest for Mist operators almost impossible. She settles on a middle distance, and somewhat self-consciously lifts her hurrying feet higher in the dismal hope she will avoid any trip wires or booby traps.

Sun Bear, Green Hawk's best shooter, steadies her shaking hands on her Sky Strike's firing grips. Above her, the skinny Apache gunship has flirted with the edge of her clear-fire zone once or twice and is now inching back into her sights.

Sun Bear looks down at the sling-tension gauge…green, 100%. Ready.

Now the gunship slips into the center of her sights. Nice shot but…too high.

The helo orbits away. Damn.

Then back. Lower, lower.

Sun Bear thinks the pilot must be looking for something. For a second she worries that she's being watched...that the Apache's gunner is ready to fire on her. But how could that be? She's totally camouflaged from anyone looking down and her cool suit's running fine.

Above, in Apache Alpha, the pilot looks at an e-Seeds plot showing several Mist operators' movements through the woods. The information is hours old. Not too definitive. She checks her ground readings for thermal or ferrous presence. Nothing.

The area she patrols is close to where the Blackhawks come and go. So, the pilot is particularly concerned about Mist attacks coming from here.

She lowers her ship another two hundred feet so her sensors can get better readings and so she and the weapons system crew can get better visuals.

Sun Bear sees the helo drop lower. Now two hundred meters, one-fifty...a hundred.

There! Sun Bear gently squeezes the releases.

Whisst-snak!

The Sky Spike rips out of the cradle.

The threat sensors on Apache Alpha detect the Sky Strike's movement but can't identify it because it has no heat signature, guidance system, or rocket propellant. So, even as the alarms shrill in the crew's helmets, the automatic defense systems on the helo can't deploy countermeasures.

The Apache pilot instinctively twists the Apache's collective to veer away. But the Sky Strike's flight time is incredibly short and the pilot's action comes too late.

The reinforced ceramic missile smashes through the floor between the two Guardsmen and severs the helo's controls.

The stricken Apache hangs in the air above Sun Bear for a moment. Then it arcs over, plunges down out of her sight into Cutter's Park... and explodes.

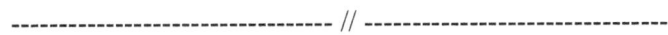

Like Mill's, Manny's eyes have been dancing between the forest edge and the ground ahead of his running feet. So he only catches Green

Dragon Apache Alpha in his peripheral vision as it curves high over his squad before slamming into the meadow behind them.

The thumping blast shakes him and almost pushes him on his face. He turns to see the burning wreck behind him and starts to head in that direction.

But his squad leader blows his whistle and yells into the radio, "Let the pick-up teams work the helo! We've got to get the area secured. Stop this stuff from happening."

The urgency in the man's voice catches Manny in midstride. The guy's right. As hard as it may be the turn his back on the burning wreck, Manny knows the more important mission lies in the forest.

He turns and waves at Mill on his right. Both of them pick up their pace…to the forest.

-------------------------------- // --------------------------------

Cheetah watches the helo burn in the distance. Closer to her, thugs hurry across Cutter's Park towards her high hide, weapons held ready.

Below her, two warrior Prides wait inside the forest's edge, well-concealed by trees and brush. Cheetah squeezes the bulb of a crow call by her side.

The squawk carries down to the Pride leaders below. They look up.

Cheetah signals the number and direction of the incoming thugs. The leaders move quickly to each Pridemate and, pointing, direct their line of fire.

Thirty meters…twenty…ten.

The Mist warriors steady their aim.

And fire!

Short, heavy arrows or "bolts" leave their crossbows.

Like the Sky Strike's, at this range, the bolts' flight times are less than a second.

-------------------------------- // --------------------------------

A small willow bush tangles Mill's feet. She slips and takes two staggering steps forward. Something whistles past her right shoulder. Bird? Rock?

To her right and left, two…then three…LEOs fall.

Arrows...Mill sees arrows...in shoulders and legs.

Another whistle...harsh, quick...passes her left ear.

They're shooting at her...fuckin' arrows, for God's sake.

Instinct takes over. She drops, bringing her M-4 up to firing position.

What about Manny?

She looks quickly to her left. He's down but in firing position as she is.

Their squad leader yells into his radio mike, "Start covering fire and leapfrog up! We've got to move in and engage them inside the forest edge."

The LEOs closest to the forest begin to fire three-round bursts from their M-4s, firing into the aspen clumps...banks of brush...trying to hit a still-invisible enemy.

Bup...bup...bup.

Manny fires as Mill runs forward.

She stops just inside the forest edge and begins to fire at likely concealment sites.

She pulls the trigger and the rifle taps at her shoulder. She shoots but she hears nothing, so focused is she on suppressing Mist fire.

Manny jogs by and she stops firing. She looks around at the forest ahead, picking her next firing position.

But before she can move, the squad leader's voice crackles in her earpiece, "Cease fire! Cease fire! Save your ammo. They've gone."

Mill realizes he's right. No arrows have zipped by her for some time and, better than that, no more LEOs have fallen.

Chapter 23 -- Decline

Philip opens the drawer of his large, old-fashioned desk. Like so many things around the church facilities, the desk had been a donation. In fact, the mismatched hodgepodge of furniture that makes up his office had all been donated over generations…and looked it.

He has never been sure such a cluttery space could be conducive to counseling the spiritually rebellious or comforting the bereaved.

Yet this battered collection is all the church has or can afford. And so be it.

His hands tremble.

It's there in the desk's bottom drawer, in a neglected corner…a "stash" of marijuana, speed, and Ecstasy that a repentant member of his congregation had given to him before entering rehab.

The woman was long gone back to despair.

While the drugs had remained in the drawer.

Two hours before, Philip's dreaming mind had finally insisted. He had to experience some of Mill's wild life if he was ever going to be a suitable lover, a real guy.

And now, at two on Sunday morning, what better place for him to experiment safely than in his locked church office? He steadfastly ignores the truth that he will have to conduct services in a few hours. It no longer matters.

He holds the plastic bag up before his eyes and shakes it. There's a little glass pipe within, the transparent bowl dark with residue.

"For the marijuana?" he asks no one.

He'll just have to try and see.

He opens the bag….

Chapter 24 - Night Fighting

Whit Chalmers' Blue Mountain Two Incident Command Team is gathered at the LEOs' base camp. Blue Mountain Two had been called up to provide support for the LEOs, a tough enough job. But now, thanks to the Mist bomb, they also have a rapidly spreading wildfire to fight.

Wildland firefighters call situations like this "an incident within an incident" and this one is nasty, dangerous. They will have to move quickly to expand operations to attack the wildfire, hopefully while the burn is still small.

Wind and dry conditions make the fire grow. Calm, cool air and rain knock it down. So, weather can be either the incident team's biggest enemy or their biggest friend.

Fire teams focus on several weather factors, including wind speed and directions and drying conditions. They combine weather information with data about fuels like wood and grass, soil moisture, and land form to predict burning rates and fire spread.

At this moment, Whit's fire meteorologist, called the "IMet", is briefing them on the weather reports for the next several days. The tall, middle-aged woman points to a bold projected image of a weather map, "….So, to summarize, yesterday the Mist-Cutter fire pushed upslope to the south and downslope to the southwest driven by north winds averaging ten miles per hour, gusting to thirty. This north-south flow is common here in this part of the Rockies in the afternoons due to the landform and differential heat distribution across the landscape. Basically the air is pulled towards the hottest areas in the afternoon. We know the pattern exists—it's predictable--but we can't easily forecast daily wind speeds and gusts. Clouds, rain patterns throw us off. So our firefighters need to be extra watchful in the afternoons. They'll have to be ready to come off the line quickly if and when the winds pick up."

The woman looks around the group and makes eye contact with the two division supervisors to emphasize her point. This wind pattern means the fire may spot unpredictably and trap unwary firefighters.

Then she turns back to the screen and points again, "Yesterday's wind gusts were created by this high pressure area moving into our area. The center has pretty much passed over us now. It's moving slowly east. For the next day or so, we won't see much wind effect from its presence, but the whole air mass is pulling air from the Utah desert and it's drier than a popcorn fart."

The group laughs grimly at her weak joke. These conditions mean the fire will grow.

"Now, here's some little-bit -better news. We have two low pressure areas coming our way."

She points towards western Canada. "This is the big one, coming down from the Gulf of Alaska."

She moved her pointer west and south, "And this is the smaller one, coming in from somewhere north of Hawaii."

She turns to the group, "I figure these two systems will merge over the Columbia River Basin and get here in a couple of days. Should bring significantly cooler air and moisture, maybe lots of moisture. Good chance of lightning as they come in. But I can't give you a track on the systems yet because I don't know how fast the high will move out…and what the two systems merging might mean in terms of speed and direction. So, guys, as always, stay tuned for the weather report. Any questions?"

One of the fire planners stands, "Okay, Joyce, 'drier than a popcorn fart' kinda works for me but for some of the more technical types here, what's your projection for the Haines Index?"

The Haines Index gives firefighters an idea of how fast grassland and forest fuels might burn.

The woman waves a stack of briefing packets, which she quickly passes into the crowd to be handed around, "Good question, Claude. Looks like a Haines of 6.3 for the next 24 hours."

A murmur runs around the room.

Whit Chalmers stands, "Listen up! The Haines number is high. In fact, it's so high our firefighters will only be able to operate safely at night and in the early morning. Between the high Haines and the unpredictable afternoon winds, there's too much chance of the fire spotting ahead and blowing up. So, for the next day or so, it's 'hoot owl' for our ground pounders and air-attack only in the afternoons."

Several people in the group nod. No wildfire, no matter how threatening, is worth sacrificing human life to stop. Night-fighting Mist-Cutter will have to do for now.

--------------------------------- // ---------------------------------

About the time the morning fire briefing ends, the start of a long vehicle convoy rolls into a large field near base camp. Busses, vans, and

130

"crummies" containing hundreds of wildland firefighters park in orderly rows.

Firefighters jump out, form lines, and quickly unload. They pass their gear from hand to hand and stack it at group campsites.

Lowboys with bulldozers and excavators roll up.

Brightly painted, compact wildland fire engines pull in. They get in line to tank up on water and fuel.

Chunky helicopters rigged for bulky water buckets drop into a nearby field. And a huge Sikorsky heavy-lift helo with a water-sucking, elephant-trunk snorkel and aerial drop tanks settles in near them.

Equipment drivers and helo load masters hurry off to the main admin tent. As soon as they check in, people and equipment go on standby and the pay meter starts running.

Wildland fires mean business…big business…millions per year to some of the helicopter, fire crew, and equipment-rental companies… billions per year to American taxpayers.

In a few hours, cooking facilities and shower units will show up. They will park in the field near the hundreds of firefighter tents that pop up like mushrooms after a spring rain.

Thyra Dexter steps down from the twelve-passenger van that has brought her buying team to the Mist-Cutter fire. She looks around and sees the normal, bustling confusion of a mobilizing fire camp.

As Thyra grabs her gear from the back of the van, she thinks, "Perfect, big operation but not too big."

She smiles, her big, bright teeth flashing, "Time to pull a few buckets of moolah from the Green River."

It would be later in the day before Thyra learned about the hundreds of LEOs nearby in their separate, secured camp. This knowledge would make her nervous. But she would quickly reassure herself that their presence simply made the situation more confusing.

The confusion should improve her chances of filling buckets without being detected.

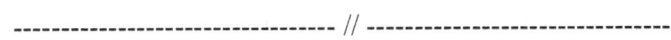

Whit Chalmers sits looking at Avery Scarrs, the Boise National Forest Supervisor. Each day's fire plan has to be signed by a local Forest Service line officer. And one of the incident commander's jobs is to convince the line officer that each fire plan makes sense and should be approved.

"So, Avery, we have all the items in the plan you asked for. Because Mist-Cutter is burning in Wilderness, we're going to limit firefighters to hand tools, small portable pumps, and hose...maybe some sprayers. We stop fire spread at natural barriers and limit the amount of burn-outs we do. No mechanized equipment except along these cherry-stem roads you have around here. And no fire retardant drops except in areas beyond Wilderness boundaries. All that okay?'

Scarrs gazes at the incident commander, using his eyes to test Whit's for commitment, "Yeah, that's fine. But I also don't want a lot of tree felling unless it's absolutely necessary. And where possible, tell the fellers to drop some of the big ones into streams. Our fish bio can brief them what to do. Is that too much?"

"No, that sounds fine as long as we can keep everyone safe."

The grey-haired, lanky Forest Supervisor nods agreement.

Whit points to a map, "Here's the fire plan for today. We're still mobilizing, so you can see it's mostly air recon and some fire scouts on the ground for the main fire. Big fire's still moving south, but with the weather, it'll probably shift west into the canyon and then towards these roads and the campgrounds just outside the Wilderness. So, as they roll in, I'm sending engines and water tenders down to secure those campgrounds and three, twenty-person crews to cut fire line along the road corridor. We have a foam-spray unit on order and they'll hit the campground structures, toilets...whatever...when they get here."

Scarrs nods, "Okay, good start. When do you plan for direct attack on the fire?"

Whit leans back in his chair, "Okay, it's mostly indirect attack for now. We've already put a couple of heli-tack crews off on the fire's flanks. The one to the east side is watching for spot fires and trying to prevent any slop over into the brush and other light fuels in the Bear Valley meadow system over there."

He leans forward and points to the map, "The crew on the west is cutting hand line and clearing fuels to protect those two wooden bridges you have...here and here. They'll also wrap fire shelters around them to block the heat. When they're done, we're going to pull the crews out so they don't get caught if the fire shifts west...should be out in about an hour."

Whit leans back again, "Okay. Direct attack. Not much for now. We've got three medium and one heavy helo working the fire itself...trying to drown it. But it's burning in heavy fuels...some of the downed logs are thirty inchers...and real hot. So, the helos are probably just making steam and holding it back a little at this point. Once the wind dies down tonight, the water drops will probably gain us some ground. And then, while they're making progress, we'll send our Hot Shot crews in to cut line along the east flank and along Castle Ridge. You can see the ridge is roughly a half mile ahead of the fire."

Scarrs finger traces the line along the map and he nods, "Okay."

"As soon as our Hot Shots have the fire line in, some of our fire-use teams will do lots of small burnouts to build black ground between the fire and the Shots' lines. Then, if the helos can catch any spot fires tomorrow, we may stop the fire at Castle Ridge. IMet says we may have wet weather coming in a couple of days. That would sure help us hold it around Castle Ridge and make mop up a lot easier and quicker.

Whit looks at Scarrs appraisingly, "Okay for you to sign the plan?"

Scarrs smiles, "Yeah, looks good."

He signs and asks, "Please let me know anytime the fire makes a run bigger than a hundred acres or so. I just like to know these things...you know us old fire horses."

Whit chuckles, "Avery, you're a legend around the fire community. You saved thirty people in fire shelters those many years back. Even doubled up a buncha lost hikers in shelters with firefighters. Those people owe their lives to you and your quick thinking. Fire guys gained confidence in their equipment and training...you know, that it worked. So, you just ask for what you want and we'll do it for you."

Scarrs looks at Whit sadly, "I also lost six people that day, Whit...for nothing...'cause some fool didn't get on the damned radio and let us know the fire was making a run at us. Damn shame...damn shame."

The two men shake their heads, grim faced.

Scarrs shrugs off his regrets, "Whit, there's one more thing. I know this operation is too small to assign an Incident Business Advisor, but I'm going to send my admin officer up to kinda snoop around. On the Boise, I like a tight-run fire operation from a cost standpoint. You can tell folks he's just around to help out and that'll be true. He looks like Santa Claus and acts just as jolly...always fun to work with. But he has a sharp eye for problems and waste. Name's Fred Pomolo. That okay?"

"Absolutely," Whit answers, "Just have him check in with me when he gets here so I'll know who he is."

The two old fire horses gossip a little more about people they know.

Then Avery Scarrs stands, "I'll be back at o-dark-thirty-early for the fire briefing. And if your coffee's any good, I'll even sign tomorrow's wildly optimistic, bullshit fire plan!"

The two men laugh, shake hands, and part company.

Chapter 25 – Posse Comitatus

Senator Charles Castwell and Mike Reinaud, his Chief of Staff, sit in the Senator's deeply padded office armchairs listening for a briefing by the Secretary of Agriculture to begin.

Normally, the briefing would have been held in one of the many Senate hearing and meeting rooms. But the matter that caused the Secretary to call the briefing is urgent and the Senate's rooms are already booked for the day. In addition, the meeting involves so many Senators, Congressmen, and staff people that few rooms would have held them all.

And they are all eager to hear.

After interminable scraping and rustling and then some microphone thumping, Secretary Calabazas speaks in his quiet-but-distinct voice, "I'll answer questions at the end of my prepared remarks."

More rustling-paper noises and then, "The White House has asked me to brief you on a Posse Comitatus request received by the Departments of Justice and Defense this morning. The reason it concerns the Department of Agriculture is simple. USDA houses the U.S. Forest Service which manages the Frank Church-River of No Return Wilderness in Idaho. Presently, a state and federal task force is in that Wilderness attempting to arrest a vicious eco-terrorist organization calling itself, 'Mist'. In addition, a Forest Service incident command team is simultaneously fighting a wildfire in the area, lit by the eco-terrorists yesterday during an attack on our law enforcement people."

"Some of you may wonder what a 'Posse Comitatus request' is. Simply put, it's when a state requests that the U.S. military become involved in local police activities to help enforce state laws. This is a very rare thing. It normally only happens when all social order breaks down as it did during the riots here in DC in the 1960s."

"There's always some sharing of resources between the military and police agencies, such as high-altitude military-sourced photos that spot marijuana gardens on national forest and park lands. In this case, the law enforcement task force headed by the Idaho State Police, the Forest Service, and the FBI has already received, and lost, some military-surveillance and security-support people and equipment loaned to them by the National Guard."

A few listeners whistle and mutter.

"The Mist attack was brutal and unprecedented. Idaho Governor Sands feels they need more resources and she has sought official permission under the Comitatus Act to get them. As of an hour ago, the

President, acting on advice from the Secretaries involved, has made the resources available to Governor Sands."

Castwell and Reinaud mute their teleconference phone.

Castwell groans, "Alert the front desk! Stand by to hear from the nut jobs!"

He smiles grimly, "Military on the home team's field. This will light off the conspiracy crazies. Fuckin' black helicopters flying over people's homes, listening to them taking a crap, and all that creepy, paranoid black-ops stuff. Watchin' for the U.N. troops in blue helmets. Damn it, I wish those Idaho cops could 'a found a better way."

Reinaud nods sympathetically, "Yeah, boss. This is gonna grow into a big pain in the ass unless the idiots get it over with quickly."

He pauses for a moment, thinking, and then smiles slyly, "But we can probably get some mileage out of this…maybe a lot. Give them a couple of days to fumble-fart around. They're sure to screw up on something major…lose a bunch more people or equipment. And then we can call for an investigation. Cite Ruby Ridge…same part of the country as this fiasco…and Waco in Texas. Talk about oppressive federal government and how you won't stand for it anymore. We might even sketch out some legislation to limit the Posse Comitatus Act, claiming it's too broad…doesn't provide limits…all that. You know like we did with the War Powers Act way back. Then we can stick it to the Commander in Chief with gusto…tag his party with the political costs."

Castwell smiles broadly at his chief of staff, "Damn, Mike, if you were a woman, I'd fuck you silly. What a great idea. Give me thirty seconds and your idea will be mine."

Both men laugh conspiratorially.

Castwell says, "Get Jamie rolling on *my* plan. And see if the Republicrat National Committee folks want a piece of the action. I'll call them if they need to hear from me."

Jamie Stairs is Castwell's energetic public affairs staff. She would have the whole media plan worked up in a couple of hours. She would even have bookings going for Castwell to appear on the talk-radio and TV-interview circuits here in DC and back in his home state of Idaho.

Mike rises from his seat and hurries out.

Castwell tunes in once again to Calabazas' words, "….should have briefing materials in your e-mail that describe our current situation…staffing, activities…all of that."

136

A low cacophony of key-clicking intrudes on his next remarks as Senators and staff sitting near un-muted phones begin searching for the Secretary's brief.

Over the din, the Secretary continues, "I ask that…be shared…as few people as possible. We didn't put any of our future plans or tactical information in the brief. But a good analyst might get some valuable information from what you have. So, please be careful who you share it with. Now, your questions please?"

-------------------------------- // --------------------------------

At the Mist safe house in Michigan, Raven unconsciously cocks her head as she strains to hear the questions coming in over the telephone connection to Secretary Calabazas. His voice is clear but many of the other voices are not.

Her fingers fly over her computer keyboard as she takes notes. She will review the briefing materials and listen to a digitally cleaned up and enhanced version of the call later.

Badger deserves an update and the Secretary has given Raven a wonderful, open source.

Chapter 26 – And Fall

One of Philip's seminary instructors had told him that the way to calm Sunday-sermon nerves was to pause in the pulpit before beginning his talk, look out over his congregation, and imagine them naked.

This way, the instructor assured him, his imagination would reduce the overdressed, proper-looking people before him to just plain folks. It would bring everyone down to their most vulnerable and least threatening dress…no dress at all.

He had tried it twice.

But instead of settling him down, each time his imagination had rendered him tongue-tied and eye-shied.

He found he couldn't look up, except for quick, please-just-let-me-get-through-this glances at the clock at the back of the sanctuary.

Even worse, his mind jumbled the sermon notes.

His tongue mumbled random pious thoughts.

Horrible.

After the second time, he had said vehemently to himself, "That seminary guy was nuts! Really, in Heaven's name, who would want to see such a fleshy mass of people on Sunday morning, or any day for that matter?"

"And worse, what about the attractive women in my congregation? I can't even speak a word without visualizing their naked breasts poking and nodding at me from the pews. How can I sing a note with the vision of their naked hips gleaming at me as they stand for the praise song?"

He had shuddered back then--after that second, halting sermon--guilt and lust jousting in his mind, safe behind his office door.

In those moments, he decided only God Himself could rejoice at such sights in church.

And only a blind preacher could calmly deliver a sermon under such circumstances.

That had been Philip's shy conclusion back then, but his reality today is quite different.

Philip has been awake all night, lit up by speed. It's the oddest body sensation he's ever felt. He is vibratingly keyed up, yet time just slowly chugs by.

He had been defiant of his Sunday obligations at 2 a.m. when he began taking the drugs. But he now wants to just dodge his way through the morning rituals, go home, and crash.

He has a problem though.

He thinks that if he tries to speak, the words will chatter chipmunk-like in his brain but then leave his mouth puddled, glacial, and slurred like a sloth's. As morning hurtles towards him, he realizes that, to deliver his sermon, he has to rid himself of this quick-but-slow feeling.

In an effort to come down, he smokes two tiny, but well-packed, bowls of marijuana. As he puffs, he has no idea what effect puffing the acrid smoke might have on him. But he feels he has to do something to quell his jittery energy.

It's church-service time. He stands and puts on the fresh shirt and sports jacket he keeps in the office closet as insurance against Sunday-morning wardrobe accidents.

He unlocks his office, walks jerkily into the sanctuary, and takes his place on the low dais at the front of the church. He sits in the Pastor's chair where any parishioner may see him, pants disheveled and face unshaven, but otherwise presentable.

He makes it through the initial hymns and announcements.

And as time passes, he feels a growing ganja mellowness, a joyful well-being that gradually quiets his nerves.

His marijuana-treatment plan is working.

He glances at the clock.

Time is slowing.

It's sermon time.

He rises and walks to the pulpit stairs.

Along the way, the coiling, congealing drugs in his body unexpectedly punch his funny button.

A giggle pops out…then another.

He mounts the stairs, one giggle at a time.

As he reaches the top stair, he runs desperate hands over his face and through his hair.

"Get a grip," he tells himself, willing the manic smile off his face, the chortle out of his throat.

Within the pulpit, he turns.

And there they are…his congregation.

He looks back at them.

And in his mind's eye every one of them is bare-butt, bare-breast, stark naked-nude.

Hair askew, Philip leers at them.

First at the ugly seated masses, then at the imaginary pretty breasts.

140

He smiles, showing his flock more tooth than his sober sides ever did before.

"Oh God," he croaks, steadying hands on the lectern, "You people are so amazingly awful looking...so amazingly naked...so tits...bare."

And with that remarkable pronouncement, he begins to laugh--loud, long, and lavishly.

A few parishioners begin to laugh, too, thinking his words might somehow be an unexpectedly entertaining prelude to yet another of his otherwise predictably boring sermons.

But Philip continues to guffaw.

A minute passes, then more.

He clings weakly to the lectern.

His stomach muscles begin to cramp.

Gasping, he bends quickly at the waist.

Out-of sight of the congregation, he bangs his head on the pulpit's edge. He drops out of sight.

The congregation hears his muffled voice, "Haw...haw...gasp...he...." and then nothing.

A church elder leaves his place by the bulky Bible lying open and ready for the scripture readings, and leaps up the stairs to Philip's prone body.

A moment later, the man's alarmed face rises up into the congregation's sight like a prankster's off-color birthday balloon.

"Is there a doctor here? The pastor needs help. And someone call 9-1-1! He might need an ambulance. I think he's laughed himself unconscious."

Chapter 27 - Pounding Ground

Mill helps secure a perimeter for the SAR teams coming into Cutter's Park behind them. It's scary, solitary work. She can see Manny on her right and another squad member to her left, but nothing of the Mist people.

She hunkers down in a shallow depression and, resting her rifle on a small branch, peers through the small shrubs just ahead of her into the thick forest. Her eyes jump from shadow to shadow, tree to tree.

Nothing. Nothing.

-------------------------------- // --------------------------------

Search and rescue efforts break down into two phases: rescue and recovery.

You rescue the live ones.

You recover the dead.

A SAR team works through the smoldering, dangerous wreckage of the Apache. It's dramatic and difficult work. But Mill stays focused on shadows and movements within the forest and spares only quick glances for the team working on Green Dragon Alpha.

Mill can't see them, but elsewhere around Cutter's Park, SAR teams rescue ten battered and burned LEOs and recover thirty-two dead, including the sniper teams. Some LEOs are not there to be found, gone MIA in the TNT blast and white phosphorous inferno. The Humvee crew that set up closest to the old panel truck is among the immolated ones.

The whole SAR effort takes less than a nervous hour. This is because, except for the blown-to-nowhere LEOs and, in one macabre instance, a severed arm with no body attached, the LifeChecs lead the SAR teams straight to their targets.

Unfortunately, very quickly the SAR teams are also helping to remove the LEOs trying to protect them along the security perimeter—those struck by arrows. Mist operators keep attacking and then fading back into the forest.

Arrow strikes take LEOs down.

Even shallow wounds from the arrows take them out.

-------------------------------- // --------------------------------

After a long, tense wait, Mill's radio crackles with her squad leader's voice, "Okay, SAR is done with the pickups. Pull back on my signal. Remember: fire only if you have a clear target. The good guys will be moving out around you so don't mistake them for Mist. I want to see you double time until you're far enough out into the park to avoid the arrows. Okay, listen up. Signal in thirty seconds."

Mill checks her gear and weapons. She tightens a strap and then stands.

Ready to go, she safes her rifle but keeps her trigger finger poised to unlock the weapon for firing. Still facing the enemy, she quickly looks over her shoulder for the clearest route back to the park.

A moment later, the squad leader sounds his whistle. Mill's radio earpiece shouts his voice, "Go. Go. Go. Pull back."

Above her, a crow's squawk.

Another squawk.

Then arrows…lots of arrows.

Mill ducks and throws herself towards Cutter's Park.

Arrows zip close to her. One slams into the stock on her M-4. The rifle whips around and twists into her pumping knees, between her legs. She goes down, rolls clumsily, and staggers back up, dragging the rifle up by its sling.

Ten feet to clear ground.

Now open space.

She's a Hell of a good target now, running like this out in the open.

An arrow touches her sleeve.

She zigzags, runs harder.

She reflects on a great, eternal truth of losing ground on battlefields.

Retreats suck.

Chapter 28 - Pounding Again

Sid Ballantine looks out across the several hundred LEOs and National Guardsmen gathered around him in a large half-circle. The group is now too large for any briefing tent, so they're meeting outside, among the trees, in a natural bowl near the LEO camp

"Folks, I won't sugar coat it. I said this before to the Blue Team. Mist pretty much kicked our asses in the first round. We took serious casualties. We don't know if they lost even one. We lost equipment, major equipment. They don't seem to have anything other than bows and arrows to lose."

A growl came from the assembled task force. Ballantine's words go down hard.

"And we can't even scope or see the bastards because of their non-ferrous weapons, cool suits, and camo. They must also be wearing scent-suppressant clothes because our sniffer gear can't pick them up either. They put our K-9s out of commission, too."

A voice yells, "How 'bout some more good news, Sid?"

Ballantine laughs ironically, "Want some? Okay, here's the good news. We *do* know they have feet because our ground tracking equipment shows them walking around and where they're going."

The group growls again. One voice shouts, "Kill the fuckers." Another yells, "Nuke 'em." A few people applaud.

"Okay, okay, Red Team folks, you want some payback. I understand."

Ballantine raises his hands, "Remember, our orders are to arrest these bastards and only kill them if they resist. At this point, I'd say they're resisting. Looking ahead, seems like our tactical situation is so dangerous that if the Mist bastards don't surrender to you on sight, you're free to take them down by any necessary force."

Sid's words are cop-speak for shooting any resisting Mist people down in their tracks. He finishes his thought, "I want 'em alive, but I'll take 'em dead, too."

The task force cheers.

Ballantine turns and gestures to Whit Chalmers who steps forward to stand next to him, "Whit's job changed when the big fire started. He and his people are supporting us and working the fire, too. He tells me everything seems to be moving along okay on the fire front, but he has something you all have to know now that we have fire in our area. Whit, please...."

Chalmers holds up a bulky, plastic-encased box, "Folks, this is a fire shelter. It can stand thousands of degrees of heat for long periods of time. In a minute, I'll have my staff come up here and give you a very quick and tailored firefighter orientation. It will cover several things you need to know when you are operating around a fire like the one we have burning here."

Whit raises the fire shelter higher, "But the things I want you to remember most about what you hear and see is how to get to safe ground when a fire's coming and how to use one of these shelters. My staff will cover the part about finding safe ground. I'm going to demonstrate how to deploy a fire shelter. You'll get to practice it yourself at the end of the briefing. Right now, I want you to watch me and be thinking about what you see before you take your turn later on."

Keeping the bulky pack raised at head height, Whit pulls the shelter out of its wrapper. He drops the container and shakes the shelter out. To the folks who have never seen one before, it looks like a really large, single-person mummy bag made out of aluminum foil.

Whit yells, "See there are four pockets, one at each corner. You step into the shelter, put your hands and feet in the pockets, and drop forward to the ground."

He demonstrates. In less than a second, Whit disappears, replaced by what looks like a giant corn dog wrapped in foil.

Whit pops back to his feet and drops the shelter away, "Remember to stretch the sides of the shelter out and as tight to the ground as you can. Minimize contact between your skin and the shelter. You know, handle it with gloved hands, boots, and all that. Also, get rid of all flammables before going in like flares, smokes, but put your ammunition under you. You don't want ammo cooking off near you when the fire comes through."

"Okay," he turns to his staff, "Come on up, Doug, and tell these folks what else there is that they need to know."

-------------------------------- // --------------------------------

After the fire briefing and shelter practice, each task force member is issued a fire shelter by Whit's team. They gradually reassemble at the natural amphitheater.

Once they've straggled back, Ballantine yells at them, "Take a break. Unit commanders, twenty minutes off, and then you get back here for an operations briefing. Everybody, take your shelters back and

146

integrate them into your gear. Remember, they go on your belts, or in an accessible pocket of your packs. They *don't* go inside your packs or some goofy place where they're hard to reach or you might punch holes in 'em."

The task force members move off, handling their shelters and wondering aloud where the Hell such bulky objects would go among all the other crap cops have to carry in the field.

Mill walks with Manny towards their tents, "When do you think we'll go back in?"

"No idea, *Chica*," he answers, "So many losses, *los politicos grandees* must be screaming. The next sortie had better be successful or a bunch 'a law enforcement bureaucrats are gonna lose their asses along with their jobs."

Mill hadn't thought about the politics of this mess. But she realizes that Manny's insight is right on. If the Cutter's Park operation doesn't get straightened out quickly and score some real successes, heads would roll. With the big politicians breathing down their necks, State Police and FBI leadership could easily turn one day's hero into the next day's scapegoat.

"God Almighty, Manny," she breathes, "Do you think they'll go after Frieda? She hasn't even been up to Cutter's Park, except maybe for some air recon."

"No, they won't go after Frieda…at least not yet. No, I'd say Ballantine's *cojones* are the ones on the choppin' block at this point. Maybe Branson's, too, but definitely Ballantine's. Besides, Frieda has bigger *cojones* than both 'a those guys. The FBI'd have to buy all new equipment to cut hers off."

Mill laughs at his craziness.

The two walk on in silence for awhile. Then Mill asks, "You know how scared I was out there on the perimeter with you? It's the arrow thing. I can kinda ignore bullets. You know, bullets're so small. Can kill you, but they're small. I can put 'em out of my mind. Arrows, though…big and nasty."

Manny laughs, "Yeah, I felt like I was in a bad western…cowboys and Indians. Guess we got a better idea of what our ancestors were up against, a couple 'a centuries ago."

He looks thoughtful for a moment or two, "Guess we better be glad that it isn't those old-time *indios* shooting at us. They were probably much better shots…had to be to survive."

Mill nods, "Yeah. And these Mist arrows are different. American Indians used arrows as long as their arms, didn't they? These are littler, shorter and thicker…heavy."

"They're used in crossbows. I heard one of the BATFE agents talking about them. He shoots a crossbow himself. Says the Mist version is custom made of Kevlar and titanium…real expensive…balanced. Never seen anything like 'em before. But, *mas problematico,* the arrowheads are barely sharpened. He called 'em 'blunts.' Meant to wound, not kill. And the heads're grooved for poisons or tranquilizers like those blow-gun darts my *familia loca* uses to kill peccaries."

"Guess that's why our guys who got hit with arrows went down and couldn't get up," Mill answers.

Manny smiles his grim sheriff's smile, "Real smart on Mist's side. Wound 'em so they can't move and they have to be cared for. Cop gets killed in the middle of an action, you can leave 'em…come back and take 'em home later. Cop gets wounded, well, four-five guys gotta work that cop out to safety."

His voice suddenly sounds a little admiring, "And the Mist arrows? They're tough enough to survive being fired over and over. So, if a Mist shooter misses, he can go pick 'em up…try again. Can't do that with bullets."

Mill mutters, "Damn, how did they get so smart?"

Suddenly she thinks of Philip and a powerful longing for him hits her, a feeling so intense it weakens her knees. Even with Manny at her side and task force cops all around, she's rarely felt this alone.

Poisoned arrows in the Wilderness.

God save us all.

She shudders.

-------------------------------- // --------------------------------

Two hours later, Mill's squad leader calls his team together. Three new LEOs have joined the squad, replacements for the people who took arrows.

"Okay, look…we have our orders. We will move up to Cutter's Park by helo in the morning. Listen up now for the sit report. This is all based on what we know of Mist's movements on the ground and whatever guesses we have of what they might be up to. Intel says there're likely less than a hundred of them, but that's not certain. Still, we probably outnumber them at least two to one. They have the advantage of knowing the ground better than we do and being prepared…dug in maybe. We pretty much own the air and have more powerful and long-range weapons. You don't share this, right?"

The squad members nod or say, "Okay."

"Thanks, here's the ops plan."

The squad leader smoothes a map out on the ground. The squad gathers around.

"Just before we deploy all this map info will download to your secure global positioning handhelds. Keep you on course. Our troop positions will show on your GPSes, too…you know, from those LifeChec bracelets. That'll keep the friendlies on your radar."

He points to the map, "Just before dawn, a National Guard reinforced platoon is going to heli-assault in along the north ridge above Cutter's Park. They will dig in there and block Mist's backdoor for us. Branson's Red Team will get dropped off east of the rocks where the sniper teams got cut off by the fire. A new sniper team will go in with them and get back on the rocks…cover Cutter's Park…to watch our backs over the black ground."

"Red Team will first drive uphill, due east and join up with a couple 'a FBI heli-assault squads coming downhill to meet 'em. At dawn, the combined force will turn, march north and force Mist towards the Guard. Oh yeah, everybody going into the woods in the dark will have night vision. The rest of us won't."

He shifts his finger to another part of the map. "Blue Team's got the flatter ground here to the west. We're gonna go in just like Red Team only we don't have to meet up with anyone. The helos will drop one group of three squads at the edge of Cutter's and three other squad groups at these openings…here…here…and here. Then, we'll form a two-file skirmish line from Cutter's over to this canyon and move north."

"Both Red Team and Blue Team will hold four squads in reserve. Branson and Tomlin will make the calls on when and where to reinforce. We'll have air cover from Apache gunships and the Blackhawks with door guns.

"Okay, about the wounded. We expect to take casualties like before. We'll evacuate the wounded to any available openings and, like before, pop red smoke for SAR extraction. Don't hang around waitin' for SAR. Get back on the line."

The tall man stands again, "Here's something you gotta know. The big bosses have a surprise for Mist…a little payback…if we need it.

Sometime around noon, if we don't have all the Mist bastards down or in custody, you'll get a radio call to pull back to your jump-off point. Or if you're already hooked up with the Guard, you'll move out with them. You'll have thirty minutes to clear the area, so get the Hell out. Make sure your buddies are with you. We'll all be tracked by our LifeChecs, so the bosses will know where you are. I want to emphasize that you don't want to be the last one out, or you'll have Blue Team Frieda's boot up your ass."

He smiles tightly, "She was very clear on that point."

The squad laughs. Mill murmurs to Manny, "I bet she was...."

He grins back, "That's our Frieda...sweet as *crema*."

"Okay," the squad leaders looks around, "Any questions, people?"

The first question is, "What 'surprise' is being cooked up for Mist?"

"Not a clue," the man answers, "Since we'll have pushed them into a smaller area by then, if the day's calm, maybe they'll gas 'em, or otherwise I guess they could use audible assault on 'em."

The "audible assault" he refers to is a noise so loud and piercing, people hearing it get stopped and dropped in their tracks. Police forces generally don't have the equipment or the need, but the military, which developed the technology for crowd control, definitely do have it. And it can be broadcast from helos.

Heads nod.

The questions and talk continue. Then it's dinner time.

Chapter 29 - From Grace

Philip looks up from a metal bench inside the Chehalis drunk tank.

Tom Purlee, the longest-serving elder at his church, stands on the other side of the bars. His voice comes hesitantly to Philip's ears, "Pastor, the police are going to let you go. No charges...at least this time. They'll be in here soon to get you processed out."

Philip nods, "Thanks, Tom. I appreciate your help. I know it was awkward coming down here."

"Oh, no," the man replies with false cheer, "I've been down to fish my brother-in-law out more times than I can tell you."

He pauses and looks smilingly abashed, "As a young man, I was in here once or twice myself. Kind of a family tradition, I guess you might say."

Tom laughs nervously.

Philip says nothing, losing his high...coming down.

The EMTs had taken a blood sample. Surely the police...and maybe Purlee...know about the speed and dope.

Philip's face flushes. Fear laced with anger rises in the back of his mind.

Purlee clears his voice, "Ah, pastor...see, here's the thing. After your...ah, problem at church. Well, we went into your office and found drug stuff in your desk."

Philip hangs his head.

Tom continues, "Ah, well...bottom line...we're not telling the police, but...well, we don't want you coming back until you're fixed up. You know, if it was just a little booze, we would want to work with you. Plenty of us in AA or have friends there. But, drugs...well, that means rehab or something for you. The elders voted...but not on the record. You can only come back if you 'get clean,' as they say, and prove it to us."

"So what are you offering, Tom? I want to be clear."

"You've been good to us and good *for* us. We'll give you ninety days paid leave...a little more if you need it. That should be enough...and then, if you're not back in good standing, we'll start looking for your replacement."

Philip stands up suddenly and takes two quick steps to the bars.

An intense headache slams his temples. His face distorts with pain.

Misreading Philip's expression for anger, Purlee scuttles back out of reach.

Through the pain, Philip tries to keep his voice clear and gentle, "No, no, Tom," he whispers "please don't be afraid of me. I just have a horrible headache."

Philip presses his forehead against the bars. The metal's cool pressure drives down some of his pain, "Tom, tell the elders my life's come adrift right now, but I'll get it back anchored again, soon. And tell them I know they are being very kind to me. I appreciate it. I can't remember much of what I did, but I imagine people were pretty shocked and upset."

Purlee clears his throat, "Well, it wasn't too bad, pastor. First you acted normal. Then you went up to give the sermon and started laughing like a wild hyena. Then you fell over. EMTs said you bonked your head. Not what folks expected for a sermon. But, well, if it's any consolation, you held their attention the whole time...."

Philip's head hurts even when he laughs gently, "Okay...thanks, Tom, for sparing my feelings. Just tell the elders I accept their kindness and I pray for their forgiveness. I will be in touch as soon as I figure out what I'm going to do."

Tom looks at Philip for a long moment, "Ah, pastor, one more thing. I'm pretty sure no one has called your wife. Most of us don't know her at all, except to talk to a few times at church. Would you like us to call her for you?"

Milly! Call Milly? No way.

Almost voiceless with panic, Philip struggles to lie as calmly as possible, "No, no, Tom. I'll call her cell phone as soon as I'm released. She's out on a field operation anyway. It might be a couple of days before she can be in range to answer."

The other man nods, "Well, make sure you call her, pastor. All of us need family near us while we work these things out."

With a wave, he turns and leaves.

Philip grits his teeth. Call Milly now? Not a chance. He had ninety days of paid exploration ahead. And by then, who knew where he'd be or how.

With her head always in her work and her crazy family stuff, depending on how his experiments went, she might never catch on to his change in "lifestyle".

Philip laughs nervously.

152

A thought slips into his mind from something Milly had told him.

Portland has only four vice cops...lots of vice...and no one knows him there.

Portland lies south, down I-5, new, unexplored territory.

Philip smiles at the jail bars.

On your way to explore Hell, it's best to have a direction.

Chapter 30 - Give Me Shelters?

Jolly Fred Pomolo smiles at the base camp's young logistics staffer, "So, I know we got a couple of pallet loads of fire shelters in here for the law enforcement people. And I know the LEOs have 'em because I've heard some of them bitchin' loudly about the weight."

The two men laugh.

"But what I'm missing is the practice shelters that got ordered at the same time. I saw a few around…in the trash and bundled up after the training. But nothing like the five hundred we got billed for."

The big man scratches his head, "I guess it's no big deal. They just cost a couple 'a bucks a piece, but I was just wonderin' if you'd seen 'em."

The young man looked baffled, "Never came in here as far as I know. They could have come and gone while I was off-shift, but most things get delivered during the day while I'm here."

Pomolo thanks him and strolls off…wondering, "Where did those shelters get to? Firefighters wouldn't steal 'em. Too small for tents…too big for condoms."

Twenty minutes later, Pomolo calls Avery Scarrs, "Hey, boss, I've been finding problems with some small purchases up here at Mist-Cutter. Nothing major…first some missing staples, pens, lunch bags…that stuff. But now some fire-shelter practice tents have gone missing. Overall, it's a couple hundred bucks here…a couple thousand there. Not really big money. But stuff *is* missing and it pisses me off that I can't find it. And you know what I always say, 'if you wanna find the bucks, you gotta follow the doe'."

One the other end of the line, Scarrs groans, "Pomolo, your jokes are beyond bad. Sounds like someone may be skimming--ordering the stuff to have it delivered somewhere else or just grabbing it off the truck."

Fred answers, "No, Avery, I don't think so. Not after the practice shelter loss. Everything I found missing before was stuff you could sell in a store or use in your outhouse. But practice fire shelters? Nobody but firefighter organizations would want 'em. In fact, they were supposedly received here to be a part of training the LEO task force to use shelters. But that didn't happen. The trainers just reused some worn-out real shelters.

"And when I went to find them in logistics, the practice shelters weren't there either. The guy said he had never seen 'em. And thinking they might have gone directly to the secured LEO camp by some mistake, I checked there. Nope. Nada. Never seen 'em either. No way for me to check if they got shipped to another fire by mistake, but the receiving slip said they were delivered and signed off here."

Scarrs sounds thoughtful, "Okay, Fred. Keep your eyes open for any other missing stuff. And, if you can do it without being seen, start pulling the original paperwork together. You know, orders, invoices, receiving signoffs…that stuff. Pull the originals and put in good copies. You might even have to create some fakes. Oh, and note when there're no signatures or scribbles no one can read. We always get asked about that by investigators."

Scarrs pauses and then expresses his gratitude to Pomolo, "Thanks for doin' this. I know it's really hard to work the documents this way because the fire admin folks have had the need to keep their originals beat into them. But the U.S. Attorney won't prosecute cases without originals, particularly the small-dollar cases. And you and I know how often those originals go missing once the fire team closes out and sends their records away."

Pomolo mutters, "Yeah, funny how they go missing…."

Scarrs answers, "Right. My thought exactly."

Scarrs thinks for a moment then says, "While you're in the hunt there at fire camp, I'll be contacting my Journey, the Mountain Toppers. We've been coordinating our work on fire costs and looking for ways to stop some of the leakage…you know, prevent the small thefts or make sure materials don't get sent to the wrong fire or to a warehouse somewhere and never seen again. Stuff like that."

Fred laughs, "Mountain Toppers! I know your bunch, boss. Half of your guys and gals can barely crawl out of bed in the morning. Bad knees…bad backs…a couple of 'em are plus sizes bigger'n me. Bunch 'a beat up smokejumpers and field people at the end of their careers. So, no way you're headin' for any mountain tops."

Scarrs makes his tone contemptuous, "Ever heard of helicopters, Pomolo? We're Mountain Toppers. We take our lives in our hands riding in those egg-beaters. Brave? Why we set the example for the younger employees. And us Mountain Toppers are hardy types. Once we get up the mountain, we like to find a rough, old stump and sit down on it to eat our lunch. Some people actually sit on rocks! Believe it! And later, after all the exertion of opening our lunch buckets and talking for awhile, the helicopter pilot comes back to pick us up. That mean bastard used to be a Marine drill instructor. He actually makes us climb

156

back in the chopper! Can you believe it? So, don't be picking on our name or casting scorn on our physical abilities. It's just not like that."

The two men laugh, and after promising to check in daily, hang up.

Chapter 31 - Fire Moves

The next morning, Scarrs reaches the fire camp a few minutes before the 0530 fire briefing starts. He slips into the briefing tent, works his way around the chatting firefighters, and moves up to Whit Chalmers blind side.

From just behind Chalmers' left ear, he growls quietly, "So, what's the sit rep, Whit?"

Startled, Whit turns with a smile, "Glad you could make it, Avery. Will you be able to stay for the whole brief?"

"Yes. And I'll walk around camp a little afterwards. You know, check in with folks. See if they need anything."

"Great. You'll get the whole fire brief in a couple 'a minutes. But, to put it simply, we stopped the fire at Castle Ridge. Some spotting and slop-overs, but the Shots and a smokejumper crew are on those."

"That sounds great."

"Well, that was the good news. Now the bad. Late yesterday, the winds shifted east and sent the main fire towards the canyon. The gusts caused a bunch 'a spot fires to jump the canyon while the main fire went in. The spots burned towards the crews and equipment on the west flank. They had a lot of line cut over there and engines with plenty of water, so the spots didn't get past them into the campgrounds. At least not much. But about dark, just when we thought things were going to calm down, that big low pressure system showed up. Lightning in several places and the winds shifted southerly. Gusted pretty high, driving the fire further down into the canyon and then up to the north. And that mess threw a lot of embers out to start spot fires to the north. And only a little rain came in with the low pressure because the high pressure to the east decided to stop and block. The in-canyon fires started moving pretty fast...."

"Damn."

"Yeah. Double damn. So now we have several fires burning, some an acre or two, and others over fifty acres. They line up roughly south to north, mostly down in the canyon where we can barely get at them, a couple 'a miles west of Cutter's Park where the cops are and a couple of miles east of our base camp here."

"Sure glad the cops got their fire briefing...."

"Yup. Anyway, we expect the fire to move north quickly today. We can't put firefighters in between the separate fires in the line because there's too great a chance of fast-moving fires burning together and trapping them. So we have to work the flanks to prevent spread and look for a stopping point like Castle Ridge somewhere ahead."

Whit puts a comforting hand on Scarrs shoulder, "Guess we're gonna burn up more of your real estate, buddy, but there you have it."

"Like you said, 'double damn.' You see any light in this tunnel?"

"Yeah, the fires should stay away from the LEOs except for smoke, which will make their air operations interesting. And we can keep the fire from heading towards us here."

Whit sees the fire planner walking up to the podium. He looks inquiringly in Whit's direction.

"Okay, Avery, so that's it in a nutshell. I'll get with you after the briefing if that's okay."

"Sure is. Talk to you soon."

Scarrs moves to the back of the room and sits.

The briefing begins.

Chapter 32 - Spread

Badger and Chronos meet in the evening glow after Hellfire.

Badger is quick to compliment the exhausted man, "Chronos, Hellfire was an overwhelming success. The thugs were driven off completely. I don't know how many of them were killed or wounded, but it must have been dozens. Our warriors are very encouraged. You, and the courage and restraint of your Pride, made it happen."

"Thanks, Badger," the man smiles, "it was a lot of sweat. And the thugs leaving gave our warriors a chance to rest and re-equip."

He sits and leans his back against a tree, "So what's next?"

Badger says, "Based on what I know from Raven, I've decided to move our Fangs into the second battle phase. I don't think we can wait any longer to see what the thugs might do."

Chronos nods, "Yeah, they withdrew fully and have had plenty of time to regroup. Nobody's on the ground near us...no skirmishers, no scouts...so it looks like they plan to come in all at once...come in blind and heavy."

"Well, Chronos, phase one surprised them. They had lots of casualties. We had very few. Advantage Mist. But we both know the long-term advantage lies with the freddies. They have the people, the equipment, and the time. And, according our plan approved by the Chiefs' Council in Missouri, from here on out, we can hide...hit the thugs and run...but we can't run away. We have to defend this ground."

The man shakes his head, "Not our usual way...."

"No. Right. Well, Raven reports the thugs have reinforced with more law enforcement people and some National Guard troops. Numbers are over two hundred now. Their base camp is also much bigger because our little Hellfire surprise turned into a big wildfire. So, the thugs have a lot more logistics capability than they did before...more trucks, helicopters."

Badger gazes at the man and says firmly, "With all that against us, I think phase two should be plan Zulu."

Chronos smiles tiredly. Among Mist's several phase two options, he likes this choice best, a strong plan based on the Zulu people's traditional battle order—the Fangs arrayed in the shape of an angry buffalo's head and horns.

He murmurs, "Good pick..." just before falling asleep against the tree he'd been leaning against.

When he doesn't reply to her next remark, Badger listens for a moment.

And then hearing his snores, she smiles tiredly and slides down to the ground.

She puts her pack under her head and, like Chronos, falls sleep for the first time in thirty-six hours. The comfort of having him near allows her to sleep that much deeper.

They both wake as bird calls answer the first streak of high mountain dawn.

Badger thinks, "A good day to die…" and then shrugs off the morbid chill that comes with the thought. She has to live if Mist's plan is to be successful.

The two War Clan leaders wake their sleeping Prides. Soon after, Pridemates move out, carrying orders to every Pride and warrior.

Follow plan Zulu.

The sun rises, chasing out the forest shadows and lighting up thick pockets of wood smoke.

A half-hour later, thanks to quick Pridemate legs, the Bull's Head rests in a broad arc a few hundred yards inside the old fir forest at the north end of Cutter's Park.

The Bull's East Horn lies along the forested ridge.

The West Horn curves a quarter mile along the banks of a deep stream that travels west from the old-fir forest and eventually drops into the steep canyon.

Half the warriors are in the Horns and half in the Head.

This plan takes advantage of the terrain. No matter from where the thugs' attack comes, the mobile prides can adapt. The Horns can swing east or west, gouging and tearing.

And, if the thugs come from the south as they did before and take the easy way up the burnt-over area of Cutter's Park, the Horns can fall on the thugs' flanks and inflict heavy damage. Or, if the thugs sweep north through the woods, the Horns can conduct a fighting retreat to draw the attackers right up into the Head.

There, massed, but carefully hidden, crossbows would inflict heavy casualties before the Head dispersed and circled with the Horns to Strike the thugs' flanks and force their inevitable retreat down Cutter's Park.

Chronos grins at Badger, "Damn good plan…."

Then he moves out to take charge of the West Horn.

Cheetah is there, at the front. And well…if the thugs take very long to get there, the vigorous woman and he might bang boots together.

He smiles, slaps his thigh, and stops himself from whistling.

Yes, his affairs are settled and he has much to look forward to.

Chronos reflects that today is a good day to die….

-------------------------------- // -------------------------------

Blue Team's first transport helo lifts off earlier than planned because the Mist-Cutter Fire is burning between Cutter's Park and the LEO camp. The firefighting activities and the thick smoke mean the choppers have to fly miles south before turning back north to approach the landing zones. They also fly at greater distances apart because of the poor visibility.

Considering the extra flight times, both Red and Blue Teams will be at least a half hour slower in assembling to assault the Mist positions than the LEO commanders had hoped. The slower pace will give Mist that much more time to be ready for them.

Mill and Manny arrive in the second wave, flying in with Frieda and her command staff. As soon as the helo touches down, Mill's squad puts boots on the ground. They grab their gear and prepare to join the squad that landed before them.

When all the Blue Team squads are in place, Mill's assault group of three squads will cover an area from Cutter Park's edge west a hundred meters. Frieda and her command center will stay near the landing zone, out in the open black under sniper and air coverage— things that would not be possible further away or inside the forest.

After sorting out their supplies, the two groups begin to separate.

Frieda yells to Mill and Manny, "Make sure you two come back. I would miss you stinkin' cow pies…."

Manny grins back, "And we would miss your lovin' words, Special Agent Tomlin."

Frieda makes a rude gesture with her forearm and fist. The whole squad laughs.

The squad leader yells, "Line up, ladies. Time to move out."

He looks south. Their assault group's third and final squad is on final approach. He turns and waves his squad towards the woods.

As they move up, Mill sees that smoke lies heavier in the forest than in Cutter's Park. She figures a lot of smoke must have moved in last night after the low front came in and the night cooled off, causing the fire to "lie down". Among the trees, the breeze has been slower to drive it out.

In five more minutes, they reach the first squad to arrive. That squad has spread out in a skirmish line from the trail's edge to Cutter's Park.

Mill's squad moves into position west of the first squad. They, too, fan out at ten yard intervals, guns pointing north.

When the third squad gets in line, the group will sort itself out into two closely spaced lines, half the people forward and half back a few yards. This configuration will allow squad members to cover one another better when leapfrogging ahead or joining forces to attack a concentration of Mist people.

Mill figures the whole spacing plan will break down when the skirmish line gets into really rough ground or has to cross through areas of downed logs and wood debris. But it should work pretty well under better conditions.

Mill looks to the north. Because of the smoke, visibility is perhaps twenty or thirty yards. Mill can't sense anything through the patchy-smoky air.

Its somber, dark feel creeps her out.

Mill speaks in a low tone to Manny on the line to her right, "Cripes, Manny. I can't even see the squad leader. We're gonna have to be careful or we'll get lost."

Manny replies quietly, "Just take it slow and careful, *Chica*. Just do your job and let the other guy do his...."

Mill smiles. This is pretty much Manny's advice at every turn. "Just do your job...."

Mill gives him a weather report, "No sign of Mist this morning...too smoky."

Manny snorts derisively.

-------------------------------- // --------------------------------

Major Carol Cain pulls back on the controls of her AC130U Spooky. Flying heavy, the Lockheed gunship lifts slowly.

"Cee Cee", as Cain is called, loves the look and touch of her recently refitted airship. It boasts new avionics and flight controls, and a new battle computer, along with numerous targeting and weapons upgrades.

164

Cee Cee turns to her first officer, Paul Tillotson, "Hey, Paul, take the controls for a minute. Remember that slight rudder vibration we had before? Gone. Smooth as silk."

Tillotson's hands move to the controls, "Yeah, Major, it's bitchin' now."

They both laugh like kids.

Their Spooky had been recently rebuilt in California. It was released to Cee Cee and her crew only three days before. After running a few test flights around Nellis Air Force base in Nevada, and getting Nellis' expert mechanics to make a few needed adjustments, they had planned to fly Spooky 0704 back to the AC130s' home base in Florida. But then the call came in for a diversion flight to Joint Base Lewis-McChord in Washington State—a call that added spice to the whole adventure.

Cee Cee says, "Damn, it's good to be alive. Sweet ship. Easy mission. Loaded for bear. We can shake her down some more and be home for the weekend."

Paul smiles, "Sure, Major. Heavy ammo load though. And ops orders were updated this morning to allow for more wait time over target. Load master and I had to short us fuel out of McChord to meet load limits. All in all, we have to stop in Boise to top off."

Cee Cee takes the controls back and dips the wings to feel the aircraft's lateral trim. "Yeah, feels heavy to starboard a little. Must be all that ammo. Well, if we use the ammo up, fuel won't be a problem on the way back!"

Both officers finish their flight checklist signoffs. A moment later, Tillotson leaves the cockpit to get them both coffees from Spooky's tiny galley.

Other than training and weapons test-firings, Cee Cee has never been on a domestic mission before. Pretty rare stuff.

And the information in the pre-op briefing had been pretty sketchy. Idaho police and National Guard were mixing it up with a large body of eco-terrorists. Law enforcement might need Cee Cee's Puff Dragon to breathe fire on the eco-terrorists.

The first AC-130 Hercules "Puffs" were used in Vietnam as aerial gun platforms. They were actually called, "Puff, the Magic Dragons" after the Peter, Paul and Mary song. Big difference though between the song and the aircraft.

Cee Cee smiles. The song was a drug-generation fairytale. The real-life Vietnam Puffs were gun-smoke-shrouded air-to-ground battleships able to reduce a village to broken masonry and ashes in minutes. And in the ensuing years, the Spookies and their sisters, the Specters, had gotten ever more deadly and accurate.

Cee Cee presses a series of buttons on her autopilot to check course and speed...right on for Boise. ETA two hours. She keys the mike in her flight mask, "Idaho Guard, this is Spooky zero-four, do you copy?"

"Spooky zero-four, we copy and have you on the scope. All green."

"Okay Idaho Guard, I show ETA your location in two hours. Do you confirm?"

"I confirm, zero-four. We'll have the coffee on when you get here."

"Roger that, Idaho Guard. Spooky zero-four clear."

The pleasantries over, Cee Cee runs the battle computer through a weapons check. All green. The 25mm Equalizer cannon, the twin Bushmaster 30mm chain guns, and the 105 mm M102 are all on line and, when the safeing keys get turned, ready for firing.

She checks the battle computer itself. The initial battle sequence is programmed in, subject to remote upgrade just before beginning their first firing run.

In Iraq and Afghanistan, she and her crew had controlled the ship itself, the cannons, and the twin 20mm Vulcans that used to reside close to the flight deck. Her crew had hosed a number of unreported bad-guy targets with the Vulcans while computers in fire control hammered known targets with the old Bofors gun and the 105.

Today she is reduced to a delivery girl. Fly Spooky there, take a nap while the computer did all the work, and then fly home. Ho-hum.

Cee Cee knew her crew felt much the same way. During a mission like this with no eyes on the ground to help zero-four's crew re-aim and dial-in their weapons, they'd get no chance to improvise. Their jobs had been reduced to making sure the guns cleared if jammed and watching the ammo feeds. Otherwise, the computer ran the guns and cannons...aimed 'em, fired 'em, and made sure they didn't get too hot...and, just to mock Cee Cee's skills and experience even more, flew the plane through the target area.

Yes, as Cee Cee saw it, she was just excess baggage for the fun part.

Unless her Spooky had an emergency. Well, in that moment, people skills could be the only things that stood between mission success and absolute disaster.

Chapter 33 - Wounds, Old and New

Mill's group is on the march. The forest floor is treacherous here—full of stump holes, downed logs, and moss-filled depressions spongy with water and mud. Water must be coming from active springs in the area.

Mill hears her squad leader's quieted voice in her radio earpiece, "Keep your line, squad. Eyes ahead but check your wings now and then."

Mill thinks, "Someone's fallen behind. Dropped in a hole or something. And the squad boss saw him."

She glances ahead right and then left. Okay, there's Manny on her right, five yards ahead. A tall LEO paces ahead on her left, similarly spaced. She momentarily envies his long legs until she remembers how much better a target he makes, topping the underbrush by a couple of feet and a out couple of yards ahead of her.

Better to be a little Milly in this mess, shorter and less visible, and a little ways back.

Little. Yes, little. It's good to be little Milly.

Something dreadful…eerie…oozes into her mind like the smoke drifting through the silent forest ahead.

The thought grips her. Small. So small. Milly is so small.

So vulnerable. So easily captured and raped…so easily spoiled.

A morbid panic sets in…builds quickly... her anxiety spikes.

Her thinking starts to fragment into jumbled rhymes as it had done before in Missoula.

An image of her father, dead, blown to bits, comes into her mind.

"Dad? So sad. Crazy mad."

Her damn mother, the Mist monster, is she here…killer with loving dream hands?

"Mom gone? So long."

Mill struggles to pull her mind together. She tries to get angry. She remembers Bill Zumo, her Patrol Captain and friend. And crazy-talking, tough Special Agent Jake Burns—her mentor and champion. Both men dead by Mist assassins.

The memories make her momentarily fierce.

But her anger quickly slips back into rhymes.

"Friends? Heart rends."

A sodden, heavy fear wells up in her, pushing out the panicky feeling.

Would she die today...by Mist hands like her friends?

The Mist killers were everywhere...invisible.

They can shoot her down...penetrate her...at any time.

Anxiety runs in hot and cold flashes up and down her back.

Her vision clouds until she only sees ahead through a narrow, fear-fringed tunnel.

Her teeth chatter.

Tears come to her eyes.

"Die? I'd rather fly."

She feels like running.

"Run? Save one."

Without thought, she turns back towards the landing site.

Unaware of her hesitation, the squad marches on.

Is this cowardice? Or is this the cumulative effects of loss...as Dr. Canot had warned...coming down on her in this moment of high stress?

This bright pebble of insight slips away, too.

"Stress? Plain mess."

It doesn't matter, life lies ahead of her.

Death looms higher and higher behind her in the darkening smoke.

She takes a tentative step, preparing to run.

She remembers Manny. Brave Manny.

He is marching away from her towards the enemy.

"Enemy? Not for me."

Her legs tremble...now her arms. She can't move.

She takes a step, then another.

She looks up. The image of Manny's face hangs in the air ahead of her, smiling his sheriff's smile.

"Sign? Align."

Suddenly the cold chill in her chest is gone.

Her mind clears a little.

Manny is her rock...her anchor. He just wants her to do her job.

He could be hurt if she doesn't do it, maybe killed. So could the rest of her squad.

And so, refocused on her friends, Mill's mind clears a little more. Her fear lightens and her anxiety drops. In moments, even if her arms and legs still shake, she can see and put two rational thoughts together. The rhymes are gone.

This is better.

170

"Now," she wills herself, "Do something…move."

She forces her body to turn around, to walk a few steps on crab feet, and then to wobbly-jog back to the line.

In less than a minute from her first panic, she's back in place and keeping pace with the marching squad. Gradually her shaking stops.

The line starts down a low streamside bank. On the other side the land rises steeply to a high bank.

As the front line of LEOs reaches the stream, a crow croak echoes from high above.

Instantly, a flight of arrows pours down on them from over the bank ahead. And then another. And another.

Arrows zip over Mill. One hums past her right ear, causing her to flinch away.

The arrows stop. None have come any closer to Mill. Several LEOs fire weapons towards the trees and brush at the top of the rise. But there are no targets in sight.

She realizes what must have happened. After a spotter saw the LEOs reach the stream, he had sounded the crow's call from high above Mill's squad.

In answer to the call, Mist bowmen fired three rounds from pre-selected positions, blindly arcing their arrows at the LEOs. Then the shooters fell back away from the LEOs guns.

She peers up into the tree crowns just ahead. There…high up! Someone in camo silhouetted for a few seconds against the sky, moving out into thin air…no, walking a rope bridge.

Mill raises her M-4, aims carefully, and fires three rounds. The Mist killer doubles over, turns, and drops feet-first into the forest below. Got 'em!

She has to get Manny! They can go grab this unsub together before he gets away. Send him back to Frieda.

She looks to her right.

Her heart almost stops.

She sees…she sees…God help her…Manny…back downwards…on the ground…with an arrow…no, Sweet Jesus…in his throat.

--------------------------------- // -------------------------------

Two bullets hit Chronos, one in his chest and the other in his groin. He takes two steps along the rope bridge. His right leg gives way.

His fall is less than a second. He lands and takes a clumsy roll down a shallow slope. He raises himself to sit, and then tries to struggle up and stand.

But his feet won't come back under him.

He's colder than his cool suit should make him. Wet under it.

A vision of Cheetah runs through his mind.

Mother…Earth Mother.

He sleeps….

Mill will never know she gunned down Bill Zumo's assassin.

She would have taken no pleasure in knowing anyway.

Manny's life was worth more than a thousand of Chronos'.

Chapter 34 - Steel Rain

Badger feels the buzz and looks at her satellite phone. There's a message from Raven on the screen, "Spooky departs BOI. ETA u 40 min." Badger thinks for a moment. What did "Spooky" mean? Clearly Spooky is an aircraft because it had left Boise International Airport, but what was it for?

She felt a memory stir in her tired mind. It was a military something, not law enforcement. That much Badger recalls. She had been briefed on military equipment that might be used against them but couldn't remember this one. Must have been one of those "barely possible" options.

Was it one of those huge helicopters?

Her veering mind finds the answer.

Oh no! Spooky means a Puff Dragon--heavy guns from the air.

She has to tell Chronos immediately. The warriors would have to hide in deep cover to escape this threat if they could even escape it at all.

Badger jumps down from her high hide near the center of the Bull's Head and trots southwest to find Chronos, regretting the Council decision not to use radios at Cutter's Park.

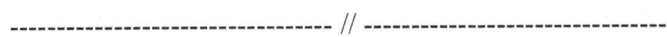

Mill kneels by Manny.

In her earpiece, she hears her squad leader, "Meacham, I've called the SAR folks for Suemez. Pop red smoke and get back on the line. I know he was your friend. But do it! Back on the line!"

Mill keys her mike. Some neutral part of her mind talks for the rest of her, "Acknowledged."

But whatever rational mind part speaks this word, it then shuts down.

Manny stares up at her, eyes bright. A little blood trickles from the left corner of his mouth.

He can't speak because the arrow has punctured his larynx. But he mouths the words, "Chica...*te amor*...do your...."

And then he's gone. His eyes dull.

Mill stares at his dead face. Manny...Manny. This is too much.

Then, a life change radiates outward from her core.

Her body shakes again, convulses.

But this time, the full weight of Mill's fears falls away. The fire of her anguish goes out.

"...do your job." She knows what her job is now.

She had been "Wild Girl Hunting" in Alaska, ridiculously hooked on booze, drugs, and sex. Mill had worked hard to put Wild Girl's wicked vulnerabilities behind her.

Now Mill wills Wild Girl Hunting to return.

Mill screams to wake Wild Girl.

But this time, instead of drugs, Wild Girl wants blood...Mist blood.

Wild Girl wants to bathe in Mist blood.

Wild Girl shakes with rage.

She *is* rage...cold rage...hot rage...berserk rage.

Her friends...death...rage.

No doubts...no pity in Wild Girl's rage.

Wild Girl looks at her gear...at her weapons.

No one can know where Wild Girl goes or what she does.

Wild Girl rips off her pack. She takes out her Kabar marine sheath knife and cuts the LifeChec off her wrist...jams it in Manny's shirt pocket.

She methodically pulls Manny's ammo from his pack, takes his knife, and pulls his Glock from its holster.

She drops these things in her pack and puts it back on.

She throws the sling of Manny's M-4 over her head and pulls it down across her chest so the rifle lies down across her pack.

She stands, handling her own M-4. She ejects the magazine and tests the spring tension to see how many rounds she has left...guesses twelve...snaps the box back into place.

One up the spout...unlucky thirteen ready for Mist delivery.

She looks into the forest ahead, gauging where the enemy might be.

She tightens her gear, then jogs ahead, maneuvers quietly and invisibly around her slowly leapfrogging squad, and runs straight north, deep into the forest.

After a hundred yards, she sees a shadow move.

Camo! She fires and the Mist shit goes down.

An arrow sails past her ear. Fire!

Another kill.

Her helmet...too heavy...brush slaps it...too noisy. She throws it off.

174

Two Mist shits run ahead of her. They go down in a burst.

Yes, this is it. This is bringing death.

Wild Girl is transcendent.

It's like she can see everywhere, all at once. She can sense the slightest movement.

Behind her! She spins and fires. Another one down.

Wild Girl screams and plunges further into the brush.

When the ammo runs out, she will gut them with her knives.

And if she loses the knives, Wild Girl will rip them apart with her teeth....

And taste blood...Mist blood.

-------------------------------- // --------------------------------

Cee Cee feels the Equalizer spooling up. The Gatling-gun cannon has five barrels compared to the Vulcan's six. And there's only one Equalizer onboard now rather than the two Vulcans her Spooky had carried before.

Different guns...fewer barrels. The sensation drifting up from the seat beneath her is therefore different, too.

She'd have to say she didn't like the difference...for one, the Vulcans' vibrations combined with the excitement of battle had always had an erotic effect on her...but she'd also have to agree that the 3,600 rounds per minute Equalizer was a great punisher on the ground.

She glances down at the gun-readiness read-out. Everything green. Ready to go.

Cee Cee's Spooky normally orbits around fixed targets. Because of the AC130s pinpoint targeting and heavy firing capabilities, it can tear them to bits from thousands of feet up. In fact, it rarely runs low-altitude missions because it has virtually no armor and could be shot down with heavy machinegun fire or short-range missiles.

This mission is different. Instead of a building or village that needed torn to pieces, Spooky is aimed at dense woodlands of several hundred acres, almost a square mile in size.

Cee Cee smiles. Her Spooky would cut that landscape to shreds in two low runs. And no significant threats. The ground pounders had reported only arrows being used by the eco-terrorists.

Cee Cee mutters, "A piece of cake."

Spooky's guns fire from the left side of the plane. So the battle computer will fly them along the outer edge of the target "box," with the box on the left side, firing down and sweeping out across the area at shallow angles.

She checks the flight vector display on the face plate of her helmet. Spooky is lined up on the target "box" and coming down to the low altitude required by this mission.

Cee Cee looks through the forward glass and sees smoke northwest of the target. That'd be the wildfire from her brief.

She checks the forward-looking radar and GPS equipment. All green. With this equipment, Spooky doesn't care about visibility. In fact, on regular operations, he does most of his work at night. Smoke's no problem.

She turns to Paul Tillotson, "Okay, We are all green. I'm starting the run. Battle computer goes live in ten seconds."

Yes, Cee Cee hates turning Spooky over to the computer. But there was no fixing that today.

The attack panel flashes "Auto On."

She lets go of the controls.

-------------------------------- // --------------------------------

Wild Girl Hunting has no idea that the recall order was sent to her GPS a half hour ago. And if she did, she wouldn't care. She had emptied Manny's M-4 and threw it away ten minutes ago. Hers had been gone awhile before that.

She's down to using her Glocks to kill Mist. With less firepower, she's taken to running from tree to tree in sudden sprints, dressed in a captured Mist camo jacket, hoping to catch Mist people by surprise. It's been working.

She has no idea of how many Mist shits she had killed or wounded.

A Mist shit runs towards her.

She drops the figure with two shots, waits for more movement, sees none, and then sprints ahead, crouched low.

-------------------------------- // --------------------------------

Whit Chalmers looks at his IMet who points to a weather printout, "Whit, the second low front has joined with the first one, just west of us. When they hooked up, the center of the low pressure shifted north. No way could we predict that before they joined. The high

176

pressure has this new, bigger low blocked on the east. Bottom line, the winds are due to start coming in from the northwest in the next hour and then blow strongly for the next twenty-four hours. Gusts up to gale force. Some light rain to begin with and then maybe a good bit more wet later. Nasty"

"Crap! We almost had Mist-Cutter trapped in the canyon on the north end."

"Yeah, but looks like the fire's gonna take a run southeast. And, although I'm not your fire ecologist, moisture or not, I think it's going to be moving fast, burning bright, and spotting a long ways ahead."

"Too true. Look, I have to get word out to the law enforcement people. They've got a big operation going and, with what you've told me, they need to know Mist-Cutter's coming their way soon. I'll get back to you later."

A moment later, Whit is on the radio to Sid Ballantine, "Sid, my weather people say the fire's about to make a run to the southeast. Shift in the wind. Maybe burn through Cutter's Park. Maybe not. But, if you can, you should pull your people out of there."

"Okay, we have everybody out now, except for some Guard units well to the north. An air op is going on. I'll send the choppers to pull the Guard out right away."

As he hangs up his phone, Sid smiles with smug satisfaction. Puff would hammer the Mist bastards down and then, good Lord willing, the fire would burn them the fuck up.

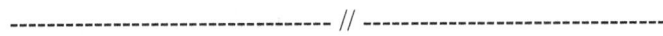

Spooky opens fire. The vibrating ship slews slightly as the Gatling guns swing back and forth firing fragmentation rounds into the forest. The hull thumps occasionally as the twin M102s fire at the hideouts.

Cee Cee calmly watches her threat screens for indications of ground fire. None.

She eyes the flight systems indicators for aircraft malfunctions. Nothing showing.

She checks the battle computer. She notes the steady reduction in ammo stores.

Her calm act is for Tillotson.

Inside, she's "as nervous as a long-tailed cat in a room full of rockers" as her mother used to say.

177

Her fingers twitch to take over the controls.
Two minutes pass.

-------------------------------- // --------------------------------

Wild Girl hears the sound of a multi-engine aircraft off in the distance. It seems to be flying well away from her, off to the east.

A sustained, stuttering scream drowns out the aircraft sound. The high-pitched noise is like nothing she has ever heard before. And then some faint thumping explosions, even a few vibrations in the ground.

Are the Apaches attacking some Mist position? If so, good for them.

In a few minutes, the noises stop.

"What the Hell was that," she wonders, "Seemed too quick for a chopper attack. Maybe some new Mist trick?"

-------------------------------- // --------------------------------

Spooky completes his first run and the guns cease firing.

The aircraft starts a wide, west turn to line up on the other edge of the target box.

Cee Cee wonders why something that involves her so little could make her so nervous.

She gently touches the controls but makes no attempt to interfere with the battle computer's careful handling of her Spooky.

Spooky lines up for his second run.

Cee Cee checks the flight path. Dead on.

She wonders briefly how long it will be before her Spooky will simply fly every mission as a drone, no on-board pilot needed.

"Certainly not before I retire," she thinks indignantly.

The guns spool up and begin to fire....

-------------------------------- // --------------------------------

Wild Girl sees three Mist figures running towards her. One in the lead and two flanking.

Some kind of commander? No way to tell.

She aims her Glock at the front figure. She can get all three of them if she stays calm and shoots quickly.

178

Wild Girl starts to squeeze the trigger.

She hears the sound of a multi-engine aircraft approaching. Same one?

Suddenly it's close…real close. And low…real low.

The three Mist shits stop and look up.

The one in the front points to a large downed log and yells, "Take cover, warriors!" then dives for the log.

Wild Girl fires at the diving figure.

Seconds later the ripping, stuttering, screaming noise engulfs them all.

The forest around Wild Girl comes apart.

Chapter 35 – Shattered Green

Mill shrugs herself awake.

Her body aches with bruises and a deep fatigue.

The killing rage is gone. Her mind is clear.

Where could she be?

Face down, half buried in dust, leaves, and needles, she tries to wiggle up and look around. Her legs won't move.

She feels around for her Glock. It's nowhere to be found.

She remembers the ripping noise…the explosions.

Must have been from heavy guns on some kind of aircraft. Had that been the "surprise for Mist" her squad leader had warned them to get clear of?

Well, it had certainly been a surprise for Mill.

She tries to move her legs again.

Numb…nothing. Is she shot…wounded?

She reaches down and feels a tree trunk lying across the backs of her thighs. Her probing fingers find that the trunk is pressing down heavily on her legs. But the cloth of her pants doesn't seem to be torn or, grisly thought, her bones bent in weird, wrong directions.

Maybe the log's weight has pinned her and caused her legs to fall asleep.

That would be the good news.

She slides her fingers up the splintered wood. She can't feel more than a few inches of it, but its curve suggests that the log is at least twenty inches around. No matter its real size, it's way too big for Mill to move by herself, particularly lying flat on her belly the way she is.

She will have to pry or wiggle herself out from under it and do it quickly. Any Mist operator coming by could kill her without resistance.

She starts pulling at the duff with her hands.

Nothing.

She "swims" her arms side to side, wiggling her torso.

Some movement but only a few inches. Hard to tell if it's real progress or not.

Mill remembers the knives. She reaches down and finds her Kabar. She digs it into the duff and jams it tight down into the harder mineral soil below.

She pulls on the handle. At first, nothing happens.

"Come on, Mill," she implores, "dig deep. Max effort or fuckin' Mist will be on you."

She grips the handle tightly and uses her whole upper body to pull--arms, stomach muscles, and back working together.

Movement! She slides forward a foot, then pulls the knife out and drives it in again. Another foot.

Finally, another max effort. Her boots pull free and sliding becomes easy.

She hurriedly frees the knife...her only defense now...rolls over and reaches down to touch her numb legs. Thank God, nothing seems broken.

In moments, the cold numbness starts to warm. Painful flashes radiate through her legs. She stifles her moans. Mist might be near...might hear.

-------------------------------- // --------------------------------

Badger can only move one arm. Her cool suit is shut down but she's not hot. No feeling at all in her lower body. Weakness settling into her. Breath shallow.

Above her is the big log she remembers diving under. She sees that it is rotten through...no decent barrier to the bullets that hammered around her. Fool for thinking that rotten wood could shield her.

She runs her good hand over her chest and feels a hole in the center...stickiness around it. Shot? She brushes away a little of the debris that had blasted out of the log onto her when she was hit.

She touches the hole again. No way to tell if what had hit her had been a bullet or shrapnel from the Puff's explosive rounds. But blood only oozes out.

Her thoughts wander dreamily. No matter anyway. She is clearly dying...paralyzed. No pain though. Perhaps the Mother will let her see Arrow soon....

She feels a touch on her face and opens her eyes.

Above her is a camouflaged face framed by the hood of a Mist forest jacket. She starts to speak to the warrior, and then realizes the person in the jacket is not wearing a cool suit.

And under the jacket, another kind of camo. Not Mist...a thug!

She sees the knife...dirty. Bloody sleeves.

Badger suddenly knows she's about to die...and waits.

But instead of cutting her throat, the thug pushes back the Mist jacket's hood and smiles at her grimly.

Badger doesn't understand. Why not death?

182

Then it hits her.

"Milly," she whispers.

-------------------------------- // --------------------------------

Green Hawk sees the big aircraft through the trees, gun smoke curling behind it, twisted into coils by the wash of the four huge fan jets. She checks her sling tension...100 percent.

She will have to time her shot exactly...count on Mother and luck for a hit.

She waits...waits...there!

Sky Strike away!

A Hellrain of bullets tears Green Hawk apart.

-------------------------------- // --------------------------------

Cee Cee looks at the battle-status indicators. Spooky has about fifteen seconds before the firing sequence runs out. The aircraft rises a hundred feet to clear a low ridge, then drops back down to five hundred feet and the optimum firing angle.

Suddenly the threat indicator lights up. Spooky rolls slightly and a horrifying vibration shakes the fuselage.

Cee Cee grabs the yoke and hits the "pilot" button, turning off the battle computer's feeds into Spooky's flight controls. She wrestles with the controls as zero-four starts to turn to the port side and the left wing starts to roll down.

She ignores the turn and fights the wing up. At this altitude, there's no space beneath them for even a shallow dive. But something is definitely pulling them down.

She glances out the left window.

Goddamn it! A solid-looking shaft is sticking through the wing just aft of engine two, the closest turboprop to where she sits. As she watches, a small fire shows around the base of the needle-like object. Whatever it was, it looks like it struck engine two's rear bearings and the damn thing is about to melt down. If it did, the whole fuckin' wing would explode.

Her Spooky would die along with its crew.

She yells, "Paul, take the controls!" His hands instantly grab the yoke.

Cee Cee's fingers dance over the throttles and emergency switches.

She shuts down engine two and hits the portside fire extinguishers.

The stricken engine rotates a time or two more and then stops.

She sees the wing behind engine two glowing through the white foam coursing over it.

My God, the fuel...the tanks are only feet away from that incredible heat!

She hits the fuel dump to empty the port wing's tanks.

She looks back behind the wing. No fire trails in the air. Looks like she got the fuel dumped in time.

Tillotson yells, "I'm losing her, Major. Airspeed's dropping. I'm barely keeping the nose up and I can't keep us out of a port turn."

Seconds after his comments, a loud alarm buzzes in their helmets and the yoke shakes. Stall alarm. They're about to stop flying and fall out of the sky. So close to the forest below, they could never recover enough airspeed before auguring in.

Cee Cee glances at the wing again...no visible cracks or metal loss.

Stop the stall!

Cee Cee has to balance the engines' output enough to keep Spooky zero-four airborne while keeping the damage caused by the missile and the drag from dead engine two from pulling the left wing apart.

She grabs the throttle for engine one and, watching the wing closely, increases it gradually to full power. No obvious cracking or tearing.

She pulls back one quarter on the throttles for starboard-side engines three and four. The left drift almost stops.

Most importantly, Spooky gains a little speed.

She adjusts the prop pitch on dead engine two to minimize drag. And then adjusts the pitch on the other three props ever so slightly to minimize vibration. No point shaking that punctured wing any more than absolutely necessary.

She watches the altimeter and adds a little power to three and four, then readjusts the prop pitch on the three working engines.

Wounded Spooky starts a slow but steady climb.

The stall alarm stops.

Cee Cee glances at the altimeter...holding the slight climb.

She looks out and down. She can see treetops maybe fifty feet below, like hungry fingers reaching up to grab her Spooky and pull it down. They must have been almost brushing Spooky's belly before they started to climb.

She keys her mike, "Mayday, Mayday, Mayday. This is Spooky zero-four. We have sustained portside missile impact. One engine out. No explosion. Firing mission complete. We are turning for Boise Guard Base, coming in skosh fuel. I will update status en route…."

186

Chapter 36 - Crucible One

Mill looks down at her mother's debris-smeared face. Her eyes avoid the woman's bloody chest...centerline hit...almost certainly a mortal wound.

Was it Wild Girl's last shot with the Glock that tore into Rebecca? Wild Girl had fired at a diving figure. Little chance that her shot at that angle would have hit Rebecca in the center chest and penetrated. But...but.

Mill put the gripping thought out of her mind. She would have to weigh the contradictory feelings of horror and triumph whirling in her mind later.

Mill looks for a more neutral thought and is struck by the coincidence of finding her mother in all this mess. But after thinking about it for a moment, she realizes that the event is not that improbable.

They were two women running around in the same, limited area, using the same paths, and travelling through restrictive terrain. So, the chances of running across her mother on a trail here were probably greater here than at your average shopping mall on a busy weekend. Well, no matter what, it had happened.

Mill stands up. She has to check for more Mist killers. She spots two dead Mist bodies a few feet away, one ripped almost completely apart by an exploding round.

She looks around the nearby forest. A few small fires burn where exploding rounds ignited the duff and tree litter. She could not be easily seen through the smoky air and shattered trees and branches. And, with all the debris and limbs down, anyone on foot would have a damned hard time getting around now at all, let alone sneaking up on her.

Mill might be relatively safe here but before her is a scene from some kind of environmental Hell.

A strong gust of wind suddenly swirls up and throws a smoky dust devil in her face.

"Damn," she says, rubbing her eyes, "Where did that come from?"

She looks into the wind for a moment, eyes slitted. More gusts slam her face.

Then she hears it...a deep moaning...snapping sounds.

She's heard this before as a kid. It's a forest fire crowning through the tops of hundreds of trees. But she can only hear it. Where...?

On the ridge above her, she sees a sullen glow, dark behind the smoke. Instants later, flame gouts up...up, up maybe a hundred feet. Then a bigger, broader, much brighter glow as the fire front crests the ridge and starts down.

The fire is moving express-freight fast. The flames will be on her soon...real soon.

She kneels down to her mother, "Rebecca, we have to move. A big fire is making a run towards us."

"Can't....Milly. Dying. Paralyzed. Good you leave."

Emotions war within Mill. If Rebecca Theophile Meacham lives, she might be able to provide valuable information about Mist. And Mill might get to know her, and her motives for leaving young Milly.

The hurt, seven-year-old girl within Mill speaks.

Young Milly says Rebecca had not wanted to be her mother, not really. Otherwise, she would never have left her.

She urges, "Leave Mom now. Let the flames eat her."

Rebecca had told her once that her father had forced Rebecca to leave. After Mill's recent revelations about her Dad, she is more accepting of her Mother's version of things...that she had been tortured and driven off. Still, the hurt of her departure and absence didn't go away.

Maybe little Milly is right.

Just do it. "Let the flames eat her."

Mill turns to go and then stops.

She can't let her mother burn up...die...without one last chance to hear the love in her voice...feel her caress.

Mill looks over her shoulder. The smoke is so thick, she can barely see. Even through that dense darkness, she sees the furnace glow rolling down the hill towards her. She has minutes at best before the fire engulfs them.

She spots a low area downslope from where the tree slammed across her legs, maybe fifty feet away. Exploding munitions must have set it alight earlier. The little spot fire had spread over a couple of hundred square feet, and then burned out. Good. Wildland firefighters know to go to the black...to the burned-over ground...to find refuge from the flames.

Mill turns to her mother hurriedly. She knows someone as badly wounded as Rebecca should not be moved. But the fire offers certain death for both of them if Mill can't get them into the black and under her shelter.

Mill stoops and gently runs her hands under her mother's shoulders, "Hold on, Rebecca, I'm going to move you."

"No, no…leave…. I won't make it. It's too much."

"Shut up, Mom."

"Okay, dear."

As Mill lifts, Rebecca's head lolls. She's unconscious.

Mill drags her carefully downhill. Thankfully, she can thread a wobbly path through downed logs and branches so she doesn't have to strain her mother's dead weight over barriers and possibly injure her more.

The intensely smoky air is now filled with small embers that burn Mill's skin and pock her clothes. The approaching fire radiates towards her, blast-furnace hot and bright.

When Mill reaches the middle of the blackened area, she's panting with exertion. Mill has seconds only. She hurriedly kicks any remaining organic soil away, creating a coffin shape of mineral soil.

Mill rips her fire shelter from her pack and, in one smooth movement, snaps it open.

She tosses away a few red signal smokes from a breast pocket. Didn't want them igniting inside the shelter in case it got too hot.

She steps into the silver bag, and, falling carefully over her mother's body, drops the shelter over them both.

The oncoming fire roars over them.

No reason to speak…no chance of being heard.

Mill lies parallel to her mother, clumsily stretching out her arms and legs to hold the shelter's edges down and keep the flames out.

A slamming, shaking wave of superheated air hits the fire shelter. One corner slips out from under Mill's right boot and lifts.

The blast furnace is just thirty feet away.

The heat inside the shelter rises fast.

--------------------------------------- // ------------------------------------

"What the fuck do you mean Mill Meacham's 'not accounted for'?" Frieda Tomlin roars at Sid Ballantine. "This is bullshit, Sid. I thought you confirmed she was out of the free-fire zone with everyone else."

"We did, Special Agent," Ballantine grits, "We had everyone accounted for based on their LifeChecs. We found hers on one of the causalities, ah, Manny Suemez. She stuck it in his pocket."

Frieda realizes her cheeks are running with tears and wipes at them angrily, "Damn you, Ballantine. I will fucking well have your badge for this. You know you were supposed to have all the squads account for their people when we got back to base…before your Goddamn gunship came in to plow those Mist fucks under."

Ballantine lowers his head to the furiously mourning little woman, "Frieda, look…I take full responsibility. Okay. But just know this. Mist tore our squads apart in field…hit and run…booby traps. And you know we had a lot of casualties…mostly wounds from those poisoned arrows…some deadfalls. So lots of people were doing SAR at the end. The squads got broken up. People in camp…people helping with Medivac…people helping the EMTs at the field clinic. We just couldn't use chain of command to find everyone. So we used the LifeChecs. Got everybody accounted for now except Meacham."

Frieda is now openly crying. She sits down, drops her head, and speaks harshly through her hands, "You find her, Sid. As soon as you can get your helicopters up to look around and your doggies on the ground, you find Mill Meacham. If it's rescue, I'm your best fucking frienemy forever. If it's a recovery, you may as well crawl in a cave somewhere and die. Because if you don't, I'm going to stick my foot so far up your ass you'll be able to tie my shoelaces with your tongue."

For all her fury, the angry woman's threat came out only halfheartedly. Frieda is that frustrated and stymied.

Suemez and four of her FBI agents dead. Meacham missing. "Goddamn locals…," she mutters.

Ballantine drops to one knee next to her. Hesitantly, he puts his arms around her and gently hugs her, "Frieda, I promise we'll find her."

Tomlin's arms slowly, reluctantly circle around the big man's shoulders. She puts her face in the crook of his neck. She cries hard for a few moments, and then mutters in his ear, "Then what the fuck are you waiting for, Ballantine? You figure this is some kinda chick movie we're in?"

Smiling so she can't see him, Sid starts to rise.

But Frieda holds on to him a little longer. She gives his neck a tight little squeeze and whispers, "Thanks."

---------------------------------- // ----------------------------------

190

Before she can jab the shelter's corner back down with her toe, a lick of superheated air catches Mill's ankle. "Ahnnn," she moans, unable to stifle the pain.

Rebecca's head turns slightly in response to her daughter's pain and she mutters something. But the fire thunders around them and Mill can't make out her mother's words.

Mill waits, draped clumsily across her mother's body.

For a time, she can monitor the intensity of the fire by the strength of the tiny beams of light that enter the shelter through pinpricks in its surface. These holes form where a shelter's outer creases rub and bounce against its carrying case. They don't present a danger unless something catches in them and causes a rip.

So, at first the pinpricks of light offer Mill a simple way to check on the fire. But after half an hour, the fire noise quiets and the incoming light wavers and then disappears, starting at ground level and moving up. Mill knows her shelter is probably getting covered by ash, a sign that the fire is burning out around them.

But she has no way to check if this is true without looking out. And there's no way she can do that safely.

The air inside the shelter is smoky and stuffy, the heat just barely tolerable.

Rebecca moans quietly.

"Theophile, what is it? How are you doing?"

"I was out of it…still can't see."

Rebecca moves her arm. Her hand touches the shelter's inner surface close over her face, "What's…what's this?"

"We're in my fire shelter. We got burned over. The worst is past, I think, but we can't leave. It's likely to still be super hot out there. Bad air. Maybe an hour or two more in here to be safe."

"I won't make it that long…I don't think. I can barely keep my eyes open….so tired."

"You've lost a lot of blood. Are you in pain?"

"No, just numb…above my breasts to down…nothing more."

Mill hugs her mother gently, "I'll be here." She laughs ironically, "Couldn't leave you if I wanted to go."

Mill hears a slight smile in her mother's tired voice, "So I have you…all to myself, huh? Guess I should give you some motherly advice…."

"Maybe not, Mom," Mill says with ironic severity, "I guess you could say I don't approve of your style of mothering."

As soon as the words tumble out of her mouth, Mill bites her tongue. Damn, why had she said that to a dying woman who could do her no harm now and nevermore?

"Oh, God, Milly," her mother answers, "In this moment, I would so like to…to relive my life, at least the part about leaving you. I should have figured out a way to get you…free when W.A. made me leave."

"Well, I'm not sure Dad…."

Her mother breaks in with a voice momentarily quick and firm, "He's not your Dad."

"What do you mean? He raised me after you…ah…ran."

Rebecca's voice catches, wavers, and fades, "Your father was cheating on me…women on the Forest Service compound. Stopped loving him…tried to hang in…but I had an affair in grad school. Guy was wonderful…Jacob Mountainspring, a native guy from Wyoming, the Wind River Reservation. He…he's your father…real father. You…you even look like him a bit. I met him at a lecture. That guy, Jack Ward Thomas. You know, he was…Forest Service Chief for a while. When this is over, go to see them…Jacob…Thomas…talk about it…all."

Rebecca's voice trembles and falls even lower, "W.A. saw Jacob and I…said he killed him…said it the night he drove me away from you. Broke my heart. You…Jacob. Always afraid to know if he really did it. You…you could find out. Cop. Do please."

There's silence as Mill tries to take all this in. W.A. Meacham not her father. Rapist instead.

A couple of missing shapes slip into place and fit firmly in her life's million-piece puzzle.

Time to offer some insight of her own.

Mill says flatly, "Mom, W.A. Meacham raped me. When I was fourteen. In Idaho…near Driggs."

Her voices breaks and she starts to cry quietly into her mother's shoulder, "I just found out he did it. Sent me over the edge."

Mill feels her mother's hand in her hair, touching her, patting her gently. Caring for her.

Rebecca cries, too, the sound so low as to be almost unheard, "Then he ruined us both…our lives. He must have figured out that…you weren't…his. Made us both…pay. Glad…dead. So…so…sorry."

Mill touches her Mother's face gently.

Words hard to say come out, "I forgive you, Mom. I always loved you. That's why…why…your leaving me was so hard. I just didn't know where you'd gone. I lost you and…then I got lost…lost myself, too."

Rebecca's hand weakly hugs Mill's head.

After a time she says, "Milly, when I go, bury me with the soil against my skin…I want the Earth Mother to touch me…please. Nothing else."

"Of course, but…."

Mill almost tells her mother that she won't die, to hold on, but it's clear she will die…and soon.

Warmth spreads between them. The two women's souls intertwine, as they had done so often when Mill was young. Both feel it, cling to it.

Then Rebecca's soul reluctantly departs, trailing off to find Arrow.

Milly hears her mother's last breath slip sighing from her body.

After that, there is only the dying crackle/moan of the fire outside the shelter and of Milly's baby-quiet sobs within.

-------------------------------- // --------------------------------

Two hours later, Mill pushes back the fire shelter nearest her head. She pushes the corner up and lifts about a foot of ash and unburned debris up with it. Daylight filters in.

She tests a breath of air. The air is still hot-smoky but definitely breathable.

Shoving the shelter aside, she stands stiffly and looks around.

Of the forest that stood when she entered the shelter, little is left. The jumble of branches and small trees that the sky cannons had cut down is gone, totally consumed by the fire. Close by, the blackened trunks of what must have been the largest, oldest trees poke up through deep ash towards the sky.

Mill is struck by their gaunt, sterile shapes.

A chill runs up her spine.

Fingers…the black-brown trunks look like accusing fingers…fingers pointing damnation to the sky.

Weirdly, Mill hears wind hum through the trees, hears words…questions, "Why? Why did this happen? Was our death…all this death…worth it?"

A moment later, she hears other trees answer, "No, nothing's worth *this*."

That she hears actual words scares her. Her heart races.

What would Dr. Canot say?

Was this some crazy quirk of her exhausted mind?

Her grief talking?

She raises her eyes. Across the landscape of Cutter's Park, the scene is the same--brown-grey smoking ash and soil.

There, too, black fingers point a warning to the sky, and speak words to her, "This must not happen again."

Mill shudders and turns away from the sights and sounds.

Mill uses her knife and her hands to scratch a shallow grave for her mother. She scrapes slowly through the burned, ashy layer into the sandy soil.

Once Mill has the ground open, she undresses Rebecca's slender body. She keeps her eyes away from her mother's grievous wound, and carefully tucks her into the soil, legs straight, and hands at her sides.

"As you wanted, Mom, safe in your Mother."

She covers Rebecca and inspects the results. She can sense her mother's body only a foot or so below the soil surface.

Not good enough. Too shallow.

Mill locates a nearby rock pile.

For an hour, she carries stones to stack over Rebecca, to protect her from animals until her remains can be reabsorbed into the earth.

She looks at the now rock-piled grave again.

Good enough.

She remembers the old words from the Bible, "dust to dust, ashes to ashes," and repeats them quietly, the words so especially true here and now.

Philip! Mill suddenly realizes how much she misses him. How she would have liked having him here. He would have been such a help with her mother's departure and with Mill's recognition of this newly sacred ground.

Philip. Time to go home to him.

Passion flashes in her tired body. She is alive. She wants Philip, now. She wants him next to her, on her, in her.

She turns on her GPS, checks the direction to base camp, and starts out.

Frieda and the LEOs will be pissed, thoroughly pissed.

Time to face some loud and discordant music. And then go home.

As she walks, rain starts to fall.

The first large drops pock the surface of the ash piles. Then more come down, raising little ash puffs before running together to pool in low spots on the dry surface. As Mill watches, the pooled drops grow bigger and bigger, sparkling like dark tears, before running down to disappear into the blackened soil.

Chapter 37 - Styx and Stoner

Philip has been ignoring Milly's calls for the last two days, letting them go to voice mail.

Now, sitting on his bed in a Portland college-district motel, he listens, starting with the oldest.

His mildly stoned mind takes in more tone than words. His brain hums along pleasantly as her voice goes from loving, to angry, to despondent. Then her messages end.

He replays the last message and actually listens to her anxious words, "Philip, I spoke to your church. They were very guarded, but said that you'd been sick...hit your head. And that you were on leave for ninety days. And then I called Tom Purlee, one of your...what do you call 'em...eldest's? No, that's not right...ah, one of your elders. I remembered him from my visits. He wouldn't tell me anything more at first. But then he broke down and told me that the elders had found drugs and paraphernalia in your office. Marijuana, Ecstasy, and speed...maybe other stuff. That you had been stoned or something when you hit your head."

Her voice gets very angry, "For God's sake, Philip...speed...dope? Philip, what's going on? What the fuck are you doing to yourself?"

Milly's voice turns desperate, pleading, "Philip I want to help you. But I can't do that if I can't talk to you, or find you. So, please, please call me. I'm stuck here for a few more days while investigators sort through what happened on this mission. But then I'll be headed home. So, please call and let me know where to find you. I'll come to you; help you, dearest, like you've always helped me. I love you, Philip. I'm scared about what you might be doing to yourself. So please call, just leave me a message if you don't want to talk."

Milly's message ends.

Philip looks at the phone, tempted to call.

No, not yet.

May not ever.

He turns the phone off and puts it in the drawer of his night table next to the Gideon's Bible.

He ignores the book.

He has a session in twenty minutes. He gets his coat.

Chapter 38 - Questions

The fire camp runs full bore. The light but steady rains and more stable air of the past several days have been their greatest allies in knocking the fire down and penning it up. The Incident Command Team has Mist-Cutter eighty-five percent fire-lined and predicts full containment in forty-eight hours.

Whit Chalmers and his staff expect to hand the fire off to one of Avery Scarrs' Type Three teams in a couple of days. The Boise National Forest's home team will babysit the last smokes and do some hot-spot mop-up until heavier fall rains or winter snows smother everything out.

The LEOs are packing up to head home. Most of the task force has already left, including Billy Branson who limped onto his shuttle helicopter with a sprained ankle and a tired smile.

Sid Ballantine and Frieda Tomlin are still on site, working with an inter-agency after-action investigations team.

Because the conflict with Mist was so violent, with severe loses on both sides, and the military was involved, the team is being assisted by experts from the Army. Mortuary teams are also on site working with cadaver dogs to locate the scores of Mist dead, their bodies killed by gunfire and burned over by Mist-Cutter.

Mill has been interviewed a half dozen times. She has stuck to a simple story.

She repeats it again now to the latest investigator handling her statement, "I went a little crazy after Manny's death. I did something stupid by removing my LifeChec. I got separated from my squad, ran ahead of them, and got into several firefights with Mist operators. I hid in my shelter after being shot at by the Spooky and overrun by Mist-Cutter. No, I can't really provide an accurate body count because things were moving so fast. Besides, I often shot at shadows. How could I tell if I hit anything? Yes, all I had left at the end was my knife. No, I didn't pick up or return with any evidence or Mist equipment."

"I feel real sorry for causing so much consternation by remaining in the free-fire zone after the recall. But how was I to know that the commanders had called in a Puff?"

Through it all, she has felt there was no reason to mention her mother, now a part of the past, dead and buried.

Besides, those final moments with her Mom were too precious to share with others, except maybe Philip, if she could ever locate her wandering husband.

The investigator taps his pencil on his pad, "Okay, Special Agent Meacham, I feel like there's more to the story. But you're free to leave camp when Ballantine and Tomlin sign off. If you remember anything more, you know how to get in touch."

She nods, "Sure, if anything comes to mind, I'll call...."

-------------------------------- // --------------------------------

Mill and Frieda sit by a small campfire in the evening light. The rains had made conditions safe for open fires. So, every evening, the steadily shrinking LEO ranks meet around small campfires to end their day and talk through their experiences of what they are beginning to call the Mist War.

"Goddamn it, Meacham," Frieda growls, "I know you're holding out on me. You *must* have an idea of how many kills you made. Every cop I ever knew can't forget his kills, let alone not know how many."

"Really, Frieda, how would I know? I was shooting at shadows most of the time...probably killed more tree trunks and squirrels than anything."

"Okay, so don't count shadows. Tell me how many you saw go down. I mean really saw hit the ground. No guesses."

Tomlin waits through a long pause, keeping her eyes fixed on Mill's.

Finally Mill drops her gaze. Truth time. "Eleven for sure. Maybe seven-eight more hits. And then, I remember Manny lying there...dying."

"I don't know," she ends miserably, "I just want to forget...."

"Mill, my friend, I will miss Suemez myself. Damn good cop. But, about Mist...it looks like you may have wiped out almost one fifth of those fucks all by yourself. Damn nice work."

"Thanks...I think."

"Yeah, don't mention it. And forget? Well, your candy-ass never will. Those Mist bastards are a part of you now...their deaths at least...and you'll remember each one...the scene, the sight picture, how they fell when the bullet hit 'em...for the rest of your life. Over the years, some will rent space in your head more than others, but they'll all be there."

"Damn," Mill says softly.

"'Damn' is right. It's the price cops pay for wanting to protect and serve but winding up killing instead. It's like you buy a beautiful

200

photograph and have it sent to your house. But when it gets there and you open the package, what's in your hand is the ugly reverse of beautiful...a negative...and the envelope has no return address. You paid so much for it, you can't throw it away. So, there you sit...the ugly fucking mess is yours. No way to give it back."

"Shit, Frieda, how do *you* handle this stuff?"

"Well, an FBI shrink told me to decide to stop remembering the negative...you know, don't daydream those memories or roll them around in my head. Sounded pretty fuckin' stupid when he said it. And it took me a long while to get the trick of it, but when I did, it helped. Still, anytime I want to conjure those dead people back to life, they're still waiting to join the ghost party upstairs."

Mill shudders, "I guess I've got more work with my counselor."

"Christ, Meacham, as fucked up as you cow cops are, you should have the same number of counselors as you do panties, one for each day of the week. Otherwise, you'll just be wearing the poor pencil-necked bastards out before they can help you. Besides, for now, you just need something to keep your mind off the Mist War...something to keep your hands busy before you get to messing in something nasty again."

-------------------------------- // --------------------------------

The next morning Mill is in the chow tent scarfing down scrambled eggs and thick, sugary pastries with coffee.

A man walks in the tent and spots her. He's no one she knows, but he walks over quickly, and sits down next to her. He leans close for privacy.

"Agent Meacham? I'm Fred Pomolo. Frieda Tomlin from the FBI told me to come look you up. She said you were Forest Service out of Missoula and ranking agent on site. She also said you had nothing to do until she cut you loose. Said you were therefore a perfect hemorrhoid up her ass, or words to that effect. She seems to like you."

Mouth full of strawberry Danish, Mill waves her hand and makes the "okay" sign.

Pomolo grins and says, "Maybe I should give you a moment."

Mill swallows some of it and mumbles through the Danish, "No, go ahead and talk. I listen better with my mouth full anyway. Just ask anybody. No interruptions that way."

"Okay. Look, I work for Avery Scarrs, the Boise Forest Supervisor. I'm his admin staff, special assistant, LEO liaison…all that kind of stuff."

Mill nods and takes a slurp of coffee to wash down the Danish.

"Well, Avery asked me to keep an eye on things around the camp. He's got a bug up his ass about cost control on fires…hates waste and all that. So, I've been looking around and I've found some problems. Nothing major, but the numbers are significant if you add everything up."

Mill's mouth is clear for a moment although it lusts for the fat, cream-filled donut on her plate, "So, if I get you right, you have evidence of theft or at least pilferage. Is it anything criminal enough to warrant investigation or do you just want me to get some statements so you can ding somebody administratively?"

"Ah, good question, Agent Meacham…"

"Call me Mill, okay?"

"Sure, sure. Well, Mill, I don't think it's significant enough on this incident. But Avery's been checking around with his Journey…you know, those roaming packs of Forest Supes that terrorize motels, spas, and restaurants from coast to coast. Anyway, his Journey has good evidence of this happening in lots of places. Small purchases that seem to disappear after delivery or are never delivered. What the Journey guys could count or guess at adds up to a bunch of money…hundreds of thousands…maybe lots more."

Mill gives a low whistle.

"That's what Avery and I think, too."

-------------------------------- // ------------------------------

Three hours later, Mill and Pomolo stand by a long table, looking at stacks of paper, some of them three feet high and tilting dangerously.

Each stack represents a different fire. Purchase orders, invoices, receipt slips, and scribbled notes from frustrated logistics officers and admin people referencing goods supposedly received but never found, are all there.

Pomolo says, "Looks like a crap detail doesn't it? You're wonderin' how're we gonna sift the pepper from the fly shit in all this mess, right? And you don't know this, but some of the paper trail is still comin' in…fax mostly. So, a lot to wade through."

202

"You must be psychic. You read my innermost thoughts, Fred."

"Yeah, well, at least everything's arranged by specific fires, one pile or group 'a piles to a fire, so we have some of the sorting already done."

"That's okay. But if I'm not mistaken, the by-the-fire significance isn't what's really important. What's important is what people or businesses got the money or who otherwise benefitted from the thefts. You know what I mean?"

"Un-huh. I always say, 'if you wanna find the bucks, you gotta follow the doe.' Pretty awful, right?"

"Yup, you read my mind again…awful."

Mill muses for a moment, "Fred, could we get a laptop in here? I think what we should do is build a database that shows the fire, the purchases, the company doing the billing, the team, the people in the buying unit, who signed off…all the pertinent stuff. And for the older fires where we have it, let's throw in who did the audit, too. Then we'll run some basic sorts and see if a pattern jumps out at us. Otherwise, I can't imagine us ever making sense of all this, at least not before any perps die of old age."

"You got it, Special Agent…oh, ah…Mill. One laptop. Want a clerk, too? You know to punch in the data?"

"No, let's keep this tight until we know what's going on. We don't know who might be in cahoots with whom."

"Sure, on my way…" Pomolo leaves the tent.

Mill sees that the big, round man moves fast but looks entirely casual. She shakes her head. She would have to study that technique. Something in the arms and shoulders maybe.

While Fred is gone, she calls Philip's phone again.

Her call goes to voice mail.

Again.

Fuck!

--------------------------------- // ---------------------------------

Mill and Pomolo knock off at eleven and then charge back into the pile of paper at six in the next morning. At seven, Avery Scarrs arrives, looking eager.

He shakes Mill's hand, "Nice to have you helping us on this investigation, Agent Meacham. Sorry to hear about your Dad. Shook up the whole Boise staff to find out he'd been killed and, you know, that way."

"Avery, just call me 'Mill', please. And thanks for your condolences."

Scarrs has such an approachable, nurturing presence; Mill has to suppress an urge to tell him her life's story, complete with updates about her mom and her real dad.

Keeping her mouth shut, she manages to sadly smile more of her thanks.

Scarrs asks, "What can I do?"

Pomolo waves at the remaining stacks of paper, "Just help us organize, Avery. I'll show you our routine. Then you bring the stack to Mill or me, whoever's on the computer. We'll do the input because we've been doin' it so far and we're pretty close to being done.

"Okay, no problem. Just call me 'Mr. Organized', but don't tell my wife or my secretary. They'll both choke at the thought."

The group digs in.

Just before lunch, Pomolo looks up from the laptop and says to Mill, "Got anymore?"

"Nope, everything's checked off my sheet. How about you, Avery?

"Done."

Pomolo leans back and says, "Ahhh, the moment of truth."

He pops his knuckles and waves his fingers in the air like a magician," Okay, let's run a few sorts and see if we strike gold. Let's try businesses first."

He presses a few keys, "Well, some multiple hits on businesses, but not many. And you'd figure there'd be some multiples because there's only so many outfits doin' fire business. So, maybe we don't have just a few, specific businesses doin' the rip-offs."

Scarrs answers, "Might be, but let's run a sort by location. You know, check for a cluster of losses on one fire or in one part of the country."

Pomolo types in a few more commands, "Okay, we do have clusters. But overall, even lumped together, the losses are fairly small…all under fifty thousand. The difference that we might care about is that the accumulated losses by fire break out into two groups. A whole buncha small losses on lots of fires, averaging less than ten thousand per fire. And then twenty or so fires where the losses jump up way up. If I was to guess, I'd say an average of twenty-thirty thousand dollars per fire, highest was that fifty thousand one…long fire, just under a hundred days of active firefighting, then a lot more in mop-up."

Scarrs says thoughtfully, "I wonder if there's a certain incident team that doing this. Could you check that higher-dollar group against which teams managed the fire, Fred?"

"Sure, hold on." Pomolo resorts the data. "Nope, lots 'a teams. Some repeats but you'd expect that with the teams rotating in and out every fourteen days. Wanna see 'em?"

"Yeah, can you do a print-out? Hard for my old eyes to track anything on a screen."

In a moment, the printer Pomolo provided with the laptop spits out a couple of pages. Avery picks them up and studies them with Mill looking over his shoulder.

After a minute or so, the Forest Supervisor says, "This is a list of at least half the Type Two teams in the U.S., mostly Forest Service but also some state, BLM, and Park Service teams."

Mill thinks and then comments, "So the only significance here is that they're Type Twos. What could that mean?"

"Well, smaller, easier fires, smaller organizations. But not much else. They get the same financial audits as the big Type One teams."

Pomolo chimes in, "But anymore they don't have the on-site admin scrutiny the big fires get. We've told the teams to cut costs, so most of them don't order Incident Business Advisors or on-sight payment teams. On most small fires, the buying unit polices itself and a clerk authorizes payment, unless the local forest sends someone in like me to help."

Scarrs nods, "Yup, that's pretty much true."

Mill smiles, "Okay, so we have some evidence that someone *may* be taking advantage of this gap in oversight. But we've got nothin' the U.S. Attorney would be interested in, at least not yet."

Scarrs offers, "I wonder what we'd get if we sorted by the names of the people in the buying unit."

Fred types furiously for a moment, "Okay, you two, look at this. When I cross-reference the fires with the bigger losses, I get a list of ten names. And one of those gals is here, Thyra Dexter. From this data, looks as though there's almost a quarter of a million dollars of losses attached to her name."

Mill asks tersely, "Is she still on site?"

Scarrs says to Mill, "Probably. We haven't released the buying unit yet. Do you want her? Fred can go get her and bring her here."

"Nope, we really have only probable cause to investigate at this point, not arrest. But, Fred, could you go and make sure she's still on site? If she's due to de-mob today, get that cancelled until we can get enough information to question her."

Pomolo leaves the tent at full speed.

"Avery, we have ten procurement-clerk names. I could be wrong but that hints that we might have some kind of network or conspiracy operating here."

Mill raises a hand for emphasis, "So, here's a head's up. It's really hard to put together a case when there's lots of people involved and lots of moving parts and pieces. You have to develop so much credible, connected evidence that sometimes the case just breaks down under its own weight. And when the dollar amounts are small, as they are here, the U.S. Attorney gets really uncomfortable about taking on such a case. Figure it could cost millions to prosecute when chances of convictions are relatively low. They usually have bigger fish to fry."

"I can imagine."

"So, the best thing we can do is get Dexter to confess. Build enough evidence from what we have here to scare the shit out of her, and hope for the best. If that fails, then we'll have to get several Special Agents pulled in to develop the evidence and put the wazoo to others on the list. Push 'em until someone pops an artery."

Scarrs smiles at Mill, admiring her tough talk as much as her trim, curvy figure. He doesn't know Mill has had motivational speech lessons from Frieda Tomlin.

"Sounds like a plan to me, Special Agent Meacham."

Chapter 39 - Caught

Thyra looks up from her desk.

Mill Meacham smiles down at her, "Are you Thyra Dexter?"

The woman examines the pretty, slender woman and smiles in return.

Then she notices Mill's hand resting on the holstered Glock at her side and the embroidered badge on her Forest Service LEO uniform shirt.

This could be that nightmare she had told Clipper Jones about, "Ah...how can I help you, officer?"

Mill leans down and speaks quietly, "I think you know, Thyra, so just listen. I want to make sure you aren't embarrassed in front of your colleagues. I'm asking you to stand and walk out of here with me, very friendly and nice. I have someone with questions for you. I'll take you to a place where no one will know what you're talking about, very quiet and private."

"Well, I...I don't know what you want, ah Officer, ah, what did you say your name was?"

"Here're my credentials. I'm Forest Service Special Agent Mill Meacham, from Missoula, assigned here with the Mist Task Force."

"And what was this about again?"

"We just have a few questions for you and, as I said, I'm pretty sure you know what it's about."

Thyra puffs up with mock indignation, "Well, I don't...and I'm not going anywhere with you."

Mill leans across the desk, smiling kindly but holding Dexter's eyes. She pretends to point at some papers on the desk in front of Dexter, and speaks in a low voice, "Listen, you insufferable lying bitch, in the past two days my best Forest Service friend was killed within five miles of here and, earlier this year, my father was blown up by ecoterrorists. I'm beyond putting up with anyone's bullshit, especially yours. This is your last chance to get up from your desk and walk out of here, being treated respectfully. I *know* you're involved in theft. I also know that *you aren't* the one responsible. Other people pushed you into it."

Mill shifts where her hand rests on Dexter's desk, and speaks a little louder than before, "If you don't leave with me now, I'm going to take you down by force, as if you are resisting arrest. I'll see that you're carried out of here in wrist and leg restraints in front of all these nice people, face down and ass in the air."

Thyra glares at Mill for a moment, and then as her bravado collapses, drops her eyes, "Okay...okay. I'll just get my purse."

Mill shakes her head, "No, no purse. Just stand up and we'll go. Your purse will be here when you get back...maybe twenty minutes. Coffee'll be on me."

"So, I'm not under arrest or anything?"

"No, not if you come quietly now. I told you, just a few questions. If you answer them to my friend's satisfaction, you'll be back at work so quickly no one will wonder where you've gone."

Thyra shakes her head and stands, "Okay, let's go."

"Just walk and talk like we're old friends, Thyra."

Dexter immediately begins to smile and talk animatedly in a raised voice, "Yes, yes, Mill, like I told you, she was way too ready to give him her number. Made me wonder how many guys she'd given that number to before. Maybe she's a little too desperate for male company, if you know what I mean...."

The two walk beyond the tent.

"Okay, Thyra. Nice job sharing gossip."

Mill points, "We're going over to the LEO camp. You'll be meeting a friend of mine in that big tent off to the side there."

"Who, ah, who would that be?"

"A really nice woman, very professional....first name's Frieda. She likes hard-working folks like you. She has the scoop, knows that you were put up to the thefts. Be straight with her, and you'll come out fine."

"I wasn't a part of any thefts...."

"No point telling me, Thyra. Just listen to Frieda and answer her questions. You'll be fine."

An hour later, Dexter walks out of Blue Team's command tent. Her back is stiff and her eyes are puffy.

Mill gets up from where she's been resting with her butt on a pallet and her back against a pile of rolled-up fire hose. She had been listening to Dexter's interrogation through an encrypted radio channel, occasionally offering tips to Frieda, "Doin' okay, Thyra?"

The woman flinches and blinks back tears, "Y-yes. You say that *person* is your friend?"

"She's one of my best friends, Thyra."

Dexter sniffs, "You need better friends, Special Agent."

208

Mill laughs. She wouldn't want Tomlin on her ass either, "Thyra, don't leave camp without checking in with me. And understand that we will be monitoring all of your e-mails and phone calls...taps are already set up. You'll be under full-time surveillance until we know we can trust you. So if you contact anyone on anything other than normal business, we'll know it. If I find out you've messed up, you'll be headed off to jail a few minutes later."

"I know, I know," the miserable woman tells her, "Special Agent Tomlin went over that *very forcefully*. I *told* her. I *want* to cooperate. I *will* cooperate. *As long as it takes* to get those fucking Green Rivers."

Mill plays along as if she had not heard Dexter's first halting, then fast, vehement confession, "Did you give Special Agent Tomlin the full list? We had most of them but we weren't sure we had them all."

"Yes, I gave *that woman* all the names I knew. She didn't show me any list you had. Just put a piece of paper in front of me and told me to write the names down. Then she made me write out a full statement and sign it. Told me to get down every detail. Said that if I didn't, she'd drive me to a supermax prison for lesbians and tell the inmates that I was in there for gutting a dyke because she had bad hair. Said I'd taste every snatch in the place, maybe more than once, before they dropped my dead body down the sewer. She actually described it."

Dexter shudders.

Pleased to keep the pressure on, Mill chuckles grimly, "Just for the record, Thyra, she meant it."

The woman's face gets a little whiter, "I *told* you, Special Agent, ah, Meacham, I'm *cooperating*."

Tomlin had volunteered to bring the heat after Mill softened Thyra up. Mill's job had been to plant the idea that the investigators considered Dexter an innocent caught up in a conspiracy led by evil-minded, uncaring people. Then Frieda would break her. The plan had clearly worked.

Mill shakes her head. She almost tells the woman to get a lawyer right away...but holds back.

Thyra had received her Miranda rights and waived them. So, what was going to happen to Thyra was now a matter for the courts.

Early in the interrogation, during its softer build-up phase, Tomlin had hinted at immunity, but had not promised it. Dexter had bought the idea that immunity would be offered to her once she confessed and cooperated.

But Dexter hadn't got an agreement in writing.

Mill figured the FBI would just play her until they had all the conspirators fully documented. Then they'd throw Dexter in with the rest to be prosecuted.

Thyra might well wind up some prison dyke's "sally" in the near future.

Mill walks Thyra back to her work tent, "Remember to act normally, Thyra. It's just another day at work. Nothing wrong. Come and find me as soon as you're off shift."

Frieda and Mill will sit down with Dexter after work and require her to read and sign her now typed-up confession. They will also give her a first set of orders and equipment for recording and documenting the other Green Rivers.

Thyra doesn't know it but she's burned…a walking crispy-critter.

Mill decides she would rather face another forest fire than Frieda Tomlin's purifying heat.

Chapter 40 – Crucible 2

Two days after Thyra Dexter's confession, Mill leaves the LEO base camp for Missoula. She will continue to work the Green Rivers' case with Frieda Tomlin, serving as the Forest Service liaison.

But she has to check in at the Regional Office with her boss, Harry Bitters, complete her after-action reports, and get personal leave approved so she can go find Philip.

During the six-hour drive to Missoula, Mill calls Philip's number five times. She leaves voice mail each time, ending with "Please call me dearest. I love you." Those words come harder and harder each time she says them.

She alternates between being utterly furious at him for deserting her and being utterly despondent that he's not with her, supporting her.

She also calls Philip's church elders, Chehalis-area hospitals, and the human resources staff at her Regional Office home base.

No more news than before.

Hurrying up Highway 97 about a hundred miles from Missoula, she gets another thought.

What she has to do would be hard, but she is almost to the panic point.

She calls Frieda Tomlin, "Frieda? Yeah, me, Mill. True confession time. My Philip's gone missing. A couple 'a days ago. Problems at church, wound up drunk or something. The church elders put him on leave. And now I can't get in touch with him. I've called him over and over for the last few days, but he doesn't pick up…doesn't call back. I could use your help."

Tomlin almost makes a crack about "no one flies off the wagon farther than a preacher" but stifles the impulse. Mill has been through too much lately for that kind of cynicism, however accurate.

Instead, the tough little woman's voice comes through Mill's iComm as crisply professional, "Okay, Mill, any chance he's been kidnapped, say by Mist operators, or come to any harm…same folks?"

"No, there's no sign of abduction or violence. I haven't been on site or had law enforcement involved, but the elders at his church have keys to his house…they provide it for the pastor…and everything's in order there. I told them what to look for. No sign of someone breaking in and tossing his stuff. Most of his stuff is in there. A few empty hangers and open spots in drawers, so some clothes and personal items are gone. Based on what he told one of them…uh, Elder Purlee…they think he might be in rehab or something."

"Is that a possibility? You know, that he's in rehab?"

"I can't see how he could do that without working through me. He's under my federal health insurance. To get into rehab, he'd have to apply through employee assistance and get a sign-off. Regional Office checked and said that didn't happen. He has no reason to spend money out of pocket when he has the insurance to cover it. I checked on his credit card and bank accounts…no recent charges or significant withdrawals."

"What if he's ashamed of what's happened and he's hiding his rehab from you?"

"Not the Philip I know. The guy would never check out that way."

"Well, Mill, not to state the fuckin' obvious, but he has checked out…for whatever reason…and won't return your calls. You don't even know that he's listening to them. Could have lost the phone or had it stolen…sold it maybe if he's hard up enough. I don't want to be too hard on you here, but if he's off on a bender, you might not hear from him for weeks."

Mill flinches and replies in a low tone, "Frieda, the guy barely drinks a glass of wine with dinner. I never saw any signs of a problem. And…you don't know this…but I had that problem once. I think I'd see the signs."

"Love is blind, Meacham, particularly yours."

Tomlin instantly regrets the harshness of her comment, but Mill can't deny its accuracy. Mill feels a rising lump in her throat and cloudiness sliding in at the edges of her vision. Panic starts to make it hard for her to speak, "Ah, Frieda, what am I going to do? I've got to get a lock on where he is at least. Find him if possible."

"Okay, he's an adult. No sign of foul play or any laws broken. Adults can do what they want. They don't have to check in. Legally, the most you can do is file a missing person's with his local police department. But don't expect that to be acted on, other than maybe a patrol spots him around some dive and gives you a courtesy call. After all, this *is* the land of the free and the home of the runaway."

"Sounds pretty hopeless."

"Yup, but there's another choice. If you were to tell me there *might* be some chance *Mist* grabbed him, I could at least get the Bureau to run a check on the location of his cell phone and ask the locals to

212

contact him. If you just happened to be in the neighborhood when the locals roll, why you might get invited to ride along. You know professional courtesy and all that."

"I see, Frieda. That way the federal government could make sure that one of its special agents wouldn't be targeted for coercion or extortion in her line of duty."

"Ah, you catch my drift."

Mill's mood lightens quickly, "Why, yes, I do. I'm a slow starter, but I finish well, if you know what I mean."

"I sure do. Possibly the slowest starter I've ever worked with," Frieda replies tartly.

"So, Special Agent in Charge Tomlin, I'm officially notifying you that I suspect my husband, Philip, may have been the victim of foul play at the hands of Mist, the eco-terrorist organization. This is based on our recent action against them and their past involvement with my family..."

"Okay, okay, Meacham," Frieda growls, "I can fill in all the bullshit. I don't need your help with that."

Mill's voice is full of dimples, "No, Special Agent, I would never question your expertise at filling in bullshit..."

"Oh," Tomlin groans, "I knew the instant I said it, you were going to move on me. Okay, Special Agent Grass-Fed Cow Pie, I officially recognize your concern. Get your ass back to Moo-zoola, or whatever barbarian crossroads you live in. And once you're clear of the bureaucrats, give me a call. I'll be able to tell you what a real professional law enforcement organization has done for you. And you may be appropriately grateful when that happens. Some gratuitous kissing of my ass will be just the ticket to ensure future cooperation."

"Bye, Frieda, and thanks. You're a great friend."

"Bye, Mill. Stop fretting. We'll find your wandering Elmer Gantry."

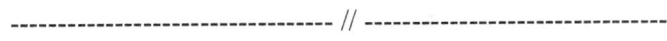

Four days later, Mill stands by a Portland uniformed officer as he knocks on the door to a low-rent motel. "This is the Portland City police, Philip, please open up. I've been asked to make sure you're okay."

No answer. He knocks again. Nothing.

Mill holds up the room key she obtained by showing the motel clerk that she and Philip were married.

The tall, black officer nods, "Okay, Special Agent, you can go in. Do you want me to wait?

Mill's throat gets tight. What if Philip had hurt himself? Worse, what if he's in the room dead?

"If you wouldn't mind, Officer Cook, could you clear the place?"

Cook looks at her appraisingly. She had been the calm professional up until now, but he sees her deep frown and anxious eyes.

"Sure, Special Agent, let me go in and look around. Then you can go in."

Mill smiles gratefully, "I would appreciate that, Officer Cook, very much. You know, it's just...."

"Yeah, I know. I'd want the same thing."

The patrolman takes the key from her hand and opens the door.

Mill peers around the jamb while he looks around the neat room, checks under the bed, and turns on the light in the bathroom. He walks back to her and hands her the key, "All clear, Special Agent."

"Thanks. I'll mention all you've done to your Sergeant."

"No need. Just glad I could help."

He touches the brim of his hat and leaves.

After the door closes, Mill looks around. She tells herself to be detached; to work the room just like a sneak and peek...see everything and disturb nothing.

She starts with the bathroom....

About ten that night, Philip opens the door, comes in, and tosses his key on the bureau. He weaves towards the bathroom.

Mill sits quietly in the room's only chair, a broke-backed wing chair in a dark corner by the head of the bed. Mill hears Philip vomit...and then again. Sounds of running water in the sink and then in the shower.

Mill waits.

After fifteen minutes, Philip comes out and, without turning on a light, throws his nude body on the bed.

He doesn't notice Mill in her dark corner. He moans and rests limply.

She leans forward a little and says distinctly, "Philip, the FDA says motel bedspreads are filled with disgusting germs and bedbugs...."

His body tenses at her words.

He turns bleary eyes to hers, and says, "Milly. I...I...."

214

She puts a hand over his mouth, "No words now. In the morning, when you're clear, we'll talk. Right now, you're just going to touch me...nothing else."

He tries to talk again, but she presses her fingers more tightly against his mouth, "Shhhhh. Sleep...and then we'll talk."

She helps him up from the bed and pulls back the covers. She slips off her shoes and climbs onto the bed, fully clothed. She pulls him down next to her and makes spoons with him, her face against his back.

She's too tired for analysis and too stressed for making plans.

Still, an oddly well-formed question comes into her head, "Is this the end of the beginning for us, or the beginning of the end?"

She doesn't know.

Lying here now, it feels like another end to her, another relationship ground to bits by the chaos of her life. And this was the best one of all....

Tears roll down her face. She makes no sound.

First Philip, then Mill....the exhausted partners fall asleep.

-------------------------------- // --------------------------------

Mill wakes the next morning and notices that Philip has apparently slept in the same position all night. She thinks, "He must have really tied one on to knock himself out that much."

She climbs out of bed, walks around it, and puts her face near his. He's breathing normally and his face has nearly normal color.

Mill smiles grimly and mocks herself, "Considering some of the things I did, I bet some mornings I looked a lot worse for wear than Philip does."

Troubling thought, followed by another.

Has she inserted herself into Philip's self-destruction? In this moment, the cheap motel room has that feel.

Mill quietly leaves and goes out to her car. She opens the trunk and retrieves the suitcase she packed for a week away. She had not known what to bring, so the case is unusually heavy.

In Missoula, she had to decide. Was this to be a hunt for Philip? That would require the kinds of scruffy, inconspicuous clothes that she would need to hang around bars and drug dens.

Or was this to be a warm and healing reunion, more of a honeymoon, requiring sexy outfits for the bedroom and dress-up clothes for dinners out?

215

As she hauls the heavy case up the stairs, she has no idea which experience lies ahead.

She opens the door and bumps her way into the room. The bed is empty. Sounds of the shower come through the open bathroom door.

Mill sees a drawer open in the scarred bureau. The clothes within lie in a muddle, not in Philip's orderly stacks and carefully folded arrangements.

Mill strips down and wraps up in a robe. She wants to be ready for the shower when Philip comes out.

The water stops. A few moments later, he peeks out of the steamy room, "I thought you'd left."

"Why would I do that?"

"Because you were disgusted with me...through with me."

"No, Philip, I'm scared. I'm worried for you and even more worried for us. But I'm not disgusted...at least not now...yet."

"I have an appointment in an hour."

"What are you saying? That we have only a short time to talk?" Mill feels her anxiety rising.

"Yes, just a half an hour and then I need to go."

"What's the appointment for? A doctor? Are you in rehab? You know, like Elder Purlee thought you might...."

Philip laughs harshly, "Yeah, you could call it rehab, I guess. Rehab for false virtue. A purge of self-righteousness. A voiding of fatuous and misplaced self-confidence. A flushing of spiritual pomposity. A casting out of trite and careful words."

He giggles, "Yes, that's my rehab."

"Philip, what are you talking about?"

"Milly, I'm on a new adventure. I'm finding my rock bottom. You know, like you did. Sex, drugs, and rock and roll. Then I want to see what comes of it. What I will be."

"Philip, you're scaring me. I barely survived doing crazy crap in college and my early years with the Forest Service. I'm still getting over some of it. And I know how dangerous it is...how edgy...people trying to exploit you, even kill you. Please don't harm yourself for no reason."

Philip looks at her warily, struggling to reject her words, "Milly, I'm so damn tired of being your rock...everyone's rock. So tired of humdrum...of a whinery of people hanging on me."

Mill's heart begins to race, "Am I a whiney person? A parasite?"

"I never said 'parasite'. And you're not."

216

But that's what you are describing. People hanging off you, using you for support, and not giving back."

"Yeah, I'm surrounded by people like that."

"Me? Am I one of them?"

"Not so much as some. But, yes, you do that a lot."

Mill flinches. Tears start in the corners of her eyes.

Philip smiles, some kindness coming into his face, "Milly, you had good reason to ask for my support. The past two months have been really hard for you and, well, your whole young life was pretty awful."

His face and tone darken, "But, going back a long time, our life together has been about you. Not me or us. Even when we were kids. I've tried to be your best friend and partner all these years. I guess I got lost in the dark energy of your life, its problems. I lost something in there."

Mill starts to cry.

His words must mean the beginning of the end.

This time she really had blown up the best thing in her life.

Philip shakes his head, steeling himself to keep from offering her comfort, "Now I'm trying something new. Confronting my devils...embracing them...or something. You can decide to stay or go...up to you."

"You...you want to do this alone?"

"Yes. I can't imagine you want to be a part of my...uh...'rehab.'"

Philip has finished putting on his clothes. He walks to the door.

Mill looks at him through teary eyes, "Do you want me to be here when you come back?"

He laughs harshly, "Suit yourself. I don't know when I'll be back. Right now, I need to get right and I have this 'therapy' session in a couple of hours." He laughs again, hand on the knob.

"Philip, how are you paying for all of this? All your money's in the bank...insurance."

"Sold my car, Milly. Figured it would make me hard to find, buy me a few weeks before you tracked me down. But, like always, you were better than that...better'n me."

Philip opens the door and leaves, closing it softly behind him.

Sold his car!

Mill angrily wipes the tears from her eyes. Goddamn him! She will *not* give up.

Forgetting her shower, she throws on fresh clothes and whips a brush through her hair.

She mutters, "If he thinks I tracked him before, he hasn't seen my fancy moves yet."

She grabs her backpack and shoves several windbreakers in different lengths, styles, and colors into it. She adds a couple of hats, picks up her keys, and runs out the door.

At street level, she quickly scans the sidewalks and sees Philip opening the door to a taxi a couple of blocks from the motel entrance. She races back to her car, jumps in, and reaches the street as his taxi pulls away.

No more Wild Girl Hunting.

Mill had left her in Idaho amidst the burned-out devastation she'd helped to create.

She smiles. She's "Milly Hunting" now. And Milly Hunting is on Philip's tail and that's where she plans to stay.

Chapter 41 – Don't Eat The Fruit From That Tree

Philip makes no attempt to hide his actions. His first stop is in a smelly, "every-hour-is-happy-hour," shot-bar in Portland's north end.

Milly Hunting slips in the back door bundled in a dull-blue, oversized windbreaker with "LA Raiders" on the back and a dirty ball cap on her head. The bar is half full with alkies lining up for their day's first double hair of the dog.

She walks casually to the end of the bar and takes a stool. Mill perches at an angle so she can just see Philip across the room over the top of two men's shoulders through a haze of fried food smoke and illicit cigarette fumes.

Philip has a couple of drinks. After downing the second one, he peers around the room, obviously scoping for narcs. Mill ducks slightly so all he can see of her is her ball cap. After a moment, she raises her head to find that his gaze has traveled beyond her to a far corner on the other side of the room.

Satisfied that it's safe to make a buy, Philip gets up and approaches a nondescript-looking man sitting in a corner booth.

Mill's frown deepens.

Philip is quite the druggy already. And the dealer...well, he looks like he could be a substitute teacher in an elementary school. Excellent camouflage.

Philip conceals money in a handshake and accepts drugs under the table with his other hand.

His moves are polished enough to make Mill even more worried.

How had Philip gotten so good so quickly at drug purchases?

She shakes her head. Maybe he's a natural. Another bad sign.

Philip slides out of the booth and turns towards her.

Mill quickly lowers her head below the level of the barflies' shoulders and waits for Philip to move past her to the back door. But when he doesn't come, she looks up. Philip is gone.

She slides off her stool and peers around the line of bodies along the bar. Nothing.

He must have left by the front door.

She moves quickly in that direction, attracting the attention of the drug dealer. He hurriedly drops his drug bundle to the floor and stares up at the ceiling, feigning innocence.

Outside, Mill peers up and down the street. Philip is nowhere in sight. There are no taxis cruising this dumpy part of Portland. So, unless he got lucky and caught an empty cab dropping off a fare, Philip is on foot and has not gone far.

Mill rushes up to the nearest intersection.

There he is two blocks down, walking slowly along.

She watches as he ducks into a doorway or alley. Probably to drop some drugs or smoke a joint. She mentally marks the spot and runs back to where she parked her car in a sleazy fast-food joint a half a block away from the bar.

There's a note under her windshield wiper from "The Mangement" promising to have her towed if she parked in their lot again. She rips the note off, jumps in, and moves cautiously out onto the street. She cruises slowly up to the block where she last spotted Philip, drives past the entrance to what she now sees is an alley, and stops.

She can see down the alley but numerous large dumpsters squat in the narrow place and, halfway down, an aging and unused roach coach obscures her view. She sees no movement.

Mill motors ahead. As she reaches the center of the block, she sees Philip at the next corner turning right. He doesn't seem to be in a hurry.

She glances at her watch. If his statement in the motel room were true, he still has twenty minutes or so before the "appointment" he talked about was due to take place.

Mill slows down for the stop at the corner. Now that Mill has seen Philip moving, she wants to stay on his tail. This means she has to hang back and try to hide in the urban landscape while keeping him in sight.

People can identify even an ordinary-looking vehicle if they see it go by too often. So Mill drives past Philip by a couple of blocks, turns left onto a side street, and parks in the middle of a line of vehicles.

Mill gets out hastily, changes into another nondescript windbreaker and hat--this one wide-brimmed so she can pull it low over her face--and grabs a plastic garbage bag from the back seat. In seconds, she appears to be scouring the street and nearby sidewalks for returnable bottles and cans.

As she reaches the corner of the street Philip's on, he passes by on the other side. She keeps her eyes on the ground and moves slowly as if aged. He ignores her and keeps walking.

220

The slightly goofy smile on Philip's face leads Mill to think he's high. He looks mellow, not manic. Grass probably? No telling.

She stays on her side of the street and begins trailing him. She works along low behind lines of parked vehicles, dumpsters, mail drops, and newspaper dispensers, bobbing a little as if her returnables search is going well.

He walks on, never looking back.

She lets the distance grow between them to the point where she can just keep him in sight. This far away, if he looks back, he's unlikely to recognize her. She will run up if he turns.

A long two-part city bus goes by and stops for a customer, blocking Mill's view. She crosses the street in mid-block to get directly behind him, gets a panic honk from a braking driver, and looks for Philip. Gone!

Mill breaks into a trot. So much for looking old and nondescript.

The last view she had of her husband, he was sauntering past an old, brick-front drug store on the corner of a cross-street. She trots up to the store and steps into the entry alcove that faces the street corner. Hoping to just catch sight of him again without being seen, she carefully peers around the bricks.

Philip is leaning against the wall three feet away from her, "Hi, Milly. I thought you might be following me."

Mill winces, feeling a little panic. He wasn't supposed to know. What if he just sent her away...got mad and said it was over between them?

She answers a little shakily, trying to make her voice both impish and chagrined, "Was I that obvious?"

"No, I didn't know what to look for and didn't care. I just thought you might be coming around that corner sometime, so I waited for you."

"You're not mad?"

"No, but since you stuck your nose in, I do have plans for you. You'll have to promise not to interfere with my 'therapy' though. Just sit and watch, the whole thing, until it's over."

"How can I promise that when I don't know what you're going to do? Is it crazy? Will it put you in danger?"

"A little crazy I guess, but not dangerous. I spent a lot of money on hookers for a few days. Got crazy dangerous a couple of times. This is better. Hurts a little but safer."

Mill gets frightened. Hookers? He gentle husband hurt?

She retorts, "Well, I won't be a part of hurting you."

Philip replies firmly, "No, you won't. In fact, I forbid you to interfere. So, if you want to come with me, do. But you'll have to follow what I say. If you don't want to come, well then, turn around and go. Don't look back and don't follow me. Even an amateur like me can ditch you now that I know you're behind me."

Suddenly anxious, Mill takes his hand, "I...I just want my Philip back. The guy I grew up with...married. You're scaring me into thinking that Philip might be lost to me...permanently."

Her husband looks Mill in her eyes. She sees that his pupils are dilated and each of his cheeks has a reddish patch, drug effects. She changes her mind that he is high on mary-jane to the more likely Ecstasy or one of its many imitators and spin-offs.

Philip says flatly, "The old Philip is gone."

He laughs harshly, "The new Philip is trying his wings. So fly with me, Milly, or be gone, too."

He giggles, "Quoth the raven, 'Nevermore.'"

Mill drops her eyes and bobs her head, acquiescing. Although she's desperately fearful and angry, she doesn't want to drive him away.

She says humbly, "Okay, Philip, whatever you want...."

He squeezes her hand as if he's going to drop it, but, instead takes a firm grip. He pushes away from the wall and leads her down the block.

Mill sees that the homes in this area are better-kept than the area near the bar. The street has a calmer, more neighborly feel.

Private homes intersperse with home-businesses. A tax service here. A small title company there.

Philip leads her to a clean, well-painted craftsman-styled bungalow. By the sidewalk is a sign, small red letters on black, which says, "Mme. S, by appointment." Mill looks up towards the house and sees none of the trappings of business: oversize mailbox, credit card stickers in windows, or an "open" sign in the window.

"What...ah, what kind of service does Madam S provide?"

"No questions, Milly. Remember you're along for the ride...no interference...no comments."

Everything seems so normal about the house...peaceful, well-kept.

Mill sighs, "Okay, let's go in."

They find no one in the entry area.

222

Philip says, "It's her home. Therapy's in the basement. I told her you might be coming. So, we made arrangements for you…to keep you comfortable while I had my session."

He points towards a door, "Come in here and I'll get you settled."

Philip opens the door and ushers her in. The windowless room beyond is small but nicely finished with tan walls and a large powder-blue easy chair in the center. Next to the armchair, a carafe of water with glasses rests on one table and nearby, on a smaller table, sits a box of tissues. Two corner shelves display what appear to be scented oils or bath products, seemingly sales items for Madam's business. Off one wall, a small door opens into a powder room, the edges of a sink and toilet visible in the shadows within.

Facing the armchair is a floor-to-ceiling curtain. But no outside light filters in through it. Mill realizes it faces the house's center.

She points, "What's this for?"

"It's an observation window. You know, like the ones above hospital's surgical suite."

He laughs ironically, "Sometimes Madam has family or friends who want to watch their loved-ones get treatment. Sometimes she has other professionals watch and give her feedback."

Mill looks at the damask curtain. It conveys a certain charm and luxury.

"Okay, what do I do now?"

"Sit down, relax, and wait for the session to begin. That's all. There are some reading materials and other stuff in the table drawers but you probably don't need them for today."

He gives her a gentle shove towards the chair, turns, and opens the door.

"Bye, Milly," he says a little sadly, "See you on the other side."

The door closes with a click.

Mill enters the powder room and uses the toilet.

When she re-enters the room, she sees that the curtain is open. Must be on a remote-control switch.

She walks forward to the window and realizes it is actually one-way glass, clear on her side and mirrored on the other. Mill stands close to the glass. She can see down into the basement.

The room below is dimly lit. It has grey, severe-looking concrete walls and a rubber-mat floor. A grey leather couch and matching chair sit in the center of the room. Here and there are other pieces of leather furniture, their purposes less clear.

Shelves run down one wall but, because of her vantage point, Mill can't see what's in them. Clothing hangs on hooks along the wall across from Mill; looking down on the clothes, she can see top edges, shapes, and textures but the actual pieces are lost in shadows.

Suddenly a speaker hidden in the ceiling above her crackles and she hears voices. Someone has turned on an intercom. Philip and a woman are talking at a distance from the microphones, their voices indistinct.

The pair walks into her view.

Philip has a leather hood over his head and nothing else on except leather chaps.

His dominatrix, Madam Scratches, is dressed in a leather bustier, naked from her waist down to her ankles which are bound into military-styled hiking boots.

Moments later, high on Ecstasy, Philip lies stretched over an arched leather couch, his arms and legs strapped to the corners. Mill watches, mesmerized.

Scratches cracks a short whip topped with several lashes. She slashes hard at Philip's leather-bound legs.

He grunts with pain. Breath whistles through his nose.

The woman hisses, "I'm going to hurt you, Philip, until you give me what I want. I want you hard and in me. I want it now. But you can't get it up, can you?

"Yes, yes, I can, Mistress Scratches. See, it's hard now. Just look."

"That's not what I want. I want a real cock. Something a real man can give me. Not a pathetic worm like you got, you useless limp-dick preacher man."

She slashes again.

The spell holding Mill breaks. She takes two quick steps to the door.

The knob turns uselessly in her hand. Locked! Damn it.

She hears the pair's voices again. Seconds later, a new more solid, heavy noise begins.

She looks back down through the window and sees Philip lying face down on the couch, arms tied tightly at elbow and wrist behind his back. His ankles are secured to the couch.

Madam's arm goes up and down, slamming his rear and thighs with a metal-studded paddle.

It's as if she's a druggist counting out doses.

Philip's skin is bright red. With each blow, he whinnies with the pain, each cry ending with an "ahh."

Not dangerous?

Bullshit.

Mill pounds on the glass.

Madam does not look up or slow the steady pace of her arm.

Mill looks closely at the glass. She might be able to shatter it. Then she sees the metal wires twining through it…security glass…tougher than she can manage. Even if she shot out pieces of it with her .40 caliber, the wires would be impossible to break. And besides, the chaos of breaking glass and bullets would fall into the basement, probably harming Philip below.

She turns and opens the drawers to the tables. They are filled with sex toys, partially used bottles of lubricants, and S and M magazines. No help in there.

"Fuck! What a nightmare," she yells.

Ignoring her husband's cries, she returns to the door and inspects the jamb. The door is firmly locked, but whoever installed the door had left the hinges exposed on the inside.

She has no tools. What to do?

Mill quickly pulls her Glock and removes the clip. The clip has a jutting, tough plastic flange at the base. She catches the edge of the top hinge pin with the flange and taps hard against the clip's side with the Glock. Slowly, reluctantly, the pin slides out. In seconds, she removes the second hinge pin and then the third.

The door sags a little in the frame but doesn't open.

Mill shoves it but it doesn't move.

Of course…the hinges will only allow the door to fall into the room, not out into the hallway.

She sticks the clip's flange into the gap in the door frame and pries. The door slips towards her, catches, and then falls in, almost knocking her down. She shoves it aside.

Mill runs out into the hall, looking for the basement door. There!

It's locked, apparently by a deadbolt on the other side.

She peers at the lock. Looks like it can be jimmied.

She races into the kitchen and pulls a bread knife from a wooden block. This will do.

She returns to the basement door.

After inspecting the lock again, she slips the knife under the door molding and up against the catch. She twists and shoves, forcing the tongue back. The lock clicks and the door swings open.

Who knows what kinds of weapons a woman in the S and M trade might have to protect herself?

Mill moves down the stairs cautiously, not wanting to startle the dominatrix and have her injure Philip.

Mill knows that what's been going on is not illegal. Most people asking for this crazy stuff follow fantasy stories and scripts of their own creation. Is that what Philip is doing too? The truth is Philip can have his ass whipped all day long as long as he wants it to happen.

She enters the room.

Scratches has her back to the door. Her arms rises and falls slowly, evenly. Philip's flesh is bright red. His moans are almost inaudible now.

Mill walks quietly up behind the dominatrix. She reaches suddenly around the leather-clad head, covers the woman's mouth, and presses the Glock tightly into the ear hole.

Mill whispers, "Shhhhh."

Scratches tenses and then relaxes. She nods.

Mill spins her around and uses the Glock to gesture first towards the door to the upstairs and then Philip's hooded prone figure.

Scratches says in a low voice, "Philip, you useless shit, I'm going to leave you alone now. When I hear you beg hard enough for my return, I'll be back."

Philip's muffled voice says, "But, you and I agreed...."

The paddle slams down hard on his beet-red buttocks. "Silence, you pig, or I'll take my piss all over you. Would you like that?"

"No, no," comes his muffled voice again.

Scratches starts to hit him again, but Mill grabs her arm. She points to the stairs again with the Glock.

The two women leave the basement and climb the stairs, Scratches clunking in her heavy boots and Mill tiptoeing behind. They reach the kitchen.

Mill says flatly, "Take off the mask."

The woman complies, revealing an ordinary looking, rather lined face. She appears to be in her thirties. She has a trim, almost skinny,

226

body with several tattoo's including one of a spider's web around her shaved pubic area.

"Okay, what's he paying you to do?"

"Why should I tell you? He's the customer. If I'd 'a known you would do this I would never have let him talk me into lettin' you watch. Most peepers just want to...."

Mill brings the butt of the gun down on Scratches shoulder. She grunts with pain and then smiles, rubbing the spot, "You might have potential...."

"Cut the crap. I'm federal 5-0 and I'm off the leash. Tell me what Philip wants...what you're going to do to him...or I'll put you out of business, personally and permanently."

The dominatrix smiles sourly and tightens her lips, saying nothing.

In response, Mill uses a snap-twisting knuckle to tap the woman on the temple.

"Ouch, damn it. Don't mess up the face. I got a boyfriend who likes me the way I am."

Mill taps her again. She ducks her head in pain.

"Okay...okay. Your guy just moved up to full bondage and pain. He likes whips and pinchers. Draws the line at anything that might leave a scar. So, no burns or cuts. Everything else is on the table."

"What's the game, the fantasy?"

"I work on him for a couple of hours, then fuck him, telling him at the end he's a good man, a real stud."

"Does he have a safety word? You know, if the pain gets too great?"

"No, he used to have one, 'midnight', but not since he moved up. Guess he likes the edginess."

Mill has a hard time asking this question, "He call you any name besides yours? You know for the fantasy?"

"No, no name. But sometimes when he's comin' he mutters something. Might be a name but I never been able to make it out."

Mill nods, "So, it isn't 'midnight'?"

The woman shakes her head, "No idea. Says it too low to hear."

Mill decides, "Okay, this is what you're going to do. Keep up the pain the way he likes it, but towards the end, do this...."

After a little more persuasion and a promise of double fees, Scratches agrees.

A few minutes later, Mill returns to the door-less window room to watch the action.

Scratches reenters the basement and puts pinchers on Philip's nipples.

For the next hour, she demands.

He tries to comply...fails...begs.

She demeans and degrades him, whips him, spanks him again with the metal-studded paddle.

She pinches his scrotum with metal clips and binds him ever tighter until his flesh bulges between the straps.

Throughout it all, Philip writhes with pain and obvious lust.

Upstairs, Mill watches with a sense of muted horror.

What could she have missed about Philip in all their years together? Why would he want such treatment? Was she the reason he found this way to "go bad?"

The questions keep rattling around in her brain while she watches her husband accept the torment he's sought and paid for.

The one question she can't seem to ask herself is if this means the end for them as a couple...the death of their marriage. Could it survive this incredible departure into depravity?

Mill looks at her watch...ten minutes to go in Philip's session. It's about time.

Scratches releases Philip and forces him to his hands and knees. She throws a choke collar around his neck and leads him like a dog around the room. All the way, she whips his back and buttocks with a knotted rope, calling him, "a bad little shit" over and over again.

Finally, she takes her "bad dog" to one of the smaller couches, this one humped up like a turtle's back. She forces him onto it, and reties him so his back arches over the cushions.

After pulling the knots tight, she walks to the wall of clothing and takes down a bright red latex suit. She slips out of her leathers.

Naked, she glances up at Mill who gives her a frowning thumb up. Mill doesn't remember that she is standing behind a mirror and her gesture will be unseen by the woman in the basement.

After rubbing a baby powder on her skin, Scratches pulls the suit's mask over her face and slides into the stretchy outfit, zipping it closed up to her neck. Once the mask is on, her face looks alien with nothing but slits for eyes, mouth, and nose and tiny holes for ears. Her body form is equally weird, utterly smooth, with its few curves flattened and pressed, molded into the suit's latex grip.

228

Scratches walks back to Philip, rubs her body across his erection, and slides her hands up and down his torso

"Feel that, loser? Want more?"

His throat totally dry, he croaks, "Yes."

She slaps his face through the hood. "Not now, little bitch. I have something special for you."

She walks to the stairs. Reaching behind some shelving, she turns on black lights positioned in the ceiling over the turtle-back couch and switches off the mini-spots in the ceiling.

She walks back to Philip and roughly jerks off his hood.

Under the black light, most of the latex suit puts off a dazzling pearl-like glow. In those places not touched by the light, dark red splotches and shadows shift as the dominatrix moves.

Philip's eyes can barely stand the bright glow of the body suit. He keeps them focused on the suit's shadow areas to avoid the blinding glow.

Philip begins to speak.

But his dominatrix says, "Shut up, scum. I'm getting you water, and then we'll finish."

She disappears into the shadows, uttering complaints and cursing his weak manhood.

Moments later, her glowing figure returns.

While drinking, Philip tries to roll his head away from the suit's brightness.

The water Scratches offers him slops over his lips. She slaps him and mutters, "Clumsy shit."

She opens a condom pack and rolls a condom on his erection. Then, throwing a dazzling leg over him, she mounts. Sliding him inside, she makes a series of quick up and down movements, settling her body over and around his penis.

He moans with pleasure as he watches her ride and flex on him. The light from the suit becomes an intense, rippling ribbon as she moves. But he can't watch for long. Eyes watering, Philip looks away into the shadows for a few seconds before looking back.

Like everything in his life now, even this vision is pleasure mixed with pain.

His luminous dominatrix begins a steady rhythm. Unlike past sessions, she drops low over his body. Through slitted eyes, he watches her glowing figure hover above him even as her hips move gently, bringing him exquisite pleasure.

It occurs to him that, after being so demonically tormented earlier, it's like being fucked by an angel.

He laughs, even more aroused.

She feels his penis start to swell within her. She puts her hands around his neck and draws her glowing face close to his, heightening his sense that a faceless angel is fucking his brains out.

Sensing from his breathing that he must be close to an orgasm, she tightens her vagina around him.

Pulled by this gentle suction, his orgasm rises uncontrollably. He can't stop…can't reverse…has to let go. Now!

Wanting him to release fully, she relaxes her grip and stops moving.

As his semen pulses out, he whispers, as he always had, "Milly."

Inches from his ear, his glowing fuck angel whispers in reply, "Yes, Philip, my love, I'm here…"

And at that moment, the biggest orgasms Mill has had in months rolls through her body.

As she shudders, a newly committed Milli clings tightly to her husband's body, unable to let go.

Chapter 42 - An Inquiry of Fools

Senator Castwell brings his gavel down, "The Joint Select Committee on Eco-Terrorism will now come to order."

Even with the gavel's loud bang, the noise in the large Senate hearing room drops only somewhat, but does not abate.

"I said this committee will come to order," Castwell bangs the gavel twice, "Sergeant at Arms, please quiet those people in the back. People who might like to carry on conversations out in the hallway are invited to leave this chamber."

A few people in the back quiet down and then find seats. Some talkers leave.

Castwell looks out across the room. Plenty of media are present, including the big networks and cable channels. He sees some of the most influential bloggers and columnists sitting at the press table off to the left. A few of his top financial supporters are seated in front rows. And here and there are public- and private-interest lobbyists of the highest standing.

And before him at the witness table are the Secretaries of Agriculture, Interior, and Homeland Security, and, best of all, the President's pet, the Attorney General of the United States—all of them the little lambs he has brought here to slaughter today.

Earlier, Castwell's Chief of Staff, Mike Reinaud, made sure that the ceiling spots were realigned to direct their full wattage on the witness table. He had done well. The harsh light makes the President's politicos look pale and causes them to sweat, sure signs of conspiratorial guilt served up for the electronic media.

In contrast, Castwell's team has made him look cool and imperious. Perfect for the cameras.

This is the highest political theater he has ever arranged.

No matter what words are spoken during the next weeks of testimony, the whole political world will know that Senator Castwell, Republican from Idaho, is among the heaviest hitters in the United States. Here's the Word people: Charles Castwell is powerful, even presidential...and for sale to the highest bidder.

Castwell clears his throat and leans into the microphone on the desk in front of him. He makes a few perfunctory thanks to the Administration for sending such impressive representatives to testify.

Then, squinting accusatorially, he asks, "Mr. Attorney General, please explain to this committee why your Administration has set out to

231

systematically tear down the fifty States' Constitutional protections, more specifically their sovereign authority to administer justice within their boundaries. And even more specifically, please tell us why the Department of Justice, acting through the FBI and numerous other agencies, and in concert with the Department of Defense, committed itself to a war…yes, a green war…in Idaho's River of No Return Wilderness. This unconscionable action has left wide areas ravaged by gunfire and burned by wildfire. There are many people dead, sir, and millions of dollars in cost that must be accounted for."

Castwell glares down at the figure seated before him, "Frankly, Mr. Attorney General, this smacks of the same kinds of abuses of power as occurred at Waco and Ruby Ridge. No, sir, it's not the same abuse. This Mist-Cutter green war far exceeds those events in cost and bloodshed. So, please, sir, provide your justifications to this committee and the American people."

The dapper Attorney General had sat quietly through the diatribe and now asks laconically, "Senator, I am eager to answer any questions you or your committee have. Was there a question embedded within that speech?"

Castwell gestures angrily, "You heard my questions. Now answer."

The Attorney General shakes his head, opens a folder with about a dozen large-type pages in it, and begins to read the Administration's carefully prepared statement, "Let me start with a summary of actions taken near Cutter's Park in Idaho's Frank Church-River of No Return Wilderness. Three months ago, the Federal Bureau of Investigation began investigating the deaths of Esperanza Angelica Pizzaro and Wolfgang Amadeus Meacham, Associate Chief and Chief of the United States Forest Service, respectively…."

Castwell leans back.

He thinks, "Blah, blah, blah. Say anything you want, Mr. Asshole General; I've already got you pinned down like a dead fucking butterfly."

He looks at his audience and sees plenty of attention being paid to the testimony. Good. It means people think this hearing is important. In turn, their focus makes him even more important.

His eyes wander to the crossed legs of a young woman in the front row. Who could that be?

Seeing his eyes on her, she obligingly re-crosses her legs, giving him a nice view. He catches a quick flash of panty beyond nicely rounded thighs. Excellent.

He smiles benignly at her and she smiles back. He probably shouldn't go there, but the possibilities are nice to think about.

He misses the place where he began his political career, his old Idaho House chamber. Back then, he could sit on the chamber floor and look up through the narrow railings into the visitor gallery one story above.

Any woman in a skirt was almost certain to give him a show. He would pass notes to some of his friends when an especially nice pair of legs came into view. To improve his odds, he made sure that high schoolers and college kids visiting from his district were always seated in the front rows and Garden Clubbers in the back. Good views of firm flesh and occasionally a little fur…obscurity for the rest.

It was nice to be the king.

Chapter 43 - Touch

Philip rests his head on Milli's naked belly, "I still don't know why you took Madam S's place. Why did you do that, Milly? I was so completely shocked when you whispered in my ear that you loved me."

Milli strokes his hair, "Well, I told you I didn't want to see you hurt. That's why I broke out of the little peeper room. But I guess I've not been too clear about the rest of it."

She pauses and sighs, "I'm still not real sure, but after I pulled her off you and had her secured upstairs...."

"You mean 'thumped'...."

"Well, yes, I did thump her a little. God knows she deserved it for thumping on you...."

"Remember, I was paying her."

"I know. As you keep telling me, you were her customer, not her victim. But I couldn't really see that there was a difference at the time."

She raps him lightly on the head with her knuckles.

"Ouch!"

"See? And that was for free. Anyway, back to your question. I put on that vinyl suit and joined in because, as soon as I had the Glock on Scratches, I realized I didn't know what to do next. And then it came to me in a flash."

She runs her hand through his hair, "Going in, I knew I wanted to be your wife, your partner. That's why I followed you and, even after you caught me following you in such an embarrassing way, I kept going."

She raps his head, more gently this time, "But what I realized standing in Madam's kitchen was that, if you're going to play out some of your fantasies, I want to play, too...with you. And the idea that you'd actually like me to bind you and spank you, while you call the shots on the whole thing, really appealed to me. And what made it all make sense was that I wanted in on the loving part, the finish, where I get to call you what you are, a good man and a good lover."

Because bondage and pain conjured up terrible old feelings around her rape, Milli had no desire to have those things done to her. And she wanted to avoid acting out any remaining grief and rage from the rape on Philip. She feared she might lose it and harm him dreadfully.

However, within her was a more positive, insightful core that liked what Scratches did. As long as Philip gave her permission to act, while sticking to whatever limits he set, she was greatly turned on by binding and spanking him.

It satisfied some deep longing within her, something to do with controlling her wandering parents, punishing them for their neglect, and then receiving outpourings of love.

Milli wriggles a little with excitement. The idea is still tantalizing and strongly appealing.

"So that's all."

For Philip, Milli's increasing dominance and willingness to play had given him the perfect combination of edge-of-sleep fantasies and chastity. He could be dominated and dominant at the same time…with his own wife. It was the most erotic situation he could conceive.

Milli and Philip had been back to Madam Scratches "studio" twice since that first day. For a double fee, the couple had learned many things about the woman's art and about themselves.

Madam S had shown Milli how to use whip, paddle, and pinch to inflict the level of pain Philip liked. And how to use ropes, shackles, and leather bonds to secure him without hurting him.

Her studio offered an almost endless variety of devices and bonds, giving the couple lots to pick from and try. They already had favorites and vowed to buy what they liked when they got home.

Now this talk had been so stimulating, Milli shoves Philip's head off her stomach and says, "Ready for a little action?"

He laughs, "Sure am."

"Let's play the one where you are stopped by a cop for a traffic violation."

"Yeah, that'd be nice. But not too tight on the handcuffs."

Milli slips into her role, "Listen, citizen, you'll do what I tell you or there'll be consequences…. Now roll over so I can cuff you."

"Okay, special agent. Ouch! Those cuffs are too tight."

"Shut up, worm. I'm going to make sure you never forget what your worthless ass is doing and run a stop sign again. You could kill some old lady, or worse, a kid that way. You are no better than pond scum, but I'm going to straighten you out."

"Yes, officer, I know I've been bad. Please don't hurt me."

Milli replies in mock disgust, a little-kitten smile on her face, "Craphead. Just do what I say…." She spanks his bottom with her bare hand. Both sting.

Grimacing, Milli shakes the sting off her hand and reaches for a narrow paddle….

An hour later, the couple rests.

Philip lights up a tiny bowl of dope and inhales expertly. He offers the little pipe to her.

She shakes her head, "Nice of you, lover, but I'm done with that...permanently."

He nods and puffs again.

Milli has been watching Philip closely over the last day, making sure his drug use stays as low as possible. After the meth and other speed, she figures he's physically hooked. But since he's not a long-term user, he has a good chance of getting clean and staying there with the right treatment. She knows the pot and E he's been using could be equally addictive, she'd been there, but not so physically so as the speed.

Once Philip's done smoking, they lie together, this time with her face on his chest, nestled together under the covers, "Philip, this question may seem premature. But have you thought about what you're going to do next? You know, about your congregation...career...all that?"

"Well, I think I might need to get my drug use under control a little. I gotta say, "going bad" is pretty hard on my body."

He laughs ironically, "I still have a hard time figuring what time of day it is. But maybe it doesn't matter to me the same way it once did."

He coughs from the pot smoke and then continues, "My career? That's over, Milly. Or at least the way I was living is over. I just can't stand the thought of going back to that awful routine, the endless rounds of comforting sinners...or people who think they are sinning."

He smiles wanly, "The drugs...Madam's whip...they created clarity for me."

"I thought you loved your church life, Philip...you know, caring for other people."

"I do...or did, Milly. But I'm so tired of the routines, the rituals, the budget fights, the annual church calendars, elders' meetings, and I...I just don't know. Being *nice* all the time. Being *good*. All of it."

"Okay, I understand. You were burning out."

"No, I wasn't burning. I was fried...broasted."

His voice rises, "And the worst of it, Milly? The absolute worst? The whole business is wrong, or at least most of it. I mean the whole

Christian practice…the way we do it. Not the part about Christ coming among us and saving us. That's true…at least for me."

"What do you mean 'wrong'? Philip, you have big degrees in Divinity and Theology. If you know what's right, why don't you say so? Tell everyone?"

He sighs, "I'm not sure people could handle knowing how simple it all is. I think people love their rituals and traditions, their elaborate divisions from others, and their routines of mock faithfulness. Those things allow them to stay comfortable, to wallow in prejudices, to poke at wounds, perceived and real, and to scratch at other people's scabs, trying to get them to bleed. How could I ever I change that?"

"Well, how about telling people about that "simple truth" thing you mentioned and let them decide."

"Okay. I'll try it on you first. Let me lay it out for you…those simple truths…stripped of all the miracles and magic names and ancient prophecies and confusing complexity."

Milli settles closer, hugging him tighter. She prepares to let his words reach one ear as plain speech and invade the other as resonance from deep in his chest.

"Here are the four immutable Christian truths according to Philip."

He laughs a mildly high, ironic laugh, "Imagine that. St. Philip speaks."

At these words, the dope takes over and he giggles for awhile, bouncing Milli's head until he finally gets a cramp in his side.

Groaning he says, "Dope finally made me think them through. Crazy huh?"

Another cramp hits and he grunts, "Cripes."

Tempered by the pain, he finally gets a grip on his giggles and says, "Whooo-ee. That was fun. Okay. More serious now. I find two kinds of people in the world…people who believe the universe was created by someone we call 'God' and people who do not. My new church is for those who believe it was created…didn't just happen. Got that?"

Milli nods.

"Okay, here are the simple truths."

"One. There is a God, the Creator of everything and everyone."

"Two. The Creator of everything created you and me for one purpose—to love the Creator—and to be personally loved by the Creator

238

in turn. Without humans in the universe there'd be no one to love the Creator. So, the sole purpose for our existence...our souls...is love."

He giggles for a moment over his weak pun.

"Three. The Creator has a role for each person, common to humanity, but unique to each person—we are to care for the Creation, including each other and the world around us. Because the Creator made it, the Creation is sacred, both the people and the world. Deserves our care."

"Four. 'Care for the Creation' means sacrificing ourselves in the great cycle of annihilation and rebirth, dust to life and then life to dust again. The Creator has built that sacrificial potential into us if we just choose to release it. But it's our choice."

He pauses then says, "So, in any future church run by St. Philip...."

He starts the giggles again, and then clutches his freshly cramping side, "Unhhh. Any new church of mine will just deal with those truths. None of the other stuff. And we will work to understand that all 'good' intentions are based on the four truths. Otherwise, it's just 'stuff' and irrelevant."

"But, Philip, isn't there evil in the world? Look at W.A.'s life and what he did to me, Mom, and others. And what about Mist, hurting people, killing people. And my Mom? And then there're earthquakes, floods, disease?"

The dope swings Philip's mood. He starts to cry a little.

"Yes, evil...we see a lot of it, don't we? For our Creator, evil is when we fail to love the Creator first and ourselves second...way second. Evil is when we don't humbly tend the garden...take care of the Creation around us. Evil is apathy. Evil happens when we don't care."

Philip sighs and wipes his eyes, "We are put together from the same stuff the Creator used to form the stars, the planets, the plants, the animals. Made us, not the other way around."

He's struck by a thought, "Dearest, did you ever realize that we breathe the same air that Jesus the Christ or Buddha did...the atoms and molecules they breathed into their bodies are in our air. We share that with them."

He stops talking and kisses his wife's hair, "A tiny part of you is Jesus stuff, literally born again in you. You...we...are sacred places where the Creator who came to live among us still lives."

Milli asks quietly, "What about souls...you know, like mine...black and heavy as coal."

"Your soul is energy, not matter. Creator laid down a law; we humans call that law the 'second law of thermodynamics'. The Creator says energy can't be destroyed, just moved around...changed. So, your soul can't be destroyed, just changed. Creator says when you're done with your body and it turns back to dust, your soul-energy gets to decide to travel to Heaven and be with the Creator or to go off on its own, be alone."

Philip chuckles low in his throat, "Could the Creator have made what's going on more obvious? Every new scientific discovery...every theorem...Darwin's evolution...confirms the Creator's intentions...power...majesty."

Milli yawns and mumbles into Philip's chest, "I wanna go to your church. Will you build it for me, love? Be my pastor?"

She reaches down, takes his genitals into her hand, and squeezes gently, "And share your star stuff with me? Someday maybe put a star baby in me?"

He smiles and yawns, too.

They sleep...deeply...filled with Jesus' breath and other star stuff.

--------------------------------- // ---------------------------------

When Milli wakes up the next morning, bright light streams into Philip's cheap motel room through a gap between the heavy curtains. Milli blinks into the light for awhile before sliding out to use the bathroom.

When she returns, Philip is awake, too, lying on his back, blinking in the light. He looks only a little hung over and therefore better than the last four mornings.

Once Philip has wiped the sleep from his eyes, Milli asks, "What's first this morning, love?"

She's afraid his answer will be what it has been, "I need a drink...," his code words for two stiff ones and a drug buy.

Instead, he says, "I'd like to try breakfast first, Milly, if that'd be okay with you. Then, we'll just see...."

"Okay," Milli replies cautiously, "Let's take it an hour at a time today."

He nods, "Let me grab a shower. Then we'll go out."

Milli dimples at him "I want a shower, too. Let's share one this morning."

240

He looks at his wife's curvy body, "As long as you take it easy on me."

He points to some reddened areas on his wrists and a few bruises on his backside where she had applied the thin little paddle a little too strongly.

"You've starting liking this bondage thing a little too much."

"You told me 'life's a learning process, Milly'," she retorts, "And remember, you're the one in charge. I'm just doing what *you* want."

"Well maybe you could do what *I* want with a little less enthusiasm."

He looks at her narrowly, "You know what I mean, Special Agent Tight Cuffs?"

Philip embraces her. They kiss lightly and then again, more intently.

He smiles at Milli wolfishly, "Maybe there's time for a quickie in the shower?"

"Ever been snapped by a wet hand towel, you worthless little bitch?"

---------------------------------- // --------------------------------

An hour later, Philip's rear end still tingles when the two sit to breakfast in the greasy spoon off the motel's lobby. It looks like it hasn't been remodeled since the 1980's. Burnt orange wallpaper is marred and ripped in a few places. The sconced lighting sags.

Even though Philip's stomach is a little queasy, they both order big breakfasts.

Their shower love-making had been brief but vigorous, ending well for both of them, but leaving them both drained of energy.

Milli smiles across the damp and slightly sticky tabletop, "How's the stomach? You look a little washed out."

"It's okay. Feels like the flu. Stomach's fluttery and my temperature goes up and down. One minute sweats and the next cold."

"Withdrawal. It's fairly easy to come off the dope and E. Harder to clean up from the speed, particularly meth. Do you want to get right before we eat?"

Milli is hoping the answer is "no", but she has to leave that up to Philip. Having been a binge addict, she knows that only Philip can get himself clean and sober. Until he decides to do that, it's going to be one fix at a time.

"Not yet. Let's see how the food goes down. I'm feeling more and more anxious, so I'll want to get something this morning. But not right away." His right hand taps the table nervously. His right leg pumps up and down out of sight below the tabletop.

Milli reaches across the table and takes his twitching hand, "I understand what's happening for you." She sighs deeply. What she's about to say is far riskier for her than entering Madam Scratches place and taking up the S and M play.

She grips his hand tightly, "Philip, I love you more than any other person on earth. I want a future with you. I want my babies to be your babies."

Her face turns grim. Her shoulders grow taut with tension, "But I won't buy drugs for you, pay for them, or help you use."

Milli takes a deep, shuddery breath, "And, my dearest, after tomorrow, I won't stay with you, either. I'm going back to Missoula, to my job. You are welcome to come with me…live with me, love me anyway you want…but only if you clean up, get sober. Do you understand me?"

Philip looks at her warily, "Why does this have to be an 'either-or'? I can keep it under control. I could make sure my habits stay out of our life, your career, all that. Just use a little when I need it."

Milli says flatly, "That's your addiction talking. Those are the same words that I would have used ten years ago, 'I've got it under control…leave me alone to do what I want'."

She shakes her head and speaks vehemently, "But I didn't have it under control. No one ever controls dope…not you, not me, not anyone. Sure, people can use less, at least for a time, but they keep using. To get off dope, you have to stop. For good. Period. I had to have the shit scared out of me to quit."

Milli gets up and comes around the table, slides into the booth next to him, and puts her arms around him, hugging him tightly. "I had no one to turn to in Alaska, Philip. Your situation is different. You have me. I was young and stupid. You're mature and wise."

She laughs quietly, "Well, maybe not quite so wise lately, I guess, but at least intentional."

An irrational anger grips him. Why can't she just let him dabble a little, dope up when he needs it, nothing more?

His eyes flash hatred but he speaks quietly, trying to con her, "I'm all mixed up. Could you stay a few more days? Bankroll me just a little until I taper off…get straight?"

"Nope. I'm getting on a plane tomorrow and going home, with or without you."

She lets go of him. Milli slides out of Philip's seat and gets to her feet. She's instantly dizzy. She hadn't realized she had been breathing so shallowly or that her vision has grown so cloudy.

This is her chronic anxiety spiking again. She should have remembered Dr. Canot's warnings about strong emotional events. And after all the fighting and deaths of the last weeks, Philip's tragic behavior probably has been doubly impactful.

Darkness takes her sight. She starts to sag and grips the table.

"Milly, what's wrong?"

Philip's voice comes dimly to her ears, which now are roaring with white noise, "Are you okay?"

Her elbows buckle. He jumps out of the booth to grab her before she can fall. He remembers Canot's advice, "Don't panic. Tell her to breathe deeply. Do what you have to do to keep her conscious. But once she's out, her breathing should return to normal right away and she'll come out of it."

"Milly, take deep breaths, love."

He kisses her hard on the mouth, willing his love into her, "Come back to me, sweetheart."

Pale dead weight, she doesn't respond.

His spirit equivocates, love and addiction at war within him, but he announces to her, "I'm ready, Milly. I want to go home …with you…get sober."

She still doesn't respond.

The café manager hurries up. Philip is about to ask her to call 9-1-1 when Milli begins to revive a little. Her eyes flutter open.

She looks around, "Oh boy, I guess I made a scene, huh?"

Relieved, Philip grins at her, "I've seen better. But this was a pretty good one."

He looks closely at her and sees her color improving.

His addiction lies for him, "I was just telling you that I would make my decision tonight."

He helps her to her feet. They both slide back into the booth.

Breakfast arrives. Milli digs in.

Philip picks at his food, his appetite as tangled as his motives.

244

Chapter 44 - Reflections

Milli stares into the steamy mirror of her Missoula bathroom. Above her, the exhaust fan hums and vibrates. With the door cracked and the dry climate helping, the mirror will soon be clear.

But not fast enough for today's schedule.

She has an appointment with Dr. Jack Ward Thomas, the former Forest Service Chief, one of the men her mother had told her to contact. He lives south of Missoula, up from the main highway to the west in hill country. She lives well north of town in a four-plex...bottom floor, three bedrooms with a big kitchen-living-great room.

Dr. Thomas' place is far enough away that, unless she hurries now, she will be late for their meeting.

She swipes at the fog with a dry wash cloth and creates a little space. She quickly applies light eyeliner and runs a brush through her hair.

She had seen a few grey hairs yesterday and plucked them out. She twists her head quickly from side to side, using a hand mirror to check for more. None visible.

Damn nuisance, that grey-hair business.

Milli walks naked into her bedroom and pulls on underwear, tailored jeans, and a ruffled western shirt. Threading a tooled-leather belt around her trim waist, she uses it to clamp her Glock to her right hip. She slides her feet into her favorite roper-styled boots and walks into the living room. By the front door, she grabs a flannel-lined denim jacket, its color matching the faded fabric of her jeans, and flips it over her shoulder.

Milli likes the relaxed dress standards of Missoula and the Rockies. They make both social gatherings and undercover work easy to dress for. She jumps in her Audi A6 and throws a little gravel getting out of the driveway.

She only has to speed a little to get to the Thomas' house by the appointed time.

She strides up the short walk and tings the bell. After a few seconds, she hears footsteps approach and then the door opens widely. A tall, solid-looking, white-haired man stands there, his face lit by a tentative grin. "Are you Mill Meacham?" he asks.

"Yes, I'm Meacham. But call me 'Milli' please, Doctor Thomas."

"Okay, Milli. I knew your father a little, although I never worked with him much. And I'm 'Jack' to everyone who knows me."

Jack looks Milli over.

He's always admired human beauty, male or female, the same way he treasures works of art in a gallery or museum--warmly objective but not wanting to possess them. He finds the woman before him doubly beautiful—in her shapely physical form and in the character he reads in her maturing face and intelligent eyes.

He looks at her clothes and admires how well put together her outfit is. Then he sees the black, thick-gripped handgun hanging at her side.

Raising his voice and hands in mock surrender, he grins, "Am I so dangerous you had to bring a gun?"

Milli laughs, "No, Doctor…uh, Jack, no, not dangerous. I'm in Forest Service law enforcement, a special agent. We have to carry our firearm at all times. Just part of the job."

Jack laughs, "Okay, I'll stop thinking about diving for cover."

Milli smiles back at him, "Do you have time for me this morning? I really came on a personal matter. I'm hoping you can help me out."

Jack looks puzzled, "Please come in. I have no idea how I can help, but I'm willing to try."

Jack leads her into his study overlooking the ranching valley below. She notes his careful walk and stiff posture, "Jack, are you hurt?"

"No, Milli. First too much football in high school and at Texas A&M. Kinda totaled my knees. And then some back trouble over the years, mostly from a helicopter crash. You know, one of those "good" crashes you walk away from. I've got some fancy nuts and bolts holding my spine together."

He grins impishly, "You know, old Forest Service Chiefs and college professors like me never die. We just crumble into little bits one day and get swept out by the cleaning staff."

Jack gestures to a photo on his desk, "That's my wife Kathy. She's off quilting this morning. But, she should be home for lunch. I hope you'll still be here. She's sure to like you. You look a bit like her daughter, Erin."

His eyes twinkle, the love for his Kathy and Erin coming through, "But until then, how can I help you?"

"Well, Jack, I'm not sure. But you and my mother met a long time ago, a year or so before I was born. And this sounds weird, but

246

what you told my mother changed her life, led to me being born, and a whole buncha other things, good and bad, happening."

He looks shocked, "I did all that?"

She grins and looks at him curiously, "Can you keep secrets?"

Jack nods his large, white-fringed head, "I had to get a Top Secret clearance when I became Chief, so someone must have thought I could. Unless something you tell me that threatens national security, I'm pretty sure I can keep my mouth shut."

Milli frowns, "Maybe some of this does. I don't know. But please hear me out…."

Jack settles back in his armchair. He loves a good story…likes to tell them, too. And he senses he's about to hear an interesting one, although one he may not be able to repeat.

An hour later, Milli finishes her story. She's covered what she knows of her mother's past with W.A., Jacob, her horrifying ordeal with W.A., Milly's rape, Mist. She's talked about the events of the past two years….the green war--death, destruction—her mother's last moments in the fire shelter.

She had planned to talk only about the Forest Service stuff, but Jack's calm presence and thoughtful questions tempted her to talk about her personal bad years. And she has done that, too, along with the recent crisis with Philip.

Her resulting tears caused him to get her water and tissues.

Now Jack bows his arms above his head and stretches carefully, "Milli, yours is one Helluva story. Frankly, although I heard rumors about W.A., those parts of your story are really hard ones to believe. Still, you seem to know what you are talking about."

He looks up at the ceiling and inspects its plaster whorls, thinking back, "I don't remember your mother, sad to say. But I do remember the lectures I was doing back then. I was going around the country trying to get people to understand what some of us had begun to call 'ecosystem management'. The idea was to bring greater harmony between people and natural resources, to get natural resource managers to think about all resources instead of just a few or one, like trees for timber mills or fish for fishermen."

He leans forward and gestures to her with open hands, "I wanted people to know that, unless we got our act together, we would lose many of the places and critters that we cared most about. Not because we didn't care…we did…but because we had built all these professional and bureaucratic silos and fiefdoms that didn't talk to one another. And each of those camps had their 'gladiators', people who battled for them in the courtrooms and in public media, confusing everyday people. They just squabbled and fought and, all the while, resources were being lost…not as much here in the U.S. where it was bad, but all around the world where it was much worse. Even while we loved the world, we were neglecting it to death.'

The big man shakes his head sadly, "I told people like your mom that something had to change. But it hasn't, not really. There's been no real progress, since then…since the 1970s. We have the technologies…the science…just not the willpower to use them effectively. Just more conflicting rules and regulations piled on…more confusion about how managers should act…or even if they should act. And, the environmentalists? After winning what you call 'the green war', they've just been going around bayoneting the wounded. Outfits like Mist reflect the most extreme example of that craziness—all their energy going to harm people when people have to be a big part, maybe the only part, of answers to every environmental problem."

Milli looks at him closely, "Well, Jack, what we can we do? Me, I mean. What can I do?"

Jack sits up as straight as his long-injured back will allow, "Well, Milli, it's time we ended the war. Whatever we've been fighting about, it's time we stopped. Maybe we don't know anything anymore but how to fight. So, somehow, some way, we have to learn the ways of peace…and then rethink this ecosystem management thing…really do it. Change the laws. Change how we work together. Do what we call 'adaptive management'; make every action we take an experiment, learning as we go."

Jack shakes his head, "Otherwise, I'm pretty sure all of us humans are going the way of the Dodo Bird and the Passenger Pigeon. It's the Darwinian imperative come home to roost; it's time for the human race to adapt or die, or better, adapt and live."

He holds up a thoughtful index finger and points it at her, "Somebody's has to lead this change. Might as well be you."

Milli starts to reply that there's no chance she could lead such a thing, but Kathy Thomas peeks in at that moment and beams a welcoming smile, "Isn't he just an old wind-bag?"

Before Jack can offer an appropriate retort, Kathy hushes him by asking, "Anybody hungry for lunch?"

Jack replies with gusto, "That'd be me."

He launches himself stiffly out of his easy chair and heads for the kitchen, charging along with a John Wayne gait.

"Did you remember to pick up my apple pie, Kathy?" he calls to his wife's receding back.

Milli faintly hears Kathy's reply, "Lunch first, Jack Thomas, then pie."

"Aw, something's not right about that," he responds fondly.

Chapter 45 - Deeper Reflections

Three days after visiting Jack Ward Thomas, Milli steps off a plane in Cheyenne, Wyoming. She picks up a rental car and heads west on I-80, planning to turn north on US 287 towards the Wind River Reservation. She would make her turn at Rawlins, a good place for a coffee stop because there was pretty much only road between that little town and Lander, hours distant.

After Milli's visit to Jack, she turned her attention to finding Jacob Mountainspring. Milli's initial records search had not turned up a man by that name living on or near the Wind River Reservation, but that might not mean he wasn't there. Many people on the res live without phones and routinely house with friends and relatives, so ordinary ways of finding them don't necessarily work.

When Milli phoned the tribal offices, a man named Jacob Mountainspring had shown up on the rolls.

But the tribes wouldn't release age or contact information, even to federal law enforcement, without a warrant. Milli couldn't get a warrant.

And what information the office had wasn't necessarily even current.

But, even more to the point, the enrolled Jacob might not be her father at all.

Milli thought res size might be a search challenge, too. Although the numbers of Arapaho and Shoshone living on or near the res numbered under ten thousand, the reservation itself was huge, over three and half million acres, an area about the size of Connecticut. Big, empty country and her biological father might be anywhere within or near it, not in the area at all, or altogether dead and gone.

After working through these frustrations, Milli had decided a visit to Wyoming would be the only effective way to find her father, if he could be found at all.

She leaves the rental car parking lot and zips onto I-80. Milli has driven through Wyoming before—a beautiful, empty state where locals measure road distances in how long it takes to drink six-packs of beer. Motoring upcountry west of Cheyenne, towards Telephone Pass and the big Lincoln head, she looks forward to the fabulous open vistas and critters on the plains beyond Laramie.

Even with all that beauty waiting for her, she doesn't relish the day's drive it will take her to get to Riverton and her motel for the night.

The gas station clerk at the Sinclair station in Rawlins flirts outrageously with Milli as she pays for her gas, some snacks, and a quart of coffee in a Styrofoam-insulated mug.

Something about the wide, empty landscapes to the east of Rawlins had reminded Milli that she would sleep in a lonely bed again tonight and that a passionate companion wouldn't be a bad alternative to a night alone.

Regardless of that thought, she has no intention to bed the cute cowboy in front of her. But she dimples at him as he hands her change.

"You hanging' around here, lil' darlin'?"

"Nope, I'm headin' up to Riverton to spend the night, then driving over to Fort Washakie. Don't know after that."

"I'd be ready to quit my job to come along, if you was interested."

Milli raises her left hand and displays the wedding set on her finger, "My husband might object. Sorry, cowboy. I know it'd be fun."

She turns and walks towards the door. Looking back, she sees him scoping out her rear. She dimples at him again and waggles a finger at his face, "You can look but you can't touch."

He laughs and waves goodbye, a pretend pout on his lips. She wonders how many times a day he used those lines and how often he got lucky as a result.

Milli heads out on US 287, possibly the least-known and most picturesque road in Wyoming. A few miles out, the Rawlins traffic disappears and Milli is almost alone in the wide-open spaces.

An occasional southbound pickup truck passes. The drivers wave. Some smile.

What an amazing place. Even complete strangers are friendly.

She reaches Muddy Gap and turns northwest, scooting along between the Green Mountains to the south and the Granite Mountains to the north. She notes that the Green Mountains aren't green and that the Granite Mountains don't seem so mountain-like.

But whatever trapper or pioneer named them so long ago probably had good reasons. They also had lots more time to contemplate their choices as they walked along at 3 miles per hour along as versus Milli who now motors at 75.

Two hours out of Rawlins, Mill reaches Lander, a small ranching community resting in the rain shadow of the Wind River Range. Tiny and isolated, the community enjoys some of the best weather in Wyoming, less-windy, warmer, and drier than most, yet still well

252

supplied with water from the snow pack on the Winds. Milli knows from some of her Forest Service friends who grew up there that the locals try not to advertise how nice the area is to live in.

Lander is the county seat for Fremont County.

Milli reaches the edge of town, and she passes the county sheriff's office. As she sees the sheriff's sign, that knowing chill surges up her neck once again. There's something about this place....

Then her bladder yells "full" and tells her that it would like her to have a chat with local law enforcement.

As she makes a u-turn, she smiles. Neck chill or not, at a minimum she can pee and refill her huge mug from the sheriff's pot, which inevitably will contain the worst coffee within fifty miles.

The friendly receptionist in a brown and tan western-cut uniform points to the ladies bathroom. Milli heads there on quick feet. When she returns to the reception area a few minutes later, she offers her badge and the woman says, "Okay, Special Agent Meacham, what can we do for you?"

"I'm looking for a local man, name of Jacob Mountainspring. I wonder if you can help me find him?"

"I'm not familiar with that name, but Sheriff Jeffers might be."

"Is he in?"

"No, but I can raise him on the radio. There was a wreck down by Atlantic City and he's there with Deputy Childers, handling the scene and traffic."

"Think I could go see him there?"

"No, that's half hour away at best. Let me try the radio."

The woman goes to the radio and calls. It turns out Sheriff Jeffers is almost back to Lander, his obligations down near the old mining town over. He tells the receptionist to have Milli sit tight until he can get there in "ten minutes maybe."

Seven minutes later, an average-sized man strides through the door. Lean, large-knuckled, and brown-skinned, he's in western dress with a handsome beige Stetson hat on his head. The only sign that he's the sheriff is the gold badge clipped to the holster on his hand-tooled leather belt, a Beretta Model 92 resting stiffly in it.

He sees Milli and strides up, "You Meacham?"

When she nods, he snaps, "Jeffers. I'm sheriff here. C'mon in my office."

He leads the way through a secure swing-gate in the counter and then towards a corner office. Over his shoulder he asks, "Need anything? Coffee? Water?"

Milli motions with her giant coffee mug, "Yeah, I'd like to fill this cattle trough."

He grunts amusement and points, "Back there. Break room. On the left."

He turns into his office and tosses his hat towards the hat rack in the corner. It misses and rolls back towards his desk. Milli hears him mutter, "Damn," as he stoops over, picks it up, and dusts it off.

Milli fills up her giant mug and walks back to Jeffers' office. He looks up from a pile of reports on his desk, waves her in, and points to a chair, "Sit."

After she does, he asks "Watcha after?

"I'm looking for a man named Jacob Mountainspring, last known to be returning to the Wind River Reservation almost thirty years ago. Native American. Probably in his fifties, average height or taller, college education in Colorado."

"Warrant?"

"No, I just want to talk to him."

"'Person 'a interest', huh?"

"That would be right."

Jeffers studies her intently. His face tightens, "I'm not big on Forest Service, especially the law enforcement. And I can't see how a federale like you would come way out here for a 'person 'a interest'."

"It's not federal. It's personal. I believe Mountainspring might be my biological father."

The man nods grimly, "Run off did he? When you were a kid?"

"No, as far as I know, he never knew I was even born."

"Why you want to find him now? Lookin' for revenge? Money? Get enrolled in the tribe?"

Milli blushes and her habitual frown deepens, "No, my Mom asked me to find him in the last minutes before her death."

Jeffers stares at her even more intently, "Plenty 'a death bed requests get ignored. Gotta be a reason *you* want to do it."

"Look, Sheriff Jeffers, you hear of the recent federal action at Cutter's Park, Idaho...you know, in the last two weeks?"

"Yeah, I heard. Buncha eco-terrorists fought the federales. Federales almost lost until the military came in and shot the woods to pieces. Big fire. That what you're talkin' about?"

254

"Yes, I was there. Lost friends there. I was in the woods when they were shot to pieces." Milli takes a deep breath and, taking a leap of faith says, "Lost my mother there."

"Lost your mother...." Jeffers thinks for a moment, "Guess she wasn't a federale, was she?"

"No, she was batting for the other side. I found her wounded, dying, after the gunship attack."

Milli stares into Jeffers' eyes, "I haven't told anyone else."

"Haven't told the Fibbies or your bosses?"

"No, it didn't matter to anyone but me. As far as everyone else is concerned, she's just another Mist casualty. No name...no identity. Just dead."

"Why you tellin' me this? Hopin' for my sympathy or somethin'?"

"No, I'm just trying to show you how important finding Mountainspring is to me. I just told you something that could ruin my career...that I have suppressed evidence in a major federal case."

She looks Jeffers straight in the eye, "I'm leveling with you, taking a big risk. How about doing the same for me?"

Jeffers considers her words. His face reveals nothing.

"What was your mother's name?"

"Rebecca...Rebecca Theophile Meacham."

He writes the name down.

After several more moments of thought, he reaches out his hand, "Show me your ID."

Milli gives it to him. He writes her name and numbers down, too.

"Okay, Special Agent, you're real law. Where you plannin' to stay the night?"

"A motel up in Riverton."

"Cancel. Stay with my wife and me. A small spread over in the foothills. Good water...little guest cabin."

Milli doesn't want to offend the man so she says mildly, "That's really generous, Sheriff Jeffers, but I couldn't impose on you and your wife."

"You can. You should. I'm half Arapaho. Born within a hunnert miles 'a here. Got my criminal justice degree at Laramie. Worked law enforcement on the res. You stay with me and Alice for a night, two maybe. I'll get this Jacob Mountainspring run down for you. I'm your best bet, Millicent. Take it or leave it."

Milli dimples at him, "Call me 'Milli' please, Sheriff Jeffers."

"I'd be 'Two Eagles' but, if that doesn't come off your tongue well, call me 'Jeff'."

"Okay, Two Eagles, I guess you got yourself a guest."

The man smiles for the first time, the corners of his mouth going down and the skin around his eyes crinkling deeply, "Why don't you walk around town, Milli? Meet back here at 5, and then head out?"

Milli looks at her watch. 2:50. Hmmm. Two hours wait. Well, she could figure out something to fill that time, maybe check for Mountainspring in the records over at the courthouse or at the Fremont County Pioneer Museum.

"Sounds good to me."

Chapter 46 - Mountain Spring

At 5:20, Two Eagles' pickup rattles over the second cattle guard on his property.

Milli has been holding back a hundred yards or so to avoid the thick dust trail his tires kick up. Because of the roiling dust, she has had no trouble following him.

She watches now as he curves left, travelling uphill towards a tall knoll where she can glimpse dark-green metal roofs and red-stained cedar walls among a grove of trees.

Two Eagle's truck disappears into the trees. Milli steers in the same direction. Moments later, she arrives in a gravel parking lot that separates the Jeffers' house from their barn. Scattered over a nearby acre are several smaller buildings and a large corral. A dozen or so mixed-breed cattle pace around the corral, momentarily interrupted by her arrival from eating at the chow bins near the corral's gate. Milli parks next to a solid-looking livestock-loading ramp and gets out.

Two Eagles, a small woman, and a taller man are waiting for her on the broad, roofed porch that surrounds the house on three sides.

Jeffers waves her up.

As she walks up the stairs to the porch, her eyes are drawn to the Wind River Mountains off to the northwest. The view is incredible. Tan-brown plains rise from below the Jeffers' knoll to steep, tree-dotted foothills, and, off in the distance, intensely green mountainsides lift up to a few snow-capped peaks. The air is crystal clear. Milli has no idea how far away the snow fields lay but guesses at least twenty miles, probably more.

She reaches her hosts.

Two Eagles points to the woman next to him, "Alice."

Milli notices that the taller man is studying her intently, but she turns first to the woman and offers her hand, "Hi, Alice, I'm Milli Meacham."

The woman takes Milli's hand in both of hers, "I'm so glad to meet you."

Alice gestures to the older, slightly stooped man next to her, "This is my older brother, Jacob Mountainspring. I believe you've been asking about him, dear."

Shocked open-mouthed, Milli can only stare at the man whose face now holds the most amazingly broad grin. Only Jacob's eyes hold a hint of concern.

Then Milli's wonderful, contagious laugh bursts out, four bell notes rising into the clear air.

At the sound, Jacob's concern evaporates. In seconds, all four people are laughing with relief and delight at family found.

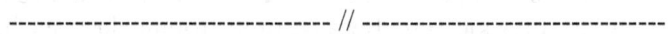

After dinner, Jacob and Milli walk to her cabin. It's well away from the main house, resting on a rock outcrop above a tumbling creek. From the chairs on the front porch, the wonderful view of the Wind River Range is mostly hidden by a dense Lodgepole Pine forest. The two sit in the chairs and, for many minutes, just let the evening hush settle over them.

After listening to bird calls and the stream's music, Jacob speaks quietly, "Milli, I want to make sure you understand that Jeff just wanted to protect me when he put you off at his office. He can be brusque when he thinks something's not right. It's the cop in him."

"No, Jacob, I had no problem with the way he treated me. He was courteous enough. Just wouldn't tell me anything."

"He wanted to talk to Alice, and then to me, first. We were all so excited, but I wasn't sure you were…ah…mine until I saw you. And of course, Alice said that not only did you look just like our mother but that she had also known you were coming for the last couple of weeks. Just didn't know when you would arrive. And of course, I had to drive down from Etete, so that took some time. I almost didn't get here before you did."

"Ah, Jacob…that part about Alice knowing I was coming. She talked about that quite a bit at dinner. I wasn't really sure…you know...about how much to believe her. Sounded kinda magical."

"It's a tradition in the family. The women say they have this gift…feelings I guess…about the future, about the importance of things or events, and about family. They can't predict when the gift will assert itself, but once it does, they're adamant about what they know."

He grins, "We men make fun of 'em. That's also part of the tradition. To get 'em fussing at us is the best part. Still, those hunches turn out to be true so often, we men listen closely before teasing the women."

Milli thinks back to the many chills that have run up her neck when something otherwise unimportant suddenly affected her, suddenly caught her attention for an unknown reason. And the many times those things had turned out to be far more important than she ever thought they would be. Just like turning into the Sheriff's Office today.

"I guess I might have the gift, too. I've had these hunches since I was a little girl. Sudden truths that would hit me with nothing to support them. I always just put it down to intuition…lucky guesses."

"Milli, I don't know how Alice's gift works. You should check with her. Sounds like you might have it. She might give you some ideas about how to develop it or understand it better. The gift comes from the spirit. In Arapaho, we might say it, *'noohóó3ei betéé3oo na'*, or 'to see with the help of a spirit or angel'. It's been a part of our traditions for a long time."

He pauses for a moment and then says regretfully, "Sounds like you had a really bad childhood after Becka left."

Over dinner, Milli had given her new-found relatives a short but clear history of her life, including Rebecca's being driven off by W.A. when she was seven and her rape at his hands when fourteen. With brutal honesty, she had covered her addictions as a young fisheries biologist in Alaska, her lesbian relationship with Tilly Corcoran in Oregon after she became a LEO, and her now-troubled relationship with Philip.

The three Wyomingites were warmly supportive. They had dealt with similar things among their extended families and offered kind sympathy and encouragement. And now, Jacob wanted to discuss his past in more depth.

"I never knew Becka was pregnant. I would have come right away. Alice kept saying I should find her, but she never told me a reason, so I never did. I didn't want to make trouble for your mom…and I never thought she would want a life with me, especially here."

"Jacob…ah, Dad…she loved you. Mom thought W.A. might have killed you out of jealousy. She never wanted to know for sure. She couldn't bear the thought of it happening. I figure if she had known you were really dead, she would have had nothing to hope for, to cling to for comfort. And I bet that among the many reasons she had for joining Mist and attacking the Forest Service was the possibility that you'd been killed or hurt by her husband."

Jacob mutters, "Revenge…."

"Yes, exactly. Revenge against W.A. for hurting you, for hurting her, and for driving her away from me. And that all got wrapped up with her passion for caring for the planet, for protecting Mother Earth."

Milli starts to cry quietly, "Her poor body...so damaged. She had me bury her with her skin against the soil. So that she would be back with her 'Earth Mother' as soon as possible."

"That would not be the Arapaho way...at least not traditionally. We would elevate the body up on a platform, and allow natural decomposition to occur in contact with the air, the sky. Of course, now most Arapaho bury their dead in European ways...cremation, underground. But I can understand Becka's intention. To get back into the sacredness of the ground as soon as possible."

"You are beginning to sound like my husband, Philip. He talks about the earth being sacred."

"Yes, he would know as a pastor. American Indian and Christian beliefs overlap in some ways. Belief in a Creator and that the creation is sacred. Belief that there are helping spirits and harming ones. There are many differences, too. Christianity doesn't hold that inanimate objects and animals have souls. Many Native American religions say they do. And some Indian religions say that one species can turn into another...fish into humans, humans into fish...and Christianity rejects that belief."

"So, Dad, what do you believe?"

"Well, I have been Christian my whole life. But I also accept the wisdom of the old ways. For people living close to the waters--people everywhere for that matter--fish aren't just food. Fish are the basis for life itself, a gift from the Creator. The old thought was that this connection is so intense, so close, the species could move back and forth, take each other's form and live with one another."

He shakes his head and laughs gently at himself, "Wouldn't that be something? I'd take off for a year, travel around on my own, chasing girls or something. When I got home, I'd tell Alice I'd been living with the fish people. And then, my sister would swat me with her broom like she used to do when we were kids."

Father and daughter laugh. Milli had sensed Alice's feistiness and has no doubt that she'd put a broom to her brother's backside, no matter what his age or dignity.

Her father continues, "But those were the old ways of understanding. For me, now, it's that when the fish die, we eat them, and they become part of us. We die, go back to the soil and water, and then the nutrients from our bodies nurture the plants and insects the fish eat and we become part of them. So, in the Creator's ageless truth, our species do indeed migrate back and forth, and become a part of each other's families and clans. It is a great truth that's hard to grasp in the span of a single human's life. But the old ones did understand this and, in their own ways, tried to explain it."

"Goodness, Dad, you and Philip would certainly agree about all this."

Jacob grins broadly again, "I look forward to meeting him someday."

Milli frowns, "I hope you will, Dad. I hope you will."

She sighs, and then continues, "My heart has really been searching for an answer to the war we've just been through, Mist against society and the Forest Service. Them killing us. Us killing them. I just can't seem to get what went wrong, and more importantly, what we can do about it…do to stop it from happening again."

"Milli, that's a lot of weight for so young a heart," he chuckles affectionately, "I have a few thoughts that might help you even if I have no great wisdom to offer."

He puts his hand on her arm and squeezes, "The Great Law of the Iroquois Nation called for decisions to be thought about in terms of their possible impact seven human generations in the future. The Arapaho people had similar thoughts…always working in the present for our young people and for those Arapaho yet unborn. This is a good thing…the long-term view, I mean. I think you Forest Service people do this in your environmental impacts statements and forest plans and all that."

"We do. Fifty years for forest plans at least."

"Well, the Iroquois people were trying to look ahead at least two hundred years, possibly more. So, a very long time. And if you don't think that far ahead, the old wisdom would say, you might disrupt the connections, both physical and spiritual, between a person and the rest of Creation, including other people."

"So, does that mean you can't act…can't use resources?"

"No, both European and Native Americans found that the Creator gave us the choice to nurture Creation…to live with it…or destroy it…use it up. And human experience says we can even change the Created web of life significantly, but not necessarily destroy it."

"I think that's pretty much what the laws require the Forest Service and other land managers to do. So, I don't understand why we had this war, this horrible loss."

Jacob looks very sad, "I only watched this conflict from my little corner of Wyoming. So I don't know much about it. We aren't very close to the Forest Service on the res. But, here's my view of what might have happened."

Jacob leans way back in his chair and points off towards the far mountains, now almost invisible in the dusk, "Americans have moved to the cities, and left mountains like those behind...left the wild places and wild animals. And as they settled in the cities, they lost their spiritual connections to the land and waters. Treated water from a faucet, not pure from a stream. Cold meat from a supermarket, not from an animal's warm body. Boxed vegetables from a road-side stand, not grown by a person's hand on their own land."

"People no longer understand that these things come from intimate relationships between people and the rest of Creation, some very sturdy links and some very fragile. No, today, people think they are entitled to clean water and air, to abundant food, because they have money or ownership...or just because they are alive."

"And so most of them no longer care, not really, about the Creation, about its deep spiritual connections to people, about the responsibilities the Creator gave people to tend to the Creation. They think they can abandon their ancient connections, do nothing, and the Creation will just move along unchanged, or even improved, without them."

Milli nods, "You sure see that in people who come to visit the national forests. Many are more concerned about where the toilets are and how trails are maintained than in the condition of the fisheries or woods."

Jacob agrees sadly, "Yes, we have that on the res, too. Poaching. Waste. And people want their creature comforts. But, I don't think the war you fought came directly from human carelessness or desires for comfort. No one wants to go back to hunting every day for meat or living in longhouses and teepees at forty below. No refrigerators to preserve food during hot weather. Hey, I like my hot showers!"

Father and daughter laugh.

Jacob's voice turns sad, "No, it's not technology or the hope for comfort. I think people just don't care about staying connected anymore."

Milli shakes her head, "Yeah, look at how wildfires are ripping up the west...well, really everywhere now. We suppressed them for so long. Smokey Bear and all that. And now, an endless succession of court decisions and new regulations keep us from putting the forests and grasslands back in their regular fire cycles, to benefit the critters and the waters. No one seems to care. We get plenty of money to fight wildfires from Congress…but little or none to restore normal ecological functions. Is it…what would you and Philip say…killing Creation?"

Jacob laughs grimly, "No, daughter, our spiritual break is not killing Creation. People don't have the power to do that. Only the Creator can end Creation. No, our spiritual break from nature is getting ready to kill *us*, the people part of Creation. Once we're done killing ourselves off, or reducing our numbers to unimportant misery, the Creation will go on without us."

Jacob's voice becomes stronger, his tone more vehement, "*This* is the choice the Creator gave us. Be bad stewards and *die*. Be good stewards…excellent stewards…and *live*. The Creator made this *our* choice, and our *only* one."

"A man I talked to only a few days ago, a great scientist named Jack Thomas, said almost the same thing. If you are both right, then the Creator…or God I guess…help us because I don't see how we can choose differently. I don't think prayer will help with the politics."

"Yes, Milli, this is definitely a place for prayer. I do pray about it. If nothing else, prayer changes the person doing the praying. And that would be a great beginning…each prayerful person changing, reconnecting to the Creation."

Jacob sits quietly for nearly a minute, and then continues, "And really, the Creator has sent the words to us, to all the peoples of the world in our different ways, to get this done. If we listen to those words, pray for the understandings that fit with our times…not necessarily those of the ancient Hebrew or Arapaho tribes…and then align science and resource management to them, we will be just fine. Pray, hold to the ideas that come, and the Creator will bless your work…."

Milli's face flushes and she thinks furiously, "Prayer! Pray to the Creator? Bless my work? What the Hell! Where was this Creator when W.A. was raping me? When Mist killed Bill, Jake, and Manny? Is this some kind of joke?"

Milli looks off into the distance…anger, rebellion, and anxiety building rapidly within her. She *couldn't* do this prayer thing. No one could make her. Her whole life had taught her that she alone had to fix things, fix herself, and now fix the green war. It would be *her* work, not some mythical Creator.

But then, as her vision gets cloudier and her breath comes quicker and quicker, a wash of reality overcomes her. She can't end the green war alone. She couldn't even keep her relationships on track…Philip…W.A…her Mom.

Crap! All the other stuff she'd tried had more or less failed. She *has* to have help…*has* to try something different.

Philip and now Jacob are telling her that she can have someone with real power on her side. Why not the Creator? The Creator's influence could do no harm and might do great good.

An intuition strides boldly into her mind. She remembers Philip's words and now her father's. Her role, like everyone else's, is to care for Creation. Surely, the Creator would back her in this!

Like a balloon popping, her rebellion vanishes. In seconds, her vision clears and her breath stops whistling through her nose.

Milli says in a small voice, "Dad, I don't know how to pray."

She sees her father's face crease in a gentle smile, "It's easy. You start with the word 'God" or 'Creator' and then just empty the contents of your heart…thanks…grief…joy…and then ask for what you want…trust that the Creator will deliver it in some Creative way."

Milli asks, "Can we do that now? Will you show me?"

"Sure. And remember, you have a husband who goes about these things far better than I do."

"I'm not sure of that. I was sure once, but not so much now."

Her voice catches, "And I ignored that part of him back then."

"Okay, that'd be something else to tell the Creator, I guess."

He takes her hands and folds them together with his, "Here, I'll start and then you can join in."

He looks up at the mountains and then down to their folded hands, "Creator God, my daughter and I are here together for the first time, talking to you. What a blessing our being together is. We love you and your Creation. We are humble people and don't know what to do, so hear us now…."

As Jacob continues his prayer, tears run down Milli's face.

She doesn't know why…something about coming home…her father's hands on hers…connection. She doesn't care.

She just lets the tears flow from her body back into Creation.

She remembers the dark raindrops hitting the ash piles near her Mother's grave--star-stuff tears flowing back to the Mother, her mother.

Milli cries harder.

And when the time comes for Milli to speak, she lets the contents of her heart flow, too…into the ears of the Creator.

Harm…and healing…flow out of her.

264

Chapter 47 - Baby Steps Along Redemption's Path

A month after saying goodbye to Jacob and her new-found family members, Milli Meacham walks briskly into the Los Angeles Federal Court House.

Sixteen members of the "Green River Mafia", as they got named by the media, are due to be sentenced today. Milli wants to be present.

Most of the other Green Rivers have accepted plea agreements and are serving time. Two members are working their way through the federal courts on their own. A few members, those with little involvement, got fired from the federal government and paid restitution administratively.

Outside the courtroom, Milli sees Avery Scarrs and Fred Pomolo. She knows Scarrs has recently retired and is surprised to see both Avery and Fred here.

Scarrs waves her over to the large group he's with, "Mill, I wanted to introduce you to these folks. These are most of the 'Mountain Toppers', members of my Journey. This was the bunch that pulled all that God-awful paperwork together for us to analyze."

Milli shakes Scarrs' hand, "Avery, I go by 'Milli' these days, two 'els' and two "eyes', no 'ees'. 'Milli' fits me better than just plain Mill. I'm not just grindin' my way through life anymore."

Scarrs laughs.

She looks around the rest of the group, "Nice to see you folks in person. You Mountain Toppers got the goods on the Green River Mafia."

Scarrs responds, "And you delivered them to justice. Great teamwork!"

Milli laughs, "You bet. You, me, Fred, and a host of federal law enforcement people. Damn lucky we got them all."

Fred Pomolo speaks up, "Nice to see you again, too, Mill...ah, Milli. I like your new nickname. In addition to your name, I heard you changed jobs, too. That you're not in law enforcement anymore. Why don't you tell these folks what you're doing? It might interest this bunch 'a grey heads."

A Mountain Topper woman, one who looks like she runs marathons and obviously dyes her grey hair blond, jabs Pomolo's shoulder, "Watch it, Fred. We're not dead yet."

He rubs it and says ruefully, "I stand corrected. The Mountain Top Floppers are all young, sexy, doing really well, and they don't want to know what you're doing now." The group laughs.

Milli blushes a little before speaking, "Well, I'm still officially in law enforcement, but I've taken unpaid leave…two years worth…to work on what people are starting to call 'ending the green war', the whole gridlocked conflict over the environment and public lands here in the U.S. My parents left me some resources and I can afford to take some time off without pay. Anyway, it turns out a whole lot of people want to end the green war. And we're trying to figure out how. I hope you Mountain Toppers will give us your ideas, or if you have some time, help us organize."

Avery says, "Absolutely. Count me in." Several others murmur their interest, too.

One of the older men, still straight-backed but leaning on a cane, asks, "So, does this mean walking away from the Forest Service traditions? You know, long hours, hard work, caring for people and resources. Time was we were able to take quick action in the face of threats, wildfire or whatever. Local managers helped local people. And we followed the direction, what's the Pinchot quote, to provide for 'the greatest good of the greatest number in the long run' or something like that? But now, everything's stuck in court or some Goddamn bureaucratic hole."

Milli smiles and says emphatically, "We want to embrace those traditions and values again, not walk away from them. And add back conditions where old agency virtues like honesty and truthfulness can flourish and get us back on track to figuring out 'the greatest good.'"

The man says, "I vote for that."

Two members of the group start to ask Milli more questions. But, before they can do more than open their mouths, a bailiff comes out of the open courtroom and begins to close the doors. Milli, Pomolo, and the Mountain Toppers move as quickly as they can into the gallery and take their seats.

The court convenes. After a few minutes of procedural matters, the Green Rivers file in, manacled and dressed in orange jumpsuits. They sit before the judge's bench with their attorneys seated behind them. As each name gets called, the Green River and his or her attorney rise, walk to the dock, and stand, waiting to have sentence imposed.

Milli sees Thyra Dexter. She's next to last in the sentencing order. Milli had heard Thyra had accepted a plea deal with lots of years

266

cut off for cooperating. But then, perversely defiant because she hadn't received immunity, the woman backed out.

Dexter clearly had no good sense. She had set herself up to get the same sentence as the rest of them were getting.

Milli listens as each Green River receives, in turn, a sentence of from six to twenty years. The judge also imposes various fines and repayment terms on them, depending on the nature and extent of that particular Green River's thefts and embezzlements.

After sentencing, each is asked if they have any testimony for the court. Most of them apologize, some with apparent sincerity, and others, it seems from their tone, so the apology will be on their record for reference at future parole hearings.

After each one testifies, the judge names their first prison destination and remands them to the custody of the federal prison system. Federal Marshals lead them away.

Thyra begins to sob when her sentence is read. When asked if she wants to testify, she simply cries and hangs her head, tears dripping. Feeling pity for the little fool as she stumbles off, Milli thinks, "First Frieda and now this."

The judge reaches the final prisoner, "John Brinksman, please rise."

A tallish, handsome man Milli has never seen before struggles to untangle his feet from his chains. His attorney reaches out and steadies him, and finally the man lurches awkwardly upward.

Clearly agitated, Brinksman angrily shrugs the attorney's hand away and faces the judge. The judge reads the sentence and then asks, "Mr. Brinksman, do you have anything to say to this court?"

Brinksman answers slowly and with great vehemence, "Yes, Sludge, I do. My sentence makes a crockery of American legal sedition. This country was founded on a Rill of Bites which guarantees fair defecation for all people...."

First incredulous at Brinksman's words, Milli, the Mountain Toppers, and everyone else in the gallery are silent, and then they collapse with laughter. The judge sternly gavels them silent, and then looks malevolently down on Brinksman.

"Mr. Brinksman, I hereby sentence you to an additional year in federal custody for contempt of this honorable court..."

"But, Sludge...."

"That's two years, Brinksman. Care to say more?"

"No, your Honor, I…I respect this court, but…but, I can't accept your drooling on my anal situation…."

"And, three! Bailiffs, get him out of here before Mr. Brinksman gets life in prison for malicious potty mouth."

Giggling loudly and hoping to avoid the judge's ire, Milli hurries out into the hall to finish laughing.

Chapter 48 - Pathways

A month after Brinksman and his bunch are sent up the river, Milli stretches comfortably in a bubbling spa in her room at a resort near Loveland, Colorado.

Tomorrow she expects Philip, Jack Ward and Kathy Thomas, and Jacob Mountainspring to join her at the remote location. She is bringing the three men together for a discussion about how to end the conflicts that led to so many deaths at Cutter's Park. Kathy's coming along just to have fun.

Tonight, Milli just wants to relax.

Above her, the steam drifts up to touch the white plastered ceiling of her large bathroom and rolls along its cedar-log walls. She bobs in the bubble-filled water and looks out through the doorway into the bedroom beyond. She admires the rough textures of its rustic, peeled-log furniture, elk-patterned bed clothes, and its wrought-iron lighting fixtures. Altogether too cozy.

For now, she has the room and the spa all to herself.

Tomorrow, Philip will arrive. She frowns. She has assigned him to a separate room. But even with that distance between them, his presence will mean troubling distractions for both of them.

Philip has just completed his second try at rehab and the couple has been living apart. Getting together this way and in this place, she and Philip will be so needy of one another.

And yet, of course, no matter how she tries to connect with him, she will be wary of Philip...of his broken promises to clean up...and be emotionally flattened by the foreboding that he plans to leave her...leave with her money...her honor.

She lowers her head under the water...feels the heat on her face, in her ears. Oh, damn. The Milli-can't-trust-Philip list may be way too long to process and still allow the three-day, working weekend to bear fruit.

"Come on, Milli," she bubbles into the water, "suck it up. Let go of Philip. Let him follow his own path, up or down. You follow yours. Trust Creator."

She shakes her head under the water, making her hair toss, slow-mo, against her face. She reflects that the "follow your own path" advice is far easier said than done.

The love of her life...the most spiritual man she knows...a fuckin' drug addict, unreliable...maybe even a little dangerous. She needs Philip now more than ever. But her best friend and husband is further away from her than at any other time in their lives.

How bad is that?

-------------------------------- // --------------------------------

By happy coincidence, at about 10 a.m. the next day the three men and Kathy Thomas arrive on the same shuttle from Denver International Airport.

Kathy gives Milli a hug and says, "Thanks for making this happen. Jack is happier than I've seen him in a long time." They chat for a few moments.

After Philip steps awkwardly out of the van's back seat, he stands waiting for the two women to stop talking. When they do, he walks eagerly to Milli, puts his arms around her, and kisses her.

The kiss proves joyless on Milli's part. Philip can sense stiffness in her body and lips. He starts to ask her a question, but she covers his mouth with one hand and says, "Later."

Philip grimaces his agreement. He has much to atone for and knows it. An easy reconciliation was too much to hope for.

Mill has their luggage taken to their rooms. Kathy goes off with her pastels and sketch book to capture some surrounding mountain sights. She is hopeful of some dramatic cloud and sunset scenes later in the day. Maybe a few good Rocky Mountain elk sightings.

Milli leads the men upstairs and ushers them into her executive suite with its four big armchairs and a sideboard stocked with fruit, coffee, pastries, and water. She will have lunch brought in today.

Kathy has offered to work on meal arrangements for tonight and their remaining days together. Milli is grateful for her help in eliminating that pesky distraction.

After everyone fills small plates and cups or glasses, Milli seats them in the armchairs and then walks to the curtained wall facing them. She grabs the curtain and pulls it back, exposing a huge window.

Philip murmurs, "Wow!" Each man has a fabulous view of the Colorado Rockies, the light and dark greens of nearby forests giving way to sharp grey granite peaks and snow fields beyond. Milli had asked for this room with the view in mind, thinking the scene would continuously remind them of what they came to discuss.

She smiles at the men, her dimples showing, "Yup, it's a great view. I never thought you three would be willing to travel all this way to

270

work on such a tough topic. I can't really express how thankful I am that you've come. Did you get to know each other in the van?"

Jack grins at her quizzically, "Yes, Milli, we did. We're quite a mixed-up bunch, aren't we? An Arapaho father you never knew about until a couple of months ago. A retired Forest Service Chief and college professor...ditto on your knowing me. And your wandering ex-pastor husband who confessed to us on the shuttle that he's just out of rehab for drug abuse. I don't know what we can do for you, but at least we'll get to enjoy each other's company in such a beautiful place."

Milli glances sharply at Philip. She had not expected him to be so forthcoming with the other two men. She notices that Jacob has reached over to Philip and is gripping his arm supportively. Philip's honesty with strangers and the obvious warmth between the two men-- good signs.

She smiles thanks to Jack for getting them started. She points to an audio recorder and three mikes on the solid-looking table in front of them, "With your permission, I want to record what we talk about. That okay?"

The men nod their agreement

"Okay, gentlemen, here's the question for the next couple of days. What can we do to fix this crushing environmental war that's been going on for the last century or so? To start, let me tell you guys what I think I learned from you.

"Jack, you think of our needs in terms of how to apply science to management, and you strongly believe laws, regulations, and working relationships need to change."

"Dad, you feel we must re-connect people back with the land and resources...re-forge traditional physical and spiritual connections."

"And Philip, you see that we need to reinvent our approach to Christianity, and maybe some other religious traditions, to give Creation its due...reinforce its sacredness. That about right?"

The three men nod again.

Milli reaches over to turn on the recorder, "Well then, let's get started...."

-------------------------------- // --------------------------------

Two months after the Loveland meeting, Milli sits with a group of thirty or so Forest Service retirees and top-echelon Legacies. Two hours of bitter conversations have led to the usual impasse over questions of how the Forest Service should change to retake its place at the head of conservation leadership in America and how to end the green conflicts.

About half the group simply wants the past to return.

And the other half doesn't care where the organization goes as long as they can retain their personal power to influence personnel choices and national politics.

The mood in the room is grumpy and mean-spirited.

Frustrated by their wrangling, Milli stands and looks around the group, "I'm fourth-generation Forest Service, great-granddaughter of a Firster. My father died in office as Chief, killed by Mist. I've been beaten up, wounded, and almost killed in the green war. I'm not leaving here today until we all agree that some things have to change and with at least some ideas how those changes can happen."

She holds up a few sheets of paper, "I've given you my best ideas about how to heal this horrible mess…at least part way. And I'm telling you that, with or without you, I plan to move ahead with what you read here. You can add to and refine what I'm showing you, or you can walk away and contribute nothing. So, you can either be a part of the fix, or you can be a part of the problem, but you can't be both."

She stares into the old, privileged, and mostly sour faces around her, "And I will guarantee you that, as I work with retirees and employee groups around the country, I will make sure they know what you choose to do today. They will know whether you decide to help lead the Forest Service into a better future…or to let it die along with the hopes of future generations."

"Okay, folks, what do you want your genuine legacy to be?"

-------------------------------- // --------------------------------

Six months after meeting with the Forest Service retirees, Milli walks into the American Wood Products Producers Association's elegantly finished board room off M Street in Washington, DC. The fine-grained wood walls glow under recessed spots. Leather chairs with the organization's vividly colored logo hand-tooled into the backs range around an oval antique-walnut table the size of a small swimming pool.

The Executive Director, Susan Beech, meets Milli at the door, "Ms. Meacham, I'm so glad you could make it."

She points to several men and woman already seated at the table, "Our Chairman is here, along with representatives from the minerals industry, the power companies, and the grazing groups. The U.S.

Business Council has sent their staff attorney who deals with public lands issues, too. The Farmer's Association can't make it."

"Susan, thanks for pulling these folks together. Would you please see that they get these handouts after we make introductions? I'd do it myself, except that I'm so nervous I might forget."

"Don't worry, Ms. Meacham, they won't bite."

"It's 'Milli', Susan. And I'm worried that they *won't* bite…on my ideas that is, not me. Plenty of people biting on me the last few months."

"Well, we're pretty excited about your proposals. So, I think you'll find most of what's said will be positive. Still, there's a lot of skepticism that any real change can happen. Things are so muddled up now…so bad. There's so much hatred and mistrust."

"Yes, indeed, things are definitely muddled up…."

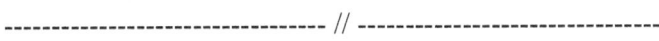

Milli looks out at a room of more than a hundred representatives of environmental groups from around the U.S. A week after the meeting with industry people, she had been invited to this national meeting between environmental activists and their funders, the big foundations and families who bankroll environmental organization all across America and around the world.

The faces before her are almost all lost in the anxious clouds that obscure her vision. Of the dozen or so she can see clearly, two representatives seem interested, two seem angry, and the rest don't seem to care at all.

Milli checks her notes, takes two deep Jesus breaths, mentally asks the Creator for a little help, and begins, "Good morning, my name is Millicent Meacham, thank you for asking me to keynote your conference. I'm not a public speaker, so I ask that you bear with me."

She shifts to her next page and clears her throat. Her cloudy vision is starting to clear. Her heart rate is dropping to normal.

Her voice strengthens, "I won't be here today, except that I need your help…your help to rebuild relationships…the connections of people to land and resources that everyone in this room, including me, care about. If we can't do that…and do it soon…our wild places…our wonderful, beautiful waters…will be degraded or lost. And, we in this room will be guilty of propelling those wonderful places and things into oblivion…."

Chapter 49 - Proposition

Senator Castwell waves a copy of American Life magazine at Mike Reinaud. "Mike, look at this woman. The article says she's Bull Meacham's daughter, leading the charge on some kind of pinko accommodation for eco-freaks. I mean she's talking about 'peace', 'justice', 'end to the green war'."

Castwell shakes his head ironically, "If that's not un-American I don't know what is. Politicians like me can only stay in office if we can exploit some fight people are having. And then there's the American Trial Lawyers Association and the lobbyists. What's this Meacham girl tryin' to do…put those generous boys out of business?"

Reinaud looks thoughtful, "Boss, we have the election coming up in eight months. Our numbers look good right now because we've been attacking the Administration on the Mist-Cutter fiasco. Looks like this Milli Meacham and her bunch could change the debate…maybe knock our numbers sideways."

Castwell stares at Milli's picture, "Damn, Mike, she's good looking, too. Law enforcement, too…got a uniform, gun, and a cop expression on her face…no nonsense like. And look at this caption 'Milli Meacham, straight shooter, the 21st Century's Annie Oakley'. No wonder people are listening to her."

Mike looks over Castwell's shoulder and whistles with appreciation, "I never figured Bull Meacham could throw a prime filly like this. I think we should haul her fancy rear end in here for a good talk. Look it over and see if she'll talk sense."

"Good plan, Mike. Make it happen."

Milli had been surprised when the call came asking for her to visit Senator Castwell in Washington, DC. Because of Castwell's gruff and public criticisms of Mist-Cutter, she thought she might have found an ally in her quest to end the green war. So, she hopped on a plane the next day to go see him.

But now, alone with Castwell in his well-appointed office, and facing one another in cushy leather chairs, Milli realizes that they hold very different views. In fact, the man's tense body radiates a cool hostility towards Milli that she finds quite uncomfortable.

"Okay, Senator, I guess I now understand that you don't like what my coalition is doing, but I'm not sure why. I mean you seem to be very upset with how the FBI and law enforcement handled the battle at Cutter's Park. And don't some of the things you said to the press imply you'd like to see changes made to prevent such conflicts in the future?"

Castwell waves off her question, "Ms. Meacham, nobody can stop crazies from doing crazy stuff. America's always had 'em. We always will. Government's job is to keep 'em from hurting other people. Stop 'em before they start. Punish 'em if they act. Didn't anybody teach you that in high school civics?"

Not fond of being patronized in this or any way, a red-cheeked Milli responds, "Senator, I don't think it's as easy as that. Wouldn't changing the way we deal with green conflicts mean that people could have other choices besides betrayal and violence, be able to work together without that sense that they should win-at-all-costs?"

"Hell, Meacham, I knew your dad. He understood that America is all about winning at all costs. You just make sure you win and the other guy loses. What's the matter with you? Can't you compete? Don't you want to be a winner?"

"Senator, it's not about that. My coalition is not advocating an end to competition, just an end to the social and physical violence of the green war and ways to deal more effectively with what fuels it. My father died because of the green war. Regardless of what he thought before Mist blew him up, don't you think he'd want something different if he was alive today?"

"Never happen, Ms. Meacham...never happen."

Castwell shakes his head, "Look, Ms. Meacham, we're probably never going to agree on this stuff. But, here, I'll make you a deal. You back off on this coalition thing you're doing for at least a year and I'll hold hearings on your ideas. At the end of the year, if you're not satisfied with where my committee and the Congress are going, you can get your gang back in the saddle and ride as hard as you want."

Milli instantly sees the smothering blanket of Castwell's proposal coming at her. All he wants is to get her coalition's efforts out of the headlines and under wraps, buried in senatorial obscurity, never to reemerge.

Time for some counter-diplomacy.

"Senator," Milli dimples, "What a kind offer. I definitely hope you'll hold hearings on our ideas in the future. But for now, I think my group would like to keep developing them with the public. As you pointed out earlier, some of them are still half-baked. We'll bring them to you when they're ready for an important body like the Senate to take a look at them."

Outmaneuvered, at least for the moment, Castwell thinks, "Damn, this woman is *good*. And she's gorgeous. I really would like her in my camp, preferably in my bed."

Turning on the charm, Castwell grins warmly, reaches across, and puts his hand on Milli's leg.

"Ms. Meacham, I could use someone like you working on my campaign, maybe serving as my personal advisor on land management issues and law enforcement. How about we have dinner this evening and we figure out how that could happen?"

"No, Senator, I'm afraid I have to head back home. Lots to do."

Castwell puts on a mock pout, "Well, Ms. Meacham, maybe next time...."

They exchange goodbyes and, after Castwell escorts her to the door, Milli leaves.

As she walks towards the elevators, Milli's back is running with chills.

"Talk about creepy," she mutters to herself, regretting the lingering sensation of Castwell's hand on her bottom, his parting shot.

Chapter 50 - Change Fire

Two years after her meeting with the environmentalists, Milli Meacham steps before a bank of microphones at the Press Club in Washington, DC. When the tumult in the room dies down a little, she turns her face away from the mikes and clears her throat nervously.

She has addressed many groups over the past two years, attended innumerable meetings and briefings, but she has never grown truly comfortable with this part of her work, facing the eager, violating press and their lens' insatiable suck. But now, experience tells her she can rely on the Creator and the hungry media mean comparatively little to her.

Mill squares her shoulders, dimples for the cameras, and begins, "Ladies and Gentlemen of the press, I'm Milli Meacham, President of the National Coalition for Environmental Peace and Justice. Many of you have covered the Coalition's work over the last year, in particular the petition drive which has garnered so much public attention. Today, I am announcing that we have met our petition goal of obtaining signatures at least fifty-one percent of all registered voters in every U.S. Congressional District. In some places, we have more than sixty percent signed up. In a few, the tally is close to eighty percent."

"In the near future, I will deliver copies of these petitions to every Congressman and Senator and to the Administration. And then, as Coalition President, I will call on those parties to quickly pass, and then sign into law, every element stated in the petition."

Milli pauses for a moment, reminding herself to slow down and breathe. Otherwise, she is likely to faint from anxiety again and blow her efforts to smithereens in front of millions of viewers. She takes a deep breath and smiles confidently, "As you know, the Coalition is made up of groups and interests from all over America, from little towns to big cities, from developers to environmentalists, from First Peoples to new citizens, from faith-based groups to atheists, and, most importantly, from those whose lives have been devastated by the long green war, of which I personally am one."

Milli smiles confidently and raises her voice, "We have agreed. There exists no legitimate political philosophy, no approach to an economy, no religion, and no society anywhere in the world that desires to destroy nature and the web of life. As the response to our petition drive shows, Americans understand this. People around the globe understand this. And our endless battles over the environment are literally killing our communities, our societies, our economies, and in some places, nature itself. This has *got* to stop."

"To paraphrase what people said many years ago, we, the petitioners, are fed up with America's green warfare and *we won't take it anymore*. And best of all, ladies and gentlemen, we don't simply have a complaint or demands, we have a plan...and we are acting on it."

"That's all the formal remarks I have today. Questions please?"

"Ralph James from CNN, Ms. Meacham. The most controversial part of your petition is the proposed Constitutional amendment. Do you anticipate that it will actually pass?"

"Yes, I do. The amendment is a simple one. It requires all governments in America to consider the needs and interests of future generations in making decisions. It further specifies that a two-hundred year horizon be used and that methods of analysis and conclusions have to be shared with citizens. We know it won't be easy to follow this direction until the procedural details are worked out by the Executive Branch and the Governors, but we know it can and will be done well. It also requires that, except in times of declared war, fifteen percent of every federal budget be dedicated to environmental and public land protection, enhancement, and management."

"A follow up, please?"

"Sure."

"This idea seems so off-the-wall to many people. Why two hundred years and why tie the hands of Congress by locking up part of the budget?"

"Well, Ralph, two reasons for the length of time. First, for the long-term decision thinking, we have over two hundred years of American social and political history under our Constitution. That history is a precious resource that no other democracy in the world has. We know how certain ideas might work, or might not work, from that history. And that knowledge can serve as a partial basis for projecting what today's decisions might do two hundred years into the future. Technology can help us, too, along with people's good judgment.

"And second, the proposal is based on the thinking of the Iroquois People, one of our proud First Nations that had a thinking-seven-generations-ahead requirement built into *its* constitution. The Iroquois government was successfully operating when Europeans arrived. The Founders learned from the Iroquois, along the older governments of ancient Athens and many other nations and peoples dedicated to democracy. The Founders used what they learned to form

280

our Constitution. So why not return to our roots and add an element our Founders left out--something they probably knew about and respected, but didn't fit with the colonial-expansionist ideas of their time? And even if it didn't suit Americans then, it clearly suits more than fifty-one percent of Americans now. So why not now?"

"As far as the budget element is concerned, it simply assures that adequate funds are aimed at what Americans want. It doesn't tie Congress' hands over how to spend those dollars or how to assign them by agency or program. Next question?"

Hands wave. "Ms. Meacham...Ms. Meacham...."

--------------------------------- // ---------------------------------

Listening Clan Chief Raven addresses the Mist Chief's Council. Her slow, careful words fill the remote Arizona cabin where they've convened.

"As planned, the thugs think...they defeated...ended...Mist at Cutter's Park. And we have stopped our attacks...our controls...on the Forest Service, the BLM...and industries for now. I have...reduced our clan's Eyes and Ears efforts...to make them...almost negligible. Based on...these limited...Listening Clan reports...the thugs, in fact...have stopped...looking for us."

The Council snaps their fingers in applause.

The Money Chief, Golden Eagle, growls, "Damn straight. We beat them again."

Raven holds up her hand for quiet, "Yes, Golden Eagle...we executed the plan. It worked. But then...something unforeseen by us...years ago in Missouri...has happened. People are coming together...for peace...to end what they call...the green war."

"Well, fuck them," Golden Eagle yells, "Who cares? End the green war? They'll talk and talk, but it will come to nothing as it always does. We'll see to that even if the normal political bullshit doesn't just do it for us."

Raven cocks her head, looking almost like her bird namesake, "I am not...so sure...as you. Millicent Meacham...the daughter of the late Chief...is one of the leaders. She and her story...have caught the people's...attention...their respect. A huge...groundswell for change...is building. Our old allies...the mainstream environmental groups...and funders...are switching allegiances. And we...we are out of the picture...and in hiding for several more years. We have to...have to stay underground…or we will surely be…found…and destroyed. As we fade, support for Mist…is disappearing, too."

The newest War Clan Chief, Fire Lance, raises his hand, "Raven, this is grave news. Perhaps it is time for you to make a proposal if you have one. Then we should pass the Talking Stick until we decide what to do."

"Yes, Fire Lance, I have a proposal. I would ask…this Council…to consider one more Strike. I believe we should Strike Millicent Meacham…end her leadership in shame if possible…and halt this so-called…Coalition for Environmental…Peace and Justice…in its tracks. Otherwise when we reawaken Mist…from its present slumber…no one will support us in our…noble cause. Developer slugs will be grinding…the Earth Mother…to pieces…and we will not be able to…oppose them. That…is my proposal. Now, we must talk…and decide."

Fire Lance jumps to his feet and, taking the talking stick, says, "I support Raven in this. Now I pass the stick."

Within an hour, the Council has agreed to Raven's proposal, and by the next day, the Strike Plan is set.

A contract killer is to be used, not an assassin from Mist's depleted ranks.

A high-profile scandal, decided on opportunistically, to go with her death.

And only one Mist contact to bring it off, the Enemies Chief, working outside the Listening Clan, using paid informants close to Meacham.

Yes, it will be high-profile Strike but with every detail neat, compact, and constrained, but, most of all, secret.

The Environmental Peace and Justice Coalition will die with this last Meacham.

And, best of all, Mist will stay fully hidden in shadows.

Chapter 51 - Moments of Truth

Two months after the Mist Council met in Arizona, Milli sits on a rocky outcrop next to the one of the many large creeks feeding the Kootenai River in northern Idaho. She watches Senator Castwell from about ten yards away as he fly-fishes in the center of the stream.

His form is smooth, mesmerizing. His long, colorful float line whips, whips through the air, then settles on the water, only to be reeled in and the whole process begun again.

Castwell yells, "You fly fish, Ms. Meacham?"

"No, Senator, not much. I like fishing a lot. In fact, even though I work in law enforcement now, I'm a fish biologist by training. But I never learned to run a fly pole well enough to catch anything."

"Who says fly fishermen catch anything, Ms. Meacham?"

Milli laughs, "Well, you seem to, Senator. And please if you'd like, call me 'Milli'. That's what I'd prefer."

Castwell gestures with his free hand, "I always accede to a beautiful woman's desires. Okay, Milli, and you can call me 'Senator.'"

He laughs at his own joke, "No, no, please call me 'Charles', but not 'Chuck'. Too easy to add words to 'Chuck', like 'up' and make 'up Chuck'. That kinda stuff plays badly in the press and with the electorate."

They both laugh.

This conversation is not what Milli had expected when she accepted an invitation a week ago to meet with Castwell here. After Milli's creepy meeting with him in DC, Castwell had been brutally hostile to the Coalition's initiative, mocking the language in the petitions and even the petition process itself. He had called it the "worst example of public interest hysteria I have ever seen."

And he's pledged to defeat any Congressional legislation single-handedly even if the other Congressmen didn't see the 'gross injustices' of the proposal and help him vote it down.

Worst of all, now, when Milli's Coalition lobbyists count Congressional noses, they find that they have a clear majority in the House of Representatives. But they are one vote shy of the sixty votes they need to get past a promised filibuster in the Senate.

One vote shy.

And Castwell is Chairman of the Interior and Insular Affairs Committee, which has the Coalition-inspired legislation bottled up.

Castwell controls the Coalition's future…controls the end to the green war.

If Milli can get his thinking changed around, not only would the bill reach the Senate floor, but its passage would be guaranteed.

And now here they are, political opponents bandying pleasantries around like old country-club chums.

Something's definitely not right about this. Milli figures Castwell has called her here for a reason and has laid down this convivial smoke-screen to soften her up. And then there was the sexual pass he made at her at their last meeting.

So, Milli waits. She will follow his lead and see where it goes, while staying ready to jet out of here if she needed to.

The man works the stream long enough to catch and release two more fish. Then he reels his line in and slogs his way out of the thigh-deep water and onto the shore. He drops his gear and strips off his hip-boots.

Smiling at Milli, he picks up a red-and white cooler and saunters over to the rock where she waits. "I've got sandwiches in here, some dessert, and a couple of beers. Brought some for you. Care to join me for lunch.?"

"Of course. That's very thoughtful of you, Sena…uh, Charles."

The ruggedly handsome man plops down next to Milli on the rock, leaving less than a foot between them. He opens the cooler and takes out two beers, twists the tops off, and hands one to Milli.

"Here's to democracy in action, Milli!"

"You bet, Charles."

He drinks deeply and nods while she drinks, too.

"Milli, I imagine you're wondering why I thought we should get together out here, away from all the interruptions and prying eyes in Washington."

"Yes, I have to say I am."

"Well, I thought we should just have a good talk…sort some things out. You know my position on your Coalition's proposal…on the amendment and legislation tied to it. Frankly, between you and me sittin' out here, your ideas are probably good ones. But they don't set well with a lot of people, powerful people. Mandatory public service for young people…smacks of the military draft we did away with years ago. Federal lands managed by local resource councils…commies tried that crap in the USSR and look where it got them. And, worst of all, a national commission like the limp-dick Postal Service or the Federal

284

Reserve running the whole shitaree and telling Congress what to pay for at every turn with no accountability to anyone. How does any of that make sense?"

"Well, Charles, most people like the idea of giving eighteen to twenty-year-olds a purpose: go to college, go in the military, go into the Peace Corps, go into AmeriCorp Vista, or go into a renewed Civilian Conservation Corp. If we don't make education or service mandatory for most young people, it won't happen."

"Goddamn socialism, if you ask me."

"Not really. We've done it many times before here in America. And, looking back, it was good for all of us. Got done what was needed at the time. When it stopped working for us, we did away with it."

He looks off into the distance for a moment. "Okay, I'll concede that the putting-kids-to-work idea has some merit. I've got a grandkid I'd like to see get up off his dead, video-game playin' ass and make something of himself. But the rest of your proposals are nonsense."

"Okay, well the idea of resource councils is working all around the country. You've got soil and water conservation districts all around Idaho for example. If we can do things like that and have 'em work, why not build even stronger ones by bringing federal lands into the councils and give the councils real management authority. Wouldn't that bring local people and interest groups together? Get them to work together when, otherwise, they're just fighting from the sidelines? Wouldn't something like that play well with your constituents, especially in little, rural towns?"

All Castwell did was grunt.

"And then there's the National Public Lands Commission. You know how you and your Congressional colleagues have been driven nuts by all this environmental conflict...by all the opposing lobbying and bills. It's so distracting and every choice seems to offend some important group. Well, why not do something different? Set up the Commission and give them direction, and then make them take all the heat, work out the gory details. Then these environmental issues wouldn't tie themselves to election politics, but, if you worked it right, you'd still have tremendous influence. Maybe you'd have even more influence, depending on how you set the Commission up."

Castwell grunts again.

Milli waits for Castwell. She has said her piece and now it's his turn.

The man reaches down into the cooler and takes out two sandwiches, and hands her one. It's roast beef and cheddar on rye bread with thick coats of mayonnaise and mustard on the bread. The flavors are excellent.

The two munch away in silence, enjoying the warm sunshine together.

When the sandwiches are gone, Castwell takes the wrappers and empty beer bottles and loads them back into the cooler.

Castwell stands up and turns to Milli. He takes her hands in his and lifts her to her feet. He continues to hold her hands high up, forcing her close to him. He looks her in the eyes.

"This really important to you, Milli, isn't it?"

"Yes, I've worked on it for over two years…the Coalition, the proposal…and a lot of people are counting on me…us, you and I…to get this done."

"Well, I'm persuaded by your words today to think favorably about what you want, maybe with a few modifications, but I want something from you in return. Here…today."

He drops her hands and slides his arms around her waist, pulling her close, "In exchange for my vote, I want a good solid fuck. Right here and for a long while…on that sandy bank yonder. Not your everyday, half-hearted fuck, but an all-out, Milli-fucks-Chuck senseless screwing. That okay with you?"

Milli admits to herself that her intuition had told her this might be coming. After all, he had propositioned her not so long ago. And he had sat so close at lunch that his elbow had occasionally brushed against her right breast.

So now it was clear Castwell had invited her to this privately owned place only a few miles from Canada in middle-of-nowhere Idaho so he could cut a political deal with her that included a tryst. Letting him hold her, she muses angrily, "Men! Pleasure…money…power… America's trinity. One simply shifts shape into another. Like fish to people…people to fish; today, here, it's power into sex and back again."

"And also here is my role in Creation hanging in the balance…so many people's trust I can get this thing done…get America back on track."

"I can't say I didn't half expect this, and I came here in spite of those feelings. And I can't call him out. No one would believe me."

She smiles grimly to herself and admits darkly, "I sure know about casual sex…how to do it and, more importantly, how to forget it."

286

"I have to give in…the best way."

Her heart sends a silent "sorry" to Philip so far away. She knows he would never understand but he had done worse, hadn't he?

And Philip would never find out…just this one time…today and never again.

Her decision made, just the thought of what was to happen causes her heart to sink, grow cold.

Her voice comes out flat, dull, "Okay, Senator Chuck, it's a deal. One senseless fuck in exchange for your vote."

He chuckles deep in his throat.

He's won again.

His fingers slide upwards to caress her breasts.

He starts to open the snaps on her western blouse….

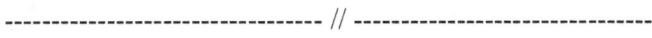

On a low ridge two hundred yards above Castwell and Meacham, Buster Hawks shuts off a digital recorder attached to a state-of-the art parabolic sound amplifier. He's caught every word the couple spoke. And he's ready to transmit those words as soon as he completes his next task.

He had tracked Meacham for weeks with a high-tech bug hidden in her Glock's grips and expensive access to her schedule. Finally, his sniper-patience has paid off. No more waiting and watching. Time to score.

Next to him, a long-lens video camera is catching all their action in high-def. Its audio track would cover the rest of his kill contract, gunshot and impact, evidence enough for proof of death.

Buster slides gently down by his Dragunov SVD sniper rifle. His is the original, Vietnam-era rig with no modifications, and none needed to do this short-range job. Most importantly, the whole weapon has been cleaned and scrubbed, including its competition-grade ammo…no fingerprints…no chemical trace…no serial numbers.

And Hawks has already planted the only evidence investigators will find besides an empty shell casing, a brushed-chrome Zippo lighter carrying the Aryan Nations logo.

He pulls the rifle in tight to his cheek with his gloved hands and aims carefully through the PSO-1 sight. The jacketed rounds in the Dragunov could penetrate two car doors, through and through. Even the bones in the fragile human bodies below would offer no real resistance.

287

Hawks wants his shot to kill them both in place, fucking. Then later, when investigators look closely, his precise ballistics would guarantee the headline-grabbing scandal his boss had paid for.

Buster waits for the best firing angle while the couple undresses by the river, climbs up the hill a little ways, and stands fully exposed to him. They stay upright for a time, the man's hands running up and down Meacham's body. Then they drop down to the ground.

He sees Meacham straddle the man. She starts pumping hard, her back to Hawks. He watches the man's hands kneading her hard, round buttocks. He's obviously enjoying her ride.

Hawks hates to shoot them before the show is over. But their position lines them up in his sights...ideal.

Buster sights carefully. He holds tight on the woman's lower back just to the right of her spine and above her hip, aiming to hit the center chest of the man writhing below her. He squeezes the trigger....

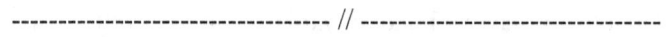

Beneath her, Castwell's hip motions get shorter, more frantic. He's about to have an orgasm, "the first of many today" as he told her.

She has no doubt "Chuck" wants to penetrate her in every way his imagination can conceive. She doesn't look forward to any of it, but still, a deal's a deal, however Hellish.

Sensing how close he is, she squeezes him tightly inside her, and begins to drive her hips side to side and rotate them, hoping to screw him fully empty as soon as womanly possible.

He begins to pant and groan, holding her eyes with his. In seconds, as she twists and turns, he groans loudly and releases himself into her.

A sudden burning pain rips Milli's right side. A huge booming sound follows. Castwell bucks hard, throwing her off. She rolls clumsily down the little hill and onto the sandy bottom below.

Dazed and lying in the sand, she grips her side where pain has bloomed. She raises her hand...blood!

Shot! She's been shot.

She checks the wound, front and back, by touch.

Clean punctures. Blood oozing quickly, not pumping.,..not arterial.

The bloody wound is just below her ribs, through muscle and soft tissue, along the edge of her core.

288

Gut shot? Bleeding out inside?

Probably but no way to tell.

What about Castwell? Every reason not to look.

The shooter must have been on the hill above them.

Damn! He would soon be arriving to check on his kills.

Milli stays down and edges on her left side over to the clothes, leaving a crimson trace of blood in the sand.

She grabs Castwell's shirt and quickly winds it around her wounded body…strains it tight. Then she grabs her pants and shirt, prone and struggling into them before adding her boots, not bothering to tie laces.

Hurry. Hurry! Where to go?

She looks around. Into the water? No she'd be a sitting duck in the shallow flow.

The rocky outcrop where Castwell and Milli had eaten lunch juts up just twenty feet away. Maybe she can hide behind its low edges somehow. But it's slim cover…equally slim promise.

She has to throw the shooter off.

No time for anything fancy…no time!

False trail?

She takes their underwear and Castwell's pants and boots and tosses them towards the river. Then she starts to belly crawl towards outcrop, kicking her feet behind her side-to-side to obscure her track.

She glances back. Maybe her kicks didn't do much, but the remaining signs in the sand do look a little more like footprints than the track of a wounded woman crawling to safety.

She crawls as rapidly as her side allows.

Her initial adrenaline is wearing off. The tissues around her wound are screaming with pain, protesting her movement with sharp stabs.

She's also starting to get shocky…clammy.

She shakes her head to clear it.

Milli hears brush snap high above her on the bank.

The shooter's coming now!

Ignoring the pain and cobwebs creeping into her brain, she crawls faster. Seconds later, she reaches the rock and slides around and partly behind it.

Peeking out, she sees a large foot step cautiously off the bank. Another boot follows.

The barrel and forestock of a soviet-style rifle, too long to be an AK but built like one, swings back and forth at the shooter's waist-height.

He stoops to check the blood that had soaked from Milli side into the sand.

Then his eyes follow the line of clothes and he stares intently out across the water.

Milli shoots him just above his collar at the base of his skull.

She doesn't feel the Glock kick or hear its sound.

She also doesn't see the man's body fall.

She just grips her side and passes out.

Chapter 52 – Something Old and Something New, Something Borrowed...

Milli rouses. She looks up. Daylight's almost gone. Her side aches fiercely.

She touches the wound through the taut shirt fabric. The blood flow has mostly stopped.

Perhaps the cold, Castwell's shirt, and the way she fell when she fainted helped staunch the blood flow. Who knows?

Some way or another she's awake but incredibly weak, cold, and stiff.

Shivers run through her body. She could use a jacket or something to warm up.

She looks over at the dead shooter on the beach. Ever so gradually, she gets to her feet and staggers over to him.

He's clearly dead, face planted in blood-soaked sand.

She makes a quick check of his pockets. The only thing in them is an extra clip for his rifle.

She checks clothing tags. His clothes and boots are all new and of the workingman's variety, available almost everywhere in discount stores. So, nothing on him to identify him. Even the cheap watch on his wrist is new. Surgical gloves on his hands.

Pro.

She stands and walks over to Castwell's clothes. He had worn a lined canvas coat earlier in the day. She locates it.

Milli drapes the coat around her shoulders, slides her left arm into the sleeve, and pulls the coat tight enough to close several of its snaps, keeping her right arm by her side, thumb hooked in her belt. The warmth starts to build a little in her chest and she gradually stops shivering.

She turns away from the stream and climbs up the bank to where she'd been screwing Castwell. He lies there on his back, eyes open in surprise--also dead, the wound in his chest almost directly over his heart. Death must have been instantaneous.

Milli mutters sardonically, "Well, that's the only real proof that the bastard had a heart."

She looks up hill towards where the shooter must have watched them and waited for his chance. Way off, she sees what appears to be a small antenna poking up through the grasses, its upper edge silhouetted against the grayish, light-dying sky.

Spotting scope? Too big for that.

She would have to go see if she wanted to know.

And if she was going to get help, she would have to make a cell phone call.

She had tried her iComm down by the river earlier while Castwell was fishing, but she had gotten no cell signal. If she is to get any kind of reception at all, it would probably only be at the top of the ridge.

So she had two reasons to make the climb.

Carefully, she begins her trek.

She first tries a direct route up, but the steepish slope stops her cold. She's too weak, has too much pain in her side…and every uneven leg lift offers the chance she will open her wound again.

She begins traversing the slope side-to-side, ten feet one way, ten feet the other, gaining an upward foot or two with each pass.

After long minutes, she reaches Hawks' shooting spot.

In the last light of the day, she sees the recording equipment and a small pack.

She turns the video recorder off.

She opens the pack and finds a small, cheap flash light, a throw-away cell phone, and several nondescript, commercially blister-packed foods…jerky…candy…an unopened bottle of water.

She opens the water and takes a sip, starts to open the candy… then remembers her wound. Possible gut wound means no food. Damn! She's so shaky she could use the calories.

She takes out her iComm. One bar of reception, then it then fades…returns again.

She tries a call to Frieda Tomlin. A text box comes up on her screen telling her "no signal."

What was that thing about cell service in the backcountry?

Oh yeah, even when voice calls couldn't go through, text messages might make it…had made it from stranded hikers and skiers even twenty or more miles away from the nearest cell tower.

Milli painfully types the message to Frieda, trying to make it as short as possible in case shorter might mean more likely to transmit. Who knew about this tech crap anyway?

She writes, "Castwell, one more dead. I'm hit. Send bus. Milli" and presses "send".

After what seems like an eternity, her phone beeps.

292

She looks at the screen. No bars at all. She can't tell if the message went or not.

Milli leaves the iComm on. She hopes that, if the message went through, Tomlin could use the FBI's satellites and locator equipment to home in on the GPS location inside her phone.

Well, if Frieda could track her iComm, help would be coming.

If not, Milli wouldn't make it through the night.

Milli would do her best to survive and give Frieda the chance. She leans back carefully against the shooter's pack and clumsily pulls the tarp's edge over her.

Castwell's coat and the tarp will have to do for warmth. She drinks a few more sips of water and closes her eyes. She starts to drift off.

What was it Philip had said so long ago in Portland, something about our bodies were only a loan from the Creator? That someday we had to pay the loan back--life molded from dust, and life going back to dust again?

Well, she was ready.

Too tired to go on.

Ready to be dust again.

After a slight prayer-smile for the Creator, Milli sleeps.

Frieda Tomlin punches a number with shaky fingers.

The call goes through

"Ballantine, this is Frieda Tomlin."

He begins to talk, but she interrupts.

"Sid, skip the pleasant puke, okay? Remember that business about my boot up your ass? Well, you get a chance to redeem yourself, once and for all. You and I probably have a very shitty mess on our hands. You move fast and maybe the shit flies on others or doesn't fly at all. So listen carefully. I got a text ten minutes ago from Mill Meacham. She's out in your neck of the woods. I've got the coordinates. She's shot, needs a bus ASAP. Make sure the medical team is good."

Sid's voice booms into her ear. She listens for a moment, and then breaks in again.

"Sure, that's bad but I got something worse, Sid. Meacham says Castwell and one other, possibly the shooter, possibly not, are dead…yeah…*your* fuckin' Senator, on site with Meacham."

The tough Special Agent listens to Ballantine's raised voice.

Then she interrupts, "Yeah, Sid, yeah…I know. This is bad shit."

He interrupts again.

"Sid, shut the fuck up. Listen, we can't fix anything until you get in one of your shiny flying machines and run your big ass up to the coordinates I'm sending to your phone. Take a small security team with the medics. If there's a shooter, the unsub might still be in the area. I'd send a FBI chopper out of Coeur d'Alene but then everything would get very official, very fast. Homeland Security and maybe the Secret Service would come in. Maybe even the fuckin' Border Patrol, too, because the drop site's so close to Canada. Everybody would put eyes on what you and I have goin' on."

Ballantine's voice is loud enough for Frieda to hold the phone a few inches from her ear.

"Yeah, yeah…all of that company wouldn't be good. And no reasons to alert Governor Sands or any of your political busybodies until you have the facts. Call could be a cruel hoax, right? Besides, after Cutter's Park, better you get to shine your badge on this one, build your macho crime-fighter image back to its former glory. So, if you haul ass up there and contact me back, well, you'll earn my undying fuckin' gratitude. And, Sid, maybe, just maybe, if we work together, we can keep this from becoming the media circus we lived through after the Mist War."

Ballantine's voice makes affirmative sounds through the phone.

"Okay, okay. Call me as soon as you land and locate Meacham."

The little woman hangs up.

She pounds her desk, "Christ, Mill, what have you gotten yourself into now?"

-------------------------------- // --------------------------------

Ballantine calls Frieda six nerve-racking hours later.

"Got Meacham. She's in surgery. Looks like she was shot in the back, low…just above right hip…came out her upper abdomen. Through and through. Doc thinks the shot might have clipped a kidney, but no sign of bleeding that way…so maybe not. Definitely hit small and large intestines. Better news. The round was jacketed and it hit her just below the last rib. So, it didn't expand at all…just bored a hole clean through her."

"Will she make it?" Frieda's voice is quiet.

"Came close to bleeding out…in shock and unconscious when we got there…but looks like she'll pull through."

"What about your big man?"

"Dead. Shot in the chest. Looks like bullet hit heart or lung, and then lodged in his spine. No exit."

"The unsub?"

"Also dead. Best as we can tell before the autopsy, Meacham shot him dead center above the collar of his shirt. Saved the taxpayers bow-coo prosecution bucks. Just won't know who sent 'em"

"Damn. Give Mill credit. She's always been a good shot. Any idea on the shooter's ID?"

"Nope. Nothing. We're sending you the fingerprints as if it was a routine background check. You know, as if it's a security clearance…that kind of thing."

"Good thinking, Sid. Keep it low profile."

"Right. Guy looks like a pro, so you might have something on him."

"So, was there anything else?"

"Yeah, a…Frieda…don't pull my head off and shit down my neck…okay?"

"No guarantees 'a that, Ballantine," the little woman growls, "but go ahead."

"Okay…good thing I'm a thousand miles away. But, Frieda, the unsub fired only one shot."

"What's that supposed to mean, Sid?"

"Ah…he fired one shot and hit both of them."

"Okay, so they were standing close together and he…."

"No, Frieda," Ballantine interrupts firmly. "Everything at the scene, and what the EMT's told me when they examined the victims, says Meacham and Castwell were naked. Meacham had no holes in her shirt…no bra on when we picked her up. Castwell was buck naked except for his socks. Underwear was spread out towards the lake…not near either one 'a them."

"Goddamit!"

"Yeah…and the shooter fired at them downslope. Woulda put Castwell on his back…if, ah…Meacham was on top 'a him. You know ridin' hi…."

"Okay, enough details, Sid. Will everyone who went out there know what happened?"

"No, the EMT's are Troopers. I got them to agree not to tell…ever. They're solid guys…they understand why. Helo pilots landed us a quarter mile away…for security. Stayed with the helo. I had them stay put while we secured the site. So, they didn't see or hear enough of anything to gossip about."

"Okay, what about the rifle? One shot…all that?"

"Ah…I took care 'a that, Frieda. Listen close. I personally took all the photos, gathered up all the evidence, and took it with me from the scene. Before I turned it in, I fired another round from the Dragunov into a sandy bank in the middle 'a nowhere. So, now evidence shows two rounds fired…one for Castwell…one for Meacham. One shell casing was laying on a tarp at the top of the hill where the perp laid down to shoot. The other casing's in the rifle. Castwell probably has a slug in him. Meacham had a through and through. Her slug's gone. Too bad. Musta landed in the river or the lake beyond it."

Tomlin grunts her understanding.

Sid continues, "And…wouldn't ya know it; the photos didn't work out…no memory chip in the damn camera. Didn't find out until I got back to base. And that was the only visual record. Perp's camera and recording equipment are on their way to you. Never at the scene as far as I can remember. Musta been found in his vehicle. Typical backcountry crime scene. No pictures. No sound. Not like in the big cities."

He laughs ironically, "Guess we'll just have to rely on my keen memory. How am I doin'?"

Tomlin feels a tremendous surge of relief and, uncharacteristically, a profound sense of respect for Sid Ballantine's quick thinking, "I could kiss you, Ballantine. And I haven't told a guy that since I banged the debate captain's brains out in the back of his daddy's hearse. Nice coffin. Soft cushions."

"Christ, Frieda, you are twisted."

"If you're lucky, Sid…I mean *really* lucky…you may find out how twisted I really am."

Ballantine's voice comes slowly, "Oooookaaaay. Let's move on to what's next…."

After some more banter, Frieda agrees to review Sid's written report. Together, they'll make sure it will bear up to any scrutiny before the media gets the story.

---------------------------------- // ----------------------------------

Two weeks later, Milli lies in a hospital bed. She still has an IV going, but the docs have taken her off the massive antibiotics she had been on for eight days. She's glad of the change because, between the painkillers and the antibiotics, her ears had rung so loudly she was afraid her few visitors would think they were sitting in a clock tower.

Frieda bustles in and booms, "Okay, you pansy-ass, you're gonna be out of isolation in an hour. Are you ready to get up out of bed and face the music?"

Milli looks at her mildly, "What music is that, Frieda?"

"You know, dereliction of duty…screwing Senators on official time…all that."

"Cripes, Frieda, keep your voice down. Not everybody has to know my life's story, or at least its most sordid details."

"Give a little credit to Auntie fuckin' Tomlin, Mill, er Milli…whatever you're calling yourself lately. Between me and Ballantine, we got a lid on the pressure cooker early. The official story is that you shot the unsub after he shot bare-assed Senator Castwell, only we left out the bare-assed part. So you got to be hero on this one with Sid a close second. And if the bare-assed part comes out, it'll be because he got wet fishing and had to change. You modestly averted your eyes."

"Sounds better and better."

"Well, I got to see the video of you and the Senator. Nice screwing technique…learned a few things."

Stern-faced, Tomlin smacks Milli's hand and gives her a waggle-finger no-no sign, "I heard the nice audio recording, too. Very high-tech, very clear. You were dumb to do it, but any moron could understand why you did what you did."

Tomlin's voice gets edgier, "I bet that bastard shoved his prick into plenty of others, so I'd get myself checked for booty bugs right away."

Milli groans and says, "Thanks for that image. I'll try to get that done as soon as possible."

"You're welcome, Meacham. Anyway, just so you know what went down, the recordings proved that your fuck-buddy Senator was unquestionably guilty of rape and sexual assault under both federal and state statutes. What does it say, 'the use of coercion to obtain sexual acts', or some crap like that? So, it was easy for Sid and me to 'convince' Governor Sands and various other important people to play the story our way. You know, keep it simple and close to the facts...unsub shooter, dead Senator, and hero Mill-ee. We all agreed to omit the recordings and certain small details like the Senator and you were shot superimposed with your clothes off and that you both displayed signs of recent sexual activity...small shit like that."

"Gee, Frieda, I don't know whether to thank you, or *shoot* you, so you'll never tell on me."

"*Tell* on you? Christ, my ass would be in the slammer for what I've covered up. I'd be doing five to twenty, suckin' prison guard dicks for breath-mint money. And you, Millicent my dear, would simply be America's next great laughingstock."

"Guess we better keep our mouths shut then, right?"

"Guess we better."

"But what about Sid? Will his mouth stay shut?"

"It'd better. He got his caped-crusader image back. And besides, if he tries to talk I'll shove one of my tits in his mouth."

Milli looks dazed, "Ah, wasn't there something about your boot up his ass a few months back? What's this tit thing?"

Frieda suddenly looks almost coy. A little smile plays on her face, "Well, it seems like working together this way has brought about a miracle. Crazy Sid Ballantine likes my action...got some of it, too. Didn't know I could still do that after so many years. But, hey, everything works."

"So, you're *lovers*?!"

"No, we're engaged."

"*Engaged*?!"

"Yeah, to be married, all that."

"*To be married*?!"

"Damnit, whatever-you-call-yourself, you keep squeaking like that and I swear I'll smother you with one of these lumpy hospital pillows. Yes, Damnit, we're engaged. And we're going to get married as soon as you get your weak ass out of here and can be my maid of honor."

"*Maid of honor*?!

Tomlin picks up a pillow from the rolling service table and approaches Milli menacingly, "I told you Meacham, one more squeak and you're doomed, you fuckin' cow pie."

Milli's life is saved when the door opens.

Philip peeks in, "Am I interrupting something?"

298

Tomlin growls, "Just your wife's murder. That's all."

"Well, okay, I'll just be going then."

He starts to duck out the door, but Frieda fires the pillow expertly and hits him in the face.

"Okay, okay. I give up."

Milli has been staring at Philip with a frown on her face. His third rehab had worked well enough to keep him clean for the last year. Now he tries so hard to meet and end each day sober.

This Castwell thing proves she had not done so well.

Philip deserves to know about her fall from chastity, "Frieda, how about giving us some time."

Tomlin looks at her sharply and leans in close, "Don't let those pain killers addle your brain. He only has to know you're a hero, just like everyone else. Nothing more."

Secrets again? What would the Creator think?

Milli looks at her friend grimly and whispers hoarsely, "Thanks Frieda, but I have a lot to talk over with my husband. So, please give us some time."

Shaking her head, the little woman stalks out.

Philip asks, "What was that all about?"

"Well...plenty, dear. So let me just say what I need to say."

The truth about what she had done to get the Senator's vote, now numerically unimportant because of the vacancy in his Senate seat, looms large in her mind. So hard to explain now...even to herself.

She *should* tell Philip. He had been through so much...brought himself back from the edge of Hell...for *her* and for their life together.

Milli pauses for a long time, considering her words and the pain they might cause Philip...how they might send him back down a druggy rabbit hole. What if the truth broke him?

A minutes passes. Then two.

Philip gets worried. He stares at her intently.

Finally Milli decides.

The dead past can bury its secrets.

And the living can move on.

In a small voice, she says, "Philip, I'm leaving Forest Service law enforcement...that whole thing."

Her voice starts to quaver, "Ah...this shooting thing...the docs say the bullet hit one of my ovaries...grenaded it. So, ah...only one left."

She cries for a few moments, and then wipes her nose and eyes.

Her voice gets stronger, "I'm thirty-five. If we're going to have a star baby, it's time for us to start. We can't do that if I'm gone all the time and if keep getting shot at and hurt. Maybe it's too late for a star baby. I would hate that. So I've got to make a change…for us, for the baby if we can have one."

She cries some more, "And it's probably time for me to do something else. Maybe my job with the Coalition can grow into something permanent. Maybe I'll be welcome in another part of the Forest Service besides law enforcement. I burnt a lot of bridges around the agency and among the Legacies getting the Coalition's work done. So maybe not Forest Service."

She covers her eyes, "I don't know. But I'm ready for something else…*anything* else. I just wanted you to know."

Philip looks at Milli, astounded, and then says mildly, "Well, that's big stuff, but not that big. I was sure you were going to tell me something really bad…about us…being over maybe. Was there anything else?"

Milli crosses mental fingers for the Creator and looks at her husband serenely, "No, dear, nothing."

She takes his hand and holds it tightly, "Now, you tell me about the new church you're planning, the Creation Chapels my father, Jacob Mountainspring, is helping you put together."

"Well, thanks to the big grants Jacob helped us get, we have twenty-six Creation Chapels opening next year…all in big cities…and a hundred more planned for next year. They'll be inter-faith, but they won't try to merge religions, just bring the different religions and traditions together. And the preaching, the programs, the staff are all outdoors-oriented. Sure, we'll still hold services and all that, both inside the Chapels and outside, with a focus on Creation learning…people's purpose and role…the web of life…all that. But the real emphasis will be on travelling out to explore Creation together…go to local places and help out…and go to far places to learn and praise. We'll all be leaving our wonderful-but-stuffy old church houses behind and reconnecting to Creation."

"Philip, like I told you a couple of years ago. I wanna join your church. Do I have to be a Christian? 'Cause you know I'm not. I may never be one."

"I know. But, Jacob and I have already agreed. For exemplary service to the faithful, you've been appointed a Creation Chapel "elder-for-life", Milli. How does it feel?"

Milli preens for effect, "Well, I'd feel fine about it if you could change the name to something other than "elder'..."

The two lovers laugh delightedly.

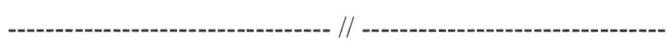

In Austin, Texas, the Mist Enemies Chief lies sprawled on the floor of his den. The poison he consumed had been fast-acting and potent. From a safe-house in Arkansas, Raven had watched him take the dose, convulse, and fall to the floor.

Raven starts the video she had shot of his actions and reviews the scene again. It looks authentic and surely, if the Enemies Chief had been acting, he would not have been able to voluntarily void his body wastes at just the right moment.

Satisfied, Raven bobs her head and cancels the internet video feed.

The Enemies Chief had paid the price of failure and, with the best kind of ending, died to make sure Mist remained secure, invisible.

Until Mist is needed again someday.

Time for Raven to go.

Raven walks to the nearest window and opens it.

She drops her robe, revealing a smooth, youthful body.

She lifts her arms up and gives a loud "ca-caw", a raven's territorial cry.

Her body begins to shimmer. It darkens and turns shiny cinder-ashy.

Raven hops to the window sill, and grips it with clawed feet.

Leaping outward, the dark spirit stretches her wide wings and flaps silently into the lowering night sky.

Epilogue

On Earth Day, 2014, both houses of the U.S. Congress passed the American Environmental Peace and Justice Restoration Act by overwhelming majorities. President Obama signed the bill into law on the same day. Thereby our country ended six generations of "green war".

The Constitutional Amendment was passed by both houses of Congress and sent to the fifty state legislatures for ratification. Thirty-six states have to ratify it before it becomes the supreme law of the land. Twenty-two legislatures have done so to date.

Milli Meacham and her beloved husband, Philip, continued to enjoy a little S and M now and then, although they had to keep the noise down to avoid waking their twins, a boy, North, and girl, Estrella.

Frieda and Sid Ballantine retired and raise hair sheep in rural Idaho. Frieda frequently accuses Sid of fucking the sheep silly. He just smiles--an expression, which, under the circumstances, irritates her to no end.

Thinking and Talking About This Book

Principal Characters

A **Deep Brown Crucible** is the third book in a series, relating the life of Millicent "Mill" Meacham, a fourth-generation U.S. Forest Service employee.

A **Deep Brown Crucible** carries forward some other key characters from the first two books, namely Philip, W.A."Bull" Meacham, Rebecca Theophile Meacham, Manny Suemez, Raven, and Frieda Tomlin. Other minor characters from past books--Golden Eagle, Chronos, and the Enemies Chief--also appear.

Actual people--Jack Ward Thomas and his wife, Kathy—appear with their permission.

Unique Themes and Plot Elements

Setting and location

Each of the three books has a unique ecological setting:

A Deep Blue Abyss – the Chugach National Forest (Sitka Spruce, Western Hemlock temperate rainforest) and many other parts of Alaska ranging from the Arctic Sea to Glacier Bay National Park.

A Deep Green War – the Siuslaw National Forest (Douglas Fir, Western Hemlock, Sitka Spruce temperate rainforest) and other areas of the Pacific Northwest, particularly Portland, Oregon. Also various locations in Washington, D.C.

A Deep Brown Crucible – the Boise National Forest/Frank Church-River of No Return Wilderness (mountain grassland meadows, Lodgepole Pine, Douglas Fir, and various other firs and spruces in a high-altitude, moist-to-dry forest) the Northern Rocky Mountain States of Idaho and Montana. Also various locations in Washington, D.C.

Plot elements

Each book also has unique plot elements:

A Deep Blue Abyss – a greedy miner conducts an illegal operation in a National Park and an epic race across Alaska is filmed to be part of a reality television show. Mill begins her first long-term relationship with Tilly Corcoran, a BLM employee

A Deep Green War – a murderous eco-terrorist organization, Mist, is discovered and Mill ends her friend-lesbian relationship with Tilly.

A Deep Brown Crucible – a horrific but purifying wildfire creates the potential for ending the "green war" and reflections on spirituality and the past form the basis for addressing and perhaps ending many of America's environmental conflicts. Mill is married to Philip, a friend and supporter from her youth.

Wild nature

The three books explore the many roles of wild nature in human life.

A Deep Blue Abyss presents nature more or less realistically. Homes for wild plants and animals. Places of beauty. Places for human challenge and growth. Source of threats to life and property. Refuge from dangers.

In **Blue**, contrasts are also made between real and faux nature. For example, the real aurora borealis lights Mill's way out of starvation and wilderness hazards. By contrast, under the neons of the Aurora Rave Club, Mill and others pursue their addictions to alcohol, drugs, and reckless, impersonal sex.

The book also draws parallels between the threats of predators like Drag Carlson and dangerous animals like bears, and between life-destroying forces like coercive, freedom-robbing governments (the fish cops) and cold, rapid-running rivers.

And finally, **A Deep Blue Abyss** makes the distinction that, besides Mill's personal addictive choices, the greatest threats to Mill come not from wild nature, but rather from the choices of developers and despoilers such as Hard Rock Gruber, Drag Carlson, and Toad Craven.

306

In contrast to **Blue**, **A Deep Green War** treats nature in a somewhat romanticized way, more specifically as a benign, intentional force.

For example, after Milly's rape, she is nurtured by Cottonwood Creek to the point where the creek bottom grips her hands to prevent her suicide. And later, the creek's waters, the sun, and the trees begin her physical healing.

And when the Mist assassin, Ekos, has to hide to avoid capture by the LEOs, Ekos takes refuge in a hollowed-out sequoia, avoids detection, and later escapes.

In counterpoint to how the giant sequoia cares for Ekos, the yellow jackets Ekos releases unnaturally against John O'Reilly kill him.

Throughout **A Deep Green War**, choices by Mist eco-terrorists represent the true threats to people and society, not wild nature.

A Deep Brown Crucible portrays wild nature at Cutter's Park as an almost sentient. Mist desires to destroy human greed and save Mother Nature. The federal government desires to perpetuate a peaceful society by capturing Mist. Mill and Manny thirst for revenge for Mist's murders of friends and family. Wild nature just wants to be left in peace. Instead, Cutter's Park becomes the unwilling battleground for the destruction Mist, the federal government, and Mill bring to one another.

At **Brown's** first crisis point, Mist's and the government's weapons have torn Cutter's Park apart and the Mist-Cutter fire has burned it up. In this moment, the blackened, finger-like trees beg a newly conscious Mill for both peace and justice.

After the second crisis point when Philip no longer supports Mill and she has to change, wild nature becomes the focus point for reconnections--spiritual, societal, and within Milli's marriage.

Themes and plot elements common to all three Mill Meacham stories

Certain key themes unite the three books. The most important of these is Millicent Meacham's personal growth and development.

In all three books, Mill's life symbolizes and expresses the forces shaping, and in many cases, paralyzing the U.S. Forest Service and America's utilitarian conservation movement in the 21st Century.

To this end, Millicent's very name comes from the marriage of two words, "Millennium" and "Innocent".

And her nickname evolves as life events shape her. The child "Milly" becomes the addicted, tough-but-tentative "Mill". And, after much travail and emotional integration, "Mill" finally develops into the competent, independent, and self-confident "Milli".

Satire and the portrayal of outside forces affecting Mill's life

To greater and lesser degrees, the three books also make common satirical points about how others treat Mill. Here are some of the satirically presented forces at play in Mill's fictional life:

- Deserted and then murderously attacked by her alienated "mother"; Rebecca Theophile Meacham whose character represents U.S. environmental interests and their conduct, beginning in the 1980s shortly after "Milly's" birth

- Kidnapped, neglected, raped, and despoiled by her "father", Bull Meacham, who represents post-WWII "modernist" resource-development forces that twist the Forest Service mission towards destruction of wild nature

- Kept in a childlike, regressive state by multi-generation Forest Service families, referred to as "Legacies" in all three books

- Dominated by Senators and Congressmen, and their staffs; people outside the Forest Service who perpetuate environmental conflicts for votes and who extract political favors from Forest Service leaders in exchange for budget concessions and personal advancement

- Administered by cowardly, politically-motivated, male and female Forest Service careerists bent on attaining as Mill puts it, "Pleasure…money…power…America's trinity. One simply shifts shape into another", rather than providing the conservation leadership and public service they are paid to deliver. **A Deep Green War's** Ham Hoggett is the best representation of this idea, although there are many others as well

- Betrayed by other agencies bent on their own self-serving missions, represented by the Alaska State Patrol fish cops in **A Deep Blue Abyss** and BLM's Tilly Corcoran in **A Deep Green War**

308

Conditions affecting Mill's life

The books also display common personal behaviors and conditions shaping Mill's life:

- Addicted to secret connections and pleasures--in Mill's case, sex, drugs, and alcohol. In the context of the Forest Service, these secret addictions represents many things, but most specifically how low-level employees inside the agency war secretly against each other and against people and policies higher up in the organization. They create betrayal by forming secret alliances with outside interests to influence and attempt to dominate other employees and programs

- Attempted to perform her duties while coping with post-traumatic stress disorder—blurred vision, hyperventilation, extreme shyness, punishing nightmares, inability to speak to large groups—these symptoms persist throughout Mill's career

- Only tentatively reconnected to her real "father", Native American human-land traditions, and her real "mother", the ages-old philosophy of non-violent, utilitarian eco-feminism, but lacking the support, resources, and drive to complete the necessary transformation

In far less dramatic and injurious ways, the same forces and conditions affect the "life" of today's post-modern Forest Service and the utilitarian conservation movement.

Over the course of the three books, Mill copes with the terrible traumas done to her, integrates and overcomes her internal conflicts, develops confidence and skill, and ultimately transforms her life and the nation. So also must the agency and the movement accomplish these things to contribute effectively to post-modern America.

Common characters

Throughout the three books, certain characters and character groups represent important influences in Mill's life.

For example, Philip truly is "Saint Philip," Milli's loving companion in **A Deep Green War** and **A Deep Brown Crucible**. He is a character with no last name who serves as Mill's supportive spiritual guide from childhood to adulthood, from friendship into marriage. His loving questions at the right time reflect the Biblical St. Philip's role among the disciples, at once pragmatic and yet idealistic, always eager to help.

In **Brown**, Philip's unfailing support falters at the book's second crisis point. Mill loses his support and the loss propels her toward independence. The loss also allows her to throw off past wounds and the resulting inhibitions that hold her back, including the crutch of Philip's constant care.

After this crisis, Philip struggles through three rounds of rehab, as **Deep Green's** Milly once struggled through three immersions in Cottonwood Creek. In the end, Philip endures. He emerges whole and able to once more take his place beside Milli. The two enter into a much more intimate relationship.

Through the three novels, Wolfgang Amadeus "W.A." or "Bull" Meacham represents the worst aspects of father and, by extension, of Forest Service leader. He is a brutal sociopath who neglects and debases Milly, Rebecca, Esperanza Pizzaro, and many others. In his work life, he conducts himself with only his personal pleasure and career in mind. His dies alone, ambitions crushed, a torn corpse in a druggies' park.

In contrast, Mill bonds with Manny Suemez, Bill Zumo, Jake Burns, and Jacob Mountainspring. Together, the four men represent the positive male influences Mill needs in her life—strength, protectiveness, self-restraint and -sacrifice, honor, dedication, and Earth connectedness.

Rebecca "Badger" Theophile Meacham represents the loving-but-desperately-lost aspects of "mother". After being brutalized by Bull, Rebecca falls into the resistance trap. She exceeds even his monumental cruelty after first deserting and then attacking the institutions and daughter she loves.

In contrast, Charli Jenkins of **A Deep Blue Abyss** becomes Mill's nurturing lover. She pleasures and holds Mill as long as she needs comfort, gently directs Mill toward sobriety, and finally releases Mill when she begins to find the strength to leave her addictions.

In **A Deep Green War**, Tilly Corcoran becomes Mill's first committed partner. Caring but flawed, Tilly can't sufficiently overcome her own ambitions to form a solid and lasting relationship with Mill. But the partnership between the two women, though temporary, gives Mill the self-knowledge that she can actually enter an intimate relationship and sustain it, at least for a time.

Frieda Tomlin represents the tough-loving, older-sister/mother Mill needs to propel her towards self-confidence and life focus. Through Frieda, Milli learns that actual toughness comes from commitment to an important purpose, "sky centeredness", not from physical strength or aggressive talk. Milli also learns from Frieda that some of her ability to love and nurture others must come from Milli being transparently honest about what those others must do to grow and mature.

Sex and sexuality

Throughout the three books, sex and sexuality are presented as confused, perverse, often violent, and distorted by power imbalances, secrecy, aggression, and miscommunications. Milli's thought about "Pleasure…money…power…America's trinity" applies to these sexually perverse aspects of the books as well as it does to the many other inappropriate ways characters treat one another in them.

For example, Milli's sexual relationship with Philip only becomes free and truly nurturing when she becomes independent and when he begins asking her for what he wants, in other words her cooperative dominance in their sex life. Until then, like so many other aspects of their relationship, insufficient communications, secrecy, and dependencies distort and warp their shared sexuality.

Extremism

The three Mill Meacham books convey numerous insights about the effects of extremism on people and natural resources. People practicing extremism display several common characteristics and behaviors: secrecy, cultism, narcissism, unconstrained need to control resources and other people, alienation from other people, dehumanization of opponents, and intense and persistent resistance to opponents.

In **A Deep Blue Abyss,** the extreme human element is Hard Rock Gruber's greed. The extreme natural element is the grueling environmental conditions facing racers and support crews on the Great Land Geo-Challenge.

Gruber's reckless greed kills Enoch Saarinen and severely endangers the rest of Mill's Green Group by sending them through Turnback Canyon. By contrast, the Great Land Geo-Challenge, though a part of a for-profit entertainment enterprise, has rules and safety measures in place to mitigate dangers to the racers and crews. It is Gruber's resistance to the race and the possibility that his illegal mine will be discovered that leads directly to Saarinen's death.

In **A Deep Green War**, the extreme human element comes from Mist's secrecy, cultism, alienation, dehumanization, and resistance to what they characterize as "development slugs and thugs", namely the business and government entities engaged in natural resource development or management. The extreme natural element is how Mist assassin, Ekos, uses natural products and conditions to kill human targets.

In **Green**, the natural elements are, in and of themselves, passive or beneficial towards people. But in Ekos' hands, they are turned into weapons. Also in **Green**, even while their losses mount, Forest Service and FBI law enforcement people are never able to develop an effective response to Mist's aggression.

This reflects the reality that, in America today, few legal, political, or social options exist to allow development and government interests to confront and resolve issues and conflicts with environmental interests holding extreme views. America's inability to work with groups like the Earth Liberation Front, the Animal Liberation Front, and Earth First! illustrate this reality.

For example, such groups have no political party to join. Because America's Republicans and Democrats display few differences when it comes to environmental issues, no party reflects extreme environmental values. Therefore, under our two-party system, environmental extremists cannot support existing political parties, or more importantly, elect people to office. And this means America's political system usually cannot accommodate an integrating public debate of environmental issues and the eventual incorporation of otherwise radical views into everyday government policies and life.

Regardless of the merits or their ideas or the popularity of at least some of their views, we treat the groups and their ideas as threats. We push them away, declare them "outlaws", infiltrate and watch them, and pursue them as criminals if they act. In a sense, in our desire to perpetuate a peaceful society and prosperous economy, we encourage both alienation of environmental extremists and resulting environmental conflicts.

Readers should be quick to note that the same could be said for mainstream America's responses to even-more-dangerous, ultra-

312

conservative interests. But retrograde radicalism or anti-brown racism, as advocated by ultra-conservatives, is not the subject of the Mill Meacham stories. This is because ultra-conservative interests, while they may at times contribute significantly to gridlock over environmental issues, rarely attempt to separate people from natural resources. Thus, they are not pro-environment and anti-human as some extreme environmental groups have become.

In **A Deep Brown Crucible**, Mist's **Green** aggression gets answered by annihilation. And although many people die and valuable property is lost, natural resources in the River of No Return Wilderness get hammered the most.

Reflecting real life, over the course of the three books, resistance begets resistance. Because of resistance, issues escalate into conflicts, conflicts into disputes, and disputes into crises or even violence and bloodshed. If disputes stop short of crisis, gridlock ensues. Gridlock perpetuates conflict but does not offer resolution. In this way, gridlock is inherently both anti-human *and* anti-nature.

And what if one side seems to "win", thus ending the gridlock? The Cutter's Park battle illustrates the futility of win-lose approaches to environmental issues. Mill and her allies seem to notch up a "win" at Cutter's Park, temporarily ending gridlock between Mist and federal law enforcement. But Mist leaders remain in place as the stewards of a secret cult, hiding and abiding, waiting for the opportunity to begin their work all over again, marking time until they can resume their vicious agenda and actions.

How do you count the costs of such "wins"?

And what are the benefits?

Are there better ways?

Thanks for reading!

Look for

The fourth Carson A. Pierce novel

A Deep Red Sunrise

<u>The fourth Mill Meacham story</u>

Action spread across four continents